That Summer in Ischia

Penny Feeny

First published in May 2011
by Tindal Street Press Ltd
217 The Custard Factory, Gibb Street,
Birmingham, B9 4AA
www.tindalstreet.co.uk

A CIP catalogue reference for this book is available
from the British Library

ISBN: 978 1 906994 18 1

Typeset by Alma Books Ltd
Printed and bound in Great Britain by
Mackays, Chatham

For Elinor, Roisin and Imogen

PROLOGUE: 2003

Every movement was familiar: the languid easy stride, the swing of the hips, the tilt of the neck, the click of the fingers to an invisible beat. The woman on the path ahead had Helena's height too, her blond fall of hair and the long lean legs that outpaced others so easily. Liddy would have to make an effort to catch her up if – and she needed to consider this – she actually wanted to. If she didn't mind risking rejection. And if it were Helena in the first place. After so many years, memories become unreliable, eyes see traits that aren't there.

The figure stopped, balanced on one leg and raised the other, stooped from her waist to remove a shoe and shake out a stone. The action transported Liddy to the little cove below Casa Colonnata: Helena skipping over the sun-warmed shingle and coming to a sudden halt, adopting the same stork-like posture, the same impatient flick of her sandal; calling over her shoulder to the children, challenging them to find where the pebble had landed. A quick glimpse of a face was all Liddy needed to be certain, to settle her disquiet, but the woman didn't turn her head. She restored her shoe and veered inland. As Liddy debated whether to follow, the wind eddied across the foreshore carrying a smack of salt and a ballooning plastic bag. The decision was made for her as Rolo launched himself at the bag and tugged her in the opposite direction. When he lost interest in it, and the scurrying trail of litter in its wake, he raced towards the sea. She just managed to unclip his leash before he dived through the railings.

Crosby beach was a Mecca for dog walkers, ploughing furrows in their Wellington boots under a blustery overcast sky. She knew many of them to nod to, and apologize to when Rolo sniffed their crotches or licked their toddlers' toes. She hadn't expected training him to be so demanding. She hadn't even been certain she wanted another dog. She'd waited a year after Flora's death before going back to Animal Rescue because there was always a chance – you couldn't keep hope down however hard you tried – that the gap in her life might be filled.

She'd chosen Rolo (part spaniel, part retriever, possibly part terrier) for his friendliness. She wasn't looking for a guard dog. They already had a sophisticated system of security lights and alarms. What she and Michael both wanted was to come home to an enthusiastic greeting, to sound and movement, to warm breath fogging the atmosphere.

Now, with her feet sinking into puddles, she felt out of her depth. Rolo was oblivious to her commands, transfixed by the power of the sea. His tail quivered at the dramatic pull of the tide. His body tensed as if a thousand electric impulses were being delivered to each chocolate and toffee strand of his coat, propelling him into the waves. When he emerged again, scattering rainbows, the fur on his belly was matted and dripping, his tail sweeping the sand. She'd have to let him exhaust himself sprinting along the beach before she tried to call him to heel. There'd be plenty of time, pacing after him, hands deep in her coat pockets, to wonder whether her eyes really had been deceiving her and why this uncomfortable prickling sensation should lodge in her brain.

A different kind of discomfort accompanied her when they set off on the return leg of their Saturday morning excursion. She'd hoped to reach home before the knot of pain swelled to intolerable proportions, but there were no short cuts. Halfway along the broad leafy avenue, something like a red-hot poker plunged into her abdomen and sent her into spasm. She staggered to the support of a sandstone gatepost, holding on to its curved finial and waiting for the worst to pass. It would, of course; she could be sure of that. This was not a new experience; it didn't get any easier.

Rolo took advantage of these circumstances to charge through the open gateway as if he'd spotted a rabbit. He started tearing chunks from the smooth, green lawn and Liddy was in no position to yank him off; when she called out her voice sounded shrill and strange. The house itself was Edwardian, grand and double-fronted, with a veranda running along one side. The upper storey sprouted gables and a turret; fetching red pantiles clad the roof. Originally built for a prosperous merchant family who'd made their fortune from jute it had since been divided into six self-contained flats. The occupant of one of the ground-floor flats appeared in her doorway and yelled at Rolo, who ignored her as serenely as he ignored his mistress. Then she saw Liddy clutching the gatepost.

'Is this your dog?'

Liddy moved by degrees from the safety of her prop to the uneven, treacherous surface of the gravel path. 'I've only just . . .' she began. 'He's still . . .'

'What on earth does he think he's doing? Digging for victory?'

'He's a bit wild I'm afraid. No one's ever trained him before.' An apology coupled with explanation was what she was aiming for; she didn't want to grovel.

'I realize that a dumb animal doesn't recognize private property. That should be your responsibility.'

'Yes. I'm sorry.'

The woman, layered in cardigans, emerged from the shadow of her porch. 'Just a moment. Don't I know you?'

As Rolo bounded up, showing no concern for the woman's awesome bulk, Liddy prepared herself for the kind of lecture she could remember well. Daphne Myers had taught generations of girls to hate chemistry, delighting in quashing the lively and the joyful, sneering at their bad breeding as if they were livestock rather than exuberant adolescents.

'Helen Liddle!' she said with the satisfaction of a person whose memory has not lost its keenness.

'Actually I sort of morphed into Liddy Rawlings a while back.' They'd had similar brief exchanges on the past few occasions they'd met – most recently in the spirits aisle at Sainsbury's, when each had refrained from looking in the other's trolley. 'I changed my name when I married.' To all intents and purposes she had changed it at school. There were so many Helens in her class they had to find ways of distinguishing one another. (Helena had chosen to add the *a*.)

Liddy was used to viewing Daphne as a figure of authority. It was almost impossible to see her as an ordinary human being, a woman with her own disappointments and regrets. She could never have imagined her showing solicitude. 'Are you all right? You're very pale.'

And this was so unexpected that Liddy, instead of saying 'I'm fine', felt her shoulders droop as she admitted, like a homesick child, 'Actually, no, I'm not.'

'You'd better come and sit down a moment,' said Daphne, waving her towards the house.

'But my dog . . .'

'Take a seat on the veranda. I'll tie him up.'

If Liddy's clear thinking hadn't been clouded by stomach cramps, would she have seen through this ruse? The lonely old woman capturing company the only way she could, like Ariadne with her spider's web. Liddy would far rather have been in her own home, lying in her own bed with a hot water bottle, but she was trapped. She lowered herself into a teak chair, its wood smooth and silvered like beaten metal. Rolo, tied on a short rein to the wooden rail, yelped, strained his neck and then gave up, burying his nose in his paws. Daphne, with no haste and much precision, fetched a glass of water and a cushion to support her back. She then sat opposite and folded her hands in her lap. 'Remind me, dear, what is it you're doing now?'

'I'm a management consultant.' Usually this was a claim she could make with pride. It indicated a person who was incisive, observant, efficient: qualities that a chemistry teacher would probably admire, and even take credit for. Management consultants were not like life coaches or psychotherapists. They didn't have dysfunctional personal lives. The fact that she couldn't handle her dog or her own fertility had no bearing on her job, although it kindled a sense of shame she wished she could suppress.

A slight frown, as if the term were baffling, possibly even as spurious as those new university subjects that hadn't existed when Daphne taught her girls how to make copper sulphate crystals: media studies, music technology, sports science. Then she recovered herself. 'How interesting. I always thought you'd do well.'

'You did?' This was not how Liddy remembered it. Miss Myers had been their form teacher in the lower sixth, had constantly despaired at their prospects, even though chemistry had long been abandoned.

'You and your friend from down the road.'

'My friend from where?'

Daphne moved only her chin. The rest of her settled in folds between the stout arms of her chair. A line of conifers marked the boundary of the garden. Further south along the shore stretched the handsome Victorian terraces built to watch the ships steam up the Mersey. 'They lived on the front. What was their name now? Ashbourne.'

'Oh, you mean Helena Ashbourne?'

'Rather a troublemaker, that girl. Clever though.'

Liddy and Helena had considered themselves vastly superior to the drones surrounding them. They'd been inseparable at school, a striking pair identified by their contrasting looks: Helena's tall, fair elegance (evident even when she cropped her hair and flirted with punk); Liddy shorter, curvier, a dark, dimpled prettiness.

'She didn't finish her degree, did she? Such a waste.'

Liddy didn't speak. Helena's abandoned degree was the least of it.

'Went off to Italy and never came back.' Daphne spoke as if Italy were (in one of her favourite phrases) a den of iniquity.

'Actually, she had to spend six months in Rome as part of her art history course. I haven't seen her since.'

Daphne was genuinely puzzled. 'Really? But I thought you were such good friends.'

'We didn't keep in touch, after that summer.'

That summer. Liddy had just graduated; Helena had another year to go. Liddy had come home and registered at a temping agency with a dismal sinking feeling. She could still recall her shock and excitement when the operator announced an international call.

'Tell me your wildest summer fantasy, Liddy.'

'Helena! Where are you?'

'Rome, of course, where d'you think? I had to book this call from a friend's apartment, so I can't talk for long. You're looking for work, right? How soon can you make it?'

'What?'

'I bet it includes lolling about on a private beach. The fantasy I mean. I've fixed us a job you'll love. Get yourself here quick as you can and you won't regret it.'

'But I've stuff to sort out and . . .'

'Listen, it's a very simple proposition. There are two families who have villas on Ischia and are looking for girls to mind their children and speak English to them. There are only three kids so it will be a doddle and we'll have a great holiday at the same time. They have a boat and everything.'

'What's Ischia?'

'It's an island in the bay of Naples. The Verduccis and the Baldinis both have loads of money so we'll be living in the lap of luxury.'

'The who?'

'Never mind the names, you'll get used to them. And it's only for the summer. What have you got to lose?'

Liddy could see the two-tone green telephone squatting on the hall table. She could hear Helena's enthusiasm, could see her own hand lowering the receiver. It was disturbing, the way the events of more than twenty years ago could seem so fresh and immediate.

Her attention had drifted and Daphne broke through by raising a voice which already creaked from a lifetime of strident hectoring. 'You haven't seen her, then, since she came back?'

'Back? You mean recently?'

'Well, yes.' Daphne enjoyed being an informant. 'Mrs Ashbourne was in a nursing home, did you not know? And the house was let until she died some months ago. I would have gone to the funeral if I'd heard about it in time. One does like to make the proper observances. I understand the daughter's been here settling things since she got probate.'

So Liddy hadn't been mistaken after all. She looked at Rolo who was snuffling at the ground beneath his paws. She imagined she saw contrition in his melting eyes. Don't worry, she wanted to tell him, it's water under the bridge now. Except, illogical as it was, the burden of guilt still weighed on her.

'It's always a pleasure to come across former students,' said Daphne.

'You've spoken to her? Helena?'

'No dear. I meant you.'

'Oh, right. Well, I do appreciate your kindness, but I really should get going.' Her pain was rumbling at a lower, more bearable note and she stood to make herself clear. 'Thank you for the drink.'

'You will be sure to call again, now you know where I live?'

Liddy nodded and grasped Rolo's collar.

'And remember me to your friend if you see her.'

In the days that followed, the past swam close to Liddy, tugged with such tenacity at the memories which had been stacked and bound and stored away that she couldn't resist turning into Marine Terrace. She hadn't realized the strangers coming and going through the Ashbournes' front door were only tenants, that the family might return. One evening after work, she strolled past the colourful ribbon of houses with their florid hedges, long windows, and graceful wrought-iron trellis-work. She stood and stared, expecting at any moment that Rolo would interrupt her meditations. She was not planning to ring the doorbell.

Her gaze travelled upwards, to what had been Helena's room. The room where they'd drunk cheap wine, deliberately ripped and re-pinned their clothes and planned outings secret from their parents (not that Helena's mother, a piano teacher with a continual stream of pupils, would have noticed). The room she had treated as her own: sitting with a towel wrapped around her head, while Helena in scanty underwear counted down the minutes until she could discover whether the henna had worked. The room where they'd devised torments for their teachers, fantasized about their careers, selected names for their children.

She became aware of a young woman ambling towards the gate. She had an air of youthfulness that Helena could not possibly have retained. She moved with the same sinuous sway of her hips, but there was also something disconcerting about her which Liddy couldn't identify. Her hair tumbled over a denim jacket, her skirt was short, her legs were bare. Joyfully, Rolo thrust his damp nose up the skirt and pressed it between her thighs.

'I'm so sorry,' said Liddy, jerking at his lead, wondering how she could explain her loitering. 'If I take my eyes off him for a second he gets into trouble. Only I was thinking how lovely it must be to look out from that balcony. You'd never get bored, would you? With the change of tides, I mean, and the light on the water.'

The girl didn't seem to be listening. She was crouching down to fondle Rolo's ears and let him lick her palms. 'He's a gorgeous dog,' she said in a tone both husky and uncannily familiar. 'What's he called?'

And Liddy felt her throat contract so that Rolo's name came out in a stutter. It might have been natural at this point to ask the girl her own, but her lips wouldn't form the question. Could Helena possibly have a daughter so grown-up? Was Helena inside the house at this moment, watching from the window? But then another dog trotted into the street from the public gardens opposite and Rolo was distracted afresh. He hared off again, dragging Liddy with him. The girl walked up the path and the door closed behind her.

PART ONE

1979 ISCHIA

I

Casa Colonnata, the Verduccis' villa, had the better view; the Baldinis' had a more conspicuous use of marble. Both were set on an elevated promontory reached by a narrow and precipitous road. The Verducci terrace caught the golden promise of the rising sun and the crimson drama of its rays sinking over the horizon. It encompassed an infinite and breath-taking panorama of the Mediterranean below and the rugged forested lands above. Standing at the balustrade, Liddy felt as though she were poised on the rim of the world. She placed her palms on the rough warm stone and drank in the sensation of time stilled, of being in paradise.

Her charges, three-year-old Roberto (Bobo) Baldini and his six-year-old sister, Sara, had woken from their siesta and clamoured for the beach. She'd assembled the necessary equipment, the buckets and spades and towels and sunhats, the bottles of water and tanning lotion and Sara's doll, and they'd wandered next door. The children had run inside and Liddy was enjoying the moment's peace. She had been here scarcely a week, but from the moment they'd skimmed across the bay of Naples and disembarked at Ischia Porto, it was as if they'd stepped into a world switched to a different time zone, a world where you wouldn't know they had clocks at all if it hadn't been for the chiming of a church bell tower. Buses pulled away from their stops with a sound like a slow snore; Lambrettas buzzed around corners like drowsy wasps; even the bars where customers stirred sugar into velvety espressos had a sleepy feel.

She was startled by a squirt of sun cream between her shoulder blades. A hand massaged it into her back with tender circling strokes. She knew it was Helena; she'd caught the scent of her. Rive Gauche by Yves Saint Laurent was just the perfume Helena would wear: light and jazzy and – what was the word? – insouciant. Liddy was still experimenting, hadn't yet found her signature fragrance.

'I didn't hear you coming.'

'You were miles away. Is it as sore as it looks?'

Helena had been in Italy long enough to acquire a honeyed glow; Liddy had freckled and peeled. 'Not really. But that feels nice; don't stop. It's so perfect here, isn't it?' She drew in and let out a long luxurious breath. 'At least, while we're minus the kids. Where've they got to?'

Helena rubbed a fresh quantity of cream on to her skin. 'They're fine. Rosaria's stopping their gobs with strawberries.' She hadn't exaggerated the families' affluence: in addition to the boat and secluded beach, the villas came with a housekeeper who cleaned and cooked and topped up the fruit bowls daily with cherries, apricots and nectarines.

Neither Maresa Baldini nor Gabriella Verducci was at home. Sisters-in-law – Gabi was married to Maresa's brother, Fabrizio – they shared long indolent holidays while their husbands negotiated property deals. They spent their days seeking therapies – Gabi suffered from intermittent eczema – immersing their bodies in mud or salt crystals and bathing in the foaming hot springs. They crooned to their children and smothered them with kisses but were too self-absorbed to attend to them for long.

A thin piercing cry rippled through the french windows, spoiling Liddy's sense of harmony. 'Sara,' she sighed. 'Mental-boy Bobo'll be tormenting her again.'

'Just leave them be.'

'It's all right for you. You got the cushy deal.'

Helena's hand slumped to her side. She replaced the cap on the tube. 'Oh Liddy, please don't start.'

Liddy bit her lip. Her room was a dream of white wicker and marble, her balcony swathed with the starry flowers of summer jasmine. And she liked Maresa. You couldn't help warming to Maresa: although she could be capricious and demanding, her generosity was lavish and her sense of enjoyment infectious (she always carried a transistor radio around so she could sing along to the songs). Bobo, however, was frustrating. '*Il mio piccolo mostro*,' Maresa called him, watching indulgently as he scribbled over Sara's picture-books or dismembered her soft toys. He was difficult to settle at bedtime and woke frequently in the night. Liddy hadn't realized, when Helena had talked her into this venture, that she would be responsible for two children. Their cousin, Massimo (Mimmo) Verducci, only a few months older than Bobo, was much more compliant and eager to please. Helena had engineered for herself the easier option and, despite their glamorous surroundings, it was beginning to rankle.

There came a light patter of feet across the terrace; a pair of brown legs sprang on to Helena's hips, reedy brown arms wrapped themselves around her neck. She tickled the sides of the child's chest and he wriggled like a little lizard. '*Madonna mia!*' she said. 'Who is this wild creature?'

'Massimo! *Sono io!*'

'*Chi?* Do I know this person?'

The little boy giggled and poked his face under the wide brim of her sunhat. 'Mimmo! *Adesso mi riconosci?*'

Helena swept off the hat and placed it on his dark curls as he vaulted from her back to the ground. 'It really doesn't make any difference, Liddy,' she said. 'We're all in this together. Come on now. Call the others and let's get down to the beach.'

The twisting flight of steps led directly on to a jetty where the boat was moored. It wasn't as grand as the yachts floating in the harbour, only a dinghy with a pair of oars and an outboard motor, but it was good enough for fishing purposes and for ferrying the children to other coves along the shore for a change of scene. Bobo led the way. Even though he had to stamp on every tread, he seemed to plunge down the cliff face as if it were a water chute. Mimmo, close behind, followed him on to the jetty where they both stopped short.

'Well now,' said Helena. 'Looks like we've got company.'

A young man was lying asleep on the coarse sand, tawny hair spread around his face like a lion's mane. He was wearing jeans and a short-sleeved shirt, but no shoes.

'Where on earth did he come from?'

'*Dài*.' Helena nudged Bobo. 'Sprinkle water on his toes.'

Bobo ran at once to fill his bucket. His idea of sprinkling was to flood the sleeper's feet in a torrent of seawater. The young man jerked upright but didn't show alarm. He drew up his knees, reached into his top pocket and tapped a cigarette from a squashed packet of MS. As he lit it, the smoke wavered and rose.

'Oh my God,' said Liddy. 'It's that guy from the club. James Knight.'

'Actually, he prefers to be known as Jake.'

They'd sampled the Vesuvio – 'So hot it erupts,' Helena had mocked – at the weekend. The club was proud to have a genuine English disc jockey spinning records on its turntables – though he confessed to Liddy that he wasn't really a DJ. He was trying to get into films and had been hanging around Cinecitta studios for months, in pursuit of work and contacts. Helena already knew this because she'd met him previously through a flatmate in Rome.

'Oh, right. Do you think he's looking for us?' Liddy hoped he was. She'd been impressed by his confident manner, the deft movements of his hands at the controls, that dazzling Hollywood smile. 'And he hasn't even yelled or lost his temper. I'd have wanted to throttle Bobo if he'd done that to me.'

'You're forgetting,' said Helena, 'that he's an actor.'

'You mean he's only pretending he's not bothered? Really he's steaming?' It had struck her at their first meeting that he showed enviable self-possession. If a scorpion rather than a lizard ran over his foot he'd probably just laugh. But she wondered whether, beneath this casual stance, she could sense a nervy twitch.

'No, darling.' Helena hopped on to the beach, unfurling her towel like a flag beside her. 'I mean that actors want to be liked. That's their motivation, isn't it? *Like* me. *Laud* me. *Love* me if you will – and I shall be as sweet as pie until you're eating out of my hand.'

'That's nonsense,' said Liddy. 'Everybody wants to be liked. I know I do. You too.' Actually she wasn't certain of this. Helena was abrasive rather than accommodating; provocative where others would hold back. She was provoking at this very moment: strolling over to Jake Knight to tell him off for trespassing, yet squatting beside him in a manner that was oddly intimate.

Liddy called to Sara to hurry up. She was dawdling from stair to stair with her favourite Barbie doll, stopping at intervals, where a platform gave a breathing space, to assess how much further she had to go. Feeling obliged to wait for her, Liddy sat down beside her basket. Bobo was already filling another bucket, his stocky legs planted like stakes in the shallows. Jake finished his cigarette and buried the filter. He and Helena were speaking in an undertone.

With a shriek of triumph Sara completed her descent and announced that she wanted to build a spa like Mamma's for her doll. Liddy wondered how anyone could enjoy being packed in mud and scoured with pumice and subjected to intense humidity, but according to Maresa: 'It repairs the condition of the skin. Also the function of the lung.' The women had remedies for nearly all ailments. They sounded like witches casting spells when they offered up their lists of ingredients: the camomile, the fernet, the evening primrose, the belladonna. 'She could open a health shop,' Helena had said of Gabi's bathroom cabinet. 'Pity she can't zap the eczema.'

Liddy helped Sara over the boulders and headed to a patch of damp sand where she scooped out a hollow into which Bobo helpfully tipped the contents of his bucket. 'It runs away,' Sara complained as her pool drained to a soggy slush.

'We should line it,' said Liddy. 'Find something plastic.'

Behind her, Jake rose to his feet. He reached out to Helena and pulled her up also. 'Liddy,' she called. 'We're going to take the boat out.'

Sara was ferreting in the beach bag. Bobo was crouched a few metres away, smashing mussels. He liked the way the viscous tissue shrivelled on contact with the air, and the fact that the shells didn't shatter instantly but required much manly pounding. Liddy rocked back on her haunches. 'Oh, okay. I suppose the kids will have to get their shoes on again.'

On a calm afternoon earlier in the week they'd crammed into the dinghy and chugged idly round the reef of rocks. At the tiller, Helena had negotiated the gullies between volcanic tufa columns that soared skywards like a Gothic cathedral, steering them through the dark shadows and back into the light. Liddy'd had to quell her nerves. She'd fixed Bobo on her lap and her arm around Sara's waist so she wouldn't tip out as she searched for mermaids. Eventually the gentle slap of water against wood had lulled her into repose. Second time around it might be easier.

'I didn't mean with the kids.'

'What?' She had misunderstood something here. Surely Helena didn't intend to leave the children behind?

Jake came over and hunkered down beside her. 'Look,' he said. 'I know we're being utterly selfish, leaving you holding the fort like this, so if you don't want us to go just say so.' He rested his hand on her forearm. His touch made her start because it felt scalding, like a poultice.

'Holding the fort?' she repeated, mystified, but seeing how churlish it would be to turn them down. 'What's all this about?'

'Something we need to discuss,' said Jake. His hazel eyes seemed to change colour according to the strength and position of the sun. 'We won't be long.'

He winked and went over to the mooring to untie the boat. Behind his back Helena mimed exasperation. Then she leapt in and sat at the prow. Jake pulled at the cord until the motor sparked into life and water churned beneath its blades. Sara jumped up and down on the spot. 'I want to go with them!' she cried. 'Take me. Take me too.' But already they were out of earshot.

The two boys were playing in the lee of the rocks, lining up lumps of fallen shale to create opposing squads of soldiers for battle. They were keeping to the shade, Liddy was glad to see, even if their aim was to obliterate each other. Sara was burying her doll. Liddy tried to help but she couldn't focus on creating the series of underground caverns. Her hands shook and her mind kept returning to Helena and Jake in the boat, to her own sense of abandonment. What did they need to discuss that was so private? They hardly knew each other. When they'd met in the Vesuvio, Liddy had been enchanted to find someone she could speak English with; Helena demurred.

'Have you got something against him?' Liddy had asked.

'No. Why?'

'You seem, I don't know . . . rather cool.'

'Maybe I'm just wary of that whole expat instant soulmates routine. Like freshers' week all over again, cosying up to types you wouldn't give the time of day if you met them in the pub at home. Know what I mean?'

'But not *him*. He's gorgeous.'

'Christ, you're smitten already.'

'No I'm not.'

'Wouldn't you rather grab yourself a sexy Italian? Dark eyes you can drown in, neat little arse but hung like a stallion. Declarations of passion in the language of romance.' There was a mischievous gurgle at the back of her throat. 'All that sort of thing.'

'I'd rather have a guy who understands what I'm saying.'

Someone was calling her name. She blinked and turned to Sara who was building a massage table, grunts collecting in her throat as she concentrated. She looked upwards, to the terrace of the villa, to see if Maresa or Gabi had come back. She suspected they'd long finished their therapy sessions and had been enjoying an extended late lunch, flirting with the waiters. No one was leaning over the terrace wall or signalling from the top of the cliff, so she swung her gaze to Bobo. To be honest, she'd recognized his high-pitched roar all along.

She was standing in the glare of sunlight. Both boys were in deep shadow and she had to shield her eyes with her hand. As she adjusted her gaze she saw that they had climbed on to a ledge a few feet up. Each had a stick in his hand and was attacking the other in mock combat. '*Guarda*, Leeddy!' Bobo called again, flourishing his weapon. '*Come sono bravo!*'

'Get down at once!' Liddy yelled back. From this angle she couldn't tell how wide the ledge was, but she didn't want to take any risks. '*Subito!*'

They ignored her, of course. She shouldn't have to manage all three of them alone. That wasn't part of the deal. She felt another rush of resentment that Helena expected her to cope, although (to be honest, again) her resentment – the maggot that was burrowing into her perfect summer and tainting it – was largely because she'd pretended not to have the slightest interest in Jake and yet had now gone off with him.

'Get down,' Liddy repeated. 'Finish your fight here, on the ground.'

Bobo was shorter but heavier than his cousin; he had also chosen a stouter stick. Mimmo's was as long and thin as a fencing rapier.

Despite his agile footwork, it snapped under Bobo's hammering and he was left holding a stub. His response was to swish and thrust it in a series of stabbing motions but he was hampered by his lack of reach. Bobo swiped his make-believe sword through the air and lunged at Mimmo's chest. The latter tried to jump backwards but lost his balance. Liddy watched, helpless, as the little boy toppled from the rocks in an arcing somersault.

2

The boat nosed across the tranquil bay. Liddy and the children were small, animated specks. Helena bit into a rosy nectarine she'd filched from the beach bag. She couldn't imagine a more delicious fruit. It was her first gift to Liddy when they'd met up in Rome. 'Try a taste of heaven,' she'd told her. It had been a new experience for Liddy too.

Jake cut the motor and began to row, the shift and dip of the oars propelling them silently through the water. After a while he said, 'Best to clear the decks, don't you think?'

Helena sucked at the sweet nectarine flesh; let it slide down her throat. She threw the kernel with a plop into the sea and licked each finger one by one; a light breeze dried them. She said, 'Why do I get the feeling you're stalking me?'

'I've no idea.'

'Can you tell me, hand on heart, that it's complete chance you've landed up here?'

'Sure. I can't afford to turn work down.'

He could ladle sincerity like syrup, but she wasn't persuaded. 'I think you're a terrible liar.'

'I'm a very good liar actually.'

A motor launch cruised by some distance away and their little dinghy bobbed unsteadily in its wake. Helena plaited her hair into a smooth rope at the nape of her neck and jammed her straw hat back on. She kept her eyes hidden behind the great dark blots of her sunglasses and waited for him to continue.

'All I want to know,' said Jake, 'is why you're avoiding me.'

'I'm not.'

'Yes you are. And you've been pretending to your friend that you hardly know me.'

'Maybe because it spooked me.'

'What?'

'Finding you on the same island, of course.'

He slowed his stroke and craned forward. 'Anyway, I'm *not* stalking you. I happened to meet the owner of the Vesuvio and wangle my way into a contract. Which is how come I'm here, masquerading as the hot catch from the UK. Basically, Helena, I need the money. A job is a job and I think I've rather fallen on my feet with this one. I'm not going to cramp your style.'

'No one ever cramps my style. You know what freaked me. We needn't go into it again.'

'Your reaction was kind of off-the-scale. You could at least give me a chance to explain.'

'I don't want to talk about it.'

He clicked his tongue as if she were being particularly recalcitrant, like a sulky child. 'Look, I'm sorry you've got this grudge against me. But if we're going to see a bit more of each other – which is inevitable in a place this small, don't you think? – we might as well make the best of it.' He dropped one of the oars to offer a handshake and the boat drifted in a circle. His touch brought back a medley of half-remembered intimacies, the slip of sweat on skin. 'Okay?' he said. 'Can we call it quits now?'

She nodded, withdrew her hand and dipped it into the sea.

'I won't queer your pitch and you won't queer mine.'

'Am I right in thinking you have designs on someone?'

'I want us to be friends, that's all.'

'Well, you needn't worry,' she said. 'I'll be the soul of discretion. Anyway, I'm not the slightest bit interested in what you get up to.'

'You really mean that?'

'I really mean that. And now I think we ought to get back.'

Jake rescued the oar and slotted it into its rowlock. He glanced over his shoulder at the picturesque cove and the two villas perched above it like nesting gulls. With a steady rhythmic pull he began to head back to the shore. The sun caught the ripple of the muscles in his arms, the clench of his knuckles and jaw, the demeanour of someone who knew his own powers of attraction. 'Talking of falling on one's feet,' he observed after a while. 'You haven't done so badly yourself. Special subject: gold-digging.'

She lunged at him. 'Fuck off! That is *not* the way to keep me sweet.'

'I'm only teasing,' he protested. 'Just a bit jealous because I'm bunked in a stuffy little room above the club. The bin lorries wake me at seven every morning and, unlike you, I overlook power lines, empty crates and the hen house.'

'My heart bleeds. What hen house?'

'Didn't you spot the *tavola calda*? They make their own pasta with the eggs. I live off it actually. It's okay. You and your friend could join me for dinner one night.'

'Thanks. We'll bear that in mind when we get bored with our four course banquets.'

He shipped the oars for the final approach, as they glided towards the jetty. 'I knew you'd come round eventually.'

The scene on the shore was peaceful. Liddy was sitting with her arms around Mimmo; the other two perched close by as if they were listening to a story. Helena stepped out and Jake moored the boat with much tying and retying of knots. A bird of prey hovered in the clear sky above them, casting a momentary shadow. Sara sprang up and ran to clasp Helena's hand.

'Hey, slow down,' said Helena. '*Piano*. If you gabble like that I won't understand a word.'

'Mimmo!' shrieked Sara. '*È successo qualcosa*.'

Helena whipped off her sunglasses and took long strides up the beach. 'Liddy! What's happened?'

Liddy was cradling Mimmo on her lap, smoothing his temple with a damp towel. On his shin was a nasty gash three inches long, a loose flap of skin, a thick rivulet of blood.

'Mimmo fell.'

'How? Where from?'

'He and Bobo were messing about. They were on that ledge up there and he lost his footing.'

'Oh Liddy . . .'

'What's that supposed to mean?'

'They shouldn't have been clambering around the rocks. Didn't you see what they were up to?'

'Do I have eyes in the back of my head? If you hadn't gone swanning off –'

Helena gritted her teeth. As a friend, Liddy had many excellent qualities. She was a spirited and willing accomplice (she also provided a useful counter-balance to some of Helena's more reckless enterprises), but she wasn't much good at taking the blame. 'Honestly! We were gone about ten minutes. I ask you to do one simple thing . . .'

'Simple!' exploded Liddy. 'I didn't even dare move him in case he had a fracture. I heard a story once of a kid who'd walked around on a broken leg for days. The bones set out of alignment and he limped for the rest of his life.'

Jake came to crouch the other side of Mimmo. 'Shall I have a look?' he said.

'Why? What can you do?'

'I might be able to tell if the ankle's sprained or the tibia's broken. At least the bleeding's not too bad.'

'So you're a doctor now, are you?'

He nodded. 'Sort of.'

'Sort of! How can you be a sort of doctor? What, d'you mean like a vet?'

'I studied medicine,' Jake said. 'But I didn't qualify.' His hands on Mimmo's limbs were soothing and the boy stopped quaking. He asked him in Italian if any other part hurt, whether he'd banged his head when he landed. He bent the boy's leg at the knee and probed the flesh delicately. 'It feels all right, but he could have a greenstick fracture, which would still need a cast. I think he'll be okay but he should get an X-ray to be on the safe side. Can you stand, Mimmo? If it's really painful he won't be able to put any weight on it.'

Helena helped Mimmo to rise. Liddy was shaking her head. 'I don't get it,' she said. 'First you're an actor, then you're a disc jockey and now you're a medic. I mean, how can that be?'

'You've got it the wrong way around,' said Jake. 'First I was a medic. Only I flunked my exams so I dropped out. I'm not proud of failing, but I was doing the wrong subject. My parents are both doctors and it didn't occur to them I might have different ideas.'

'I didn't think acting was something you could just walk into either.'

He grinned. 'It isn't. It's bloody hard to crack. But, you see, I'm shameless.'

'How the hell,' said Helena, unable to decide which of them she was more annoyed with, 'are we going to get him up to the villa?'

'I'll carry him I suppose,' said Jake. 'If you'll lift him on to my back.'

The ascent seemed steeper than ever, each flight an obstacle which Bobo and Sara greeted with shrieks of dismay. When their straggling procession finally reached the terrace, they found Gabriella reclining on her steamer chair with a glass of orange Aperol and a copy of Italian *Vogue*. She was wearing a fine cotton kaftan with concealing sleeves, and her head was wrapped in a turban which accentuated her thin, arresting face. Gabi exuded the sense that, despite all her privilege, she was trapped in a life that didn't suit her; she had no energy for the demands of husband and son. She turned reproachfully: they had come back too soon, she hadn't finished her magazine, and she wasn't yet ready to be disturbed. Then she saw Mimmo's condition and leapt up. '*What* have you done to my baby?'

'Gabi, I'm really sorry. He's had a fall.'

'*Come?* How does this happen?'

'He was playing with Bobo on the rocks and we didn't realize. We didn't see . . .' Helena hated sounding so ineffectual, but she could only report what Liddy had told her. On the way up Mimmo had clutched Jake's neck and occasionally yelped with pain. Now he sat on one of the wrought-iron chairs clasping his knee and dripping on to the terrace tiles. His face was ghostly with shock.

'You were not watching him?'

'It only takes a minute. We tell them not to climb, but –'

Gabi peered at Jake, his shirt smudged with blood. 'And who is this?'

'An English friend. Jake Knight.' There was no law against them socializing, no need to apologize for his presence.

'There were *three* of you,' Gabi said, 'and nobody noticed what they were doing? You were amusing yourselves in some other way perhaps. You were –'

At this, Jake stepped forward. His Italian was better than Helena's and with charm and fluency he depicted their sojourn on the beach: the bathing, the games, the construction of spas and saunas and pirate ships and army barracks; how Mimmo's tumble was an unforeseen unlucky accident; that the damage was probably not as bad as it looked.

Gabi said, 'I shall take him at once to the clinic.'

Helena said, 'Do you want me to come with you?'

Gabi pulled her sleeve over a flaking patch of dry skin. 'No,' she said. 'Your friends should leave. Sara and Bobo must go home. I shan't need help. *You* may do as you please.'

What Helena would have liked to do was go for a long walk, up into the dense wooded mountainside where wild boar still rooted for sweet chestnuts and tawny owls nested, where she might find shade and tranquillity, but she was concerned for Mimmo and didn't want to look callous. Nor did she want to spend any more time with Liddy and Jake. Liddy worried at issues like a terrier: the afternoon would be analysed and dissected and gnawed at until she could find an explanation that satisfied her. She was never prepared to acknowledge that some things were just random. So Helena slung her beach bag over her shoulder, retired to her room and drew savagely on her cigarette. She sat on the bed and kicked her espadrilles, faded, salt-stained, the heels downtrodden, to the far wall. She picked up a book and began turning the pages without reading them. That poor kid. In her mind she could see him suspended in the air, the slow-motion crash, the damage that could have been so much worse . . .

When the knock came it startled her, interrupting her drowsy stupor. The visitor didn't wait for a response. Fabrizio Verducci strolled through life helping himself to whatever he fancied: a wealthy aristocratic wife, building projects underpinned by money and connections, the best view on the hillside. The weekend before he had relieved his son of the cone of nuts he'd been holding and tossed them one by one into the air. 'See if you can catch them in your mouth,' he'd said. Mimmo couldn't. Fabrizio could. So he ate all the nuts.

Lean and lanky with a commanding presence, he was the kind of man who made a room seem smaller. As Helena stirred and uncurled her toes, he ducked through the doorway and sat at the end of her bed.

'Where is everybody?'

Her vision was bleary. 'What time is it?'

His watch was expensive, a bold face in a gold link chain. 'Not long after seven. Too early for bed.'

'I didn't mean to fall asleep. Have I got the day wrong? You shouldn't be here.'

'*Facio un ponte*.' The season was full of religious holidays, which could be bridged into long weekends. 'I've only just arrived. See. I haven't even had time to change.' He was wearing a light-coloured linen-mix suit, workday shoes.

'Were you expecting us to meet you? Gabi didn't say.'

'No, I took a taxi. A surprise for you.' He grinned and moved much closer; his hand lingered at her thigh. Downy brown hairs escaped his starched cotton cuff. 'I missed you,' he said.

Helena's mouth was dry as ash. She picked up the bottle of mineral water she kept by her bed and swigged it. 'You did?' Her breathing was swift and shallow.

'Of course. You should have stayed in Rome. Then I could see you every day.'

'You wouldn't though. You'd've kept cancelling me for more important appointments. Anyhow, we've been through this. It was getting so hot in the city. Everybody else was leaving and I had to find work or I'd have been under pressure to go home. And this way I can get to know Mimmo. You already told me Gabi won't care: you have your "arrangement".'

She knew he considered her too close for comfort, but he couldn't deny the added frisson of danger that made the sex so exciting. His hand inched up her leg and he bent his head to nuzzle her throat. Although she could feel herself arching her spine and stirring her hips in response, she pushed him away.

'But we are alone, yes?' he said.

'They might come back any minute.'

He mimed an exaggerated sigh. '*Va bene*. But now, I have something for you.' He patted his suit jacket and pulled a slim rectangular box from his pocket.

Helena squirmed. 'You don't have to give me anything. You know that.'

'I'm tired of seeing that old shoelace around your neck.'

She called it her lucky charm: a leather thong threaded through a lustrous green pebble she'd found on the beach at home. Fingering its smooth cool surface, she accepted the gift with her other hand but didn't open it. 'There's something I have to tell you.'

He was quick to react to her tone, his playfulness dissipated. 'What?'

'The reason Mimmo and Gabi aren't here is because they've gone to the doctor.'

'*Porca miseria!* What for?'

'It's my fault,' said Helena kneeling on the bed so that her eyes were level with his. 'This afternoon on the beach Mimmo hurt his leg on the rocks. He was play-acting with Bobo and slipped and lost his footing. It was a stupid accident. Gabi's taken him to get the wound dressed and X-rayed. I'm truly sorry.'

'He's not badly hurt?'

'I don't think so, no.'

Fabrizio jumped up. He ran his fingers through his hair. He began to pace the room, his shoes ringing like blows on the marble tiles. He wanted every detail. 'You are sure there was no concussion? No bones are broken? There will be a scar?'

'Well, that depends whether he needs stitches . . .'

'This should not have happened. It is not a good omen.'

Helena should not have been tempted by the boat. 'I guess I'm useless at this lark,' she said. 'Gabi was really cross; she wouldn't let me go with them and I don't blame her. I shouldn't have taken my eyes off him for a second. But you must know that I would never deliberately . . . I mean, I'm really fond of Mimmo.'

'To be fond,' he said, 'is not the point. The point is to be responsible. This could have been a disaster.'

'Yes, I realize that.'

'You should have stayed in Rome,' he said again.

'Look, if you don't trust me to look after your son you can fire me. I'll understand.'

He held her face between his hands, clamped his mouth on hers in an impatient kiss. After pausing for breath he said, 'Is that what you think I should do?'

'It's up to you.' She held out the box he had given her. 'You'd better take this back, anyhow.'

'*Che cazzo dici?* Why?'

'Because I cocked up and you've probably spent far too much.'

'It's no good to me.'

'You could give it to someone else. Gabi.'

'She already has one similar. In fact' – he gave a wry smile – 'it would be better if you don't wear it in the house. Now, let's forget this nonsense. Go on, open the box.'

On padded white satin lay a strand of rich blue beads. Helena lifted it out with an admiring gasp. 'It's lovely,' she said.

'Lapis lazuli. The colour of your eyes. Make sure you take good care of it.' He covered her hand with his own and looked at her sideways the way Mimmo did sometimes when he'd been mischievous.

'Don't worry, I will.' And she stowed the necklace in the drawer where she kept her contraceptive pills and her cigarettes, beneath an innocent pile of knickers and T-shirts, where she assumed it would be safe.

3

Three upturned espresso cups were aligned in the centre of the table, one of them covering a fifty lire piece. Small change was like gold dust in Italy that summer. Once obtained, coins of twenty, fifty or a hundred lire were rarely relinquished, but Jake had persuaded Liddy to supply one for his conjuring trick. She and Helena were supposed to be guessing which cup it was hiding under. Jake sat back and folded his arms as if he had all the time in the world, though his break from the turntables was more than half over. He had already baffled them with card tricks, with the transfer of aces from one pile to another. 'Go on,' he'd say. 'Cut. Now, cut again.' And each time, there it was: the ace of hearts. The fifty lire piece had travelled too. He had found it beneath the ashtray and inside a matchbox. At one point he'd bent down and retrieved the coin from Liddy's shoe.

Staring at the cups she said, 'Whichever I choose will be wrong.'

'Actually,' said Helena, 'you've got a thirty-three per cent chance of being right.' She'd seen these tricks before. Not so often that she knew how they worked, but enough to know that she didn't really care now that she was on her fourth gin fizz.

'Well, I'm going to go for the least likely.' Liddy pointed. 'That one.'

With a smirk of complacency he lifted the cup.

'You cheated.'

'How? How did I cheat?'

'You tell me.'

'Never,' he said, shaking his head, 'give away the tricks of the trade. Try again.'

Liddy was wrong the second time too. She picked up the third cup and snatched back her money. 'You're pretty good. Did it take ages to learn?'

'I've spent an awful lot of my life hanging around, that's all.'

'You could go professional.'

'Yeah. I could be one of those guys you see on street corners, plying their trade at a little folding table, drawing the punters in.'

'Or a magician? Or a children's entertainer?'

He flicked back his fringe, a mannerism that gave his face an edgy profile in the lambent outdoor lighting. 'Thanks, but I don't know whether I should set my sights so high.'

'Shit, I'm sorry. I didn't mean to cause offence.' An embarrassed silence settled on the table.

Helena spun her empty glass; she crossed and uncrossed her legs, scarcely disguising the fact that she was bored. Evenings at the Vesuvio were quite different from what she was used to. The clubs at home in Liverpool – fetid cellars awash with spilt beer and tight black leather – had a raw energy quite missing here. Young men and women swayed together under the coloured lanterns, dancing languidly, as if the heat of the day had induced a torpor that couldn't be shaken off; even the smoke from their cigarettes drifted in lazy spirals. When they needed privacy they slunk into the corners of the courtyard and hid among the pots of passion flower and jasmine; in the dark, hot tongues probed, moist hands strayed.

She pushed back her chair. 'Off to the loo,' she muttered. 'I'm sure Jake can spin a few more tricks while I'm gone.' She didn't add – although she felt like it – anyway, three's a crowd.

In the dankness of the ladies' toilets she splashed water on her face. Then she wandered through the main entrance out on to the moonlit street. A brick wall extended at right angles from the premises. A haphazard collection of scooters and motorbikes sprawled against it as randomly as if they'd fallen from a great height. A couple of young men in tight shirts and tighter trousers were admiring a Suzuki 500: its polished chrome chassis, the fat, red belly of its engine. Something in their manner made Helena wonder whether the bike actually belonged to them, even though they were brazen enough to be hauling it from its station in full view of the road. The snap of her lighter alerted them and one of the pair strutted towards her. He had a slight cast to his eye and a golden medallion blazing on his sternum; his cheap aftershave was already overlaid with grease and petrol.

He addressed her in the old-fashioned plural. '*Volete fare un giro?*'

'A ride? With you? *No, grazie.*' She was slurring her words but her accent had given her away. Now, as an unaccompanied foreigner, she was presented with further tempting invitations. His tone changed from insolent to ingratiating. He offered to take her to a club where the drinks were half the price of the Vesuvio, to show her the magnificent slopes of his cousin's vineyard, or the spot where the thermal waters foamed into the sea. Feigning reluctance, she turned him down. His friend, struggling with the starter motor, growled with impatience.

'Are you *stealing* that bike?' asked Helena.

At that, the man grabbed her wrist and began to pull her towards it. Surely, she thought, it's not big enough to take three people. What could he have in mind? Was she to be sandwiched between them, driven to the top of the mountain, raped and abandoned? Not that she felt threatened just yet – the pair didn't seem competent enough to be organized criminals. When he refused to release her, however, she shouted and waved her cigarette in his face. Already some drops of oil had spilled on the tarmac.

'*Attento, la benzina!*' he hissed.

'Then let me go!' said Helena, trying to wrench her wrist free, and inhaling so that the tip glowed red and dangerous.

Another man appeared in the club doorway. At this point her delayed sense of panic asserted itself. She couldn't possibly take on three of them. There wasn't any exit available to her and she wouldn't get far on foot. Were they really thieves? Should she take the initiative and warn someone? She yelled anyway. '*Aiuto!*' She supposed she needed help; her captor was refusing to relax his grip.

The man in the doorway rushed forward. He was not, it transpired, an ally of the other two. Instantly his fist shot out, whistled past Helena's cheek and thumped the exposed chest a fraction to the left of its medallion. Helena was let go, shoved aside so fiercely that she teetered against a mud-spattered Vespa. This in turn jostled a second scooter, causing a ripple effect of rocking windshields and handlebars. In a kind of syncopated harmony the stranger's fists continued to thrust and parry while his opponent ducked and stumbled. Then came the sudden roar of an engine firing.

Powered by this success, the first man straddled the Suzuki and opened up the throttle. The second threw a futile, wayward punch and leapt on the pillion seat. The bike screeched down the road and around the corner.

Helena discarded her cigarette and massaged her bruised arm. Fabrizio would say she took too many risks but, really, how could you know that nipping out for a breath of air would get you into trouble? The stranger, brushing his sleeve but not looking at all dishevelled, came over. His eyes were large, brown and anxious. A black moustache hovered above his mouth with a sense of impermanence, as if it had been recently acquired and might as easily be ditched again.

'*Questi uomini, le hanno dato fastidio?*' he asked.

Did they bother her? Not any more. 'Thank you,' she said. 'For the heroics. You were terrific.'

He replied in careful English. 'You are not hurt?'

'No, no, I'm fine.' She attempted humour. 'Shaken, not stirred.'

He didn't understand it. 'You would like to drink?'

'Yeah, guess I could do with a beer. What about you? Are you okay? Hope you didn't get too battered.'

'Me? No. *Coglioni* like that are no problem.' She frowned at the graze on his knuckles, but he misinterpreted her concern. 'They are not your friends I hope? You do not know these men?'

'God, no, never seen them before in my life.'

'*Allora, andiamo.*' He clasped her elbow and steered her back inside.

The tiled floor of the bar was slick with the spillage of beer and the splash of rainbow-coloured cocktails. A huddle of young men brandished bottles of Peroni to punctuate their anecdotes and she wondered whether one of them was the rightful owner of the Suzuki. Already the incident was receding; it had happened so quickly she wasn't sure if she could remember the sequence of events. She might have imagined the whole thing – as if the wobbling scooters had been an illusion and the skirmish pure shadow play.

Helena's new escort passed over her drink. His shirt collar was unfastened, his face above it soft and plump. His jeans were particularly well-pressed, despite the dust-up. He was either married or living at home. She pictured his mother, a widow naturally, rigging up the ironing board in the kitchen of their three-room apartment, bringing her weight to bear on the crease of his trousers, guiding the point of the iron into the corners of his collars and cuffs.

'I am Enzo,' he said, proud of his English. 'You?'

'Helena.' She waved her bottle and drank directly from its neck. 'Well, Enzo, thanks for that amazing rescue. I really didn't have a clue what was going on . . .'

'Ouf, is nothing,' he said modestly. 'You are on holiday, I think?'

'Actually I'm working. My friend and I, we look after the children of families who have villas here.'

'Yes, I have seen you with them,' he said, slipping back into Italian. 'I didn't think they could be yours.'

'You've seen us?' Should she be disturbed by this? 'Where?'

'At the port sometimes. In the playground. This is a small place and I'm often outside on the street. In fact, two days ago you greeted me.'

'I did what?' She tried to imagine why she would hail an unknown man. She tried to remember what she might have been doing at the time, but the days blended into one another, into a soup of sea and sun and small children's incessant demands for *gelato*. Perhaps that was it? Perhaps her protector was really an ice cream vendor. 'What do you do?'

'I am a *carabiniere*.'

'Oh my God!'

The girls often saw pairs of *carabinieri* patrolling the port area, conferring beneath shop awnings or beside their powerful, gleaming motorbikes. Helena had been in Italy for long enough to know that the police expected to be taken seriously – they didn't wear their guns, their polished boots, their aura of menace for fun – but sometimes sheer devilment made her want to tease them. She must have tipped her hat in a mock salute, but she could never have recognized him again. Didn't men in uniform realize they all looked the same? Your eye was so busy being drawn to their shiny boots or the swagger of their epaulettes, the face was an afterthought. It was good to know that he wasn't merely decorative, leaping to her assistance like that (though she did consider his performance a little over the top).

'A policeman is never off duty.'

'Ah, now you want to see my *permesso*. They always used to tell us that in Rome. Keep your papers with you, you never know when someone will ask for them. I'm afraid I don't, though. My friend Liddy's taken charge. I've such a bad record for losing stuff.'

He nodded. 'The only reason I need to see your papers is if you are in trouble.'

She cocked her head and rubbed the mouth of the bottle. 'Is that an invitation? Only I might not be so lucky second time around.'

He didn't get her jokes. He was a serious young man, well, youngish; probably in his late twenties, which accounted for his gravity and the quaint old-fashioned quality that must come from spending his whole life (apart from military service) within an area of thirty-odd square miles.

Jake's voice crackled over the loudspeaker. He spoke in a laconic drawl with the mid-Atlantic accent he'd devised for this new persona, this parody of a DJ. It made no difference whether he was understood as long as he sounded authentic. 'Now it's time to get grooving, folks. We're heading back to the sixties and the sounds of the late, lamented king of rock'n'roll, Elvis Presley.'

'You want that we dance?' said Enzo.

Helena's response was noncommittal but at the first beat of 'Suspicious Minds', he caught her around the waist and spun her into the music. She could just make out Liddy sitting at the table, scanning those who passed near enough for her to see them properly. Liddy's short sight had always been a joke between them. There's no way she'll be able to identify me, she thought in amusement. No way she'll believe I've been dancing with a *carabiniere*. She tried to harness her giddy feet to the slow rhythm of the music, letting Enzo steady her. He was very correct, she had to admit: his hand light but firm in the small of her back, his cheek a respectful distance from hers. And so chivalrous!

Muscling in, saving her from those creepy youths, an instant avenger. She giggled at the memory. And if she had not been quite so drunk, a glimmer of self-preservation might have surfaced, might have warned her not to mess around. Instead, she thought, what the hell, I owe him a kiss at least, and moved her lips closer. She was taken aback by his response, the passion of it, the way he devoured her.

'I can see you again?' he asked when she pulled away in alarm.

'You don't have a girlfriend already? A, what's it called, *fidanzata*?'

'No.'

'Why not?'

'*Boh*, I'm very busy. Italian girls, you know, they like a lot of attention. Also I have not found the right one.'

'So you'll make do with a foreign girl in the meantime?'

He smiled as if he had only half understood. 'I may telephone you?'

She imagined Fabrizio's reaction, his blustering indignation because he knew he had no right to be jealous. 'Oh, I don't know if they'd like that, the Verduccis I mean. We're supposed to look after the children most nights.'

'But not every night?'

'Well, no.'

'So you could meet me again, here?'

'Yes, I expect we'll come back to this place from time to time.'

'When?'

'I don't know right now.'

'Tomorrow I am on duty, but the next week? Tuesday?'

'No, I don't think . . .'

'Maybe is better after all if you give me your number.'

This was getting complicated. A gentle disentanglement was what she was aiming for, but Enzo was already borrowing a Biro from the barman. He patted his pockets in search of something to write on but there was nothing to clutter the clean line of his trousers. He held out his palm so she could scrawl her number down. Another drink, another dance, and a layer of sweat would, she hoped, render it illegible.

Jake's session had come to a close. The evening was winding down with a medley of sentimental Italian ballads looping around the tape deck.

People were drifting out into the street, into waiting taxis. Helena was nowhere to be seen. Liddy, peering unsuccessfully into gloomy alcoves, wondered what on earth could have happened to her. There appeared to be a small riot going on outside the club, bursts of altercation, accusations of theft. Perhaps she was caught up in it. Before she could find out, she stumbled into Jake. He had a bottle of J&B whisky in his hand. 'I've got some catching up to do,' he said. 'Want to join me?'

Liddy didn't much like the taste of whisky or its viscosity. She made a half-hearted excuse, citing Helena's absence.

Oh,' he said, 'she's probably bunked off with her dancing partner.'

'Who?'

'Didn't you see them smooching together? Cheek to cheek?'

'She might have told me! I'll have to go back by myself now.'

'Do you want me to get you a cab?'

There was definitely a fracas on the forecourt. 'Later,' said Liddy. 'Maybe I will have a drink with you first.'

'Great! Come on up.'

Which was how she found herself in his room above the club. The ceiling was low and sloping. The tap dripped in the corner basin. The air swathed them in hot, thick folds like a blanket even though the window was open. Crammed on to a table were Jake's possessions: packs of cards, a travel clock, a radio, and a selection of books – she balked at the titles: Goethe's *Italian Journey*, Norman Douglas's *South Wind*, and Malcolm Lowry's *Under the Volcano*. Clothes poked from a chest with two ill-fitting drawers; the bed – cheap metal mesh – was unmade.

'I travel light,' he said, watching her face.

'I didn't mean to be nosy.'

'I'm not into possessions. One suitcase, that's all I need. Then I can just get up and go.'

'Sounds like you're always doing a moonlight flit.'

'It's called keeping your options open.'

'And the books, are they for show?' She picked up the Lowry, its silver spine proclaiming it was a Penguin classic.

'Who the hell would I show them to?'

She put it down again. 'You must be awfully clever.'

'Hey.' He patted her shoulder. 'I'm the product of an expensive, wasted education. Officially I'm a black sheep. Loitering around film studios was not what my family had in mind for me. Still, one of these days I plan to write and direct, and in this industry it's all about the people you know. You have to be what the Americans call "good in the room". Not that Hollywood interests me.' He poured a shot of whisky into a tumbler and added a dribble of tepid water from the tap. 'Is this okay for you? Can't face going back downstairs for ice.'

Since she wasn't going to drink it anyway, she nodded and sat gingerly on the edge of his bed. Jake came to sit next to her and clinked glasses. Close-up she could see the sheen of perspiration on his upper lip, his mouth almost womanly in its winged bow shape. He drained his whisky in one rapid gulp and poured another. She began to chatter, a string of nonsense, gush she often came out with when she was nervous. She could see he wasn't listening to anything she said.

He removed her glass from her unresisting hand and set it on top of the pile of books. She knew what was coming next and the few remaining seconds of anticipation felt delicious to her. Even more delicious was the pressure of his lips and the thrust of his tongue. She might have been composed of chocolate. Her bones lost substance and since they could no longer support the rest of her, she collapsed backwards. That Jake was dextrous she already knew; that he could unbutton a blouse so adroitly or unwrap a skirt in such a fluid sweep took her by surprise. She felt as though she were being skinned like an apple, the ribbon of peel spiralling away in a single piece. Balanced on one elbow, he examined her body as a doctor might, tracing the rise and fall of her sternum, her diaphragm, the swell of her hips and pubis, until his hand glided between her legs.

The outside clamour receded. The tingling at her nerve endings was filling her brain, driving out everything else. Jake raised his head from her breast. 'Are you sure?' he asked.

Much of Liddy's previous experience with schoolboys and fellow students had been of intercourse as a race against time: urgent, unfettered, up against a wall or under a pile of party coats; over and done with. There had been little enjoyment in it. 'Quite sure,' she said, thinking how perfectly simple were the ingredients of a holiday romance, how effortless the process of seduction. 'Please don't stop.'

He was shedding his own clothes now. Their flesh bonded with soft slurping sounds that made them both chuckle. She dug her fingernails into his back and gripped him with her knees. He moved with a steadily increasing rhythm until she thought the feeble bed would collapse beneath them. It bucked and creaked and even seemed to give a curious hoot of triumph.

Afterwards they propped themselves up against the hard, unyielding bolster. Jake lit a cigarette and stroked Liddy's curves with his free hand.

'Okay?' he said.

'Yes, great.'

He peered at the travel clock. 'Can't keep you here all night.'

'It's all right.' She could lie there for ever, quietly fizzing.

'You know what I'd really like to do . . .' He had a butterfly touch, delicate but ticklish. 'Is to find somewhere cooler than this joint, out of doors, say, somewhere I could explore every inch of you, somewhere we could screw each other into oblivion. How about that?'

Liddy swallowed. He was drumming on her ribs now, a light tapping rhythm that was causing her insides to dissolve again just as they had begun to rally and regroup. 'I thought you weren't interested in me, you didn't want me.'

'Why on earth would you think that?'

She considered. 'It's just, I suppose, because we've never actually been alone together . . . I thought you preferred Helena.'

'Oh . . .' He swung his legs off the bed and into his jeans – no underpants she noted, admiring his trim, creamy buttocks. 'What has she said to you?'

'Nothing. But when you went off together in the boat the other day, I assumed it was because she was more your type.'

'My type?'

'Well, she's so slim and sexy. I'm dumpy in comparison.'

'Dumpy? Are you fishing for compliments here?'

'No!' She blushed and fumbled for her clothes.

'Here, let me.' He slipped her knickers over her feet, caressing her calves and thighs on the upward journey, smoothing the cotton into place in tantalizing slow motion. 'As for the boat . . . I just wanted to check I had a clear field.'

'What does that mean?'

'That I fancied you right from the off, but I didn't want to tread on any toes.'

'But why couldn't you just ask me out straight? You don't have to get Helena's permission!'

'It was a bit more complicated than that.'

'I don't see why it should be. You can say anything you like in front of her. And me. We're best friends, we're really close. We tell each other everything.'

'Perhaps not quite everything.'

She halted, with one arm stuck in a sleeve. Jake drew the blouse around her shoulders, bunching the material tightly so she was cocooned and he could tug her closer. He kissed her eyebrows, her eyelids, the line of her cheekbones.

'So tell me,' she murmured, though reluctant to destroy the moment. 'Explain.'

'You'd better ask her. As you said, she's your friend.'

Ambling down to the bar the following morning to buy ice creams for the children, keeping tight hold so they wouldn't trip off the path or run under the wheels of a car, Helena said, 'Where did you get to last night? I was looking for you everywhere.'

'What?' This was the wrong way round. 'No, hang on a minute. I was looking for you.'

'You can't have tried very hard.'

'Jake said you'd gone off with someone.'

'Who?'

'I don't know. Some bloke you were dancing with.'

Helena rolled her eyes. 'Oh, that was awkward. He saved me from these creeps who were hassling me, but then he homed in on me himself. *And* he turned out to be a policeman. I don't think I handled it very well. I only escaped by giving him the Verduccis' number. I could have done with rescue actually.'

'Did you get caught up in all that stuff going on outside?'

'The stolen Suzuki? Yeah, I saw them take it.' She grinned. 'Mind you, so did Enzo and he didn't realize what was going on either. He thought they were after me.'

'Enzo?'

'Jesus, I just told you! The *carabiniere*. Whatever you got up to has addled your brain.'

This was it, confession time. 'Actually, I went to bed with Jake.'

'Ow!' Bobo had kicked a shower of gravel in an upward spurt, which struck Helena's knee. After rubbing at it, she said, 'Well, congratulations.'

'Don't be so sarky. I wouldn't have done if I'd thought it would upset you.'

'I'm not upset.'

'You're not ecstatic, are you? Why do I get the feeling there's something odd going on? I mean, I thought we didn't have any secrets. I told you all about Phil.'

'Phil?'

'The bloke I went out with term before last. The economist. And about Steve.'

'Who's Steve?'

'Oh for heaven's sake, Helena, don't you read my letters? I read yours. Over and over. Especially when you first came out here. I was so envious of you! And I was so pleased when you fixed up this job. But you had some kind of thing with Jake in Rome, didn't you? I don't understand why you didn't let on.'

Helena stopped in a swirl of grit. She let go of Mimmo, who'd been limping slowly because he still had a thick crepe bandage wrapped around his leg, and fastened her hands around Liddy's hot pink cheeks. 'He was the last person I expected to see on this island,' she said. 'And I've already told you we were part of the same crowd. So yes, we did hang out together for a while. But it's hardly significant.'

Bobo began to complain and pull Liddy forward again. 'Then he *is* one of your cast-offs,' she said, jerking herself free. 'Why couldn't you have been straight with me and admitted it from the start? What else are you hiding?'

'Nothing important.'

'So there is something!'

'Only that he blows hot and cold a bit. I think he has insecurity problems actually.'

'Don't we all?'

'Yeah, sure.'

'I don't get it . . . what am I supposed to do now?'

'If he's a good lay,' said Helena coolly, 'you might as well enjoy it.'

Liddy shook off Bobo's clutch and ignored his persistent wails. 'What, do you think I'm like you? A thrill seeker? Pants down, fanny out for anyone. Well, I'm not.'

'Nor am I.'

Helena's glance was getting frostier by the minute. The space between them on this dusty road, on this muggy overcast day, doubled and iced over. 'Have it your own way.' Liddy resumed her march with Bobo and Sara. They arrived at the bar and ordered *gelati* in advance of the other two, who lagged behind because of Mimmo's leg.

Liddy began to feel contrite. Sucking her lemonade through a straw, squinting through her glasses, she watched Helena and Mimmo's slow progress. She forced herself to rise as they came closer. 'Oh my God, I don't know what got into me. I can't believe I said that. I'm so sorry.'

Helena appeared to thaw. 'We always agreed we'd never quarrel over a bloke.'

'And we won't. Look, I really didn't want to make you feel uncomfortable about this.'

'Uncomfortable?'

'Out on a limb or whatever. I mean, if you found someone yourself, if you were keen on that police guy –'

'Well, I'm not. And if he happens to phone the house any time you're there, you must tell him I'm not in. Have you got that?'

4

The terrace of Casa Colonnata could have been designed for parties. It ran the width of the house and projected like the prow of a ship out to sea. A long dining table and a bar trolley offering beer, wine, ice and *aperitivi* stood beneath the vine-covered columns that gave the villa its name; two barbecues, one for meat and one for fish, were awaiting a match. Rosaria, the cook for both households, had enlisted her niece, Cristina, to help with the preparations in the kitchen. They were absorbed in gutting and filleting, peeling and chopping.

Cristina was a voluptuous teenager with thick, unruly hair who looked far older than her years. She was in a truculent mood. She'd arrived in an old dun-coloured Fiat with a dent in its back wing, driven by her father. The tension between them was evident as soon as they got out of the car, when he had pushed his fist into the small of his daughter's back as she shuffled grudgingly to her duties. In his other hand he bore aloft a plywood crate that emitted little cheeps of life. Liddy had found this disturbing – especially after hearing that Rosaria would deal with the slaughter: wringing the birds' necks at the same time as keeping her niece under scrutiny and away from an unsuitable new boyfriend, a feckless labourer the family deemed unworthy. Bent over the onions, Cristina's eyes streamed with tears. Rosaria's apron was spotted with blood.

Depending on your state of mind the kitchen was either a cornucopia or a battleground: those tiny, whole birds plucked naked and rammed on to a skewer; gutted sardines spliced with bay leaves on pointed sticks of willow; glossy dark chicken livers piled in a sacrificial heap. Stirring their claws sluggishly in their box of ice, but doomed to be griddled alive, were several dozen langoustines. Liddy had never eaten a songbird or a langoustine, but she didn't want to admit this to anyone else.

She had brought the children to the party early so that Maresa and her husband, Piero, could ready themselves without interruption. Unlike Gabi, Maresa soaked up the sun and her skin was a deep, oiled bronze. Even so, she would spend hours adding layers of make-up and choosing her outfit: 'For a social occasion, is important to make an effort, no?' Sara was wearing a smocked tartan dress, which Liddy thought fussy but which Maresa had insisted was charming; Bobo was in a fetching playsuit fastened with far too many buttons and therefore a nuisance. Under Liddy's supervision both were tottering through the *salone* with bowls of crisps.

Jake was standing by the table with a beer in his hand. He had been helping to set up the drinks but wouldn't be staying because he was due at the club. 'Have you noticed,' he said to Bobo, 'that everything on the table is round?'

Bobo mounted one of the chairs for a better look. There were slices of beef tomatoes like cartwheels, discs of grilled zucchini and *melanzane*, overlapping circles of salami and mozzarella, globes of marinated onions and artichoke hearts, and plump, glistening olives.

'Not quite true,' said Liddy, pointing at some stalks of asparagus.

'There's always an exception,' said Jake, as Bobo continued to study the feast. He appraised Liddy and noted approvingly, 'You look great. Nice frock.'

The white cotton dress had a low back and broderie anglaise edging. She spun on tiptoe in order to display the flare of its many gores and toppled against him. Jake's arms closed around her and she felt a glowing rush of joy and emotion. There had been times in the past when she'd fancied herself in love, but now she could see that they were just practice runs: like weak instant coffee compared to the dark espresso of her current feelings. This was it; this was true passion. A cynic might have suggested that sunshine, scanty clothing and steamy nights made an irresistible combination but, to Liddy, Jake was one of those people who are touched by magic.

'Let me mix you a drink,' he said. 'Gin fizz? Whisky sour? Bellini? Negroni? What do you fancy?'

More bottles were lined up than required; Fabrizio was a lavish host.

'You're twisting my arm,' laughed Liddy as he arched her backwards for a kiss. 'Go on then. Gin and It would be nice.' It was an hour off sunset; the time when the light was at its most entrancing, burnishing everything it touched so that the whole world seemed crystallized, exquisite.

'With an olive?'

'Just a slice of lemon, please.' She took the glass from him, ice cubes clinking, savoured the dry vermouth on her tongue. Bobo ran off to the kitchen in search of more circles.

'I could do with a fag,' Jake said, digging his hand into his pockets and bringing out a lighter. 'Shall we see if Helena has any?'

'She went out with Fabrizio. They're not back yet.' They had gone to collect an order of fireworks. Fabrizio wanted to set off a display at midnight to augur well for the rest of the summer.

'She might have left a pack in her room. Come on.'

Rosaria usually tidied the villa in the mornings, but since then Helena had discarded a bra on the floor, thrown nectarine kernels at her waste bin and extinguished a fag-end in the dregs of a tumbler of Punt e Mes. Liddy straightened the coverlet on the bed before sitting down and closing the novel that she'd left open, its spine cracking. Meanwhile, Jake opened the central drawer of the dressing table, where hairpins lodged in combs, hoop earrings latched on to silver chains and shoelaces snarled with belts. He dug out a notepad and pens, a book of matches, a roll of film, two halves of a thousand lire note and a couple of Tampax. He wrapped the film in the torn note and tied it with a shoelace like a gift. He scribbled *Kilroy Was Here* on the notepad.

'That's the sort of thing Helena would do.'

'Exactly.'

'But I'm not sure you should be going through her stuff.'

'I can't make any more mess than this and I'm only after a smoke, for Christ's sake.' He was opening other drawers now, rummaging through clothes and underwear. 'Eureka!'

'Good,' said Liddy. 'Let's go.'

'What's the hurry?' Jake crossed to the window, checked the road winding down the hillside. 'No sign of them coming back yet.' He put the pack of MS into his pocket and returned to the dressing table to close the drawer.

'Are you going to steal them all?'

'Think about it,' he said. 'It's much easier to replace a full packet than one that's been opened and raided. I thought you wanted me to be discreet.'

'It's a bit late for that.'

'Okay then. I'll give her something in exchange.' From a different pocket he took a parcel of silver foil.

'Is that what I think it is?'

He exposed the small black nugget of cannabis resin and held it out for her to sniff. 'She told me she'd run out so I said I'd cut her in if I managed to score. Nipped over to Naples a couple of days ago and got lucky. She'll be grateful.'

'Are you sure?' said Liddy doubtfully.

'Of course! I brought it over specially to give to her tonight. Since she's not back yet, it'll be a nice surprise.' He slipped it beneath the clothes, but the drawer jammed when he tried to shut it. 'There's something wedged at the top.' With a sharp jolt he freed the blockage. A narrow box flipped up and over, spilling its contents: a finely wrought necklace of blue beads. 'Ah. Lapis.'

'How do you know?'

'It's written on the box.' He grinned. 'I wonder why she doesn't like it.'

'What makes you think that?'

'Well, have you ever seen her wear it?'

'No, I suppose not.'

'It seems a shame, it's a fine piece.' He was reaching around her, his light stubble grazing her cheek. When they parted she found he had fastened the beads behind her neck. He stood back a pace in admiration. 'Mmm. Looks really good against your dress.'

The mirror confirmed this. The dress was pretty but the necklace lifted it into something more stylish. She tilted her chin and beamed at her reflection. He kissed the corner of her mouth and was pulling her towards him again when someone pounded at the door.

Liddy froze, but the person wrestling with the handle was only Bobo. He launched himself at Jake with a welter of demands.

'*Basta!*' said Jake. 'In English, now.'

'I want . . .' His face flooded with pleasure as he found the word. 'Ma-jeec. I want majeec. Majeec, majeec.'

Jake obligingly discovered a cigarette behind the boy's ear and allowed him to light it with matches lurking between his buttons. This took a while as his babyish finger and thumb struggled to grip the wax stalk of the matchstick. At last there came a burst of flame and Jake inhaled deeply. 'D'you want to see another kind of trick?' he offered, lifting Helena's cartwheel hat from its hook and slapping it on to his head.

With the cigarette poised between two fingers of his right hand, he rested his left on his hip and sashayed from wardrobe to bed and back again. In perfect mimicry of Helena, he drawled: 'Whenever I fucking see that fucking guy I want to slice his fucking balls off. Know what I mean, darling?'

Liddy and Bobo giggled.

'And toast them,' Jake continued. 'Or pickle them. Simmer them in fucking vinegar till they shrivel up.'

In truth, Helena had said something very similar a week ago, when Rosaria had taken a call from the hapless policeman, Enzo. 'Tell him *ha sbagliato numero*,' she'd hissed. But now Liddy defended her. 'Hey, that's cruel. You're talking about my best friend. She might be critical but she's not vindictive.'

Jake swept off the hat with a flourish. 'You're right. She's too lazy. All mouth and bull, that girl.'

'*Ancora*,' begged Bobo.

'Another time,' Jake promised. He pointed at Liddy. 'I could do her next if you like.'

'Don't you dare. Come on, we're getting out of here.' She linked her arm through his and tugged at Bobo's warm sticky hand, chivvying them both back to the terrace.

The guests began to arrive before Fabrizio and Helena returned, overdue, with the fireworks. These were neighbours and fellow holiday-makers, other women who sought beauty therapy in the mornings and played cards all afternoon, other men, like Fabrizio and Piero, who cruised out to sea and fished with harpoons for octopus and giant squid. Darkness had fallen and strings of coloured lights swung on both sides of the terrace. A record spun on a turntable in the corner of the *salone* and the chords of a romantic lament drifted outside to be drowned by conversation.

'Protect me from the wrath of my wife,' Liddy heard Fabrizio say to Helena. 'Take care of the barbecue.'

While the adults mingled and their children scampered between legs clad in tight-tailored trousers, Helena wielded a pair of tongs and rotated charred pieces of flesh over the coals with a dreamy expression on her face. She hadn't changed for the party. She was wearing a stained denim skirt and her hair needed brushing: a couple of leaves were caught in its tangles.

'She could damage someone with that instrument,' said Jake. 'It's not a branding iron.'

'You could offer to relieve her,' Liddy said.

'I would if I had the time, but I've got to be going now.'

'You haven't had anything to eat yet.'

'I'll go and see if any of her skewers are ready, shall I?'

As he approached the barbecue, Helena whisked around, the metal jaws of the tongs glowing red in her hand, and a sardine fell into the flames. Jake touched her on the shoulder in a comradely gesture. Then he grabbed a chunk of bread and gave a jaunty wave of farewell.

Some minutes later Helena accepted an empty platter from Fabrizio and loaded it with silver sardines and langoustines the colour of coral. As she bore her bounty across the terrace, she noticed Liddy. There were other bodies between them: a woman with rampant black curls, a balding man whose paunch threatened the buttons on his shirt, the doctor who'd treated Mimmo. Liddy raised her glass cheerily but Helena blinked as if uncertain of what she was seeing. Then she plonked the fish in the centre of the dining table and stormed up.

'Take it off.'

'What?'

'You know what I'm talking about. Take it off.'

'No I don't.' Liddy was indignant. Helena had a smut of smoke on her jaw and a wild-eyed look, as if she were high on something other than alcohol. Liddy felt Bobo attach himself to her leg.

'Go away, Bobo,' snapped Helena. She took Liddy's arm and steered her around the side of the villa where they would not be seen. The child started to follow but then ran off, drawn like the guests to the aroma of barbecued fish. They were clustering at the table, stripping the backbones from the sardines, ripping heads and legs from the langoustines.

'What's the matter? Why are you so pissed off? Is it because Fabrizio made you do the cooking? I feel bad about not helping but I didn't want to stink of charcoal and I wouldn't have been any good anyway. I think it's because they're whole bodies, heads and everything, and I find that difficult to contemplate to be honest.'

'What makes you think you can go into my room and help yourself to my things?'

Liddy's hand crept to her throat. 'Oh Lord, I'd forgotten, Hel. I'm sorry.'

Helena's voice soared in astonishment. 'You went into my bedroom and ferreted about in my cupboards and put on my jewellery and now you say you've *forgotten*?'

She gulped. 'It wasn't like that.'

'No? What was it like, then?'

For a moment Liddy wavered, then she opted for belligerence. 'As if you haven't done the same to me! Rooting about, borrowing my tights and scarves and things.'

'Only when you were around. I'd never sneak your stuff if you weren't there.'

'I don't sneak! It was Jake's idea.'

'Oh. How convenient. Blame someone else.'

'If you don't believe me, why don't you ask him?'

'You know perfectly well that he's gone. You've just said goodbye to him.'

Helena had manoeuvred her against the wall, next to a wooden shutter that was pinned back, and she clung to it as if it were a raft in a turbulent sea. Her tongue tasted sour and her eyes smarted. She didn't want to spoil such a glorious romantic evening but she had no idea how to restore things to the way they were. She put up her hands and fumbled with the clasp of the necklace. 'I can't undo it,' she said tremulously. 'Can you help me?'

Helena twisted a hank of her own hair with a ferocity that suggested she'd like to be wringing someone's neck. 'Tough,' she said. 'You must have been wearing the damn thing for a couple of hours already. You might as well keep it on for tonight. What do I care?'

A noise, a snigger, a movement behind a pillar, alerted them. Liddy turned, expecting to see Bobo, but it was a sullen Cristina, released from the kitchen to dispose of some bones. When their eyes met, she had the distinct impression that Cristina had been watching the whole thing, relishing their argument. Snoop, she thought crossly.

Helena was more direct. She let her hair fall and went to accost the girl. 'What do you think you're doing, skulking around like that? Eavesdropping. It amuses you does it, to spy on people?'

'Leave her,' called Liddy. 'She doesn't understand.'

'She understands a lot more than she lets on.'

Even without knowing the words Cristina must have grasped their intent, but she leaned against the pillar with her arms folded: irritating, implacable.

'This is none of your business,' Helena continued. 'How come you've got so much free time anyway? You should have better things to do.'

'*Come lei?*' said Cristina.

Like you? The girl's tone was soft but carried a sneer in it too. Liddy supposed she despised them because they were transient foreigners whereas she, with her broad hips and plump swelling calves, was rooted in the land. She'd still be here at the end of the summer.

It was hard to tell in the dark, but Helena's face blanched and the insult whistled between her teeth: '*Stronza!*' Then she whipped around and stalked off.

Liddy wondered whether she should be grateful to the girl for deflecting Helena's anger, or whether she should apologize on her behalf. She left the shelter of her shutter and cleared her throat, but Cristina cast her a look of contempt. She hadn't flinched when Helena called her a bitch and she wasn't about to bother with Liddy. She picked up her empty pail and rounded the corner of the villa.

Back on the terrace, the record player had been rearranged so that its speakers faced outside and the Italian ballads had been replaced with the soundtrack from *Grease*. Liddy hadn't yet eaten, but as she picked over the debris on the dining table, the son of Gabi's pharmacist asked her to dance. He was only eighteen but considered himself to be blessed with the skills of John Travolta. When she finally agreed he tossed her around the dance floor as if she were attached to a length of string.

Some of the older guests had moved indoors to continue their animated conversations on the subjects of politics – what a *casino*; economics – where *did* all one's money go; and sheer unadulterated braggadocio. Piero Baldini was giving an animated account of a fishing trip: 'It was this long, I tell you, the very devil of a beast. I had to shoot three times to kill him, harpoons hanging from his wounds like San Sebastiano.'

Liddy began to enjoy the dancing. She'd drunk enough not to be self-conscious and she forgot she'd been feeling dizzy with hunger. Nevertheless, when she saw Helena standing beside the dying embers of the barbecue her hand rose to conceal her throat. Her enthusiastic partner whirled her like a spinning top. Mid-pirouette, her fingers became trapped in the rope of beads, which snapped and scattered blue balls of lapis like bullets.

Helena didn't leave her spot by the balustrade, didn't move to collect a single rolling stone. Everyone else did. All the other partygoers chased the beads across the terrace flags and the living-room rug. Gabi, who had been in deep discussion with the doctor, finally broke off to see why her guests were crawling around as if involved in some new parlour game. Various among them were tipping their finds into Liddy's cupped hands. Maresa had been orchestrating the recovery. As she rose from her knees, her upswept hairdo began to wobble. She patted it steady and said, 'We need a bowl so they don't end up all over the place again.'

Gabi fetched a glass dish from the kitchen and carried it over to her.

'I think we got all the pieces,' Maresa said with her customary confidence. 'But they should be strung on stronger thread next time.'

Gabi gazed in puzzlement at the contents of the dish. 'But this is my necklace.'

'What?' Liddy stepped sideways, knocking over a glass of red wine. 'No, no, it can't be.'
'It is,' said Gabi. 'I know my own jewellery. How did you come by it?'
'I . . . I borrowed it.'
'You *borrowed* it? When?'
'Today. I . . .'
'This is not borrowing,' said Gabi. 'This is stealing.'
'I didn't know it was yours. I . . . I just found it.'
'Where?'
After a few moments' silence, she gave an indefinite sweep of her hand. 'Outside, on the path. I can't imagine how it got there unless one of the children . . .'
'You didn't ask if it belonged to anyone? You simply put it on?'
Fabrizio entered the room and boomed: '*Attenzione!* It's midnight and we are ready for the fireworks.'
'I wasn't thinking . . . I'm truly sorry.' Liddy proffered the bowl to Gabi but she rejected it.
'There is no time for this now. We will discuss it later.' With an eloquent shrug, as if she were overburdened with inferior jewellery, she returned to her hostess duties, ushering her guests outside again.
Fabrizio lit a taper and set off the first firework against the backdrop of the sea. It exploded in a stutter of bursts like gunfire and shot skywards in a dazzling magnesium flare. The rest were similar: some stars, some stripes, all noisy. As the company stood around watching – and shrieking at particularly violent explosions – Liddy went up to Helena. 'You knew,' she said.
'Knew what?'
'That it was Gabi's necklace.'
'No I didn't.'
'Why was it hidden away then, like you didn't want anyone to find it?'
'I don't believe this,' said Helena. 'Are you trying to accuse me of stealing the bloody thing?'
'Well, that's what Gabi's just done to me.'
'And you think it was undeserved?'
'Yes I do!' She stalked away in a show of indignation and took shelter from the fireworks beneath the colonnade. In the intervals between

explosions she heard a clatter and raised voices; her attention was drawn to the bright rectangle of the kitchen window. She peered in. Rosaria's arms were plunged into the foamy washing-up in the deep stone sink. An unforgiving light shone on the table, still littered with carcasses of one sort or another because Cristina's duties had been interrupted. Her hands were fluttering in a parabola of uncertainty and denial as Gabi, a whip-thin streak of scorn and condescension, interrogated her. Liddy couldn't hear the words and wouldn't have been able to follow them anyway, but the scene itself was consoling.

5

The treasure hunt was Jake's idea. The bounty wasn't hard to source: boiled sweets and toffees were the currency of the island. Every time the girls took the children into a bar and ordered ice creams and cappuccino or bought postcards or stamps or sun cream, every time they handed over crumpled thousand lire notes, the till would spring open to reveal an assortment of pick'n'mix. There were no coins in the loose change compartments, only a handful of *gettoni* for telephone calls and lots and lots of coloured paper wrappers containing fruit jellies, mints, chocolates, or powdery tablets tasting of violets or roses. They'd grown used to the sight now. Indeed, the children expected it: why *wouldn't* you prefer to be given an edible treat as change for your shopping?

The best spot for the treasure hunt, according to Jake, was a beach they hadn't been to before. It was further along the coast than the little coves they usually frequented, a twenty-minute trip with the outboard motor. They only used the oars for the final approach. When they struck sand they helped the children out and waded with them to shore, then pulled up the boat and fastened it to a stake. The sheer cliffs enveloping the beach were scarred with narrow fissures and a few larger crevices through which a man might squeeze. Some of these openings widened into grottoes containing shallow pools, silent except for the slow, steady splash of water dripping down the walls.

'See what a choice I have for hiding-places,' said Jake. 'Only you mustn't watch where I go or finding the treasure won't be a surprise.'

Mimmo glanced from left to right. 'There are people here,' he said.

This was true. A tortuous path zigzagged uphill through shrubs and scree to join the road. A handful of other holiday-makers had parked at the top, struggled down and laid out their rattan beach mats.

'Well, yes. So?'

'So they will eat our sweets.'

Over the past few days the temperature had been building to torrid heights. The sunbathers lay sweltering and lethargic in the sultry afternoon. 'Trust me,' said Helena. 'They won't be interested.'

Liddy slipped out of her dress and said to Sara, 'Come on. Let's go swimming.' She pitched into the limpid water and rolled on to her back, sculling lightly with her hands, kicking her feet, demonstrating to Sara how to float. Jake went off with the sweets. Bobo and Mimmo began to dig in the sand, turning their backs as instructed (although Bobo kept peeping under his armpit).

Helena lay down. She hadn't forgiven Liddy for the incident with the necklace, even though Gabi had eventually found her own undisturbed and been persuaded that any similarity was coincidental. It was an alarmingly near miss and it didn't help that things were getting heavy with Fabrizio. For months it had been a game, an aberration, a taste of forbidden excitement that she couldn't confess to anyone. Now it wasn't enough: they both wanted more. She'd broken off from him once already – that misjudged interlude with Jake – but it hadn't worked. She was having difficulty imagining the end of the summer, leaving him for a tame return to her old life – but then she was having difficulty concentrating on anything. Although she tried to run alternatives through her head, she felt sluggish and indecisive.

She thumbed through her paperback novel (*How to Save Your Own Life* by Erica Jong), but couldn't find her place. The print blurred in the white-hot light. The air was stickier than usual, and she was thinking how the chance to nap would be bliss when the others converged again: Liddy shaking her hair so that a cascade of droplets danced around her shoulders; Jake with his empty bag; Sara wrapped in a brown and orange towel like a chrysalis. She put aside the unread book and looked up.

'Picnic first,' said Jake. 'Games after. That's the deal.'

Helena handed around panini rosettes filled with slices of salami and Provolone. The children bit into them with relish. Bobo dropped his on to the sand and had to be given another; then he demolished the first one anyway. She pulled a watermelon from her basket along with a knife. She laid it on a slab of rock and plunged the knife through the thick, dark green rind. Juice spurted and showered them all and Sara screamed.

'Here,' said Jake. 'You're doing it all wrong.' He took the watermelon from her and carved it neatly into a dozen slices.

Mimmo collected up the seeds and arranged them into a pattern, a spiral that began by winding tightly around itself, but then grew into wider circles and ended with an arrowhead pointing towards the entrance to one of the caves. 'This way to treasure,' he said.

'Don't go into any of the caves by yourselves,' said Liddy. 'They'll be very dark inside and dangerous and you might get lost.'

'I swear,' said Jake, 'that I haven't hidden the sweets anywhere you can't get to easily. I'll wait here by the boat while you see what you can find. When you come back I'll be able to tell you whether you're doing well or whether there are any more hidden. Don't forget to take a bucket.'

'We'd better split up,' said Helena to Liddy. 'I'll take the boys if you like.'

They headed for the rocks, passing a circle of young men playing cards and two or three extended families also sharing a picnic. A couple writhed in the privacy of a low-set parasol. The boys stared in fascination at the bare gyrating feet as if they recognized them – and indeed, something about the solid shape of the girl's calf rubbing against her boyfriend's hairy shin put Helena in mind of Cristina – but when Bobo reached out mischievously to prod their soles, she quickly led him onwards. For the best part of an hour they rummaged under boulders and pushed aside clumps of tough scrubby daisies, filling their buckets.

'You could open a shop,' said Helena, when they emptied their finds on to the mat and began sorting and counting them as if the toffees and fruit *caramelle* were indeed real currency.

A fight broke out between Bobo and Mimmo, the latter accusing the former of stealing some of his sweets. Bobo's cheeks were too bulging to reply. They started to attack each other: a vicious barrage of punches landing wherever they could make an impact. They kicked and thumped and clawed, but Bobo's mouth was too full for him to bite. It was Jake who finally pulled him off. He carried him to the water's edge and dunked him in the sea. The other holiday-makers watched in amusement as the child, coming up for air, spewed out a stream of boiled sweets. Helena retched.

'Are you all right?' asked Liddy. 'You look a bit green.'

'I've never been able to watch people throwing up, that's all.'

'Put your head between your knees then. Anyway, he isn't being sick. He's just getting his comeuppance for being such a greedy little monster.'

'Jake encourages him. He makes him worse.'

'Oh, I don't think that's fair . . .'

Twelve curved strips of watermelon rind were scattered around the picnic basket, like unattached smiles, a legacy of teeth marks in their pink gums. Liddy began to gather them into a plastic bag along with the empty cans of Fanta and hundreds of sweet wrappers. Every now and again she gave a little tut of impatience. Helena lay down again on her stomach and closed her eyes.

'Elena, Elena!' A small sticky hand was pulling off her sunhat, tweaking her jaw. She moved her arm lazily and tickled the barrel of Mimmo's ribcage. At the shoreline she could see that Jake and Bobo were still engaged in their mock water fight and Liddy had gone to join them.

'Play with me,' said Mimmo.

'First let's have a little siesta.'

'Hide-and-seek.'

'Haven't we done enough seeking today?'

'*Please*, Elena.' He rolled off her and rested his chin on his knees, above the livid red gash on his leg. He infused his voice with passion and persuasion just as his father did and it made her laugh.

'Oh, all right then. I'll count to a hundred very slowly and you must be very clever. Hide somewhere that won't be easy for me to find.' She watched him run off and then buried her face in her arms.

She'd started to count; she remembered when she woke with a jolt that she'd got to 59. The trouble was she didn't know how long she'd been asleep. Not long, she decided, spotting Sara behind her, rearranging Mimmo's pattern of melon seeds. '*Dài*, Sara,' she said, raising herself on her elbows. 'See if you can find Mimmo for me.'

'No,' said Sara. 'I don't want to.'

'I'll buy you *gelato*.'

'Only for me? No one else.'

'No one else,' Helena promised.

She had just settled herself comfortably again when Liddy and Jake returned, swinging Bobo between them as if auditioning for an ad for seaside family holidays. Helena cringed.

'Where are the others?' asked Liddy, dropping on to a beach mat.

'Mimmo wanted a game of hide-and-seek. I said I'd count to a hundred.'

'How long ago was that?'

'I'm not sure, I think I dropped off, but it's okay, Sara's gone to look for him.'

Jake screwed up his eyes against the sun. 'She seems to be coming back.'

Sara was weaving and looping in a dance she'd invented, twirling her imaginary skirts and an imaginary baton. She thought the faces turned in her direction were admiring her; she curtsied.

'Well. Did you find him?'

'Who?'

'Mimmo, of course.'

'Oh . . .' She pursed her lips. 'Where's my *gelato*?'

'You only get the ice cream if you find him.'

'But I'm thirsty. Can I have a drink?'

'We haven't any drinks left.'

'Looks like you can't get out of it now, Hel. You'll have to go after him yourself.'

'Ouf, he'll only be behind a rock or something.'

'You don't think he's lost, do you?' said Liddy, shifting the straps of her bikini so she wouldn't get white lines marring her tan.

'How could he have got lost? There's nowhere to go.'

'Isn't that what we're always saying about Bobo? How on earth could he have done this, smashed an unbreakable toy or got a bean stuck up his nose or whatever?'

'They may be cousins,' said Helena, 'but Mimmo is not Bobo. He's quite sensible.'

'He's three and a half.'

'Quit needling me, will you.'

Liddy was suddenly all sympathy. 'Hel, are you feeling rough?'

'Yes. I am, as it happens. Thanks for your concern.'

'I hope it's not some nasty virus.'

'It's a fucking hangover, you idiot.'

Liddy nudged the straps further down her arms. Jake said, 'Do you want me to go and look for him?'

'Yeah thanks,' said Helena.

Jake set off for the far corner of the beach, skirting the card players and the other family groups. He didn't hurry.

'When I said he was only three, what I was getting at was that he can't swim yet. Not like Sara.'

'So?'

'So if he were to get inside one of those caverns which has water in it . . . I mean you don't know how deep it might be. Suppose he fell in?'

Helena jumped to her feet. 'Okay, okay. Why do you have to be so neurotic? The poor little sod wanted to play a harmless game, which, actually, as if you didn't already know, involves *not being visible*. I expect he's really proud of himself.'

'Okay, keep your hat on. I'm sure you can leave it to Jake then. He'll know where to find him.'

'No,' said Helena. 'You stay here with the stuff. I'll go too.'

The beach wasn't large: a narrow band of shore flanked by two sheer gullies, the ascent steep and overgrown. In late afternoon the cliff threw its silhouette over the sand; the sun, though burning elsewhere, sank from view. The courting couple had already disappeared with their parasol and the other sun-seekers were readying themselves to leave. Helena could see Jake ahead to her right, talking to some of them. They scratched their chins and conferred with their companions. She scrambled over a pile of sharp shale, wishing she'd thought to put on her espadrilles.

She kept thinking she could see Mimmo – the flash of his royal blue swimming trunks, his wrist poking from behind a boulder or underneath the boat. She kept expecting him to spring from his cover at any moment, unabashed delight in his eyes. By now he should have lost patience, he should be running up to them in triumph. 'Look at me! I outwitted you. I was too clever to be found!'

Unless he couldn't get out. Unless he was trapped.

At the rock face she peered through a dark crack that was surely too small even for a child to wriggle through, then moved on. The surface was pitted like pumice: some cavities extended only a metre or so; others were more menacing, leading to infinite blackness. Could Mimmo have been tempted to hide here? She squeezed through a jagged aperture and shouted his name several times; a hollow echo floated back to her. Warily she progressed along a dark, constricted passageway. The wall glistened and was wet to the touch. She wished she'd brought a torch, but who thinks of taking a torch when visiting a Mediterranean beach in August? She'd begun by crawling but soon had to inch along on her stomach, her hands scrabbling against the clammy rock. There was an unpleasant putrid smell; something soft and wet clutched at her face.

No, she decided, calling his name one last time, Mimmo would not be in a place like this. He was too sensitive a child and the gloom would terrify him. There wasn't enough space for her to turn around. She had to retreat backwards, scraping her knees and elbows and hoping she wouldn't sting herself on jellyfish or sea urchin. It was with relief she reached the strip of white that indicated fresh air and daylight.

The next cave was potentially more dangerous. Although it seemed shallow at first glance, a tunnel at the back was full of water, like a mouth ready to swallow. She was glad when Jake appeared at her side. 'I don't think I can do this,' she said. 'I'm sorry. I'm not usually squeamish, but . . .'

'It's okay; I reckon I can fit inside.'

'Are you sure?'

In answer he stuck his head and shoulders into the maw and she heard a splash. 'Jake? Are you okay?'

When he re-emerged he was shivering, despite the suffocating heat. 'Inadvisable,' he said with a grimace.

'You couldn't have missed him in there, could you? I mean, is it deep?'

'You don't need deep to drown. A couple of inches will do. But I don't think he would have gone in. It nearly scared the pants off me. And it *was* only a game you were playing, right?'

'Right.'

A game. An innocent session of hide-and-seek. Mimmo had probably fallen asleep somewhere, tired of waiting for discovery. Yet Helena felt as if a line had been crossed and in a single mind-snapping instant their quest had become a manhunt.

'I expect he wandered off and lost his way,' Jake said. 'He tried to be too clever. He'll turn up.'

'You already asked if anyone had seen him?'

'Everyone I bumped into.'

'Everyone?'

'Sure. There's only that lot left now.'

The posse of young men were the last to pack up their possessions, pulling on their bleached jeans, leaving their shirts unbuttoned. They were picking their way back towards the path. Jake's gaze followed them. 'It's the only other place he might have gone.'

'What is?'

He jerked his thumb. 'Up the hill. There's plenty of undergrowth. Quite a lot of scope for hiding, I should think.'

'But he knew he wasn't supposed to leave the beach. It was one of the rules.'

'No one obeys rules in this country. Anyway, there's nowhere else he could be. So it's either that or he's been abducted.'

'That's crazy.' Helena watched the young men begin their climb, stumbling occasionally and dislodging showers of scree. The bushes surrounding the track were unidentifiable scrub to her eyes; they also looked tough and impenetrable.

'You never know. Your Fabrizio could have made some dangerous enemies.'

'Oh, for God's sake! He's a bourgeois architect who married a bit of money. He doesn't bury bodies in concrete.'

'He'd probably be prepared to fork out a ransom to get his little son back, though. Not like old man Getty.'

'The Verduccis aren't that rich. Piero Baldini is wealthier.'

'Come on, *no one*, not even a desperate, destitute, mentally defective Sardinian bandit would try to kidnap Bobo.'

'Sorry, Jake, but I'm not in a joking mood. This is too traumatic. Give us a fag, for Christ's sake.'

He nodded towards Liddy who was serenely contemplating the gold-tipped sea, unaware of the turmoil behind her. 'I left them over there by the basket. And I think you should get her to go for help.'

'You don't think he's gone far, do you?'

'If he climbed up that way and got to the top, he could have wandered off in any number of directions.'

'We should never have come here,' she said. 'Gabi'll go bananas.'

'No excuses, Helena. You made your own bed, you lie in it.'

'Fuck off.'

'I will. I'll get up to the road and thrash about in the bushes on the way.'

She'd never wholly trusted him, found him too glib and unreliable, yet in this crisis they'd both been pretending wasn't a crisis, he was redeeming himself. She couldn't have handled it without him. 'I'm sorry I snapped. It's just . . . this is . . . I am . . .'

'Sure. Better get that search party organized.'

'I will.'

When Helena returned to Liddy, Sara was still complaining of thirst. Bobo was joining in. 'We'll be leaving soon,' Liddy told them. 'Jake will take us home.'

Helena withdrew a cigarette from Jake's pack and gagged because it tasted so foul. 'Actually,' she said, trying to sound casual so the children wouldn't fret, 'he's gone up to the road to look for Mimmo. In case he went further than he meant to along the path.'

'Oh Lord.' Liddy threw her dress over her head and struggled into it. 'He really is lost then?'

Helena bit her lip. 'He wasn't supposed to leave the beach.'

Liddy stretched behind her back to pull up her zip. 'You should have been watching more carefully.'

'That would have been cheating.'

'Oh get real, Hel. You didn't want to play the game with him at all. You were snatching extra sleep.'

'So I'm tired, I had a bad night. Okay, I've admitted it. But the point, the important thing, is that we have to find him. I'm going to join forces with Jake again. Can you get back to the villa and alert everyone?'

'Can I what?'

'Tell Gabi what's happened.'

'You want *me* to tell Gabi?'

'Is that a problem?'

Liddy mulled this over. 'She'll go bananas, won't she? And you don't want to be in the firing line.'

'It's not about that! I thought you'd need to get the kids back anyway so it made sense for you to give her the message. And I can carry on looking for him here.' She started to pull on her shorts. 'And somebody should bring a torch so we can look in the caves again.'

'Well, it can't be me,' said Liddy.

'Why can't it be you?'

'Because I can't take the kids home in the boat.' She scuffed the sand with her bare foot, not meeting Helena's eye.

'Why not?'

'Because I'm scared to be in the boat by myself.'

'But you'll be with Sara and Bobo.'

'That makes it worse. Suppose one of them went over?'

Helena gaped. She turned to Sara. 'You know this is an emergency? You will take care of your brother? You won't do anything stupid?'

'*Certo*, Elena,' said Sara demurely.

'It's perfectly calm,' Helena said. 'All you have to do is follow the line of the coast back to the villa. We've done it a thousand times and it will be easier with fewer people on board. They've got life jackets, for goodness' sake.'

'I'm sorry,' said Liddy. 'But I can't take the risk.'

'So what are we going to do?'

Liddy picked up a towel, shook it out and folded it into a neat square. 'I don't know.'

'Well we can't stay here for ever!' They were speaking too rapidly in English for the children to follow, but the corners of Sara's mouth puckered; Bobo cried that he wanted to go home.

'You could take them,' said Liddy. 'And I could help Jake.'

Helena stared at her friend's stony face. 'Looks like I don't have any choice.'

'You'd better come back,' added Liddy as Helena untied the mooring and refloated the dinghy.

'Come back? Good grief! We'll probably bring a flotilla of yachts, a squadron of helicopters, and every damn *carabiniere* on Ischia. Do you really think Gabriella Verducci wouldn't go the whole hog? Will you help me push?'

The sea lapped gently against the wooden panels of the boat. Helena lifted in the children and then their possessions. She climbed into the stern and jerked the cord of the motor. The hem of Liddy's dress was getting wet. She gave a final shove and leapt backwards. Helena tried to shout instructions but her words didn't carry over the noise of the engine. Part of her felt trapped in a nightmare, a surreal fantasy. Here she was with two attractive children bouncing across a turquoise sea, while their cousin had apparently been whisked into thin air. Or was he floating face down in a subterranean pool? Or being bound, gagged and blindfolded in a bandit's lair? No, that was nonsense. Mimmo had probably twisted his ankle in a rabbit hole. Could any child be more accident prone? He would reappear.

6

The climb from jetty to terrace had never seemed so daunting or taken so long. Sara was carrying too many items and kept dropping one after the other. Bobo whimpered that he felt sick. 'I feel sick too,' Helena said. 'And I didn't even eat any sweets. We have to hurry.'

All was quiet in Casa Colonnata, so she proceeded to the Baldini villa where Maresa and Rosaria were discussing at great length whether they should have *scaloppine* with lemon or Marsala for dinner. Sara burst into tears as soon as she saw her mother and Bobo ran to bury his face in her lap. Maresa stared at Helena who was looking, she knew, even scruffier than usual. '*Che succede?*'

'Where's Gabi?'

'She will return soon. Tell me what's wrong.'

Perhaps it was better this way, easier to explain to a person one step removed. Even so, she didn't mean to blurt out the news so crassly. 'We've lost Mimmo.'

Rosaria screamed. Maresa, ever practical, said, 'Where? In the playground? The shops?'

'No, we were on the beach, not this one, further around the coast and –'

'In the sea?'

'No, no, definitely on the land. We were playing hide-and-seek but somehow he managed to hide so well that we haven't found him. We're afraid he might have got stuck somewhere. Jake and Liddy are still looking, but we thought I should bring the children back. And raise the alarm.'

Maresa's hand tightened on Sara's shoulder. 'I will telephone the police, *immediatamente*,' she said. 'Also my brother. You should go and wait for Gabriella to return.'

So Helena, after explaining how the beach might be accessed, sat chewing her fingernails on the front steps of Casa Colonnata until a car drew up. It was a car she'd noticed before. She'd never caught close sight of the male driver, but his very existence had freed her from guilt when Fabrizio came into her room late at night or they had a fast fuck in the shower. It didn't free her from guilt now. There was no one else to blame for Mimmo's disappearance. She had no excuses.

Gabi was parting tenderly from her chauffeur. She was taken aback, as she stepped outside, to find Helena, but she approached her coolly. 'You have no keys?' she said. Then, glancing around: 'You are alone?'

'Yes, I came back to tell you. Mimmo . . .'

'What?'

The car reversed down the drive, as if trying to make an unobtrusive exit.

'He's, um, missing.'

'Missing! What does this mean? Missing?'

'From the beach. We've been searching everywhere. Maresa's already called the police. Let me show you where we went, where we think he might be. If your car's working.'

Gabi's Alfa Romeo was parked under a lean-to in an attempt to keep off the sun. Its fender, poking forward, glistened in the late afternoon heat. 'Why do you think there is a problem with my car?'

'Really, I don't. I . . .'

Gabi fished in her bag for her keys but didn't enter the house. She unlocked the Alfa. 'Get in!' she ordered. 'We must hurry, yes?'

The leather seat scorched the backs of Helena's legs. 'Yes.'

Gabi revved the engine so loudly neither of them could speak until they were out on the road. She gripped the steering wheel as if it were Helena's throat, her thumbs splayed white against its rim. 'How is this possible?' she demanded. 'You have one simple job. To take care of my son. Twice now you have failed to do this.'

'We were playing a game,' Helena pleaded. 'Hide-and-seek. I didn't expect him to be so good at it.'

'Everyone knows,' said Gabi severely, 'that when you play hide-and-seek with children, you must watch where they go. Else you will find them too quickly.'

'I know. I'm so *so* sorry I didn't do that.'

Gabi had the slender bones of a greyhound; her features were finely chiselled and her profile always had a certain precision. Now her nose quivered, her chin was thrust forward at a furious angle, but her eyes were dry. When panic mounts, Helena realized, it drains the body. There was no saliva in her mouth to swallow; no tears available – nor any relief they might bring.

Jake was waiting for them on the road above the beach. Helena had been imagining this moment: imagining Gabi slamming on her brakes, Jake semaphoring, indicating a weary bundle beside a clump of oleander, coming up to say: 'It's all right. He's over there.'

Instead he stooped to the car window and admitted: 'I've had no luck so far, but the police have sent for reinforcements.'

Further along they could see a police car, two motorbikes. Gabi manoeuvred herself stiffly from driver's seat to a standing position. She leaned against the Alfa's bonnet as if she needed its support. 'What is he wearing?' she asked in a tight voice.

'Who?' Helena was confused. She thought she might be referring to Jake whose T-shirt was black with a motif of snarling fangs: a souvenir from his stint as an extra on a B-movie about werewolves.

'My son.'

'Oh, er, his blue swimming trunks.'

'And that is all?'

'Yes.'

'No shoes?'

'No.'

Gabi shaded her eyes and stared down the cliff. The scrubby undergrowth was the kind that would rip into your flesh. The rough ground would be painful underfoot.

'It's possible he's still on the beach,' said Jake. 'Liddy's down there with a couple of *carabinieri* they sent over. At least there's no tide to cut him off. But the most likely thing is that he's fallen and got trapped somewhere. If there's enough manpower we should be able to find him.'

Another police car, noisy with siren and flashing lights, drew up. Gabi demanded a helicopter patrol and at least two motor launches. Helena wondered that she could even consider the horrendous prospect of drowning, but Gabi was a woman with a mission – one who couldn't conceive of letting a single opportunity to find her child pass her by.

A mixed line-up of volunteers – fishermen, farmers, holiday-makers and policemen – spread over the hillside, armed with sticks to prod the terrain. Motorbikes cruised up and down the twisting roads, calling at local bars and hamlets to see if anyone had come across a small child – *un ragazzo sperduto* – wandering and disorientated. Divers in wetsuits with torches on their foreheads investigated the grottoes along the shoreline. The helicopter swooped and whirred overhead.

The day dimmed and the sun set, throwing deep shadows across the surface of the land, though the humidity continued to increase. More torches were called for. To Helena, scuffling along the route she'd been designated, these efforts seemed increasingly futile. Mimmo, as everyone agreed, was no daredevil. He was spirited, but cautious. He had a measure of his mother's highly strung disposition and his father's acute pragmatism. He didn't take unnecessary risks. He couldn't have achieved this mysterious absence all by himself: a three-year-old hadn't the stamina to outwander the patrol of several dozen adults.

She poked her stick into a patch of myrtle, checking for snakes. It was possible a dose of venom had paralysed Mimmo, but there were few options left. In the distance she could see the wide beam cast by the lights of the motor launches. The wind was beginning to get up, to whip the sea into a foaming frenzy that could steal a small body from a cave and sweep it carelessly into deep water.

By now Fabrizio had arrived. He'd roared down from Rome and abandoned his car on the Naples quayside so he could take the hydrofoil, disregarding the chance that it might not be there in the morning. Helena would never forget the uncanny pallor of his face when he sought her out, or the droop of his shoulders: all his bravado, his certainty, knocked out of him.

The words rasped in his throat and he wouldn't meet her eyes. 'What were you doing?'

How many times could you tell the same story? 'I was counting to a hundred.'

'And that is all?'

'We'd already had a treasure hunt for sweets. He knew all the hiding-places and I thought he'd squeeze into one of them.'

'Children do not vanish from the face of the earth.'

'I know.'

She felt a pelting of gravel at her back and swung around, but it was the work of the wind – once skittish, now fierce and blustering. Rain rattled on the tops of the patrol cars, where the *carabinieri* had gathered to confer. The officer in charge broke away from the group and came up to Fabrizio.

'We have to call off the search,' he said. 'We can't make any headway in these conditions. The sirocco is coming.'

The sirocco, swirling up from Africa, mottled the landscape like rust, carried such a quantity of sand and grit you felt you were being pricked by a thousand needles when it blew against your flesh. It stung your eyes until they were raw, and clogged your airways. Midnight's temperature could be as hot as midday's, the humidity dense.

'In these conditions,' echoed Fabrizio, 'you would leave a small boy to fend for himself?'

'We've been searching for five hours. We've covered the hillside and we don't believe he can be found here.'

'Then where is he? What about the helicopter?'

The neighbours and volunteers were shuffling back to their vehicles, spreading their hands apologetically: the weather was too bad, the night was too dark. Rain would hamper progress, obliterate tracks, footprints, leads.

'We'll recommence at daybreak,' promised the officer.

Helena sat in a corner with her legs crossed and her shoulders hunched. There were two young women – prostitutes, she guessed – corralled with her in the holding cell. Although political prisoners had once been incarcerated in the fortress of Castello Aragonese, it was now a tourist destination and Ischia's detention facilities were minimal. Suspected criminals would be escorted off the island to Naples where the prisons overflowed, but Helena had committed no crime. The other women, sucking on unlit cigarettes, chatted to each other as if this were a regular occurrence. Lighters and matches had been confiscated and she could hear an agitated male voice howling down the corridor: '*Fiammiferi, portami dei fiammiferi.*' As if! she thought. The man's cry sounded as though he were offering to burn the place down.

After a sleepless night of recriminations, she'd been brought to the police station along with Liddy and Jake. They'd been interrogated separately and then the others had been let go. The police claimed they wanted to ask Helena more questions. In fact, they'd ignored her for hours. From time to time she dozed; now it was morning again and finally – finally – something was happening. She was tapped on the shoulder and escorted to an interview room. The light was switched on. A glass of milk was set in front of her. She stared at it. What she really wanted, she thought, retching at the sickly smell of the milk, was a mirror, a comb and a damp flannel. She didn't think of herself as vain, but she felt dirty, as if her flesh were crawling with lice and covered in smut.

The glass was still full when the door opened and an officer entered, pulling on his jacket as if he'd arrived late for his shift. He sat down opposite her and opened a notebook. She looked up, shocked into exclamation. 'My God! Enzo!'

His face registered dismay. 'So it is you. I hoped there had been some mistake.'

Can I see you again? he'd asked at the Vesuvio, his jaw taut with the tingle of aftershave, his eyes brimming with . . . what? Ardour? Curiosity? Desire? A man on the lookout for a mate. She hadn't exactly stood him up, but it must have been obvious from those unanswered phone calls that she was avoiding him. And what would he have offered: a decorous *passeggiata* culminating in *caffé* and *gelati*? A visit to the widowed mother who kept antimacassars on the backs of her chairs and caged canaries? A race across the island in the moonlight on his Kawasaki? Discomfort trickled between her shoulder blades. Not this, she thought, he can't have expected this. She reached for his hand, which he instinctively withdrew. 'What's going on, Enzo? You have to help me.'

'You can speak Italian please,' he said.

'Why d'you make me wait so long here? Why not the others? What am I supposed to have done?'

'We must investigate.' Lines of distaste ran from his nose to the corners of his mouth. His shirt had been immaculately laundered; Helena supposed any contact with her would sully it.

'I've already told you everything I know.'

'We are appealing for witnesses, for anyone who was on the beach that afternoon. Some we have identified, but it's a slow process.'

'I don't know what more I can say. How does locking me up help you find Mimmo?'

'We need you to remember.'

'Remember what? There's nothing I've left out, honestly. Look, this is ridiculous. You've no grounds to keep me here. Somebody needs to contact the British Embassy in Rome and get me a lawyer.'

'I'm afraid it's not so simple.'

'You can't hold me without charge. Come on, Enzo, you'll get into trouble.'

'The trouble is not mine,' he said gravely.

'God, don't you think I feel as sick about this business as everyone else? Mimmo was . . . is . . .' She swallowed, unable to continue.

'I am here as a friend,' he said. 'An adviser. This meeting now is entirely informal. Everything will be over very quickly if you tell us where they've taken him.'

'What?'

'Where have they taken him?'

'I don't know what you're talking about.'

'The kidnappers.'

Helena had not slept for two nights. The world was spinning on an unfamiliar axis. 'What kidnappers? Why do you think he's been kidnapped? I mean, I know it's a handy explanation but it doesn't mean it's the right one. If I could focus properly I might be able to come up with something else, but as it is . . .'

'You should drink the milk,' he said.

'I can't. It makes me want to throw up. Can I have a coffee?'

'Okay. I will tell them to bring you something.'

At the doorway he regarded her with a puzzled look, as if she had somehow changed into a different person. She had to convince him they were all barking up the wrong tree, barking mad in fact. He exchanged words with the man standing on guard and came back to her. 'The coffee is coming,' he said. 'And a croissant.'

'Thank you.'

'I will pay for it myself.'

'You don't have to do that.' She raised her arm to push her hair back from her face and caught a rank, unwashed odour. There was no window in the room, no way of telling the time of day or the temperature. The freedom of the boat, the beach, the sea were in another world: where she should be, out there with the rest of them. 'All I care about is finding Mimmo. Why won't you let me help?'

'Now it's difficult,' he said, sighing. 'While we have the sirocco, visibility is poor. We aren't able to use the helicopter. You have made a terrible mistake.'

'I know I've made a mistake! You can't arrest me for it.'

'There is evidence,' said Enzo, 'you have been consorting with someone who is known to us as a dangerous person.'

'I haven't *consorted* with anyone!'

'The night at Vesuvio,' he said. 'I saw you myself.'

'You mean those thieves? Brazen bastards. But I'd never seen them before! You know that perfectly well. This is complete nonsense.' She paused. 'Is that all you've got on me?'

'We are speaking to a witness who may be able to confirm the conversation. In any case, we must separate you from your accomplice.'

'I don't have an accomplice!' She was in a madhouse, most definitely. Still, she felt grateful that Enzo was her interrogator. When the espresso and *cornetto* were brought in, she gave him her most appreciative smile – even though the pastry crumbled to ashes in her mouth and the coffee, despite three packets of sugar, was thin and bitter.

'You must understand,' he said, his palms flat and steady on the table top, 'these are bad times for this country. We have the Red Brigades. We have the bombings in the north, we have the kidnap and murder of Aldo Moro. These are political crimes, but there are also men who are unscrupulous, who will do anything for money. They may have tricked you, pretended they want to know your movements, the boy's movements, for another reason. We don't say yet you are wicked, maybe you have been foolish. But we have to keep you under observation. Then, if you can lead us to them, the result is simple. We will let you go.'

'But I don't know these people you're talking about. Why d'you keep going on about kidnappers anyway?'

Enzo's expression was solemn. 'The family have received a ransom note.'

'Jesus!' She was stunned to hear Jake's hypothesis had taken shape. Then she rallied. 'How do you know the note is genuine?'

'Why shouldn't it be?'

'Well, what does it say?'

'I can't tell you.'

'Why not?'

'I can't compromise our investigations.'

'Have you done a handwriting test? Have you checked it against the writing of everyone else in the villa? In both the villas?'

He was picking at a scab on his chin. He had held her once. She tried to recollect the pressure of his hand, the warm tickle of his moustache, but it was no good; the dance had been too brief.

'This is no concern of yours.'

'Except I think someone might be trying to get at me.'

'Who?'

Gabi was the most likely person. But would Gabi be so vindictive as to forge a ransom demand? Wouldn't her priority be the safety of her son? Unless – and here Helena could empathize – it was the only way to persuade the police to take the quest for Mimmo seriously. She recalled how quick they'd been to call off the search when the weather deteriorated. 'I don't know! I don't know anything.' She was overwrought; she could feel tears rising.

He passed her a tissue. 'Signor Verducci will procure you a lawyer,' he said. 'One who will speak good English and be able to express to you the situation. But let me go over again the circumstances, so you will see how serious this matter is.' She covered her eyes; she didn't want to look at him. 'A child in your care disappears. The family is well-known and well-connected. A note is delivered. We know some characters, petty criminals, who could be involved in this affair. You have been seen talking to one or two of them. We draw conclusions. If you help us with our enquiries we will show leniency.'

She plucked the tissue into small white scraps; they drifted from her lap to the floor. 'When?' she demanded. 'When was this supposed encounter? Maybe I was just being polite. Someone asks me something, talks to me, I talk back. It was the same with you, remember?'

Enzo stiffened. 'This is not appropriate conversation.'

'You're trying to frame me.' She stood abruptly but hung on to the back of her chair, as if it might protect her. Enzo also rose and made to approach. 'If you come near me,' she said. 'I'll scream the place down. I'll say you tried to rape me.'

'There is a guard at the door,' he said. 'No one will believe you.'

Why had she thought him kind? He was rigid, inflexible, a tin-pot tyrant. She took the hem of her T-shirt in her hands and tried to rip it. She tugged at the waistband of her shorts – already tight and uncomfortable – and the button snapped its thread.

'Elena, don't do this.'

'Let me go!' When no one came she shrieked again.

'I think you are ill,' said Enzo.

She had backed herself against the wall. Wasn't this the moment in the movies when the overhead lamp began to sway? When the tormentors moved in and slapped their victim's face with gun butts or wet leather gauntlets? She focused on the lamp in its yellow silicone shade. It should be hanging straight down on its cord, stilled by gravity; instead it was swinging as if someone had given it a push. The walls were listing too, closing in on her. As she fainted she thought she heard him call out to the guard, something about a doctor, but her grasp of language was slipping away.

7

The fat policeman dealt out the photographs like a pack of cards: a series of profiles and full faces. Liddy picked them up and studied them one by one. She tried to seem intent and purposeful, but these men all looked the same. A pair of ears reappeared several times, mouths were set in a straight unsmiling line, deep-set eyes squinted and defied her to identify them. The photographs were spread across the glass top of the dining table in the Baldini villa. Around the edges of the prints, through the thick, green-tinged glass, Liddy could see her knees pressed tightly together facing the relaxed legs of the man sitting opposite. On her right, at the foot of the table, sat a scrawny, quietly spoken interpreter.

The note had come this morning, left by the gatepost. Fabrizio had spotted it, a tatty leaf of paper in a plastic bag to keep off the rain. At first nobody believed it was real: the writing was so ill-formed and childish it could have been Sara's. But some of the information was chilling: the description of Mimmo's swimming trunks; the assurance that he was enjoying his favourite *biscotti*; that further instructions would come. Maresa wailed but Gabi's reaction had been frighteningly quiet. She left Casa Colonnata open, unlocked, and got into the car with Fabrizio. He'd stormed off with his foot flat on the accelerator and his hand on the horn. The Alfa Romeo twisted around the corkscrew bends like a demented firecracker.

Bobo and Sara were now locked in the kitchen with Rosaria to keep them safe and Maresa – who considered, as Mimmo's aunt, that she had equal investment in the drama – was on the phone in the hallway. She marched back and forth, thrashing the extra-long cord in her hand like a gaucho's whip or twining it from wrist to elbow like a lasso. Her body had a language of its own: her shoulders shuddered, her torso rippled, her arms and legs trembled with emotion. And all the while she kept up a relentless flow of questions, demands, suppositions and predictions.

How could Liddy possibly concentrate on the task in hand against such a background? She was shipwrecked and adrift in a place that was suddenly, unbearably foreign. When she'd had Helena to cushion her against any strangeness, Ischia had been breathtakingly beautiful, but now that she'd been whisked away it had turned sinister and threatening.

It was the first thing she asked when the fat policeman arrived. 'Where is she? What have you done with Helena?'

He dug his thumbs into his broad leather belt. 'My colleague is conducting her interview,' he said. 'And we are trying to locate anybody who may have observed the boy. We have to examine all possibilities. In the meantime, I have something to show to you.'

Liddy dreaded being presented with an item that had belonged to Mimmo: a lock of hair, say. Or something worse. Instead, the photographs had been produced.

'This is a small island,' the policeman said, through the young clerk. 'It isn't Sicily or Sardinia. We are not accustomed to crime. They come here from Napoli to steal and make trouble. If the boy is in Ischia we will find him. The problem will be if he has already left, been taken to the mainland by boat, for example. But we are in contact with the police there. They will inform us of any sighting . . .'

'The note . . . doesn't give you any clues?'

'The note we are examining. Meanwhile, will you please look at these?'

'Why?'

'There is the possibility you may recognize one of the faces.'

'From the beach, you mean?'

'Or in the town. Or at the port. Someone who was looking at the boy? Who was acting suspiciously? He might have spoken to your friend.'

'My friend?' She thought longingly of Jake, the way he tossed back his head when he laughed, his clever conjuring.

'The English girl.'

'Oh, Helena.'

'So which one?'

'Which what?'

'Which man did you see talking to your friend? This one perhaps? Or this?'

'I don't know.' Truth to tell, she and Helena were often accosted in public places by swarthy young men, offering them drinks or cigarettes or scooter rides or the benefit of their superior knowledge. Even in the late seventies, in this secluded southern backwater independent women were a rarity. Not that their attempts at independence fooled anybody. Liddy now felt, more than ever, like a helpless schoolgirl.

'Does it have to be one of these?' she begged. 'Only I'm finding it quite difficult to tell them apart and we come across new people all the time. I don't want to get anyone into trouble . . .'

The interpreter, having trouble playing both roles, was becoming more flustered.

'But you want us to find the boy?'

'Of course!'

The detective's eyes were like currants poking through the glazed crust of a teacake. The rolls of flesh at his neck padded his vocal chords, gave his speech a warm mellifluous tenor, in contrast to the translator's squeak. 'There's no hurry. Take as long as you need.'

A decision was clearly expected. Anybody can make a mistake, Jake had said once. They'd been in the courtyard of the Vesuvio. She could recall the weight of his arm circling her waist, but she couldn't remember the context of their conversation. What's unforgivable, he'd continued, is sitting on the fence.

Liddy's hand skated over the blur of faces. 'This one,' she said.

'Thank you, *signorina*.'

She didn't like the tone of his voice. Even less did she like the expression on his face. It was too triumphant. What was there to feel so pleased about when Mimmo was still held captive? She watched him pack up his box of tricks and lumber to the door. The pair could see themselves out. She sat waiting for several moments to be sure they had gone, until she was startled by a series of crashes outside. She crossed the room to look through the long windows. Three large pots containing lemon trees had blown over and smashed on the terrace. The terracotta lay in jagged shards; earth and exposed tendrils of root spilled over the flags. Dimpled yellow globes rolled and bounced and came to rest under the heap of canvas chairs that had also been bullied by the sirocco. She opened one of the windows a crack and the wind seared her cheek. She pulled her head back at once like a tortoise and closed it again. She could hear Bobo's renewed cries from the kitchen, more ferocious than ever: '*Lasciami andare! Lasciami andare!* Let me out!' His fists thudded against the door.

Rosaria, widowed and childless herself, always indulged the children. She didn't try to remonstrate or influence their behaviour; she simply stopped their mouths with food – home-made *grissini*, candied fruits or salted almonds – like plugging a bottle into a baby. Her methods were no longer working: Bobo was stuffed to the gills and cross that he was being sidelined in this great adventure. He had thrilled to the hum of the helicopter blades and the power of the motorbikes; he'd wanted to play with the guns in their black holsters. At first, as a miniature model of machismo, he'd been found amusing, but this was a serious business and he couldn't be allowed to become a nuisance; hence the indignity of being locked away with his sister.

Finally he succeeded in shooting out of the kitchen and along the hallway. Rosaria, with no great enthusiasm, panted in pursuit. Maresa slammed down the phone. '*Mannaggia la miseria!*' she shrieked. 'Is there no end to all this!'

'I'll get him back,' offered Liddy. She soon gained on the boy who'd run outside but was being driven off course by the wind. The gates at the end of the drive had been left open. The road wasn't busy, but it was full of blind bends; a low barrier was the only indication of the sheer drop beyond. She put on an extra spurt of speed and hauled him towards her just as an old *camionetta* trundled past, laden with firewood. As she carried him writhing back into the house, he closed his teeth on her upper arm. The attack and the pain shocked her into dropping him. He rolled away and hid under the glass dining table.

His bite had stamped a perfect circular mark; in places the skin was punctured and little beads of blood had formed. She confronted Maresa. 'Look what he's done!'

Maresa's hands flew skywards. 'What a disaster we're having! One thing after another!'

'I think I should see a doctor.'

'A doctor? Are you sure? It's only a little scratch.'

'You never know with bites,' said Liddy. 'They can get infected and I haven't had an anti-tetanus jab for ages.' She grimaced. 'And actually it's quite painful.'

'I will deal with it,' Maresa said irritably. 'Come with me to the bathroom. I know how to dress wounds and I have a comprehensive first aid box.'

This was true. Potions and lotions, ointments, unguents, cotton wool, gauze, lint, plasters, painkillers, scissors, tweezers – Maresa's first aid collection was as magnificent as her cosmetics. 'Truly, you cannot get tetanus from such a shallow piercing,' she said. 'I will use witch-hazel to counteract the bruising. And iodine to stop infection. Be sure to keep it clean and the mark will fade speedily.' Her handiwork was neat: a large pink rectangle hid every scrap of the bite. 'We are all under stress at this time, including the children. You must understand this.'

Liddy, still agitated, said, 'Can I go out for an hour or two? Will you be able to give me a lift to the Vesuvio?'

Maresa considered. 'Very well. So long as we know where you are.'

Leaving one child sulking under the table and the other arguing with the maid, they both got into the car. Halfway down the hillside they passed another police car making its way up. Maresa slowed and glanced in her mirror, but it proceeded on to Casa Colonnata.

Jake's room was locked and empty. Liddy tracked him down in a nearby bar he'd taken to frequenting, a dark and virtually deserted place. Garish lights flashed on the pinball machine in the corner; yellowing flypapers flapped from the ceiling; a pair of old men rattled backgammon dice. He turned his head but didn't get off his stool when he saw her.

'Hi.'

'Hi, you.'

'Want a drink?'

'Coke, please. Lots of ice.' She kissed his cheek and murmured, 'I thought we could go up to your room.'

'No chance. You've no idea how stifling it is up there under the eaves. We'd suffocate.'

'Oh.' She held the cold glass against the side of her neck. She hoped he'd ask how she'd come by her plaster, but when he didn't she gave him the full story anyway. 'I save his life practically and he takes a lump out of me! Why couldn't they have stolen him instead of Mimmo?'

Jake hadn't shown much interest in her wounding. 'Because he's bonkers. You know that already. Have they let Helena out yet?'

'No.' She moved her stool to close the gap between them and her knee jogged against his. 'I don't understand what she's supposed to have done.'

'I guess they have to look as though they're taking action and she's an easy target.'

'They think people might have been watching us with the children.'

'People? Who?'

'The kidnappers, I mean. That they'd been following our movements, the beaches we went to, that sort of thing. Like it's supposed to be significant we went somewhere we'd never been before.' She paused. 'That was your idea, wasn't it?'

'What are you getting at?'

'Nothing. I simply –'

He was defensive. 'Look, I'm not hiding anything. I've been straight with everyone. I've not been sneaking around behind people's backs, like some I could mention.'

'What's that supposed to mean?'

'Just forget it.'

The strap of her sandal loosened and it fell from her foot. She rubbed her bare toes against his leg but he didn't react.

'So abduction's the top theory today, is it?'

Her eyes widened. 'Didn't you hear? There's been a note.'

He mocked her excitement. 'A note!'

'I think that's why they haven't let Helena go. They're trying to get her to remember something.'

'Even so, I'm surprised Fabrizio hasn't stormed the citadel and set her free. You know, the knight in shining armour scenario.'

Liddy sucked the last dregs of her Coke through her straw. 'Knight in shining armour? What on earth are you talking about?'

Jake's face was more flushed than usual, his eyes bloodshot. We're all functioning below par, thought Liddy.

He ordered further drinks and offered one to the young barman. The latter inclined his head in acceptance, pushed the glasses along the counter and went back to reading the *Corriere dello Sport*.

'And I thought you were best mates,' Jake said.

The hot air was like cotton wool. It filled her lungs so she couldn't breathe. She'd hoped for comfort but he was unusually distant, making her feel troublesome instead of a perfect joy. And now he was implying her friendship with Helena was not what she'd thought.

'Well, she's a bit of a dark horse, so I daresay she had her reasons.'

'Reasons for what? For telling you something she's been keeping from me?'

'Keeping from everybody, sweetheart,' said Jake, tapping his long, deft fingers on the counter top. 'Only I saw through her.'

'What, because you're the wizard with X-ray vision?'

'Because I'm bloody observant, that's why. I have to be. Studying people's mannerisms, working out their motivations . . . It's all grist, isn't it?' At the far end of the bar, a German youth, bent under the frame of his backpack, was reaching for his beer. Hunching his shoulders, Jake copied the motion exactly. 'I've made a habit of keeping my eyes open – whereas you are pretty little miss head-in-the-clouds.'

'Don't patronize me.'

'Okay, sorry.' He deposited a kiss, which was too light to be sincere.

'Don't leave me in suspense either. Tell me what you're getting at.'

'Helena and Fabrizio . . .'

'Helena and Fabrizio what?'

'Helena and Fabrizio fuck.'

'Each other?'

'Well, yes.'

Liddy inhaled the bubbles from her Coke by mistake. Spluttering, she set down her glass. He thumped her on the back. Her throat was raw with coughing. 'Do you mean that she's been sleeping with him right under Gabi's nose?'

'I imagine they employ some discretion.'

'But how could she not notice? Her husband and the au pair . . .'

'I think you'll find there's a long-running tradition. It won't be the first time anyone's asked that particular question. Anyway, *you* didn't notice either.'

'No . . . but . . .' It was becoming clearer now: Helena's curious reluctance to get involved with any of the men they met at the club and her caginess on the subject of boyfriends in general. 'Oh God.' She wrung her hands together. 'She's been using me.'

'How?'

Liddy loved the way Jake raised one eyebrow incredulously. She loved all his mannerisms, the way he bared his teeth or pinched the bridge of his nose, the way he could adopt any accent. She was, she knew, besotted. 'As a decoy of course! If there are two of us, she doesn't stand out so much, does she? When she talked me into coming to work over here, I thought it was because she wanted my company. Whereas all the while I was just a handy alibi . . .'

'Fido,' said Jake.

'What?'

'It's only a nickname. No need to get hot under the dog collar.' Was he trying not to smirk?

'Fuck *off*! Did she really call me that? I hope you stood up for me.'

'I couldn't. I didn't know you at the time.'

In Liddy's gut a fireball of fury was gathering strength. Her so-called friend had not only lied about her affair with Fabrizio, she lied about Jake too. The pair of them had probably been in bed, post-coital, when Helena had mocked and derided her. And on how many other occasions? With how many other people, here or at home? So many possibilities, of slights imagined or endured, overwhelmed her. 'Right. I'm nobody's stooge. If that's what she thinks of me, I'm going to have it out with her.'

'They won't let you.'

'Why not?'

'Well, for a start they've probably got her under lock and key so you can't just waltz in. And this being Italy, they'll be inventing the law as they go along.' He jiggled his beer and spoke wearily. 'Actually, they don't need to invent it. It's so convoluted that all you have to do is stick a pin on any page of the statute book and you'll find the obfuscating bit of bureaucracy that you need.'

She wished he wouldn't use long, difficult words. It was so pretentious. A nice simple phrase – like, I love you Liddy – would do just fine. And if at that moment he'd offered any hint of a caress, any proof of his feelings, she'd have stayed put. They wouldn't have to struggle against the torpor of his attic room, they could go down the Vesuvio's cellar where bottles of pop and Peroni were stored, where once they'd sneaked behind a tower of crates and he'd pinned her to the cold wall.

She slid from her stool, but he didn't move. His elbows were slumped on the bar. God knows, they were all exhausted, but she'd have appreciated the reassurance that they'd get through this together.

'See you later, Lid,' he said.

She didn't like being called Lid; it made her think of dustbins. She shuffled towards the door, past the German youth and the backgammon players, hoping he might call her back. She turned when she heard him speak, but he was only ordering a whisky.

'We're running out of ice,' said the barman regretfully.

It was not an afternoon to be on the streets. A child's buggy was bowling away from its mother's grasp, old men were clutching their hats to their heads, dogs were beaten into the gutter by the wind. Shop awnings bellied like spinnakers with bright bold stripes; some had been torn from their moorings and dangled like tattered flags of battle. Pink and green plastic bags sailed across the creaking treetops. If Liddy had a coin, she would have tossed it: heads for Helena, tails for home. But Jake was right; she couldn't march into the police station and stage a scene. Possibly she'd been let out now anyway, possibly the police car they'd passed had Helena inside it. If she hadn't been distracted by her throbbing arm and her need for Jake, she'd have paid more attention. She'd expected to spend longer with him, she'd expected to return, soothed and sated, to face the impossible Bobo and the perfectly horrible distress of a family whose child has gone missing. Well, she wasn't soothed and sated, but her need to get back was as urgent as her need to leave in the first place. She hailed a taxi.

They were there again, waiting for her, the fat detective and his side-kick. He's come to arrest me, she panicked. He's going to haul me off to the cells like Helena. I should have stayed with Jake.

The hallway was wide and filled with flowers and mirrors, but it didn't feel welcoming. Maresa intercepted her. 'You were not at the Vesuvio.'

'We were just having a drink in a bar.'

'He said he would wait for your return. He wants to see you in private. I think they may have some leads but they are telling us nothing. Whatever he asks about Mimmo you must answer, even if it doesn't seem important.'

'Of course I will.' One piece of information had come to light since her previous interview, but would it interest the police? Would they see Helena's relationship with Fabrizio as part of a wider conspiracy? Unlikely. No doubt they had mistresses themselves and regarded infidelity as perfectly natural and completely irrelevant.

The detective rose. He'd changed into short sleeves, and a dark thicket bristled on his arms. The buckle on his belt shone with an eager glint, like his tiny eyes. '*Di nuovo*, *signorina*,' he said.

'Again,' echoed Liddy feebly. At least he wasn't brandishing handcuffs or a revolver. He'd probably forgotten to ask her something.

'I am going to Gabi,' said Maresa. 'Until her parents arrive she needs me. You have no idea what agony the poor woman is going through. I shall take the children with me,' she added as an afterthought. 'You will have the house to yourself.'

They took up their previous positions, facing each other across the big table, the interpreter at the far end. 'What do you want from me now?' Liddy said.

When he smiled his jowls overlapped his collar. 'You have been very helpful, *signorina*. I have passed on your information and we have good hope of catching the criminals.'

'And rescuing Mimmo?'

'Indeed – though we are still looking for clues. We have searched the room of the English girl. Unfortunately we have not found her papers.

This is important to establish her identity.' He tapped his pen against his teeth. She wondered if he had done this once too often as one of his upper incisors had a jagged piece missing. The hair on his arms crept under his watch strap and over the backs of his hands; would it feel soft and furry or stiff and coarse? Would anyone's brain be in good working order if they hadn't slept properly in forty-eight hours?'

'Oh . . . right.'

'Do you know where they might be?'

'No,' said Liddy. 'I'm sorry, I don't.'

'You can show me yours, however?'

'Do you want me to go and get them?'

'Please.'

He didn't accompany her. Liddy went to the white lacquered chest in her bedroom and pulled out the document folder that she'd offered to look after. She balanced her own stiff navy-blue passport on the palm of one hand and Helena's on the other: she deserved to suffer a little longer.

She returned to the policeman and he spent a long time thumbing the empty pages, writing down the number. 'I could confiscate this,' he said, waving it in her face, 'if I thought you would leave the country. We may need to see you again.'

'Believe me, I'm not going anywhere. My boyfriend is here. I have the job too.' She made it sound as if she were settled, a fixture, and he must have been convinced. He took his leave with elaborate formality but no further threats.

She took her passport back to her room and stared into the open drawer. In truth, she felt as if there were a great yawning abyss around and within her. She was astonished her voice hadn't shaken with the force of her rage which, now the interview was over, sprang back at her, redoubled. Fido! She couldn't bear the idea of the two of them laughing at her and she was so livid with Helena – for her deception and disloyalty – she needed to do something wicked and destructive, like punching a hole through the crown of her straw hat, or shearing her favourite skirt into ribbons. Since she could hardly rush over to Casa Colonnata brandishing a knife, she made do with the closest thing to hand: Helena's *permesso di soggiorno*, folded into her passport. Liddy went out on to the balcony and began to shred it, tossing the fragments into the air. The action was petty and pointless but every rip gave her a shocking satisfaction; she enjoyed the fleeting sensation of power.

As the confetti danced in the wind currents above her head and shoulders, her grip on the passport slackened. It had been tucked under her armpit but now fell on the ground and lay open at Helena's sly, taunting smile. Liddy nudged it with her foot, about to trample over her friend's face with the contempt she deserved, but a sudden fierce flurry sent it skating through a gap in the balcony railings. She gazed in horror as the passport swooped, was buoyed for a moment in the air, and then plummeted down the cliff, beyond recapture.

8

They had gone on an excursion to Castello Aragonese earlier in July: two families, two cars, three children shrieking on the back seat. Gabi and Maresa had stepped daintily on to the pavement and surveyed its rocky outcrop, shielding their eyes. They had shuffled their elegantly shod feet.

'Maybe another time,' said Maresa.

'We've visited before,' agreed Gabi. 'To us it's nothing new.' She tweaked the collar of her shirt to protect the back of her neck.

'You take the children,' said Maresa to her husband, although they too were looking daunted by the climb. 'We'll meet you later.'

'You'll love it, Bobo,' Piero told his son. 'There's an entire museum of torture instruments. And the castle was full of prisoners, you know, in the *Ottocento*, before Garibaldi liberated them.'

At this point, Sara allied herself with her mother. She would prefer to go shopping. '*Vieni con noi*,' she begged Liddy, her brown curls bouncing, and she, too, joined the women.

After they had crossed the causeway, Piero hoisted Bobo on to his shoulders and tackled the first flight of steps in his soft-soled Gucci loafers. Fabrizio, Helena and Mimmo followed. The rough-hewn staircase was treacherous underfoot. It wove around corners and beneath archways and finally led through a damp and cavernous tunnel to the fortress at the summit. It was a day of intense fragrance and colour – of wild jasmine and honeysuckle, of a cobalt sky and a cerulean sea – but buzzards hovered in the motionless air high above their heads, rodents scurried into shadows. Helena couldn't share Bobo and Mimmo's enthusiasm for the macabre. The place made her shiver.

On their way back down, Piero insisted there was a further spectacle they shouldn't miss. He led the way past dangling creepers into the ruins of the old convent of the Clarisse. They stood in a small, roofless chamber, facing a line of stone seats like choir stalls.

'Now, *ragazzi*,' he said with an eager grin. 'You must guess for what purpose the nuns came here.'

The site was deserted. It was possible, if you tried hard enough, to imagine the nuns of three centuries ago, the flap of their skirts and the heavy clump of their boots as they traipsed up and down bearing water from the spring. Mimmo inspected the row of cubicles, finely carved and rendered but cubicles nonetheless. The round seats had large holes in their centres, reminiscent of the ruined baths all over Rome – Terme di Caracalla, Terme di Diocleziano – with their detailed mosaics, their elaborate drainage systems and their well-appointed communal latrines.

Piero lifted Bobo on to one of the seats. Mimmo balanced on another.

'This was their washroom?' Helena leaned against a column dividing one stall from another. 'And these were the toilets?'

The two men met each other's eyes and burst out laughing, slapping their knees with pleasure at their joke.

'Completely incorrect,' Piero gloated. 'This was their cemetery.' He described how, when a member of the order died, they didn't bury her. They balanced the corpse on one of the cradles so her flesh would drop through the hole as it disintegrated. The living nuns would kneel and pray for their sisters' souls in front of the unlovely spectacle of mouldering bones.

The little boys' eyeballs revolved, their mouths gaped. Gabi would have objected to such gruesome talk.

Helena said, 'It's different now, isn't it? We value our bodies more than our souls. That's why we pamper them so much.'

Fabrizio had decided this was provocation. As Piero led Bobo and Mimmo down the steps again he pulled her back – to make the point that every inch of her sun-warmed flesh, each tendril of hair and bead of sweat, the tongue he tasted with his own, was greedy for the moment. Entirely temporal.

It had come to haunt her: the notion of the decaying corpses, the penance of the living. In future she'd be more respectful, she wouldn't be so quick to ridicule. It was yet another resolution to add to the list of changes she would make in her life when she got out of here. *If* she got out, that was. If.

She was in the interview room again. Dirt outlined the cracks in the tiled floor; paint was flaking from the walls. She thought it might be afternoon; she'd lost track. When she came round after her faint, she'd been offered a slice of pizza. Cold and unappealing, the chewy crust with its smear of tomato purée now lay discarded. It had been brought to her in a wet wrapping of wax paper so she assumed that out in the real world it was raining – washing away any traces of Mimmo's journey. Any clues.

She'd tried to appeal for help from Fabrizio, but she hadn't been able to see him alone. He couldn't possibly think she had anything to do with Mimmo's abduction. It was far more likely that he was the one with the dodgy contacts: building contractors annoyed they hadn't got a lucrative deal or an official in the planning department unhappy with the value of his bribe. There could be any number of people with a grudge against a successful architect whisking contracts away from his competitors, any number of henchmen who wanted to curry favour with their bosses. The police were probably in the pay of the criminals anyway. How convenient to have a foreigner to blame.

This scenario of corruption was so vivid in her mind that, when the door opened, she scraped back her chair with a grating squeal and launched into a rant. 'This is unforgivable! You can't lock up innocent people just to show that you're doing something. You have to have grounds for suspicion. Don't you have any sense of justice in this country? Or do you always fall in with the wishes of the person who pays you the most money?'

'You feel better now?' said Enzo.

'No. Not really.'

'You lacked nourishment, I believe. You have eaten the pizza?' With a fastidious pinching of his fingertips he dropped the debris into the metal wastepaper bin.

'Yes. It was *uno schifo*. Disgusting.'

'Elena.' He shook his head in sorrow. 'You are in great trouble.'

'I *know* that. People have been telling me nothing else.'

'Sit down.'

'No.'

'I don't want you to faint again.'

'Twice in one day would be something, wouldn't it? Still, I've eaten that horrible pizza now so I'll be all right.'

'You should show more respect.'

'Why? Because you wear a uniform and I don't?'

His cheeks were plump as a baby's, as Bobo's. That must be why he'd grown the moustache, though she couldn't imagine it fooled anybody. His eyes were liquid as a puppy's. He looked altogether too conciliatory, too amiable a type to have joined the police force. And yet he wore an unpleasant sneer which she hadn't seen before. 'Because I have power over you,' he said. 'It's better if you do as I say.'

Mini-Mussolini, thought Helena as she sat down again. She'd been in Italy long enough to have encountered the pace of its bureaucracy. Even if Fabrizio were at the front desk right now with two lawyers and a wad of 20,000 lire notes, the formalities would take hours to complete. Then they'd have to get the release papers stamped and the office that did the stamping would be closed for the rest of the day. And when it reopened it would find it needed a particular shade of ink which was out of stock at the stationer's. And someone would have to be persuaded with lavish charm, or money, or the promise of a coveted ticket to a football game or a boxing match, that an approximation would do: that crimson, cherry and maroon were all shades of red and a red stamp was all that was needed to free her, so *please* . . .

'We have a problem with your identity,' Enzo was saying.

'My what?'

'You have given us the name of Elena Ashbourne.'

'Yes.'

'But we cannot find your papers.'

'Oh shit!' She almost laughed with relief. So this was the reason for the delay. She hoped she looked normal and not as if her face were stuck in a phoney rictus. 'That's because Liddy took charge of them when we were travelling down here. She's much more organized than I am. I just never got around to taking them back. She should have my *permesso* somewhere.'

'We have asked this,' said Enzo. 'It appears she does not.'

'That's odd.' She stared at him. 'Well, she'll have my passport anyway.'

'No.'

'What d'you mean, no? Of course she does. I'm pretty certain she didn't get around to giving it back to me.' She faltered; it was hard to be sure of anything.

'We have searched your room. There were no identity papers.'

'So why don't you search hers? I can't think why she's pissing about. She kept both our passports in one of those transparent zipped pocket things. She's tidy-minded, you see, and –'

'She is not under suspicion.'

'What do you mean, under suspicion? Why are you just going for me? Why not both of us?'

'You know this already,' said Enzo, while she tried to decipher his expression. Was it hostile, disapproving or merely exasperated? 'You were seen talking to the man we are associating with this business.'

'Outside the Vesuvio? But I already told you –'

'No, there is another occasion.'

She flapped her hand. 'According to who, your mysterious witness?'

'Not mysterious, Elena. Your friend.'

'What friend?'

'Elen Liddle.'

'*Liddy* told you this nonsense?'

'She has identified the man from photographs we showed her.'

'But that's ridiculous! She couldn't identify a hobgoblin. She can't wear her contact lenses because of the dust and half the time she won't wear her glasses. In other words, she's blind. She's lying. Hadn't you thought of that?' Her mouth was unaccountably dry; her breathing erratic. She'd always thought of Liddy as staunch, happy to follow her lead. Not that she'd ever ordered Liddy around and expected blind obedience (though she had sometimes talked her into doing things against her better judgement). But anyway, if anything went wrong – as it had done now, spectacularly – Helena would always be the one to take the rap; it didn't bother her, it didn't detract from her image. By the same token, if necessity demanded, Helena might tell a lie. Liddy would not.

There had only been one exception, a moment of self-sacrifice on Liddy's part, when they were at school. She could recall the cold touch of the glass as she cupped her hands against the window to spy Liddy alone in the centre of the classroom, bent over her desk, covering sheets of foolscap with her neat but childish handwriting. Helena had already been given the maximum number of detentions that term and another would have led to suspension. In any case, Liddy was the one who'd been caught red-handed. The lookout had spotted their form teacher, Miss Myers – all sailing cardigans and swaying beads – stomping down the corridor. Liddy had seized the eraser and rubbed off most of the scurrilous limerick Helena had composed on the blackboard. Unfortunately, words such as 'Daphne' and 'dildo' remained. Miss Myers was not known for her sense of humour. She'd assumed Liddy was scrubbing away her own work and for some reason she'd admitted to it.

Enzo shrugged. 'She gave us her word.'

'Well, it's nonsense.' Helena pondered the possibilities. 'And she'd make a lousy witness anyway. If there wasn't an interpreter she probably misunderstood what you were asking. It's not valid evidence.'

'There was an interpreter,' Enzo said. 'But, in point of fact, we are not using her evidence to detain you. We don't need it.'

'You don't?' She was puzzled. Did this mean they were finally going to let her go?

She'd had plenty of time to weigh up her options, to consider what might happen over the rest of the summer and she'd realized that once Mimmo was recovered (and she couldn't contemplate any alternative), the holiday was over. She thought it just possible – years hence – she'd be able to look back at her sojourn on Ischia and think, Yes, that was fun: the swimming, the snorkelling, the dancing, the picnics. But not yet, not for a long while, because this ugly mess would blot out all the good memories.

A knock vibrated at the door. Enzo went to answer it. Helena knotted her hands together and strained to hear the conversation. After a few moments he came back to her and said, 'There has been a development. I am needed elsewhere.'

'You mean you've found out something? Or you've found Mimmo?'

'I'm sorry, I cannot explain more.'

'Why not? Why do I have to be kept in the dark?'

He ignored her plea. 'Later they will come for you.'

'*Who* will come for me? My lawyers?'

'The police escort. They will take you to Naples.'

'Naples! Whatever for?' She held herself a little straighter, although a bite festered on her shin that she longed to itch. 'The Verduccis haven't got the power to throw me off the island.'

'It is we who are taking you into custody.'

She didn't understand. 'You? Why? So that I can go on "helping you with your enquiries"? Or for my own safety? Don't tell me there's a lynch mob out there.'

'And we will make the formal charges.'

'What on earth do I have to do to prove I'm not part of some half-baked conspiracy?'

'We take drug offences very seriously in Italy,' said Enzo.

'Drug offences?' Her hands flew to her mouth. 'I don't know what you're talking about.'

'We have found a substance in your room. This has been tested and found to be cannabis resin.'

Helena said quickly. 'It's not *my* room. It belongs to the Verduccis. It's their villa; I'm just passing through, aren't I?'

'Do you deny the cannabis is yours?'

Never confess. That was something else she'd been warned. Don't make life easy for the bureaucrats and with luck they'll give up on you. 'Of course I deny it.'

'Oh Elena . . .' He sighed and spread his palms in a helpless gesture. 'Why will you not co-operate with us? Why do you make everything so difficult for yourself?'

She squared her shoulders and glowered at him. For a moment she thought he might try to touch her in some demonstration of sympathy. Instead he said, 'I hope you do not regret this,' and left the room.

9

There had been storm casualties all along the windward side of the island: sailing masts snapped, shallow trees uprooted, laundry whipped from the line. On the terrace of Casa Colonnata Rosaria's broom had not yet cleared the damage; she'd swept away the broken pots and spilled soil but the flags were discoloured with a fine coating of red Saharan dust. Both families were gathered there, discussing tactics. Gabi was wearing several layers of clothing; although the sky was grey she refused to take off her dark glasses. Liddy was trying to occupy the children with colouring books.

No one was certain who heard the car first. Possibly it was Bobo, always alert to engine sounds. Without waiting for Rosaria to announce him, a *carabiniere* came around the side of the house. He wore a flourishing moustache and a spotless uniform; he was turning his cap between his hands. Liddy immediately thought the worst; couldn't bear to look in Gabi's direction. Gabi had half-risen, but halted as if her joints had seized up and she couldn't move any further. Fabrizio supported her elbow.

The policeman smiled. 'I have good news,' he said.

A collective gasp, a sibilant intake of breath.

'Well?' demanded Fabrizio.

Rosaria also appeared from the side colonnade. She was leading her niece, Cristina, by the hand. In turn, Cristina was leading a small boy dressed in an over-large shirt, Mimmo.

'*Santa Madonna!*' Maresa hailed them, crossing herself.

Speechless, Gabi sank back into her chair. Fabrizio stepped forward to claim his son, but Mimmo clung to Cristina.

There followed such outpourings in Italian that Liddy could make little sense of what was being said. Eventually it became clear that the police had nothing to do with the child's recapture. He had been found in the chestnut woods on Cristina's family's land and she had contacted them. Nobody knew how he'd got there or whether the kidnappers had abandoned him because of the weather conditions and the extent of the rescue operation. And he couldn't tell them.

'*Dimmi, piccolino, come stai?*' said Fabrizio. He stroked his limbs and tried to scoop him up but Mimmo wouldn't leave Cristina's side. The girl chewed her lip and shifted her weight from foot to foot. She'd smartened herself for the occasion in a cotton dress sprigged with tiny flowers and her colour was heightened. Liddy noticed the policeman stood close by, as if she and not Mimmo were in need of protection.

'We should call the doctor,' said Maresa. 'He has to be checked over. You don't know what they've been doing to him.'

'Are you hungry, *ciccio*?'

No response.

'Are you hurt? Maybe your feet? Your head?'

Piero went inside to make the phone call. Bobo and Sara didn't want to be left out of the drama. Bobo balanced on the rim of the terrace wall and pretended to fall off; Sara claimed to find a splinter in her finger. 'Oh it hurts so much! Please do something. No, no, don't touch it!' Liddy was the only person who responded.

By degrees Mimmo and his saviour were coaxed into the embrace of the assembled family. Fabrizio opened a bottle of French champagne and insisted Cristina drank a glass; the *carabiniere*, Enzo, too. The heroine of the occasion was invited to tell her story again, with more detail this time. Maresa translated for Liddy and she learned how Cristina had gone to feed the pigs and stumbled on this wild dirty creature wrapped in a piece of sacking. How she had fed and bathed him and found him something to wear but, like his parents, she'd not been able to get a morsel of information out of him. She had shown Enzo and his colleagues the hollow in the undergrowth where the boy had sheltered, but the force of the sirocco had brought down branches as well as leaves. There was no trail of clues to analyse.

'Don't they have any leads at all?' asked Liddy.

'Yes indeed!' And Enzo explained through Maresa that thanks to the English *signorina*'s identification they were investigating the movements of some petty local thieves. The kidnap appeared to be a sign of the times – *questi brutti tempi* – a copycat crime, but the police didn't believe they were dealing with hardened professionals. They'd decided this abduction was most likely opportunist, a poor, sloppy business; the note was obviously the work of an amateur. Their enquiries were continuing, naturally, but he was extremely satisfied with the outcome so far.

Liddy, squirming at her alleged part in the process, was far from satisfied, but at this juncture the doctor arrived. While he examined Mimmo in a quiet bedroom with the shutters closed, Liddy sought out Fabrizio. The contrast between his previous black fury and his present euphoria was striking. His usually haughty face looked as if it could crack with good humour.

She waylaid him as he lit a cigarette. 'What does this mean for Helena?' she asked.

Fabrizio removed a speck of tobacco from his lip before answering in mild surprise. 'Elena?'

'Yes. What's going to happen to her? Don't you feel responsible for her? I mean, I know I do.' This was bold. She wouldn't have dared to sound so accusing if she'd still regarded him as her friend's employer rather than an unreliable lover.

'I am finding her a lawyer,' he said. 'The best in Naples.'

'Aren't you worried about her?'

'Naturally I'm worried.' He scratched his head as if deciding how much to tell her. 'But she is an adult, is she not? She makes adult choices. And Mimmo is a child. We don't know how much he has suffered and we have to make him well.'

'At least he's alive and safe,' said Liddy. 'Whereas Helena's in trouble.'

'And this is my doing?'

'You could have stopped the police taking her in. They'd have listened to you.'

'Some things,' he said, 'are out of my control. I am doing what's within my scope and my son must be my priority. When you have children of your own you'll understand.'

'I suppose you didn't really love her,' muttered Liddy, thinking she had already lost his attention.

'Love!' The word in his mouth was as piercing as the splinter in Sara's finger. 'What is this to do with you?'

'Don't worry. She didn't spill the beans. I worked it out.'

He could be arrogant and over-bearing and she'd always been a little in awe of him, but no longer. There was vulnerability too, and she could begin to see what it was, besides his more obvious charms, that Helena had fallen for.

'Love is a very splendid thing. But we should distinguish, should we not, as the Greeks did, between the different kinds of love? Between love and duty.'

Sod the Greeks, thought Liddy. 'And don't you have a duty towards Helena who was under your roof?'

'And didn't she have a duty towards Mimmo? My wife and I, you know, we have discussed this many times and we cannot avoid the conclusion that Elena is responsible for her own – what do you say? – predicament.'

All the while, Fabrizio's fist had been clenched around his lighter. He rolled it around his palm and snapped at the wheel with his thumb. 'I offered to stand bail for her,' he said. 'Unfortunately there is a problem with her papers.'

Liddy swallowed, said nothing.

'She will be freed. After all, she is British and her misdemeanour is stupid only. But when? *Boh*, I cannot say.' And he stamped out his cigarette, flattening the remaining white column with his heel.

Two days later Mimmo had still not spoken. The doctor reassured them that he was physically sound, but that he should not be pressed. When his nerves recovered, so would his speech. The waiting was hard for them all. After they had finished their lunch of chicken *cacciatore* – everybody talking at once to make up for Mimmo's absolute silence – Maresa took Liddy aside. 'I want to speak to you when we have settled the children for their nap.'

When she was certain Bobo and Sara were sleeping she ushered Liddy into her bedroom. 'Do you want coffee?' she said as if it were a sudden afterthought. 'Camomile? Something else?'

'No. I'm fine.' She sat on the white wicker chair because she found her legs were shaky.

Maresa opened the shutters on to the balcony from which Helena's passport had plunged. 'We have been making careful consideration,' she said.

What was it about the words 'careful consideration' that sounded so ominous? Did they always have negative connotations? Was it ever possible for somebody to say: After careful consideration I believe you are absolutely the right person for me/this job/this course/this once-in-a-lifetime opportunity? Instead of: I'm sorry, but . . .

'*Mi dispiace*,' said Maresa. 'I know the children will miss you, but after what has happened, we believe, all of us, that it's best if you leave. Truthfully we will not be able to let them out of our sight from now on. As you may imagine! And now we are in August, our husbands can take holidays so we have less need of your help. This isn't what we arranged, but we must be philosophical, don't you agree? We will not be unreasonable. We will give you time to pack, to prepare for departure. We will pay the money we owe you. You can go tomorrow, yes?'

Stung into defiance, Liddy said, 'I'll leave tonight if you like.'

'Are you sure? Where will you go?'

'I'll find somewhere.'

'You know it is the high season. The hotels may be full.'

'I can stay with my friend.'

'Oh . . . yes.' Maresa's coal-bright eyes softened at the thought of Jake. She'd been beguiled by his knack of charming older women. In her opinion, it appeared he didn't share responsibility for what had happened on the beach. Briskly she added, '*Allora*, that's settled. Good.'

They agreed it would be better if she left before the children woke, to avoid prolonged and distressing farewells. Liddy did wonder if this would look as though she was slinking away like a thief in the night, but she suddenly longed to be with Jake.

Deposited outside the Vesuvio, she began to struggle with the weight of her suitcase up the stairs to his room. At the turn of the first flight she collided with someone descending and the case sprang open. As her clothes and shoes tumbled out in hectic disarray she burst into uncontrollable sobs.

The young man, who'd been skidding down the narrow treads, was dismayed and agitated by her reaction and hurriedly stooped to pick up underwear and stuff items back into the case. 'Don't touch my things,' wailed Liddy and while he may not have understood the words, he seemed relieved to snatch the excuse to move on. A door opened on the floor above and she heard Jake exclaim: 'What the fuck?'

She gathered armfuls of clothes – so carefully folded an hour ago – while he leaned over the banister, shaking his head in perplexity. Once she'd collected everything, she snapped the locks shut again and clambered up the final flight. 'Please hold me,' she said, swallowing tears.

'What is it? What's the matter?' She butted her head against his chest.

'Hey, don't take it out on me.'

She longed for him to soothe her with kisses, for his lips to press gently on her eyelids and wet lashes, but his manner was distracted and perfunctory. With reluctance he carted her luggage into his room and shut the door. She clung to his neck. 'I will explain,' she promised. 'But please can we go to bed first?' She wanted to feel him inside her, his thin sheet wrapped around the two of them like a cocoon. She wanted to keep him bound so tight he couldn't steal away. She wanted him never to leave her.

She threw herself on to the sagging mattress and pulled him down to join her. She fumbled with his button-fly.

'Sorry, sweetheart,' he said. 'I'm not in the mood.'

'But you're *always* in the mood. You're Mr Permanently Randy.'

'Not tonight, Josephine.'

His cock was limp and soft against her palm, unresponsive. She could smell whisky on his breath. Scarcely an inch of J&B remained in the bottle on the bedside table. 'You've drunk all that this afternoon?' she said, shocked.

'I had some help.'

'Who?'

'Just Guido.'

'Who's Guido?'

'My indispensable purveyor of ice.'

Why did he have to talk in riddles all the time? Couldn't he see how upset she was? Then she recalled the man on the stairs and his hasty exit, as if already late for work. She'd thought there was something familiar about him. The angle of his shoulder as he bent to pick up her clothes mirrored the way he'd hunched at the counter, turning the pages of his newspaper. 'Oh, you mean the barman?'

'Yeah . . .' He reached over her for the bottle. 'But if your need is greater than mine . . .'

He was shirtless and, catching the sharp tang of testosterone, she longed to lick and groom him. 'You know I hate the taste of whisky.'

'Fair enough.' He leaned back against the bolster, his flesh smooth and tanned, his profile even and regular as a Botticelli painting. She wriggled until her head lay in the crook of his arm. A long mirror set into the wardrobe opposite reflected the two of them: Jake detached, Liddy still hoping she could kindle his interest. A cobweb netted flies in the corner of the sloping ceiling, a small truck droned past outside. His eyes flickered to her suitcase. 'Perhaps now you can tell me what all this is about.'

'It's awful. I've been sacked.'

'Really? I thought everything was okay now they'd found him.'

'They don't trust me, do they? And they're frantic because Mimmo can't speak. If you ask something simple, like whether he's hungry or thirsty, he might nod or shake his head but he doesn't answer. They keep testing him, which makes things worse – he just opens his mouth like a goldfish.'

'So they haven't found out how he disappeared from the beach?'

'No, they seem to have some suspects though.' She gave up trying to snuggle against him; in any case the sheets were tangled and knotted and digging into her back. She sat up, cross-legged. 'Some small-time crooks who panicked. They think they couldn't get him off the island because of the sirocco so they dumped him. I expect they'll find out the truth soon enough.' She wasn't sure she cared any more. Mimmo had been restored to his family, but the relationships in her own life were collapsing like cards. 'The funny thing is,' she added, 'the person who brought him back was Cristina, Rosaria's niece. You might have seen her at the villa. She helps out sometimes.'

He poured the last dregs of whisky into his empty glass. 'The one whose father ferries her in that rusty old saloon? Has to watch her into the house.'

'Yes, he's scary, isn't he? It's because he objects to her boyfriend, thinks he's not good enough. What's a *burino*?'

'*Burino*? Oh it means like, country bumpkin.'

'Well, that fits. Apparently he's a semi-literate peasant with a tribe of younger siblings to provide for. No prospects and not much sense.'

'That sounds harsh! According to whom? Rosaria?'

'No. She let the side down herself. Marrying beneath her and then getting widowed. It was Maresa who filled me in. There aren't any sons so Cristina can't afford to waste her time with no-hopers. She needs to find a decent bloke who'll keep the farm going.'

'So the father's after funds, is he? And is Cristina going to get a reward?'

'She says she doesn't want anything. She's just God's instrument so they should make a donation to the Church. I mean, they're all over her of course . . .'

'For now.' He rested the glass on his diaphragm. 'I wonder if the police will get to the bottom of it, they're so bloody incompetent. At least it lets Helena off the hook.'

'Oh Lord, you don't know, do you?'

'What?'

'They're holding her on drugs charges.'

The drink spilled as he bolted upright. 'For fuck's sake!'

'They found the stuff you put in her drawer.'

'You're saying it's *my* fault?'

'Well, if you left the dope there and she didn't know . . .'

'Oh, she knew all right.'

'How can you be so sure?'

'Because she thanked me for it. And we shared a couple of spliffs once or twice.'

'Where was I?'

'Probably on your high horse, claiming you didn't hold with mind-altering substances.'

'Well, they're trouble, aren't they? Look what's happened. What are we going to do now?'

'Do? What can we do?'

This was not what she wanted to hear. She needed to rely on him. There wasn't anyone else. 'Well, for a start, I'll have to find another job. D'you think there's anything going at the Vesuvio?'

'No.'

'Couldn't you ask them if they wanted a singer, say?'

He turned his head, squinting at her. 'Do you sing?'

'A bit.' She attempted a few bars of 'Killing Me Softly', but her voice sounded weak and fragile and she let it trail away.

'Don't forget,' he said, 'this country's the cradle of opera. Everybody sings all the time. What makes you special?'

'Are you being unkind on purpose?'

'That's the shit performers have to put up with. You haven't tried to earn a living yet, have you? It's tough out there.'

'It's not a career move. I just want to make enough money to get by.'

'Why? Why don't you go home?'

Bile rose in her throat, as if he'd punched her in the stomach. 'Is that what you think? You don't want me to stay?'

He got up to locate his cigarettes. A whisky stain was seeping down the front of his jeans, the top buttons still unfastened from her failed attempt at arousal. 'I thought it would be easier for you. Things don't work out, you cut your losses.'

'Is that what you're going to do?'

'When?'

'When you don't get picked for a part. When you find you're not going to make it as an actor, after all.'

A whiff of sulphur as he struck a match. 'I'm not planning on going back to England if that's what you're getting at.'

'I thought,' she said, 'if I could get a job in a bar or as a tourist guide or something we could spend more time together. And I want to be here for Helena. It *will* get settled, this business. Fabrizio's going to buy them off or whatever and it was the tiniest amount of hash, after all.'

'Well, they'll release her eventually,' said Jake. 'But you've no idea of the red tape involved.'

'You mean she might miss some of next term? That's awful.'

'Is it? I wouldn't know. I'm a dropout too.'

'But it would look bad if I left now wouldn't it? Like I was running away.'

He despatched three perfect smoke rings. 'This is one major balls up.'

'So could I stay with you for a few days while I try to sort stuff out? I've got a bit of spending money left.'

'Here, you mean?'

'Yes.'

'No, afraid not.'

'No, I can't stay with you?'

He was pacing the room. She watched him meet the wall, turn and turn again. He stretched his arm above his head to touch the slope of the ceiling. 'This is a goddam garret. It isn't feasible for two people to sleep in it. Plus, I don't get to bed till about four in the morning, as you know. What would you do with yourself?'

'I'll try and get a job with similar hours to yours.'

'You'd be better trying to do the opposite.'

'Don't you *want* to spend any time with me? I thought . . . we were . . .'

'What?'

Lovers, she was going to say, but was that true any more? Had he ever felt as she did? Hadn't she always been disposable? Suddenly she was struck by a new notion – one that was so obvious she couldn't believe she'd overlooked it. 'Oh my God, it was Helena you really wanted! All this time . . . All this time you've been hanging around with us you were just making do with me. Using me. I've been so naïve. I was the second choice, wasn't I? A substitute.'

She waited for a comforting denial – No, you goose, it's not that at all. After a beat, Jake said, 'My point is that living in a place as cramped as this would only be bearable if we kept different hours.'

She said stiffly, 'Will you at least let me leave my suitcase? I'll move it out as soon as I've found a *pensione*.' She could picture it already: a shabby room with a washbasin, a wardrobe and a narrow single bed; cheap, off-white tiles with a smattering of dark chips so the track of squashed ants would go unnoticed. The sort of room that made you feel like a poor relation in a Victorian novel, knowing that up on the hillside there was life with maid service, rich food and a private beach. She'd have to live off takeaway slabs of pizza and stodgy rice *supplì* and hang around the Vesuvio, tormented by Jake's combination of cruelty and tenderness until she couldn't stand it anymore.

'Please don't cry, Lid.'

'Please don't call me Lid.'

Helena wasn't expecting a visitor. There were three regulars: the lawyer, an aide from the British Consulate, and Fabrizio. Fabrizio couldn't come often. She knew he was working behind the scenes on her behalf; and she knew that he was angry with her. She was angry too – with Enzo and Liddy particularly, even (shamingly) with Mimmo and Jake, but most of all with herself. She was immersed in a cloud of anger so scorching, so white-hot, she ought to be combustible. It intensified after her dreadful transfer from Ischia to the mainland: the pitching boat, the stifling heat, the stench of rotting fish carcasses, razor-clam shells, sardine heads – no wonder she was sick again. And it built to a climax when she realized there would be no brisk exit from this incarceration. Delays abounded. There was the process of proving her identity, of obtaining her birth certificate and a new passport. Then came the problem of tracking down the local prosecutor, who was on holiday, and the question of discovering precisely which officials might be persuaded to smooth her path. Helena wanted to yell from rooftops, but money and influence talked quietly, slowly.

When they said she had a visitor she supposed it was the doctor. She'd been examined briefly on admittance, when she'd been in an awful state, filthy and covered in vomit. She was waiting for the promised follow-up. But the person sitting on the grey plastic chair at the grey plastic table wasn't the doctor, the lawyer, the aide or Fabrizio. It was Jake.

'What on earth brings you here?' she said.

Jake, at ease in so many situations, looked uncomfortable in a jacket and tie: he kneaded his knuckles together. 'I felt I should see how you're doing.'

'You needn't have bothered.'

'Prison diet seems to have agreed with you anyway.'

'Actually, it goes straight through me most of the time.'

'Oh . . . well . . .'

'I'm not getting any exercise. That's why I'm putting on weight. You don't have to rub it in.'

'Pretty rough, is it?'

'You could say that, yes. Half the time you don't even get any sleep.' She'd never been anywhere so noisy, so clamorous – yet she was even more disturbed by the acquiescence in the dull, defeated eyes of the Romany woman who shared her cell. 'How come they let you in anyway?'

'Oh, I'm the new John.'

'John?'

'From the Consulate? He couldn't make it today.'

'I don't think he is called John, actually. Still, it's good that you haven't lost your touch.'

'Yeah, it was a classy performance. Anyway, now I'm here, is there anything I can do? Messages to the other side, that sort of thing?'

Helena bit her lip to stop it trembling. 'I just want to get out.'

He dropped his gaze; it was rare to see him at a loss for words.

She added, 'I shouldn't even be in here, but you can't get bail if you've no ID. Perhaps you should wring Helen Liddle's neck for me.'

'Too late I'm afraid. She's already gone.'

'Really?'

'The Baldinis decided they could dispense with her services, no surprises there. She hung on for a while – I know she wanted to see you – but her money ran out. Anyway, she said she was going to write. Didn't you get a letter?'

'There was one full of gush about how she didn't mean things to turn out the way they did, the conspiracy theory was none of her doing: blah, blah. I wasn't planning to reply.'

'It wasn't all her fault, Hel. You kept her in the dark about Fabrizio. That was the trouble.'

'I had to! Because of the kids. How was I to know she'd turn around and stitch me up? I don't understand why she wanted me out of the way. She already had a clear field with you.'

'I don't suppose she was *trying* to get you into trouble.'

'It's remarkable what a person can do these days without even trying.'

He laughed. 'Atta girl!'

A spark of pain was fizzing at Helena's temple, the start of another headache. She knew she should appreciate this visit. Jake had made an effort to masquerade as John: kempt, scrubbed, not quite so dissolute, but within moments of leaving her he could saunter into the street, sling off the jacket, wrench off the tie. Ever the chameleon. 'So what are your plans, now love's young dream has gone?'

'Actually, I'm leaving too.'

'How nice to have freedom of movement.' Did that sound bitter? Fuck it, she *was* bitter.

'Look, you'll be out soon, whatever happens. Flying home to the wonderful new world of Mrs Thatcher and her apparatchiks.'

'With a blot like this on my copybook?'

'You just have to reinvent yourself. I do it all the time.'

'I know.' She added, 'So then, where are you going?'

'First back to Rome for an audition, though they're shooting in Spain. Hope to talk myself into some sort of role at least.'

'If the producer fancies you enough.'

'Or the director. Or his assistant. I'm not proud.'

'Tosser.'

'Hey.' He stretched his hand across the table as if to make contact, but she kept hers folded in her lap.

'You'll get me into trouble; they'll think you're passing me another banned substance.'

'Shit. I am sorry, you know, for leaving the dope in your drawer in the first place. Only . . .'

'Forget it, Jake, it's done now. You can't change anything.'

He fidgeted on his chair, sat on his hands as if to keep them under control. 'Nobody took over your room yet, did they?'

'What, you think the Verduccis would bus in another nanny after this?'

'No, I meant the room in Rome, in the apartment.'

'Why?'

He flashed his most charming smile. 'Thought maybe I could take care of it for you. Freshen up the bed linen, dust the furniture.'

'Is that why you've come to see me? Because you need a place to doss? Because you think I'm-all right-Jack here in my comfortable spacious cell!'

'No!' He appeared hurt. 'It's just that, while I'm still around, I'd like to help. Make things easier. Couldn't I be of any use?'

'To me?'

'Yeah.'

She considered. 'I doubt it. You're as much of a liability as I am.'

'Oh . . . right. Well then, I guess I'd better be off.' They were surrounded by hard, echoing surfaces and his words reverberated. Helena didn't respond. Jake looked rueful.

When their time was up and they were escorted in opposite directions, she didn't give him a backwards glance. She struggled to put one foot in front of another, overcome by an onslaught of tiredness that made her want to sleep for a century – though she couldn't fathom why. It had not yet occurred to her that she might be pregnant.

PART TWO

2003 LIVERPOOL

10

Even at a distance, Allie recognized the dog. There was something about the way he blundered through the grass, trying to do three things at once: cock his leg, sniff out a rabbit, chase a ball; something about the agony of indecision tearing him from one objective to the next that made her empathize. In a world full of choices how *did* you stop yourself zigzagging from game to game, goal to goal? How did you pick up a steady trail, make progress? He was a handsome dog, too: his glossy coat brindled with chestnut and ebony, his ears like silk pouches. She couldn't remember his name or she'd have called out to him. Coffee? Toffee? Or a word ending in *o*: Cosmo, Jojo, Rudolfo?

'Rolo! Here, boy! Rolo!' His owner was a struggling figure, too far off to identify, but probably the same woman who'd given Allie such an odd look when they first met (so odd that she'd quickly hidden her left arm behind her back). It had been one of those mildly embarrassing encounters that human beings don't handle as well as animals. The dog had licked Allie's thigh with unabashed enjoyment. The woman had started to jabber about the view from the house as if she'd stood on the balcony for hours, watching the tides ebb and flow – as if it wasn't blindingly obvious she'd talk about anything other than her randy pet. Allie assumed she was a neighbour and would have introduced herself, but the moment passed when the dog sped off in pursuit of a Jack Russell.

Allie was a few yards from home, from what had been her grandmother's house. She had memories of childhood stays, of the piano with the brass candle-holders that had since been sold, of the piano stool that was big enough to hide in, but it was years since she'd visited. She was still finding her bearings. She had walked over the railway bridge and along the front carrying the shoebox with care. Everything else – wallet, keys, phone – bounced between her shoulders in her drawstring backpack. Her pace was slower than usual because of the box and because the wind was gusty too, eddying across the Mersey, surging through the grass on the foreshore, billowing through the public gardens, scattering petals. It was early evening in early summer, a time of year that offered freshness and promise, when possibilities are limitless, when Allie, like Rolo, might pick and sample and chase her tail until she'd found what she really wanted to do.

Rolo bounded forwards and raised his paw to her leg in greeting. In return she ruffled his head and scratched between his ears. 'Good to see you again, boyo,' she said, and proceeded to her gate. He followed. 'Hey, there, you can't come with me. Your owner wants you back.'

The woman was now close enough for Allie to see her concern. 'Don't worry,' she called. 'He's not doing any harm; he's such a friendly dog.' At which, Rolo, responding to the praise, threw himself at Allie in an exuberant display of affection, knocking the shoebox from her clasp. It rose in an ungainly arc and somersaulted into the fuchsia hedge. The fuchsia branches bent and unburdened themselves; the box crashed to the pavement. Rolo's plumed tail swept from side to side.

The woman stopped, stricken. 'Oh my God!' she said. 'I'm *so* sorry. What has he done now?' She was wearing light-coloured, expensive-looking trousers but she knelt at once to assess the damage.

'Just as well we taped the lid shut,' said Allie as she exposed a jumble of broken china. 'If any tiny fragments or shavings go missing it can make all the difference when you're trying to put something back together.'

The woman opened her handbag. It was more like a briefcase, Allie noted, with its divisions and pockets distinguishing the requirements of a well-ordered life. She was able to claim her purse immediately. 'Look, wouldn't it be easier if I paid for a new one? I'd be more than happy to.'

'No . . . no, you can't.' They were both squatting awkwardly on their haunches, face to face.

'It's the least I can do. I mean, it wasn't horrendously expensive, was it?' She replaced the purse in its section of her bag and took a chequebook from another. 'Not . . . hundreds?'

'A few,' nodded Allie, picking up the box and rising to her feet. Could it really be this easy to get people to write cheques? Why wasn't everybody walking around with broken pottery?

'Oh . . .' Allie waited to see how she'd go about withdrawing her offer. She was flapping her chequebook with a worried air. Her pale linen knees wore patches of dust. 'Look, I can't tell you how sorry I am. Rolo's a delightful dog, but I have such problems controlling him. I would have taken him back to the Rescue Centre, only I'd feel such a failure. I've trained other dogs successfully, just not this one.'

'He's sound,' said Allie, who was beginning to wonder how many times a person could apologize before the words stopped meaning anything. 'I need to clean up a bit. How about you?' She didn't expect her to say yes. She assumed that if she lived nearby she'd head for her own bathroom, but when her invitation was accepted she was obliged to lead the way up the overgrown path. The previous tenants hadn't shown much interest in gardening. Sprawling shrub roses intertwined with brambles; peonies flaunted their frilly heads amid clumps of thistles and ragwort. A small-scale wilderness; Rolo was enchanted with it.

'I don't think he should come into your house. I'll tie him up in the porch.'

Allie swung her backpack from her shoulders and fished out a door key. 'Sure. He can't do any damage out here. Actually, there's not much harm he can do inside. The place is hardly furnished.' She couldn't make the visitor out: she looked mature and confident, yet as soon as she walked into the hall her eyes were spinning in their sockets and she was flushing like a schoolgirl. 'There's a basin in the loo on the right. I'm taking this into the kitchen.' She put the shoebox on the table and tossed last night's takeaway containers into the bin. She rinsed the dirt from her hands and switched the kettle on.

The woman was surveying the cooker and the outdated cupboards and the sink unit overlooking the backyard as if she were calculating their value, as if someone who lived in such a shabby, unreconstructed old house couldn't possibly be in possession of a porcelain figurine worth hundreds of pounds.

'It needs gutting really,' said Allie. 'I'm making tea. D'you want some?'

'Thank you, yes. You're in such a good location here.'

'I haven't really got to know it yet. The house was my grandmother's, but she was in a nursing home and rented it out. She died earlier this year.'

'Oh, I'm sorry.'

'It's okay, she'd been ill for ages. Where do you live?'

'A bit further up the coast in Blundellsands. Rolo brought me on a long walk this afternoon.'

'I always wanted a dog of my own,' said Allie. 'I used to adopt strays sometimes.' She had wistful memories of a rough-coated Irish wolfhound nuzzling her palm, of a litter of chocolatey Labrador puppies in a hay barn, of a mongrel collie she taught to perform handstands – none of which she was allowed to keep.

Her visitor took a decisive step into the room and sat down at the table. She opened her bag and pulled out her chequebook again. She laid it flat on the oilcloth, which was patterned with bunches of red cherries. The blind at the window had the same pattern, but Allie never rolled it down.

'I'm Liddy Rawlings and my cheque won't bounce, I promise. I'll write my address on the back. Now, if you'd just let me know how much to make it out for and who to . . .'

'No really,' said Allie. 'It's too awkward. You mustn't.'

'Indeed I must.'

'But I don't know what it's worth. It would only be a guess. It's not mine, you see.'

Liddy Rawlings laid down her pen. 'It's not yours?'

'No, I was collecting it for my mother.'

'And your mother is?' She took up the pen again and Allie noticed a slight tremor in her fingers.

The kettle was taking ages to boil, perhaps she'd over-filled it. She hitched herself on to the counter top, dangling her legs; she was enjoying herself. 'Helena Ashbourne. But it's not hers either.'

Liddy's tone was flat as if she were trying to keep it neutral, to stifle any emotion. 'So why did you pretend it was worth so much?'

'Oh but it is! I wasn't pretending. It actually belongs to someone who lives near the station. It was on my way home – I'd been into town – so I'd agreed to pick it up. But what I never had a chance to say was that it's been broken already.'

'Broken already? I don't understand.'

'And it *is* valuable. It wouldn't be worth Mum's time mending it otherwise. And for the owner it has sentimental value and stuff, so she's doing it as a favour too.'

'You let me believe Rolo had destroyed something precious.'

'No I didn't. The important thing was not to lose any bits. I think we managed that.' She jumped back down to the floor and flung a couple of tea bags into a pair of chunky mugs. 'D'you reckon he'd want a bowl of water?'

'Yes.' She balked momentarily at the size of the mug she was offered. 'I expect he'll be thirsty.'

Allie ran the tap into a deep enamel bowl and carried it out to the porch in the crook of her right elbow. Water slopped over the sides. When she came back, Liddy was gazing through the grimy kitchen window with a dreamy expression on her face. She turned to Allie and said, 'I should have taken it to him myself. Are you all right? Have you done something to your arm?'

'It was a birth injury.'

'Oh my goodness.' For some reason, Liddy looked more disturbed than most people did when she told them. 'I'm so sorry.' There she was, apologizing again. 'I didn't mean to pry. I thought maybe you had some sort of sprain . . .'

'It's okay. I'm used to it. Explaining myself.'

'It's none of my business. I really shouldn't have asked –'

'Erbs palsy,' said Allie. 'It's when your shoulder gets stuck during delivery and the nerve endings are damaged. Mine wasn't too bad as they go, the nerves were stretched, not torn and I've had loads of physio and stuff. It's more common than cerebral palsy actually, but no one's ever heard of it. Anyway, I don't class myself as disabled. I've got restricted movement but I'd rather be seen as normal.' With her left hand she picked up a teaspoon and rattled a rhythm against her cup.

Liddy Rawlings was impressed. 'That's amazing. I'm sure I couldn't manage it.'

'I ought to be good,' said Allie. 'I'm a percussionist. If you can have deaf musicians you can have musicians with defective arms.'

'Really?'

'Like Paul Wittgenstein. Ludwig's brother. He was a famous one-armed pianist.'

'Really? Do you play in an orchestra?'

'A band. I started on drums when I was really young because the exercise was good for me and it developed from there.' She stopped. 'I mean, I *was* in a band.' She had to remember to use the past tense. Two months on, it was still raw, the break-up. She could explain her injury to strangers but wasn't yet ready to talk about her relationship. People said it was like losing a family when a band fell apart. They hadn't become enemies, she and Sam, but after a slow and painful deterioration they'd opted to go in different directions. She wouldn't dwell on the fact that his direction involved a new team, another ready-made family of guitar, keyboard and drums. While he continued to surf the high of performance, she was drifting. Unleashed.

'Oh dear, what happened?'

'We weren't getting anywhere so we split.' Quickly, she added, 'It's commonplace, I know. I'm not after sympathy.'

Liddy was taking polite sips of tea. Allie swigged hers and suspected the milk was on the turn: there was a sour, acidic aftertaste. The fridge wasn't working properly. Nothing in the house was working properly – which was part of its attraction. Living in squats and crappy student accommodation, she was used to low standards. She preferred places and things that were a little beaten-up.

'At least the timing wasn't too bad,' she went on. 'I can hang out here for a bit and look around for work. And I've got a few contacts. This is music city, after all.'

'Where were you before?'

'Birmingham – I stayed on after uni – but I've lived all over.'

'And your parents?'

'Mum has a cottage outside Oxford, but she'll be coming up here from time to time to work on projects for the Conservation Centre. Like I said, she restores stuff.' She tapped the shoebox. 'That's how I came to collect this for her: another project in waiting. It's all I do right now, run errands.'

'I was never an arty type,' said Liddy with a little sigh. She rotated the pearl stud in her ear. All her mannerisms were neat and precise, as if every action required weighing and measuring. From the earring she moved on to her tea, turning the mug between her hands as if she were considering something of major importance. She edged it across the cloth until it exactly covered a bunch of cherries. 'Now this may sound awfully cheeky, but would you be interested in walking Rolo for me?'

Allie'd had her share of diverse jobs. No waitressing or retail, but she'd been brilliant as a play scheme co-ordinator, running percussion workshops, less than brilliant as a call centre operative, reasonably efficient as a postwoman. Dog-walking: how hard could it be? And she couldn't be any worse at it than Liddy Rawlings, who'd almost scuppered a fine eighteenth-century figurine. 'Well, I suppose he likes me.'

'Absolutely!' Liddy was fired with enthusiasm. 'He's really taken to you and it would make my life so much easier. I've got a couple of reports to finish by the end of the month, which means bringing work home and trying to fit everything else around it. To know Rolo was getting enough exercise would take a weight off my mind. I'd be *so* grateful and I'd pay more than the going rate, whatever that is. I haven't used a dog-walker before. We generally manage between us, my husband and I, but he's had to go away a lot recently so . . .'

'Afternoons would be better for me,' said Allie, thinking that she too would have plenty of pent-up energy by then.

'Excellent. I'll give him a quick morning outing and then he can have a nice long ramble with you. He loves the beach, but you have to watch him with babies. And I try to avoid gateposts and gardens. As soon as he spots a nice green sward he thinks it's an invitation to rip it to pieces. I hope . . . I hope he won't be too strong for you.'

'You'd be surprised how strong I am.'

'Yes, I'm sure.' She stood up. 'I really should be going.'

You could smell the money on her, thought Allie. It was in her fancy watch, her gold bangle, the supple, tan leather belt, the swing of the jacket she'd unbuttoned but not taken off. It was even in her suede walking shoes. It made her look out of place as she went back down the hall, pausing at the living-room doorway to cast her eye over the cheap Ikea sofa and bookcases.

'The tenants left some stuff behind,' said Allie. 'The drum kit's mine though. It's been customized with an extra foot pedal. I have kick-arse legs.' She stroked the taut skin. 'I still practise. You have to keep your hand in, even if there's no one to play with.'

'Right,' nodded Liddy, as if taken aback by the kit's splendid shiny majesty, its contrast to the faded fittings and the cobwebs trailing from the ceiling. 'That's such a fine cornice, isn't it, all those lovely acanthus leaves.'

'I know, it needs redecorating. I've got a lot of sorting out to do.'

'Not by yourself?'

'Well, it is my house.'

'Oh I thought –'

'What?'

'Nothing. Just that when you said it had belonged to your grandmother I thought perhaps your mother –'

'No,' said Allie with glee. She'd not owned much in her life before so it was exciting to have an inheritance. 'She left it to me. I might let Mum use a spare bedroom for her projects if she pays her share of the bills. I'll be getting some other lodgers too.' Rolo was scratching at the front door. As Allie opened it he leapt to devour her face. 'Enough!' she said curtly.

'I know this will be hard to believe,' said Liddy, 'but I train people for a living. Training packages are part of what we offer as management consultants. But there's theory and there's practice. There are people and there are dogs. There are dogs and there's Rolo. It's so hard to get a grip on a maverick.'

'I'll give him a go,' said Allie.

Liddy delved into another of her handbag's pockets and produced a business card. 'By the way, what should I call you?

'Oh . . . Allie's fine.'

'Ali? Is it short for Alice? Or Alison?'

'Allegra.'

'That's pretty, so musical.'

'It's Italian. I was born in Rome.'

Liddy's grip on the card faltered as she handed it over. 'Really?'

'Yeah, but because of the treatment and things we ending up coming back to England. I'm sure it was better for me, but I do think sometimes, you know, it would have been nice to have lived there a bit longer.'

'Don't you ever go back?'

'Nope. When I was growing up we always chose holidays we could drive to, or get the train. Mum doesn't fly, you see. She's got this thing about confined spaces. She won't go in lifts in case she gets trapped.'

'Oh dear . . .' Her feet shuffled on the step. 'That's an awful shame.'

'Is it? I dunno. I like trains. Don't you?'

'Rolo! Sit!' He was winding his lead around her legs, unbalancing her. 'Look, when would you like to start? I'll need to give you a key and the code of the burglar alarm.'

Allie didn't waste time wondering why this stranger was so trusting. Her mother would have been much warier: she had a very cynical view of human nature. She hadn't been the least bit surprised when the band split. 'I've no plans,' she said. 'I can come tomorrow if you like.'

11

The beach had an untamed aspect, even on calm days, even when it was peopled with suburban commuters and their well-mannered pets. Shaggy tufts of marram grass and spiky clumps of sea holly fringed the coastal path. At low tide the sand was studded with empty shells, dead jellyfish, washed-up bottles, the dirty spoils of the estuary. But beyond this debris was the infinite pull of the horizon, the Irish sea, the Atlantic Ocean, America.

Allie thought she'd like to go to America. Or Europe. Or anywhere really. She hadn't travelled much. She was made aware of the gaps in her experience when friends related stories from Australia or India or Mexico, but it wasn't a lack of spirit that held her back. It was, well, the usual things: lack of money, for a start, and possibly a lack of purpose too. When the band was rehearsing, when they had regular gigs lined up and were working on their demo, she didn't want to disrupt progress. She didn't, let's face it, want to be replaced. And Sam wasn't a traveller. Sam could spend all day capturing one song and would only perceive time passing in terms of cigarettes: his roll-ups diminishing, getting skimpier and meaner until he was down to his last shreds of tobacco. She windmilled her right arm and pitched the soft ball several hundred feet along the shore. Now it was over, she didn't have to worry about deserting Sam.

Rolo ran for the ball like a bullet, but dropped it several times on his return, either in exchange for a more appealing substitute or because he felt compelled to sniff another dog's arse or charge the incoming tide. Allie didn't let his bad behaviour bother her. She shrugged off the uptight glances; she was used to shrugging off glances. She knew you couldn't tell anything from appearances. Besides, she'd been taking Rolo out regularly for several days now and they were getting to know each other. She'd developed a routine which he appreciated, and she tried not to be late because he was always waiting – as if he could tell the time.

She'd been taken aback at first by the number of clocks in the house. Anal or what? was her first thought, but Liddy had explained they were made by her husband's company. They were an old, established firm, she said, but shrinking. Clocks were objects of beauty, a magnificent marriage of craft and engineering, but everybody was going digital. It was a struggle to find new markets.

Liddy Rawlings didn't talk much about herself, but she was very solicitous of Allie. Was she lonely in her grandmother's house? Did she need the name of a good electrician? Did she want to be recommended to a temping agency? Did she have any memories of her early life in Italy? Some days Liddy got back late and Allie didn't see her, but her money would be left in an envelope. She'd also encountered the cleaning lady, buffing wood and brass, dusting and winding the clocks. The cleaning lady didn't care for dogs, she'd made that clear. She didn't appreciate grains of sand or dollops of mud tracked on to her spotless floors. Allie had made a mental note to bring Rolo home later on her afternoons.

A red and blue kite was flapping in the sky above her head, but the wind was too light for it to soar. A boy in a baggy tracksuit was cursing its feeble progress. It looped and fluttered in a half-hearted way and then dived on to the wet sand. Rolo pounced. Allie and the boy sprinted in tandem and collided. Allie hauled Rolo away. There was a tiny tear in the red section of the kite's taut cloth.

'Fuckin' mutt,' said the boy. 'Look what he's done.'

Allie reckoned the kite had been ripped before and mended. 'You don't know that was his doing. He barely touched it. Anyway, you can fix it easy.'

'What makes yous the expert? What d'you know about kites?'

'Well, I can see this is ropey weather for flying them.'

'She was doing well. It int about wind anyhow, it's about air currents.' The toe of his trainer kicked a spray of sand into Rolo's eyes as Allie was clipping on his lead. He writhed and howled in pain.

'Hey, don't take it out on the dog!'

The boy's face was narrow, foxy; his voice cracked as if it were breaking. 'Only had it a few weeks. Another new one's gonna cost a bit, like.'

'Give over! A piece of tape should do the job. It's what you used last time.'

He scowled as he bundled it under his arm. 'Did not.'

She rummaged in her pocket and came up with a fifty-pence piece. She was angered by his blatant attempts to get money out of her. 'Keep the change and buy yourself some sweeties,' she snapped, turning away and yanking Rolo to follow.

'Spazzer!' he screeched after her.

She didn't feel inclined to stay on the beach after that. Besides, her trainers were damp. The clouds were massing, low and heavy; midges hung in the air in gauzy clumps. She didn't want to get back to the house too early because of the cleaner so she wandered the shady streets instead. Cherry trees in full leaf draped their branches over the wide pavements. The mist from a sprinkler hose refracted the light into a thousand prisms. A paunchy man in shorts was shearing a laurel hedge; the leathery shoots settled at the foot of his ladder. Some way off came the jingle of an ice cream van, dawdling near the school gates.

A motorized wheelchair was rounding the corner; its occupant elderly but vast. What a neat contraption, she thought. Then, somehow, Rolo's lead got caught beneath the wheels. The motor stalled, the chair stopped. Allie, who reckoned she'd done well up to now, better than Liddy anyway, was put out. Rolo was trapped.

'I know that dog,' barked the old woman.

'He's very striking, isn't he?' agreed Allie.

The woman's glasses had jolted off her nose and danced on the end of a chain. She fixed them in front of her eyes and glared at Allie. 'Don't I know you too?'

'I'm sure you don't.'

'Which school did you go to?'

'I went to five different ones. Which do you want to know about?'
'You don't come from around here?'
'No.'
'But the dog?'
Rolo was straining and yelping pitifully. 'I'm employed to walk him,' said Allie. 'I'm going to have to push you off his lead or he'll strangle himself.'
'I wonder,' said the woman in a way that sounded more like an order than a request, 'if you would be so good as to push me the rest of the way home. I wasn't happy with the noise the engine made when it cut out. I think it will need looking at.'
Kites and wheelchairs, thought Allie. Bloody hell.
The woman had two plastic carrier bags on her knee. Once they were in motion again their contents clicked lightly in harmony. 'It's not far,' she said. 'You need to turn into the third driveway on the left.'
Rolo's lead was looped around Allie's right wrist, her hand was guiding the wheelchair. She remembered Liddy's warning: avoid lawns and gateposts. That was going to be difficult. She began to struggle with the weight of her passenger as the wheels floundered in gravel. The woman held up her hand as if halting traffic and got out, transferring her shopping to the seat. 'If you could bring this up to the back door, I'd be grateful.'
'You can walk!' exclaimed Allie.
'Dear girl, I cannot walk and carry shopping at the same time. Will you help me get it into the house?'
As Allie steered, Rolo headed straight for a patch of bare earth, rutted and uneven, and began to dig.
'That's exactly what he did when he came before! With Helen Liddle.'
'Who?'
'Helen Liddle. You must know her. You're walking her dog. Tie him up, will you, before you bring the bags in.' Allie curled her fingers around the handles. 'And be careful you don't drop them.'
'Do you mean Mrs Rawlings?'
'Yes perhaps I do. It's not easy to follow these endless name changes.' She mounted the steps to her door grumpily, swaying like a galleon.
Allie followed. Endless was a bit of an exaggeration, wasn't it? 'I

thought most women kept their names these days. I certainly will, but then mine's quite nice.'

'Really? What is it?'

'Oh . . . Ashbourne.'

'I knew it. Helena Ashbourne?'

She was startled. 'I don't get . . .'

'I have a memory for faces, you see. I'm Daphne Myers.'

'Right.' Should this information be significant? They were standing, too close for comfort, in a gloomy hallway. 'Where would you like me to put the bags, Daphne?'

'In the pantry. Through that door over there. You should find adequate room on the shelves.'

This was a pantry unlike any other that Allie had seen, an archaeologist's delight. There were tins on the higher shelves – peaches, carrots, new potatoes – that were practically pre-war. There were jars of lurid pickles she just knew would taste disgusting. There were packets of biscuits, rice and semolina years past their sell-by date. On the slate slab meant for cooked meats, eggs and cheese, Daphne was down to her last bottle of sherry. As Allie unpacked the other bottles – more sherry, gin, tonic, cheap wine – Daphne commandeered a German Riesling on its way to the fridge and waved a corkscrew. 'You've been so helpful,' she said. 'Let me offer you a drink.'

'No, I'm fine. I must get Rolo back . . .'

'I insist. News of old girls is always welcome.'

'Old girls?'

Daphne pulled the cork and passed Allie a hock glass filled to the brim. The sip she took was warm and sticky, like watered down syrup. She was more accustomed to sinking pints of Grolsch. After a session on stage, beer was the only drink thirst-quenching enough.

'I was sorry to hear about your grandmother.'

'You knew my grandmother?'

'Parents' evenings,' said Daphne smugly. 'Over the years. I was your mother's form teacher in the lower sixth. Pity she never achieved her potential.' She gravitated towards her over-stuffed living room, a minefield of fringed rugs, occasional tables and footstools, unsteady lamps and ornaments under a layer of dust.

'How do you know what she's achieved? Actually, she's incredibly successful in her field. She's . . .' She didn't know why she was arguing. It was none of the old woman's business.

Daphne's throat opened and contracted and her glass was empty. It happened so quickly Allie was reminded of a toad shooting out its tongue for a fly. And, like a toad, she sat, squat and brown in her myriad cardigans, licking her lips. 'It didn't take me long,' she said with pride, 'to put two and two together. Seeing you with that dog. You look so like your mother, as I'm sure you've been told before. And she was always very thick with Helen Liddle. The staff had high hopes of her, you know. Academia beckoned, but I doubted she had a suitable disposition. So, tell me, what is she doing now?'

'Liddy Rawlings,' said Allie, 'was a friend of my mother's?'

'Oh yes, the pair of them were thick as thieves.'

Daphne refilled her own glass and tried to top up Allie's. She moved it away in refusal and a flow of wine splashed down her T-shirt. 'Are you . . . are you sure about that?' She tried to recollect. Yes, she had definitely given Liddy her mother's name. And she must have known the house: she hadn't been assessing it in the way of an initial visitor, but looking out for something she could identify.

'Your mother isn't here?'

'Not at the moment. She's based in Oxford.'

'Oxford?' Daphne Myers sounded impressed. 'You should tell her to call in on her next trip. There'll always be a glass of something and a Ritz cracker. I'm sorry I didn't ask if you were hungry.'

'No thanks,' said Allie, putting down her glass on a book of crossword puzzles. 'But I still don't understand . . . If Liddy and Mum were at school together, how come she never *said*?'

Squeezing through the obstacle course of a lifetime's clutter, Daphne made her way to an enormous bookcase. 'Let me show you.' She heaved an exceptionally wide photograph album from the shelves. 'It was necessary to use those rolling camera shots to fit the whole school into the picture. Now what years are we looking at, mid-seventies, yes?'

Allie was partly repelled, partly intrigued as she turned the pages. Daphne's finger landed on the back row of a sea of identical uniforms. Allie peered closer at the two girls she indicated. They were standing next to each other, one a head taller, both scowling. She would have been amused if the proof had been less disturbing. But, even a quarter of a century later, there was no doubt about it: Liddy Rawlings and Helen Liddle – her mother's erstwhile best friend – were unmistakably the same person.

Liddy'd had an exhausting week. She itched to pour herself a gin and tonic as soon as she got home but she had a complex about drinking alone. She was upstairs, changing from a stiff-collared blouse into a loose-fitting polo shirt, when she heard the key in the lock, the scrape and skitter of Rolo's claws. She hastened downstairs and skidded on her way through the large square hall, where the parquet was polished to a high shine. Allie was filling Rolo's bowls in the kitchen. The girl's resemblance to Helena unnerved her anew, transported her back decades. When she straightened up she towered over Liddy. That was when she noticed the stain down the girl's front, the reek of alcohol.

'I was going to suggest a gin,' she said. 'But if you've already . . .'

Allie didn't register the implication or the wrinkling of her nose. 'I don't drink gin,' she said, with unusual belligerence.

Liddy clinked ice from the dispenser in her brushed steel American fridge. 'Something soft then? I have mineral water.'

Allie took the bottle she held out and drank directly from its neck. Her face had a healthy glow, a youthful sheen, but her eyes were frosty. 'I don't know why you didn't tell me,' she said.

'About what?'

'About you and Mum.'

The lemon Liddy was slicing bounced from granite counter top to limestone slabs. She retrieved and rinsed it, glad of the distraction and mercifully relieved that Allie now knew, that she didn't have to go through the awkward, shameful explanations involved in setting out their story. She couldn't help wondering how Helena had reacted, what attitude she'd taken when she heard the two of them had met. 'What did she say?' she asked, dropping the lemon segment on top of her ice.

'Oh . . . that you were friends at school. Thick as thieves or something.'

The tonic bubbles fizzed and hissed. 'Nothing else?'

'Well, she showed me some photographs.'

'She's here?' Presumably she'd come back to collect the broken ornament or whatever it was and Allie had told her about their encounter. And if she'd only mentioned their schooldays, did that mean she'd sheared Ischia from her memories? Was that a good sign?

'Who do you mean?' said Allie.

'Helena, of course. Your mother. It's been such a long time, but I'd love to see her again. It's sad when you lose touch with people, especially friends you've been very close to and fond of. Maybe it hasn't happened to you yet, but –'

'You must have visited my house when it was my grandmother's. I mean, like loads of times.' Allie shook her head in perplexity. 'That's weird.'

'Sometimes you don't want to rake over old ashes.' Liddy made a wry face. 'You're afraid of getting burned. But, now Helena knows, I'm glad we can start afresh.'

'Knows what?'

'That you're walking my dog.'

Allie was lolling against the breakfast island with her hands behind her back: her default position. From this angle it was possible to see that the left arm was a few centimetres shorter than the right – though most eyes would be drawn to her slim and shapely legs. No wonder she wore such short skirts – if it *was* a skirt. 'Oh I see!' she exclaimed. 'But you've got it wrong. I told Mum about Rolo, but she doesn't know anything about you. It was this old woman who told me.'

'What old woman?' Even as she asked the question, Liddy suspected the answer. The same old woman who had first set her off in the direction of Marine Terrace. Daphne/Ariadne poised in the centre of her spider's web.

'She said she was your teacher in the sixth form. Daphne Myers.'

'They didn't have much to recommend them, our teachers. Where on earth did you meet her?' She groaned. 'Oh no, Rolo didn't slip the leash again, did he? I *told* you.'

'In the street,' said Allie. 'She recognized him. She asked me to help her with her bottles.'

'Bottles? Oh, I see.' Liddy topped up her gin. The great appeal of a colourless drink was that no one could see how strong it was. The fragrance of juniper was comforting, old-fashioned. She held it in her mouth, let it spill over the edges of her tongue, glide down her throat.

Allie pulled her hair back from her face, so that her cheekbones jutted like her hips. 'You and Mum, you were really good mates, right?'

'Yes, we were.'

'So what's the mystery? Why didn't you stay in touch?'

In the dining room, hall and living room three clocks chimed in unison. The handsome clock on the kitchen wall with its bold numbers and brass and walnut surround was silent – and two minutes behind.

'Well, I think,' said Liddy, 'what probably happened was you.'

'Me?'

'Yes. Helena never told me she was pregnant. We lost touch before you were born and I suppose we took different paths. When *were* you born? I mean, when's your birthday?'

'Twenty-first of February.'

'Oh, goodness!' She hadn't expected such an early date. She didn't know what to make of it. She tried to recall when they'd arrived on Ischia, to calculate whether Helena could have been pregnant already. 'I don't know why she didn't let me know. I'd thought we didn't have secrets, but then I was naïve. There was *lots* she didn't tell me.'

'She wasn't keeping anything secret,' said Allie. 'She didn't know herself.'

Liddy didn't believe that for a moment. She thought of the years since her marriage, all those false alarms and wasted pregnancy kits, the hormone injections, the courses of IVF that didn't work and would probably never work now.

'How could she possibly not know?'

'Because she was on the pill. Still taking it and getting periods. It can happen apparently. I was a real shock.'

'How did she find out?'

'She saw a doctor,' said Allie, as if she couldn't believe the stupidity of the question. 'She kept fainting and stuff.'

Liddy ran her finger around the top of her glass and it made a low humming sound. 'Do you know where she was when . . .?'

'Did I know she was in jail for smoking weed? Yeah. She still smokes sometimes, actually. So do I.'

'I wasn't prying,' said Liddy. 'It's just if you hadn't already been told . . . I got into enough trouble with your mother before you were born and I've regretted our falling out ever since. I'm sure you'll have heard her say that life's too short for regrets. Too short to bother with people you've left behind.'

'Something like that, yeah.'

'I suppose she didn't mention my name or tell you what we were doing in Italy?'

'Oh, were you on the art history course too? She did tell me that loads of the other students smoked but she was the only one to get caught.'

'No, I studied straight history. I joined her later in the summer. Has she . . . is she very resentful?'

'No. Why?'

'When something happens,' said Liddy, 'or doesn't happen for that matter, you can't help thinking, why me?' She glanced fleetingly at Allie's shoulder. 'You must know the feeling.'

'Oh, she was really upfront with me,' said Allie. 'Obviously, she got pregnant by accident, and she admitted that if she'd realized soon enough she'd have come back here for an abortion. But she couldn't get out, could she? She was trapped, so . . . It's kind of odd to think I might not have been born but it doesn't affect the way we, like, relate now. Shit happens and you deal with it. Sometimes, when she's mending stuff, putting it back together, she leaves the join showing. She says it's more honest that way.'

If she'd been my child, thought Liddy, I would have told her she was the most wanted, loved and cherished creature on the planet. I would have . . . Her hand tightened on her glass. The ice cubes had melted. Rolo had spread himself on the cool tiles of the utility room, his tongue hanging sideways in his mouth, panting. The light filtered through the slatted blind with a greenish, underwater tinge. If Helena hadn't been remanded in custody, she'd have come back to England for a termination and continued her degree, Mimmo's unexplained abduction a minor diversion in her career trajectory. The girl with the freckles and the tousled hair would not be standing here in this kitchen. Liddy had been responsible for Helena's arrest and hadn't been able to shake off the sense of guilt ever since. But look what else she had done: she had caused a life.

She felt an overwhelming need to sit down, but the kitchen was only furnished with bar stools, temporary perches for those who are always busy, about to rush off to an appointment or answer the phone. 'Why don't we go somewhere more comfortable?' she said, hoping she sounded light and informal.

They settled themselves at opposite ends of the sofa in the sitting room, with a prospect of the restful, green garden beyond. Liddy had employed a designer who'd recommended that people who didn't have the time for pottering about with secateurs should eschew short-lived flowers and problem-rife rose bushes in favour of tranquil swathes of foliage, using height, habit and leaf-type to create variation. She occasionally wished she might look out on to a splash of vibrant colour, but she knew, deep down, that this would be vulgar and inappropriate. If you consult a specialist (as she would often tell people), there's no point in ignoring their advice.

She was struggling to find a place to begin. She'd imagined this moment often in the past two weeks, this point of revelation, but it had arrived with unexpected suddenness, thanks to Daphne Myers. She fidgeted in her corner, trying to get comfortable. She stroked the nap of the chenille cushion, watching the way shade changed with the direction of her thumb. She had to concentrate on this fresh and powerful information, this whole new spin on her alleged betrayal.

'If she told you about the, um, drugs,' said Liddy, 'then she must have told you everything else. I mean, about the kidnapping and so on.'

'Mum was *kidnapped*?'

'No, no . . . the child we, I mean, she was looking after in Ischia.'

Allie looked even more perplexed. 'But she was in Italy!'

'Ischia's an Italian island. We were both working there.' Liddy wanted to pat her hand, those bitten fingernails.

A tremor was running through Allie's body. 'She never said anything about you.'

'No? Well, that's because she blamed me.'

'Blamed you for what?'

'For getting her arrested. She didn't realize they didn't give me any choice, that I was forced, basically. Police detectives, they trap you into saying the wrong thing, especially when you're as young and idiotic as we were. I didn't understand they were trying to implicate her or I wouldn't have co-operated. You have no idea . . .' This was absurd. She was getting agitated about the past, something she had no control over. This was against the rules, not 'good practice'. Unnecessary. Stupid.

'I haven't a clue what you're talking about,' said Allie. 'She got busted, remanded and released. It happened to lots of people in the sixties and seventies. Right? Okay, it was more complicated for her because of being pregnant, but you've now come up with this whole other story. Like you actually *wanted* a part in the action.'

'No, no.' Liddy bent her head, massaging her temples. She couldn't confront the girl's open, angry confusion. 'It's not that. Look, do you have to get back? Don't rush off. My husband's away so I'm by myself. Stay and have a meal – I'll ring the pizza place, or would you prefer Chinese? – and I'll explain everything. I promise I've no axe to grind.' She rose and fetched a fan of takeaway menus from a drawer in the hall table.

'What's to explain?' said Allie, accepting a leaflet but not reading it.

'Well, that summer in Ischia and the way it all went wrong. It was a seminal year you know, 1979, and not just for us. Everything was falling apart and there've been such changes since . . .' She sighed; a whole generation had grown up in the interim. 'But actually, the main problem back then was that I didn't know about Helena and Fabrizio.'

'Who's Fabrizio?'

'She didn't even tell you his name?'

Allie's face took on a stubborn cast, just like Helena's.

'I suppose it ended a long time ago. Maybe you never met him?'

'I don't remember anything before we came back to England. I was only two.'

'But you must have wondered what had happened to your father?'

'Not for ages, no.' Allie unfolded and refolded the leaflet in her hand, tamping it down to a tiny rectangle. 'In the beginning we hung out with other single parent families, shared houses and stuff, so our set-up seemed quite natural. Mum didn't want a semi-detached life; we managed perfectly well. Then she hooked up with Ian and he became my stepdad. They split when I was eighteen but I'd left home by then. And I still saw him quite a bit anyway.' She paused, lowering her defences. 'To be honest, it's only just begun to matter because he's moved to Edinburgh and has a new family and . . .'

'You've started to get curious?'

'His twins are gorgeous but, you know, we're not actually *related* so when I see them it brings it home to me. That I don't have many blood relatives, I mean.'

'So what has she told you?'

'That my biological dad was an Italian communist without a bean in the world or any sense of commitment – except to his cause. He'd given me a gift for music, but that was all.'

Liddy gaped.

'And there are only two of us,' Allie said, 'so I need to trust her, don't I? It's not like he's on my birth certificate or I've got any records to follow up. She said there was no point trying to find him.'

Liddy pretended to study the menu, waiting for her power of speech to return. When she glanced up, Allie's gaze was steady, questioning. 'You met him?' she said. 'You actually knew him?'

'Fabrizio? Yes. But he wasn't . . .'

'Wasn't what?'

'I don't think I should interfere with whatever your mother told you.' Helena must have had a spectacular fall-out with Fabrizio to have misled Allie so. 'Goodness, she'd know her own love life better than I would. Like I said, she kept me in the dark about all sorts of things.'

'You can't bring him up and then not tell me about him.'

Liddy reached for the phone and placed an order with no reference to Allie, who waited, frowning. Then she said, 'I can only tell you what I was aware of, what I saw happen. It won't be a complete picture. But it might be of some help, I suppose . . .' Once again she was shouldering a responsibility she hadn't chosen, but she'd gone too far to back-pedal. Maybe, if she trod carefully, she could even put things right.

12

As soon as she passed through the double doors into the street, Helena felt disorientated. She stood with her back to the Conservation Centre, its brick walls sandblasted to their former rosy glory, and tried to make sense of the vista before her. She puzzled over the smoked glass and steel Millennium House to her right, the plethora of bars and cafés – even a hotel – to her left. She remembered an open derelict site with cars parked at random and unlicensed stalls selling cheap crockery. She remembered vacant buildings with ravaged pediments where pigeons and starlings roosted, squirting thick grey-white slime down the sooty façades. She remembered a walkway on stilts weaving across Roe Street to Williamson Square, ascending and descending to no purpose. The landscape of her youth had changed beyond recognition.

Rebuilding was galvanizing the city and even if some of the new edifices did look like cheap plywood sheds with stuck-on fretwork, they were a testament to change. The concept of restoration was one she was ambivalent about, despite the nature of her day job. This, she'd come to by chance, seeking work she could do from home. She'd found she had a knack for what she described as 'cobbling things back together' and it provided an income more reliable than her erratic endeavours in ceramics. She'd let her mind roam while touch and sight concentrated on the particular, on flakes of porcelain so small she'd wear a jeweller's eyeglass, so delicate she'd use tweezers, a fine-haired dusting brush.

Tonight she would be staying in the old house. It was strange to think of it as belonging to Allie, but it didn't trouble her. She didn't care who slept in the bedroom above the wrought-iron trellis that was sturdier than it looked (as she and the friends who'd scaled it many times could attest). She didn't miss the view of the river, its nuances of light and shimmer. The past was a place she'd left behind. It was up to Allie to take decisions now; though she hadn't made much progress.

'I'll get friends to move in,' she'd said to start with. Then: 'I'll advertise for lodgers. It always worked out for us, didn't it?' Then: 'I'll need to fumigate and redecorate. Some of the rooms are rank.' Now it was: 'I'm going to have a holiday first and mull it over.' She'd reeled off the names of the friends who might go with her, but her plans were hazy. InterRailing in Europe was mentioned as a possibility.

'When?'

'Oh . . . soon.'

'How long will you be away for?'

'I think the ticket lasts three weeks. Then I promise I'll come back, look for jobs and all that shit: but right now there's no point, it's a bad time of year.'

'Really?'

'And anyway, I never touched my round-the-world money before.' She'd started her round-the-world fund at sixteen, along with several of her friends, some of whom held out only until they were seduced by a figure-enhancing pair of designer jeans. Others subsequently swapped photos of themselves at the summit of Ayres Rock.

'Do you want me to bring any stuff for you in the car?'

'No, I'm all right.'

So Helena had restricted her possessions to one small, wheeled suitcase and taken the train. And she'd agreed to follow her appointment at the Conservation Centre with a suspicious-sounding meeting that Allie had set up. 'Do I know this person?'

'It's a surprise, so you mustn't ask any questions or you'll spoil it.'

Her phone vibrated in her bag. She pulled it out and clicked on to the message. As she expected, it was from Allie: R u free yet?

Just finished. Where are you?

Lees sports dept buying trainers. Can u come here? Bit of a q.

Helena stood poised at the edge of the kerb. Four buses, spouting black diesel fumes, filed past before she could cross the road. At the end of its long, retractable handle her suitcase listed and rattled on the paving stones. Milling around her were women with flapping carrier bags, truanting teenagers with skateboards under their arms and red-faced men staggering from the sour, yeasty-smelling doorways of old pubs. She hated shopping; it was such a monumental waste of time. On the other hand, Lee's was nearby, a two-minute walk across the square; she'd pass it en route to Central Station and the train home. Allie was probably bored awaiting her turn. She had the impatience of the young; she might as well keep her company.

She entered the department store through the menswear section. It was tranquil and well-ordered: sober jackets on rails, stiff shirts under Cellophane, ranks of twinned cufflinks. There were very few customers but Helena managed to tangle with one as he stepped away from a carousel of cotton chinos. She apologized quickly and moved on through luggage and handbags.

'Hey, wait.' She turned; the man was striding in pursuit. 'Did you drop this?'

He was waving an envelope that had fallen from her pocket. It had contained her train ticket, but was now empty. 'Thanks,' she said. 'But it's only litter.' As he was still holding it out, she took it and scrunched it into a ball.

'Well, you never know . . .' The man was shorter than Helena and slightly younger. His hair was cropped so close it looked mossy, much softer than the stubble on his jaw. He wore a linen jacket over jeans and a relaxed air. 'It could have been your lucky Lottery ticket.'

'Or not.' Looking beyond him, she searched for signs to the sports section.

'You're lost?' he suggested hopefully.

'No, I've just forgotten where the escalators are.'

'There aren't any.'

'Oh.' She grimaced at her memory lapse. 'Well, that just goes to show how often I've been here recently, doesn't it?'

'The lifts are over there.' A set of doors was hissing open, women with buggies piling in.

'I think I'll take the stairs.'

'Where are you going?'

Was it any business of his? 'I'm meeting my daughter in the sports department.'

'But that's on the third floor.'

'So?'

The square shoulders of his jacket rose a quarter of an inch. 'Bit awkward with a suitcase, I'd have thought.'

She said coolly, 'I don't do lifts.'

'Ah. Then let me take it for you. Save you the hassle.' He didn't wait for her to agree. He seized the handle and trundled towards an arriving lift. 'See you up there.'

Before she could protest, he'd been swallowed into the aluminium cave. Fuck! thought Helena, taken aback by the speed of their encounter. I've been robbed. She had to admire his methods: his simple device of picking her pocket and fabricating an excuse to waylay her. Her preferred outfits were at the eccentric (she would say distinctive) end of the spectrum, but she'd dressed more tamely than usual for the meeting: a silk vest, a chunky resin necklace, matching earrings. Did they make her look wealthy? Whatever did he think she was carrying in her luggage? More jewellery? A laptop? Instead he'd find dishevelled tops and trousers crammed in with pyjamas and underwear. She hoped he wasn't after the underwear.

She didn't trust people on the whole – she had cultivated an in-built bullshit-detector – but she could at least give him the benefit of the doubt as she clattered up the three flights of stairs. If he really was performing a favour he'd have arrived ahead of her; he would be waiting. The lifts and the stairs both opened into the café. Customers carrying cups of tea and coffee, glasses of apple juice and mineral water, plates of sandwiches and chocolate éclairs sought free tables. There were families spilling over from Toys and Babies, a handful of pensioners, and lots of mothers with grown daughters devising wedding lists. You could see how the latter would slip into the frame of the former, how the skin would crease and the chin sag, how the hair would coarsen and the knuckles swell. She rarely spent time examining her own reflection – she didn't want to see her own mother's face staring back – and she felt a rush of sympathy for Allie. There was, however, no sign of the man. Well, what did she expect? Cursing, she gripped the strap of her bag which lay diagonally across her chest to keep it safe and turned away from the café. And then he was standing in front of her, nonchalant and (possibly) a bit smug.

'Phew!' he said. 'I thought I'd lost you. Next thing you'd have called the police.'

'No,' said Helena. 'I never have any truck with the police.'

'You were quicker than I expected.'

'Well, I walk a lot. I'm quite fit.'

When he grinned she felt foolish as if she'd been throwing out chat-up lines. She stiffened her stance but he didn't appear to be the kind of man who was easily cowed. 'I missed my stop and got whizzed up to accounts.' His upper incisors dipped below the rest of his teeth, giving him a wolfish look. 'Sorry if I gave you a fright.'

'I'll get over it.' She pulled her case safely away from him. 'Thanks for being a good Samaritan.'

He leaned against the wall with his hands in his jacket pockets and watched her weave through the ranks of expensive gym equipment. She made a point of not looking back.

The sports shoe section was busy, most of the chairs were taken. A petulant four-year-old boy was doing his best to kick a crouching assistant in the teeth. More fathers and sons here, Helena noted, than mothers and daughters. Then she spotted a couple on the far side of the department who were not so obviously related. The older woman was small, sturdy and had something of a wren or a robin about her: the full breast, the slim legs arranged at an elegant angle, the bright darting eyes and hands fluttering like feathers. Whereas the girl – what on earth was happening to her vision? – the girl was Allie.

Allie was wearing an outfit that wasn't her usual style or colour. She favoured dark sludgy hues and rarely wore white – but this was an ivory dress that floated below her knees, that turned the tomboy into a picture-book princess. Her hair was french-braided too, something she couldn't have done herself. No wonder she hadn't recognized her. This was a changed, more feminine Allie: a newly single, proud house owner; not the grungy black-clad drummer, pale from nocturnal living.

As she was about to hail her, Allie turned to the woman beside her. The woman (responsible perhaps for this astonishing makeover?) was extending one of her twirling hands in a gesture Helena found vaguely familiar. The vagueness lasted all of three seconds. It was followed by a sensation of chilling clarity: Liddy. Two decades on but, in spite of a little extra weight and a little more polish, indisputably Liddy. How on earth had she met Allie and what were they doing in town together? This could not be a coincidence. This could only be . . . She continued to stare, but didn't move forward. Allie was bending over an object in her lap. Helena's phone buzzed. Without taking her eyes off the couple she fished for it in her bag. Then she scanned the message rapidly: where r u?

Two sales assistants edged past her carrying the component parts of a scaled-down snooker table. Under their cover Helena turned and made her way swiftly back to the staircase.

The man in the linen jacket was still there. 'Are you all right?' he said. 'You look as though you've seen a ghost.'

Allie was in the bath when she heard someone enter the house. The tub was a pale, vomit colour, a relic of the seventies, and she was torn between replacing it and turning it into a retro feature. The shower, poised above it on a wonky support, didn't work. Liddy said she knew a plumber who could look at it, but she'd also said the whole bathroom should be gutted and while she was about it she might as well convert the box room into an en suite. I don't have the money, Allie had told her, but Liddy pointed out that wasn't relevant. The bank would give her a loan, money was cheap and home improvement was a sound investment. People Allie's age and younger were becoming property millionaires overnight.

The water sloshed around her as she pulled herself into a sitting position and listened. She could hear footsteps making their way through the hall. They might belong to Liddy – who was looking after a spare key – but they'd only parted an hour ago. She hoped her mother had finally turned up. They'd had a bizarre phone conversation when she'd failed to materialize in Lee's. Allie had given up sending texts and dialled Helena's number. 'What's going on? I've been waiting ages.'

'I've been humping this case around like Quasimodo. Couldn't face the stairs.'

'I'll come down then. I've nearly done here. But I need to find a new backpack for going away. You could help me pick one.'

'Best not,' her mother said and then they lost contact. When she tried redialling there was no answer.

She'd felt a bit of a fraud suggesting help, with Liddy at her elbow. She was much more useful at shopping than Helena; she knew exactly where to go and what to look for – though her thoroughness could become tiresome. In Comet, seeking a new toaster, Allie didn't see why they couldn't just pick the cheapest and be done with it, but Liddy had other ideas. Did Allie want a chrome or ceramic finish, a two or a four slice? How about a slot which could adapt to the thickness of the bread? After a while, Allie had switched off.

She had to admit Liddy was a good listener, though. (Helena never listened, her thoughts were usually elsewhere.) She'd shown exactly the right amount of sympathy when she'd told her about Sam, as if she truly understood the awkwardness of breaking up when your partnership is professional as well as emotional, when you could still play music in tandem but your bodies shrank from contact. During their last few rehearsal sessions, Allie used to hammer herself into a state of physical exhaustion so she could collapse anywhere but their shared bed.

Liddy also understood Allie was in a unique position and this was just the right stage to seek out her origins: she might be minus a job and a boyfriend but at least she had a home to come back to. She'd encouraged her to buy the InterRail ticket and downloaded some European timetables. She'd described the two villas she might visit on Ischia and evoked both the beauty of the island and the horror of losing the boy on the beach – the mysterious incident Helena had paid for so heavily. 'I wish she'd got in touch just once,' she said. 'All I ever wanted was reconciliation.'

Allie hauled herself out of the bath and dripped on to the scuffed cork tiles. Some of these were pockmarked with the dark circles of cigarette burns; others were chipped or curling at the corners. There was a crack at the side of the mirror and one of the basin taps leaked. Liddy had let her take a shower – powerful, exhilarating – after she'd been caught in the rain on one of her walks with Rolo; it had been blissful. There was no question about it: she should refurbish the bathroom first . . .

'Allie?' That was definitely Helena.

'Coming.' She grabbed the dressing gown hanging from the hook on the back of the door. Liddy had insisted on buying it for her at the same time she'd chosen the white dress. 'I had one like this once,' she'd said of the dress, 'with a flared skirt and everything. Fashion always goes round in circles, doesn't it? It will look quite different on you. You're so willowy.' The dressing gown, a deep aubergine velour, was chosen 'so you can have something to snuggle up in'.

The sensation of being pampered could come perilously close to suffocation – but Allie hadn't owned a dressing gown since she was ten and its velvety softness was a treat against her damp flesh. She fastened the belt with one hand and left the steamy bathroom to go downstairs.

When Allie was younger, she learned to read her mother's mood from her hats. A beret at an angle, fixed with a giant pin, meant she was buoyant and vivacious. A straw panama tipped back was a good sign, as was a neat felt bowler. But there was danger in headgear that obscured the face – a wide floppy brim or the pulled-down peak of a cap. These were associated with silence and ill temper, with slammed-down saucepans, with barking answers to tentative questions. When she walked into the kitchen she could hardly fail to see that Helena had a rakish fedora slanted over her brow. With her wide trousers and silky top she looked like someone out of a slick thirties' comedy caper: Katherine Hepburn or Myrna Loy. The hat was new, the price tag still swinging from the brim. At the sight of Allie in her purple robe, Helena laughed. When she'd finished laughing she clutched the edges of the table and swayed a little.

'I thought you didn't want to go shopping!' Allie burst out.

'Allegra, are you begrudging me a hat?'

'No, but . . .'

'You're cross because I laughed at your dressing gown? It just looks a bit . . .'

'A bit what?'

' . . . I don't know. Matronly, I suppose. Headmistressy.'

'Like Daphne Myers?'

'Who?'

'She was a teacher at your old school. I met her the other day.'

Helena digested this. 'Oh Lord, yes! She sent a card after Grandma died. Writing all over the place as if someone had given her pen and paper and then blindfolded her. Always was a bit of a cow.'

'Well, she's a bit of an alkie now.'

'That accounts for the handwriting.' Helena took off her hat and spun it on her forefinger.

'Have *you* been drinking, Mum?'

'Sorry, sweet, I met someone.'

'You *met* someone?'

'Is that so odd? It happened to you and Daphne Myers.'

'But you were supposed to be meeting *me*.'

Reaching across the sink Helena rubbed at the windowpane in an attempt to clear the grime and look out on to the brick-walled courtyard. Buddleia had rooted in the cracks in the paving and bees were bouncing between the flower spikes in heady delight. 'I think they must be swarming nearby,' she mused. 'Unless they're wasps. There could be a wasps' nest somewhere. You haven't been stung, have you?'

'Who was he?'

'Who?'

'The person you met.'

'Why do you think it was a man?'

'The hat's a giveaway.'

'Damn.' She punched the crown and then patted it lightly. 'Is it? Quite fetching though.'

'Yeah, it's cool.' Allie stroked the sleeve of her dressing gown in the same manner. 'But I'm pissed off you stood me up.'

'No I didn't. I cancelled. This guy I bumped into, Simon, asked me to help him pick a hat. We bought one each and then we went for a drink and it turns out he's a lecturer. Another bloody academic. I can't escape them. I must have a face that reads: queue here if you want a good bitch about the tribulations of pursuing your own work amid the demands of admin and callow students and the failure of anybody else to appreciate your importance.'

'Mum, you can do without someone like that.'

'Well, he wasn't a sniveller, thankfully, and I needed a drink anyway. I'd had a shock.'

Helena's voice had changed. It wasn't light and breezy and self-mocking; it had gone hard and gravelly. A bee had flown in and settled on the cherries on the oilcloth. Allie overturned an empty mug and tried to trap it, but missed. It zigzagged towards daylight and batted its body against unyielding glass. 'A shock?' she said.

Helena plucked her wallet from her bag and began circling the table. Every time she completed a circuit she laid a ten or twenty pound note in front of Allie. On her final lap she emptied the wallet of small change on top of the piles of notes. Then she flicked Allie's braid, the end of it wet from her bath. 'Nice hair,' she said.

'What's all this about?'

'This place is a tip,' said Helena. 'But certain things stand out. That toaster's snazzy, isn't it? Classy coffee-maker too.'

'The old toaster was a burnt-out wreck,' Allie protested. 'Like, dangerous.'

Helena raced on. 'I know you can't afford to replace everything at once, but if you'd only asked me I could have helped. Anyway, take that to be going on with and I'll get you some more later.'

Allie stared at the cash. 'I don't understand. Is this for the kitchen or are you boosting my round-the-world fund? I appreciate it's really generous of you and everything but . . .'

'I want you to give it back,' said Helena. 'I don't want you to be beholden.'

'But I'm not! Well, hardly. I earned this dosh. I've been dog walking every afternoon for the past three weeks. I don't know what in hell you're on about.'

'Allegra . . . darling . . .'

She must be drunk, thought Allie. She's all over the place. Unacknowledged, however, was the suspicion that she knew exactly what her mother was getting at. That somehow she'd found out about Liddy's attempt to make amends and this was making her very unhappy indeed.

'I think you've got the wrong end of the stick.'

'What, the sharp pointy end that cuts your palm to ribbons?'

'All she wants to do is –'

'She?'

'You know who I'm talking about. You must do or you wouldn't be behaving like this. Liddy told me it was her fault you got locked up. I understand why you feel the way you do about her, but it was a long time ago and it's silly to have an ongoing feud, isn't it?'

'I don't have a feud! Good grief, I haven't even thought about the woman in twenty years. I just don't like the underhand way she does things.'

'Like what?'

Helena clamped the hat back on her head. All Allie could see was the deep shadow it cast over the upper half of her face, the truculent swing of her earrings and her fast-moving mouth. 'Like ingratiating herself with you, for a start. Buying you little sweeteners, softening you up, turning you into some kind of doll.'

'I'm not a doll. For God's sake, Mum.'

'Look at those twee plaits. Raggedy Allie! All you need is bright spots on your cheeks and a frilly pinafore and you'd be a dead ringer for that *Play School* programme you used to watch when you were little.'

'Stop it! That's vicious. We were only messing with my hair. She was showing me how because I can't do it myself. Braiding, that is. And I told her to leave it in yesterday because I liked it. All she's done is give me bits of advice about the house, like any neighbour.'

Helena's manner calmed. She rested her folded arms on the table and said, 'Neighbour?'

'She's from that posh bit, Blundellsands, but it's not far when you're walking a dog. She used to live nearer, didn't she, when you were at school together? Her parents have moved down to Wales, but she showed me their old house. She said she'd never expected to find herself living so close to where she grew up.'

'Half the residents of Merseyside live within a couple of miles of where they grew up.'

'And when she said she'd like to see you again,' Allie persisted, 'I thought I could be the go-between . . . I thought you'd act like two civilized adults. I wasn't trying to start a riot.'

Helena covered Allie's left hand with her own. 'Hey, I'm sorry. I didn't mean to explode like that. It's alarming to realize how deep old wounds can be. But I couldn't have seen her or been civil to her, if I'd come across her without warning. I daresay you had good intentions but, you know what, good intentions can be downright meddlesome. We'll let it pass now, shall we?'

'What about the money? Do you want it back?'

'No, darling. You keep it. Buy yourself a hat.' She took off her own. 'Really, it's yours. Put it towards your trip. How are the plans coming along?'

'Fine. You'll be proud of us. We're going to do loads of cultural stuff, not just lie about all day.'

'The ticket takes you all over Europe?'

Allie nodded.

'So where are you off to?'

'Oh . . . you know, Paris, Munich, Vienna, Venice . . .' She hesitated, the list was long enough surely? 'We're still working out the details.'

13

Liddy was the youngest member of the book group. She was treated like a mascot, willing but inexperienced compared to the rest: all formidable quasi-retired professional women. When she floundered, they might throw her lifelines or conciliatory remarks, but they were confident in their superiority. She rarely held her own in their discussions, either because she hadn't time to finish the selected book or because their vocabulary unnerved her and she didn't like to admit her ignorance. Really, she should have left and found a more companionable group, but the whole point was self-improvement.

Tonight it was her turn and she wasn't feeling up to it. She'd had a terrible day. In the morning, within moments of arriving at the premises of a small IT company seeking to restructure, she had injured herself. Twisting, bending, swivelling – she couldn't say exactly which motion had been to blame – she'd felt a searing pain and her legs had given way. She was used to living with a nagging backache, but this sensation was different. She lay on the grubby floor in one of her favourite suits while strangers stood above her discussing the likelihood of a slipped disc and whether they should call an ambulance. She hated the indignity of her situation. It wasn't fair that such a small, awkward movement should have such a powerful effect.

'Don't be too sure,' said the sales manager. 'I knew someone who tripped on uneven ground and knackered their spine. In a wheelchair for life now.'

Liddy assured him she would be fine in a moment. She had no history of slipped discs and as soon as the pain subsided she'd be back on her feet. All of which happened in due course, although the pulled muscle (for that was the diagnosis everyone agreed on) continued to grumble and bite through the rest of the day. She was considered heroic for battling on with her assignment, but she was determined to erase the embarrassing image of three men helping her into a standing position as if she were some decrepit crone.

Once home she found Michael had already gone to play golf and he would spend the rest of the evening in the clubhouse so as not to disturb her guests. She picked up the phone, thinking to ring him to compare notes – his hobby had cost plenty of muscle twinges – but his mobile was switched off. Then she contemplated trying to cancel the book group. But seven calls issuing the feeble-sounding excuse that she'd hurt her back – 'It was absolute agony this morning, I was completely felled by it' – sounded, well, unconvincing. She replaced the receiver and swilled down two extra-strength paracetamol. She shut Rolo in the utility room and lined up her most fragile cups and saucers on a tray. She arranged superior biscuits, bought yesterday from the delicatessen, on a white porcelain plate.

The novel she should have read by now was *Under the Volcano* by Malcolm Lowry. She remembered it being amid the pile of Jake's books in his room above the nightclub. 'Vesuvio,' she'd joked at the title. 'Popacatepetl actually,' he'd said. It had stuck in her mind, sparked her curiosity, but she hadn't followed it up. In fact, she'd forgotten about it entirely until her turn to choose. It was a twentieth-century classic, which was a point in her favour; on the other hand, they'd probably already digested it along with *To the Lighthouse* and *Ulysses* and *Herzog*.

However, the women with the long flapping skirts and the sensible wide-fitting shoes took her suggestion in their stride and those who already knew it were happy to revisit. She suspected they got through at least three books a week anyway. They didn't struggle, as she did, to finish one a month. She would sit mute with admiration listening to Beatrice's acrobatic sentences or watching the elegant, pincer-like movements of Janet's fingers when she wanted to illustrate a point. It wasn't that she ever needed to name-drop philosophers, but the art of casual referencing seemed to be worth acquiring. An over-anxious girl becomes an over-anxious woman; Liddy had grown deft at compensating strategies.

She filled the kettle with water and waited for the doorbell. No one was more than a polite five minutes late. Felicity was first to arrive. She had an insubstantial look: flyaway hair the colour of a mouse and chiffon scarves that fluttered like pennants around her neck, a voice as light and thin as her freckled arms. She might sound quavery but her opinions were immovable, set in concrete.

Liddy swung open the door and put on a brave smile as a shower of needles stabbed at her spine. 'What a lovely mac, Fliss,' she said, believing that payment of a compliment is always a good beginning. It shows the other person you are on side.

'Perfectly useless,' said Felicity. 'Doesn't keep me dry at all. Or anything else for that matter. I borrowed the Lowry from the library, put it in the pocket and now the pages are curling with damp. I expect they'll make me pay for a new one.'

'I didn't quite get to the end of my copy,' confessed Liddy, 'but I figured it didn't matter too much. It's obvious what's going to happen, isn't it?'

Felicity toyed with the ends of her scarf. 'But isn't it your turn to lead the discussion? To give an overview? I should have thought you'd put yourself at a disadvantage not reading the whole thing.'

'I injured my back,' said Liddy, making an exaggerated grimace of pain as she hung Felicity's mac from a high hook. She'd meant to share a confidence, not set herself up for disapproval. There was no point in bemoaning how busy she was because she knew Felicity wasn't free from commitments either. She was caring for a recalcitrant mother in the early stages of dementia in a small terraced house that was far from luxurious. For this reason Fliss never hosted the book group.

The rest of the members arrived within moments of each other. Liddy ushered them into her sitting room where they chose their favourite spots as if they had been allocated by divine right. She went into the kitchen to fetch the cafetière and the teapot. Her copy of *Under the Volcano* was also on the tray; tucked inside the cover were some notes she had made on a piece of paper. She handed out cups and biscuits to her guests, letting them relax against the cushions and spill out snippets of gossip as a necessary overture. She chose to perch on a straight-back dining chair, partly because she wouldn't have been able to get up from the sofa and partly in order to lead the discussion – though it soon ran away from her.

The book group liked nothing better than argument and analysis. Felicity stressed the novel's autobiographical elements; Beatrice dwelt with relish on the protagonist's spiral of self-destruction; Janet wallowed in the themes of guilt and repentance. Liddy, troubled and disturbed by what she'd read and by the inevitability of disaster, kept quiet. She had a picture of Geoffrey Firmin in her head, sitting over his glass of mescal at seven in the morning, and what she was most worried about was the fact that he wasn't wearing socks – though she couldn't explain why this troubled her and it seemed too trivial to mention. Some passages had been so hallucinogenic she'd had to skip them and she wasn't sure whether she'd followed the plot or even if there *was* a plot. As the women's exchanges intensified, she lost concentration and was unprepared when Janet suddenly turned to her and said, 'Is that why you chose it?'

'I'm sorry?'

'Because Lowry's a local author?'

'Is he?'

'Well, more or less. He came from Wirral, New Brighton. Didn't you realize?'

'Actually,' said Liddy, 'it was more that it was a novel I'd always meant to read. I saw it recently on a table of second-hand books outside the Oxfam shop. And I bought it because –' Did she really want to confess she thought it might have been Jake's copy? The same Penguin edition certainly, but to think she might open it and find his name inscribed inside was plainly preposterous. '– It reminded me of someone,' she ended lamely.

These women – Felicity and Janet and Beatrice and Pauline and Ruth and Mary and Lucinda – with their keen, lined faces and brains stuffed full of strong notions and classic literature were as susceptible as any to the concept of a lost love.

'Who?' asked Janet at once.

'An old boyfriend?' said Ruth. 'Before or after you met your husband?'

'Before.' She would not have told them otherwise.

'First love,' said Felicity dreamily.

'More of a short sharp shock really,' said Liddy. 'Wildly unsuitable.'

'A Geoffrey Firmin type?'

'Oh no! At least I don't think so . . .'

'What happened to him?'

'I've no idea. He was an actor. For ages I kept expecting to see his name in the credits for something.'

'If he'd been successful you'd have heard more of him. My niece tried acting for a while.' Ruth spoke with a condescension that Liddy found irritating. 'It was a total disaster.'

'Well, that's how he started out but really he wanted to be a screenwriter. It was his ultimate ambition. For all I know he could be in Hollywood now.'

There was a moment's silence as they considered this prospect.

'Well,' said Janet, 'I'm sure everybody's past has a whatever happened to whatshisname? Easy enough these days to find out. Have you tried Googling him?'

One or two of the others looked horrified, but Janet was addicted to the internet. She played bridge and Scrabble online and had sold off an accumulation of china on Ebay.

'I don't know if . . .'

'It could hardly be construed as disloyal. Even if you track him down you're not obliged to contact him.'

'Haven't you heard about the trouble caused by Friends Reunited? All these thirty-somethings revisiting their youth, ditching their marriages and running back to their teenage sweethearts?'

'It wouldn't be like that,' said Liddy, holding her cup stiffly. 'Anyway I doubt it'll be easy to find him. I don't know what name he's using.'

'What do you mean?'

Ruth intervened. 'Actors can't have an equity card the same as somebody else's. You have to pick a stage name or add an initial or something.'

'Then you could try variations. What was he called?'

Liddy's hoot sounded more like a yelp of pain, even to her own ears. 'Do you think I would tell you? No, picking up this book just gave me one of those jolts into the past that are hard to shake off sometimes. I expect now I've read it, it'll go away.'

They didn't look convinced. She didn't convince herself. She knew that as soon as they left – and yes, this time she would accept their offers to help clear away since her muscle spasms were slowing her down so much – she would go and switch on her computer.

Under the Volcano was thrust back into handbags and Liddy felt a frisson of regret that for her this was a tale still unconquered. She poured herself a very large brandy and took it upstairs to her study, along with an extra cushion. Michael's was adjacent, his desk a proliferating mess of documents that only he could decipher. When they first met he'd called her his saviour because she'd been brought into the firm to salvage his paperwork. That was ten years ago, her mission accomplished within months; she would have found it unsettling to share their working environment for longer.

She calculated that she had an hour to spare before he came home and anyway her search would mean nothing to him. She wasn't ready to admit it, but the temptation to seek out Jake was spurred on by her failure to appease Helena. She found it hard to believe she'd refused to see her. Point blank. 'No,' Allie had said on the phone. 'She'd rather not.' Any rebuff would be hurtful, but the contemptuous, 'She'd rather not,' rankled, made her feel inferior and disposable. She'd thought her attempts to reconnect had been subtle and unthreatening. It wouldn't have mattered if she hadn't become so fond of Allie: looking forward to rubbing down Rolo with her, sharing a drink, hearing her throaty laugh.

She typed Jake Knight into Google and slumped in disappointment: only a couple of irrelevant results came up. She tried James Knight and found a saxophonist, a firm of accountants, a tennis player, a doctor. She followed up the doctor – he could have gone back to medical school to complete his qualifications – but the dates were wrong. Next, she keyed in actor/film/TV/screenwriter as an extra filter, wondering if throughout cyberspace lonely people were scanning the internet for evidence they had once been loved. Not that *she* was lonely – or unloved, for that matter, although the blot of infertility was staining her marriage. Michael couldn't see what the fuss was about, the hunger inside her. And if he couldn't understand, that was already a rift, wasn't it?

A link to a film production company looked hopeful. She clicked on it: the titles indicated the type of corporate training films she used herself in the workplace. She swilled her brandy and felt the alcohol surge to her fingertips as she tried to open a PDF and cross-reference the company. Her computer was slowing down. It needed upgrading. The one in Michael's study was newer, faster, but it was too risky to use it now when he might be back at any moment. She chewed her knuckle in impatience as the file downloaded.

The company's website appeared to be under construction and, according to the small print, registered in Australia. Well, he'd always said he'd never come back to Britain. She scrolled through the credits and gasped: there he was, listed as director. Of course it could easily be a different James Knight, but along the bottom of the home page ran a montage of photos and she was almost certain she recognized his face. Australia was so far away it couldn't do any harm to send an enquiring email. They wouldn't know where she was writing from and even if they replied she wouldn't have to take it any further. She could nurse the information secretly while she waited to see how Allie got on. Information was power – hadn't Jake once said that? It was worth hoarding.

It took a good twenty minutes of false starts and unconvincing lies to compose her message. 'I have come across your training films,' she typed, 'and would be interested in more information about them. As consultants we are involved in putting together packages for our clients and we are always looking for new production houses. Are you using the same film unit and director? In any event I shall look forward to hearing from you.' At least she'd given nothing away; no one could guess at an ulterior motive.

She leaned against the cushion at her back. In the excitement of getting nearer to her goal, she'd forgotten her excruciating collapse that morning. She felt better – a fact worth celebrating in itself. She tipped her glass and swallowed the rest of the brandy. Now came the big question: was she really going to send this email? Didn't it need a bit of tweaking? Wouldn't it be better to sleep on it and save it for another day? Wouldn't it be more sensible to delete it altogether?

A taxi throbbed in the street outside. The front door slammed. Michael was back. She could hear the clank of his golf clubs as he deposited them in the corner of the cloakroom, the snuffling of Rolo's greeting, his heavy tread as he went through to the sitting room to pour himself a nightcap. She suspected he'd already had several pints in the clubhouse. They both drank too much. When she'd been preparing for IVF she'd abstained totally, but it hadn't made any difference. Afterwards, alcohol had comforted her.

She expected him to switch on the television, wrinkling his nose at the scent the visitors had left behind. The chairs were still arranged in a circle because she hadn't felt up to pushing them back into place. While he was reorganizing them she could save the message into her drafts folder. It was too abrupt, it needed more explanation.

'Good chinwag then?'

He must have crept up the stairs; she hadn't heard him approach her door. She swung around too quickly in her seat; all of a sudden the pain sliced into her again. She gave an involuntary cry.

'Something the matter?'

Michael was a large, rumpled man with a lived-in face and an unexpectedly tender touch. She would no more want to hurt him than to hurt Rolo. 'I pulled a muscle this morning,' she said. 'Or trapped a nerve or something. It's been agony.'

'D'you want me to fetch you anything? Hot water bottle?'

'I tried that. And painkillers. I think they're wearing off, that's all.'

'You could rub in some muscle relaxant.'

'I thought we had some in the bathroom but it must be finished and I couldn't get out to buy more because I had the book group coming.' She knew she sounded woeful. What would be nice, she thought, is if he would pick me up, carry me into the bedroom, undress me and give me a massage. In the past, that's what he would have done. When they couldn't get enough of each other. When love-making was an adventure and a passion, before it became a chore regulated by thermometers and hypodermic syringes and stupid sticks you had to pee over. Now sex was a means to an end and pleasure had been leached from it.

Michael entered the room and swayed a little. His breath was malty with Guinness. He bent over her and nuzzled her neck. 'I'll make it better,' he crooned in her ear.

She squealed again, which he took to be protest. He glanced at the screen. He couldn't have had time to read the message, she told herself afterwards, and anyway there was nothing incriminating in it.

'I'll take care of it, love,' he said reassuringly, and clicked the send button.

PART THREE

CASA COLONNATA

14

A school party, a phalanx of skinny limbs and bouncing backpacks, filed past the kiosk ahead of them and was swallowed into the ruins. Shrieks of laughter spun and eddied in the hot air but might have belonged to ghosts: in the maze of fallen masonry and ancient brick walls no one was visible. Unlike the Forum and the Palatine where crowds thronged as thickly as they did in Roman times, Ostia Antica was practically deserted. Rows of Doric columns guarded grassy roofless temples. The curving rows of the amphitheatre banked upwards, glistening white and vacant. At ground level a desultory spray of sand masked the fin of a mosaic fish, the tail of a dog. At waist height a marble counter beneath an archway indicated a 2000-year-old bar. A fringe of cypresses sealed off the modern world.

Allie settled herself in the shady corner of what had once been a public bath-house and flipped open her water bottle. The excited children sounded distant and unreal; close by insects rustled through dry leaves. She'd left Dom and Meg wandering around the old market place, holding their cameras aloft like talismans against the sun, pointing and shooting. She hoped they wouldn't hurry to find her. She didn't usually crave solitude, but she hadn't anticipated her current situation.

There had been four of them to begin with. Four girls meeting at Victoria to board the boat train to Calais at the start of their expedition. It had not worked out as planned. Paris proved too expensive so they'd taken the TGV down to Nice. Nice had promised much: a budget hotel room with four beds, basking sunshine, an astonishingly azure sea, an abundance of vivid flowers spilling from baskets, clumped into galvanized buckets, bursting from terracotta pots. They'd snacked in ethnic cafés, danced in dim-lit cellar clubs and got headily drunk.

And then Char had her bag stolen with her money and her passport and her precious InterRail ticket in it and everything was soured. Jess had gone on about the idiocy of keeping all her stuff in one place and the row had further spoiled their harmony. They'd spent two days hanging around the Consulate and the police station, filling in forms. Char declared she wasn't in the mood for any more holiday: she would go home, claim on her travel insurance and splash out at the Leeds Festival or something instead.

Allie and Jess and Nita continued around the coast into Italy and stopped to take stock in Florence. Wilting in a slow-moving queue in the Uffizi cloisters, besieged by touts offering handbags, cigarette lighters and cheap pizza deals, Jess had suggested they scrap the rest of Italy – 'too many fucking coach parties' – and travel east. Allie was furious. She'd set her heart on getting to Rome, and then, if appropriate, suggesting that Ischia might be a good place to chill for a few days. But the others had dismissed her objections and they'd ended up shuffling through the galleries in miserable, mutinous silence.

It was later in a bar, when all three girls were resolutely *not* discussing their itinerary, that they met Dom and Meg. They overheard them discussing Vasari's *Lives of the Artists* and debating whether it had altered their views of the works.

'Hey,' said Jess. 'Weren't you guys in the Uffizi this afternoon?'

'Man, what a scrum!' said Dom. 'But we've got this pass so we can go again. Get there, like, really early tomorrow morning. Off to Rome the day after.'

'So are we,' said Allie. 'I mean . . .' She frowned at her friends' blank faces. 'I mean that was our original plan. Only . . .'

'I'm ready for another drink,' said Jess. 'Anyone else?'

By the end of the third litre of wine Dom and Meg were inviting Allie to join them and Jess, relieved, was saying: 'No worries, Al. You know you wanted to go down there. And we can hook up later on in'

– she screwed up her face as if imagining the mass of interconnecting railway lines – 'maybe Krakow or somewhere.'

Which was how Allie found herself in the silted-up ruins of the ancient port of Ostia with a couple of earnest postgraduates in hiking boots whom she hardly knew. She could hear Dom calling her name – *Allie? Allie!* – the sound of it bouncing off the marble columns, getting closer. Then he was standing in front of her. With legs apart, arms akimbo, and a neat pointed beard, he was a series of triangles against the clear blue sky. 'There you are! I was getting worried.' Since the moment they'd mounted the high steps of the train at Florence station, he'd treated her like a bird with a broken wing. 'Sure you're okay?'

'I'm cool, thanks.'

Meg joined them. A frizz of brown curls bubbled on her head; she spoke in a soft plaintive monotone. 'Don't you think this is such an amazing place? Abandoned all those thousands of years ago and still nobody comes here. It just aches, doesn't it, with loss?'

'In point of fact,' said Dom who carried a small library in his backpack, which wrenched his shoulders into military stiffness, 'some rather crude reconstruction has been attempted in the past. Sections of walls randomly rebuilt. You wouldn't get away with it these days.'

Dom and Meg were avid sightseers. They bought passes that gave you entry to the maximum number of museums. They consulted guidebooks and printed pages off the internet and bound them into a folder between coloured dividers. They drew up schedules and calculated timetables. They were in their early twenties but reminded her of her teachers. They also had a surprising capacity for alcohol, which was why they'd been such good company that first night. After a session getting wasted, they were able to wake up fresh and lively and with perfect recall – which Allie thought was an unfair advantage.

'The problem,' Dom said, lowering himself to her level, 'is that we could lose each other in this place if we're not careful. You should make sure you keep your phone switched on. Now it costs silly money to make the call, so what I propose is we ring each other's number a few times and then hang up.'

Allie was mystified. Dom often came up with curious penny-pinching suggestions. Some, like filling your water bottle from a street fountain, were sensible – if obvious. Others, like validating your bus ticket at the end of your journey to gain you more time, were unnecessarily complicated. 'How does that help?' she said. 'If the person doesn't answer, how do you know where they are?'

Dom licked his finger and held it up. 'No wind, you see. Listen to the crickets! You'll be able to hear the ringing miles away and you can go on calling until you track each other down.'

'Why don't you just shout the person's name? Like you did before.'

He rolled his eyes. 'You didn't answer.'

'Actually,' said Meg, 'I've got a whistle.' She ferreted in her backpack. 'It's one of those things they recommend you keep with you as a woman traveller. You should really have one, Allie, since you're by yourself. Here, take it.'

It dangled from a piece of white ribbon. Allie blew a piercing blast and thought how useful it would have been when they were arguing interminably in Nice and Florence.

Meg pressed her hands over her ears. 'At least we won't lose you again.'

'Time for a break anyway,' said Dom, sitting cross-legged and gulping his water.

'It's brilliant, isn't it,' said Meg, 'to have the whole place to ourselves. I wonder how it will compare with Pompeii.' She peeled an orange in neat strips and insisted on dividing and sharing the segments equally. 'How well do you know it, Allie?'

'What?'

'Pompeii.'

'Oh, but I don't. I've never been there.'

'But your father's from Naples, right?'

'My father?'

'Yeah, that's what you said last night.'

'Christ, did I?' She swallowed a too large piece of orange and choked. 'No, no, you've got that wrong. My dad lives in Scotland.'

Meg pursed her tiny mouth in her heart-shaped face.

'I didn't mean, I don't actually know . . .' It was the sambuca's fault; disgusting, sickly drink.

'Your *biological* father,' said Meg helpfully. 'You're looking for your roots.'

A lizard scuttled into a crack in the stone, a dark safe crack beyond prying eyes and predators. Allie downed some water to soothe her throat. 'Oh my God, I do come out with utter crap, don't I? Sorry, guys.'

'We'd be happy to help, you know,' Dom said. 'Naples is a big place and quite dangerous in parts. You don't want to go tramping the streets there on your own.'

She was trying to laugh it off. 'But now I have my whistle!'

He fingered his beard, drawing it into a peak. 'Even with a whistle.'

'Are you sure that's what I said? Only, the man I think might be my father – and I know it sounds ridiculously Victorian or soapy or something – but anyway, I understood he came from Rome. That's the reason for the trip: I was born here.'

'So why are you going to Naples then? You could just look him up in the phone book.'

Well, she'd tried, but his name wasn't listed. And how could she have phoned up out of the blue, blundered into a stranger's life? This was an enterprise that needed cautious tactics: one step at a time along the route that had led to her existence. And it had fitted in well with the general holiday plans until they got screwed up. 'I'm going to Naples for the same reason you are. To see Pompeii and Herculaneum.'

'Right.' Meg nodded, flashes of sunlight sparking from her frizzy halo. 'And then?'

'Well, then I'll do what we fixed up in Florence. Get the sleeper north and meet the girls in Romania or wherever.'

'Saves paying for a hotel,' observed Dom. 'Sleeping on the train, even cheaper if you don't book a berth.'

Allie winced. She wished they'd stop crowding her. And it didn't help that they had all sorts of stuff on her because they could remember what she'd let out when she was lashed and she couldn't. Plus, it made her queasy to be with a couple who held hands all the time. Holding hands had never been Sam's style. He didn't care for public displays of affection; you might alienate your fans. He'd always introduce her in a casual offhand way: this is Allie. She's on drums. Not: she's the girl I love, the girl who warms my bed, who scores my songs, who never misses a fucking beat. Not that she wanted to be reminded of Sam – which was another problem with being in this awkward configuration of three.

Meg tidied away her orange peel and took out her notebook. 'I've got down Villa Giulia for tomorrow,' she said. 'We can catch the train late afternoon and get up early for Pompeii first thing the next morning. Apart from anything else, you wouldn't want to be traipsing around it in the midday sun.'

'You don't have to wait for me. I'm not really a morning person.'

'Nonsense, we'll make sure you're awake.'

'And entry is majorly expensive,' said Dom, 'even for concessions, so you'll want to get full value from the visit. And after that . . .'

'Actually,' said Allie. 'I might give myself a day off, take a boat out to one of the islands for a change of scene.'

Meg cocked an eyebrow. 'Oh, which one?'

With a sudden whooping, an outcrop of the school party chased each other past the entrance to the bath-house. Allie watched their stampede and mumbled, 'I was thinking of Capri.'

15

Allie woke in an unfamiliar room in the spare light of dawn. It had been cheaper to book a triple. (No worries, Dom said. We don't mind if you don't.) Her bed was in a corner alcove, at right angles to theirs, and nearer to the bathroom. They were both sleeping face-down. Meg muttered and kicked at the cotton coverlet. The alarm wasn't due to go off for another hour, but already there were brakes screeching and gears grinding from traffic at the nearby intersection, the gurgle of plumbing and the rattle of news from televisions turned up too loud.

She thumped the pillow which was giving her a crick in the neck and it bounced like rubber under her palm. She knew Dom and Meg were well-intentioned. They were members of Greenpeace. They'd protested against the war in Iraq (well, who hadn't?). They were a source of information (in English). They didn't fret or miss trains or lose their possessions. But she didn't think she could handle another minute of their company. If she didn't bail out now, their nerve-jangling pedantry would flip her into a pit of despair.

She stole into the bathroom with a pen and her diary. *Dear Dom and Meg*, she wrote on a page ripped from December, *I'm making an early start and didn't want to wake you. Hope you have a great time checking out Pompeii.* She paused. They might think she was going on a day trip. If she didn't return as expected, they might report her missing. She could hardly say: please don't try to find me. She wasn't going into hiding. *Many thanks for everything* should do it. You wouldn't write that to people you were seeing later for supper. She added a couple of kisses after her name so it looked more affectionate and crept back into the bedroom. Dom had turned over; his beard was jutting towards the ceiling, his arm was trailing to the floor. Luckily there were clean clothes at the top of her backpack. She buckled the straps silently but the teeth of the zipped section grated. A feral cat yowled below their window.

Allie felt shitty, leaving her pathetic message by her empty bed and slinking out of the door, but she couldn't see any alternative. She knew they'd keep on at her until she agreed to stick with them and then she'd hate herself even more for not taking the initiative. That's your trouble, Sam had told her, shortly after composing a totally weird and to her mind totally wonderful new song. You don't strike out often enough. Beat your own path.

In the small reception lobby, she paid her third of the room bill to a wall-eyed porter. Then, in the gentle warmth of a new day, she made her way to the ferry terminal.

She was unprepared for the staggering beauty of the bay of Naples, even as glimpsed through the smeared and spattered windows of the hydrofoil. Why didn't anybody *tell* me? she marvelled. When the dark mossy folds of Ischia reared before her she felt a curious tingling in the pit of her stomach. As they approached she made out bright clusters of buildings stacked above each other, canopies of palms and umbrella pines punctuated by slim columns of cypress. Yachts with their sails furled rocked gently within the perfect circle of the harbour; a large cruise liner had anchored further out to sea. Gulls screamed overhead and dived at floating scraps of litter.

The gangway unfolded on to the quayside and Allie waited her turn to disembark. The bustle around her didn't tally with Liddy's description of sleepy tranquillity. She had to leap out of the way of a speeding Lambretta and by mistake tagged on to the tail of a tour group who were mounting a coach bound for the gardens of La Mortella. Everybody, it seemed, had a destination in mind, they all knew where they wanted to go. Allie, who had no idea, decided she should calm her stomach with breakfast. Once she'd safely crossed the street she had a choice of bars, but she picked the most basic: a long, plain counter with snacks trapped in display cases, a handful of tall plastic stools, a couple of fruit machines in a dark recess. The clientele here was mostly bus and cab drivers with dark glasses and tanned forearms. They were tossing back espressos and munching slices of pizza: the air was scented with marjoram, roasted tomatoes and black coffee.

Allie pointed to the biggest custard-filled *cornetto* and took it, with her café latte, to a small round table. A folded newspaper was lying on the surface. A man standing nearby, burly, paunchy, tucked it under his arm and indicated with a flourish that the table was hers. Then he took off his sunglasses and grinned at her. She smiled back. She saw him again, outside, when the caffeine and the sugar boost had done their work. He was standing at the door of a bus, calling across the piazza to a colleague. His whole manner was genial and good-humoured so, when he swung with surprising agility into the driver's seat, she pointed at Liddy's rough sketch map and asked if he knew the Casa Colonnata.

'*Certo*.' He beckoned her on board.

Allie hesitated. Wasn't this a little too easy? She'd strolled off the boat, over the road and into a bar, and chosen a bus at random. There were others, nosing off in different directions. She wondered how the villa could be so well known. Perhaps he hadn't understood her. 'You go to the Casa Colonnata?' she repeated. 'This is the right bus to take me there?'

He nodded again. She had to move forward because the doors were hissing shut. It didn't occur to her, until she'd swayed into a seat with her backpack caught awkwardly between her knees, that there might be more than one villa with that name. Or a boutique hotel? Still, it wasn't such a large island; at worst, she would have to sit out the journey and ride back to the port again. Once beyond the town, the bus laboured up a winding road. Some of the bends were so sharp it was amazing its tail didn't swing off the edge. Drivers hurtled downwards with their hands on their horns. Occasionally a camper van straddled both lanes and forced them to a crawl. The passengers sat and gossiped. Every now and again the affable driver would stop at some apparently arbitrary point and let one or two of them off at the verge. Allie relaxed and turned her attention to the landscape. Everything would be fine.

They passed terraced vineyards and olive groves, torrents of rambling roses and incongruously planted billboards. Sometimes she caught glimpses of the sea below, a marvellous intense blue. A roadside stall offered slices of pink watermelon and baskets of white eggs. At a shrine to the Madonna, plastic lilies mingled with fresh carnations, their petals crisping at the edges in the growing heat. The bus lurched around another corner and the driver jerked his head in her direction and called, 'Casa Colonnata.'

Allie stood and peered out. She could see a development of several villas, white cubes and rectangles slipping down the hill. 'Is it one of these?' she asked the driver as he pulled over. 'How will I find it?'

He shrugged, not understanding, and repeated himself.

She thanked him and descended because there was nothing else she could do. Other people followed her, began to walk off along the paths that linked the villas. She accosted a woman humping a bag nearly as heavy as her own, containing cleaning products and equipment. 'Excuse me,' she began. 'I'm looking for a place called Casa Colonnata. Do you know it?'

The woman looked surprised and extended her arm. '*È tutta la zona.*'

'But that's impossible. They can't . . .'

Allie was surrounded by a maze of buildings which not only looked identical with their white stucco walls and pots of geraniums, but had the same name too. How did anyone find their way home? Eventually, Allie deduced the name applied to the whole estate. She was probably in the wrong spot entirely. This was why she shouldn't have travelled by herself: she had no one to bounce ideas off, no one else to blame for stupid mistakes.

She took out her phone and switched it on, half-expecting an aggrieved text from Dom. None came. He probably thought it would cost too much. And if she rang Liddy now for further directions, wouldn't that cost a fortune too? Anyway, she wouldn't be able to help. She had talked of chestnut forests and rocky cliff-side tracks, of the small shop and bar serving scattered habitations. Over decades a place was bound to change. It was possible that the old villas had been demolished and built over with all these new holiday homes.

It was a weekday, not yet the height of the season. A few of the villas showed signs of occupation: chairs pushed back from a table beneath a loggia, a parked car beginning to sizzle, freshly watered hanging baskets – but many had their shutters sealed and their ornamental fountains switched off. The cleaning woman and the other passengers had dispersed. A ginger cat lay under a bush buffing its whiskers.

Allie calculated that she was on the outer edges of the development, that if she struck seawards, she might yet find what she was looking for. Eventually the villas became more spacious and set further apart; some had swimming pools. A tree drooped apricots over a gateway, but she wasn't sure if the fruit were ripe. In any case, she was more tired than hungry: she should have checked into a room, rested and come out later.

She rubbed perspiration from her face, shaded her eyes and looked ahead. Here the roadway branched and took on a different tenor: older, grittier, the trees more mature. A long driveway dropped to her right, the gates latched but not locked, the gateposts topped with carved pineapples – just as Liddy had described. 'You'll come to the Baldini villa first,' she'd told her. 'It was very glitzy in its day.' Glitzy was not the word Allie would have used. It looked dated, the stucco discoloured, but it was heavily muffled with lush creepers which gave it a romantic air. Her spirits lifted; she carried on.

Until she met Liddy she'd assumed that Rome had been the arena of her mother's tribulations. She'd swallowed the story of the naïve student, the drugs bust, the rubbish boyfriend because the focus had always been on her own condition – the effort and willpower needed to overcome it. But now there was a new dimension – a whole new location, in fact – and she was standing in front of it: the Verducci villa, the original Casa Colonnata. It wasn't quite as she imagined. For a start, it wasn't as grand as Liddy had suggested. Allie had pictured a Palladian-style temple topped with a dome, like the White House. Instead, the roof was flat and the columns were more like slender poles, wound about with sweet jasmine. Tall electronic gates barred entry, although there was a bell she could ring and an intercom to speak into. Did she really want to confront the owner? She'd rehearsed all kinds of excuses in her head but they sounded far-fetched and unconvincing. Besides, the door would probably be answered by a housekeeper who, like the woman on the bus, didn't speak any English.

Anyway, she'd seen the villa and it was just a nice holiday home with a spectacular view. Without the view it would be nothing special. Like any other dwelling, it would be a repository of memories only for those who had spent time there (or who had – possibly – been conceived in one of the rooms overlooking the sea). She turned to leave and noticed an American-style mailbox beside the gates. Discreetly, she opened it. Her hand settled on an envelope and drew it out. The name wasn't Verducci. Well, didn't that answer her question? Somebody else had bought the place and was spending enough of the year there to receive post. She returned the letter to the mailbox and set off back to the bus-stop. She'd find somewhere to stay, wash and brush up. She could do with a drink first though, something to eat too. Maybe those apricots would turn out to be ripe after all . . .

She didn't reach the apricots. Approaching the Baldini villa from a different angle, she spotted a car parked under a tree. Allie wasn't much good at identifying trees. Or cars, since she didn't drive, but this one had a Fiat Punto logo and a Naples number plate. It didn't look anything special, not like a Maserati or a Porsche or the type of flamboyant sports car she would have expected of one of Liddy's Baldinis. No doubt that family had moved on, too.

She could see a figure beyond the Fiat, unravelling a hosepipe. A young man was dragging it to a raised area away from the house. Keeping as close as she could to a hedge of oleander, Allie took a parallel route. Peeking through a gap in the narrow leaves, she glimpsed a swimming pool, bordered with mosaic tiles and half a dozen inviting sun loungers. She'd spent the past ten days in cities, amid crowds and tall buildings which, however historic, had pressed in on her until she'd sensed a physical constriction in her chest. And here, within a few yards, was the most delightful empty pool. She imagined submerging herself, washing away the grime and the altercations and the setbacks. She was a strong swimmer. Swimming lessons had begun early as part of her treatment. She had no fear of waves or cold temperatures and often braved the Atlantic or the North Sea in conditions which would chill the less intrepid. Battling the elements was an invigorating exercise; leaping into this pool would be a wonderful indulgence.

The maintenance man was hosing down the tiles, topping up the water level. He was wearing ripped jeans and flip-flops, no T-shirt. As he ambled around the perimeter to turn off the tap and coil up the hose, he passed near enough for her to see the dirt on his heels. She was dirty herself: no chance to shower this morning and too much tramping about in the sun. She held her breath. When he finished and crossed the drive towards his car she sneaked further along the hedge in the opposite direction to make sure she wasn't visible. She curled herself like a cat in what was more or less a ditch and kept her head down. There came the tinny slam of a car door, the stutter of an engine; she heard him drive away.

Emerging from the bushes she found herself at the far end of the pool, beside the shower. It rose on a tall stalk like a sunflower, ready for bathers to rinse themselves before they plunged in. She eased off the backpack which had begun to chafe her flesh, leaving a nasty weal, and perched on the nearest sun lounger. It was so tempting: the prospect of lovely cool water sluicing her face, pattering down her front. She needed something to revive her, to stop the heat overwhelming her, sealing her eyelids, confusing her brain. She would lie down for a moment and consider the risks.

If asked she'd have said she'd dozed for about five or ten minutes, but sleep had overtaken her so rapidly she lost all sense of time. In any case she couldn't see how far the sun had moved because it was obstructed by a tall silhouette.

The silhouette shrank to her level and said in bemusement: 'What the fuck?'

16

If you woke to find yourself in paradise, thought Allie, it might be like this. She was floating on her back, wearing the swimsuit that had been squashed beneath everything else since Nice. When she kicked out, a rainbow of droplets poised, crystalline, in the air. Changing ends, she couldn't make up her mind which aspect she preferred: one gave her a backdrop of roses, their honeyed petals quivering in a heat haze; the other a viridian line of evergreens against the immensity of the sky. Folded in readiness on one of the chairs was a sherbet lemon towel, much more luxurious than the scrappy old thing she'd brought with her.

Max was fetching the drinks. 'Chilled beer,' he called across the veranda. 'Good for you, yeah?'

'Perfect for me,' Allie said. If she dipped her forehead backwards into the water, she could see him receding into the villa, albeit upside down. She thought briefly of Jess and Nita stuck on a rackety Slovenian train with unyielding seats and no air-conditioning. She thought, even more briefly, of Dom and Meg trundling the well-worn thoroughfares of Pompeii, navigating coach parties and tour guides, trying to imagine being swamped in a torrent of molten lava, and felt a moment of pity. She'd lucked out, hadn't she? Who would have thought it? She rolled on to her front and plunged into the deeper end of the pool, aware of the pressure in her ears and lungs, but enjoying it for the sense of release when she burst upwards again, her hair slick against her skull, her eyes taking a second or two to focus – once more – on paradise.

Max was carrying an open bottle of Peroni in each hand. He stooped to offer her one.

'It's okay,' she said. 'I'll get out now. Boy, that was terrific.' She beamed as she hauled herself up the aluminium steps and wrapped herself in the thick towel. She was a little dizzy from the sudden onslaught of air in her system and the astonishing good luck of her situation.

Max had declined to go in. 'Reckon I need to eat first. Swimming on an empty stomach is as bad for you as swimming on a full one.'

'So's drinking,' said Allie, tipping back her bottle. Rivulets of water were running down her neck. She draped the towel over her left shoulder, disguising her arm in its folds.

'Shall we go rummage around the kitchen, see what we can find?'

'Sure.' She'd agree to anything he suggested. 'Should I get dressed first?'

'Up to you.'

'Then I won't.' He was half-naked too: the faded jeans slung low on his hips. 'Plus I am truly starving.'

She followed him through the side entrance into the kitchen. In the middle of the table a paper bag spilled panini. Allie picked one up and took a bite. Max rooted around in the fridge. 'I went out for the bread and the beer,' he said, 'but I forgot to check whether there was any, like, real food.' He produced a length of salami and dangled it from its string before her nose. 'You are sleepy,' he said in an exaggerated accent. 'You are vairy vairy sleepy . . .'

'Piss off!'

He lobbed the salami into the air. 'Catch.'

By sheer fluke of timing she reached up at the right moment and it sailed into her hand. Max produced plates, knives, plum tomatoes, and opened a jar of artichoke hearts. He recaptured the salami and started slicing it.

'Can we eat outside?' she said. 'You know, like a picnic?'

'Sure. Grab a couple more beers and I'll bring the plates.'

At the table on the terrace, sunlight threaded through the vine leaves; a few metres away came the faint slap and suck of the water against the pool filters. Inside the villa, perhaps because of the gloom and the silence, Allie had felt uneasy; here she was more comfortable. In any case the silence was now broken. Max had slotted The Strokes' *Is This It* into a CD player.

'Have you *really* met them?' asked Allie. 'I mean, like more than once? Properly?'

'That's such a British word, isn't it? Proper. Properly.'

'You haven't been winding me up?'

'We have some friends in common, been to some of the same parties. You're a fan?'

She wiped a dribble of olive oil from her lip. 'I think they're amazing. Truly. I mean, they've, like, woken up the whole scene, given us such a charge –'

'Us? Who's us?'

'Oh well . . .' She began to explain. About the three years she and Sam had spent assembling the band, the difficulty of finding time to rehearse when they were supposed to be studying for their finals, the thrill of getting bookings for those early student gigs, the pleasure of creating a song together. Part of her was excited to be talking about music again – tempered by a nagging awareness, like toothache, that she was now one stage removed from the creative process. But he was listening, really listening.

'Let me get this straight.' He tipped his head sideways. His dark curls reminded her of The Strokes' drummer, Fab Moretti. (She always paid particular attention to drummers – somebody had to.) Sam had limp silky hair, the colour of the Golden Virginia he smoked. 'Are you saying you're, like, the new Meg White?'

She picked up a tomato and rolled it around her palm. 'I'm not claiming anything. I can't, I've been made redundant. Some people might think a girl drummer's a big deal but basically you're background. The main egos are strutting out front.'

'Hey, don't put yourself down.'

'Well, it's the English malaise. Don't aim too high, then you won't get knocked back. You won't be able to do everything you want in this life so don't even try. It's different if you're American.'

'I'm not. I'm Italian.'

'Sorry, my mistake.' She rolled the tomato across the table towards him and his hand closed over it instantly. You could call it harmony, she thought, and wondered what he'd be like to jam with. He'd told her he could strum a guitar a bit. 'I've a mind like a sieve at the moment. Besides, you do such a great impression of a New Yorker.'

He grinned. 'Maybe that's because I *am* a New Yorker. Did you want another beer yet?'

The alcohol had already induced a state of enjoyable torpor; she felt warm and weightless as if she were still buoyed up by water. She twisted a drying strand of hair around her finger and closed her eyes. 'Mmm, that'd be great.' The empty bottles clinked as he swept them into his hand. She sat upright. 'Hell, that was rude! Sounded like I expected you to wait on me or something. Let me get them. They're in the fridge, right?' She grasped the empties and shoved his shoulder gently so that he sank back into his chair. He had the kind of skin you wanted to touch, firm and taut with the sheen of richly polished walnut – and the kind of bearing that made pushing him down a satisfying thing to do. He was so obviously (like The Strokes) from a moneyed background. Even the ripped (designer) jeans were an amazing fit; the flip-flops were Havianas. How on earth could she have thought he was the pool maintenance man?

She padded back into the villa. She needed the loo and wandered the hallway, furtively peeking through doors, trying to guess which had been Liddy's room. There were mirrors everywhere and she kept being startled by her own reflection. It was hard to believe that she had gained entrance to this place so easily. She was staggered by her own brazenness.

'Who the fuck are you?' he'd said, and she hadn't even wondered why he'd addressed her in English.

'I'm Allie. Allegra.'

'Oh.' He'd waited while she unwound herself. 'I wasn't expecting anyone to arrive so early.'

'You weren't?'

'No. And heck, I'm sure I would've remembered if he said a British girl was coming.'

'How d'you know I'm British?'

'The accent?' He considered. 'And the skirt. No other girls wear skirts that short.'

She stood up and tugged it down. He had risen too. 'Who said? Who are you talking about?'

'Bobo. You are a friend of his, aren't you?'

'Do you mean Bobo Baldini?'

'Sure.'

Wow, thought Allie. He really exists. The toddler who'd so frustrated Liddy was now a grown man, coming back to the family house for the summer. Weird.

'He hates the nickname, haven't you found? Insists on being Roberto, or Bobby for choice, because it makes him sound like de Niro or someone.'

'Where is he?'

'Oh, he's arriving later with the others. Didn't he tell you there was a whole gang coming out for the weekend? One of those get-togethers that really should have been arranged in advance, but hey – it's more fun, isn't it, if we're all spontaneous together? That's the way we do things in Italy. Barely controlled chaos.'

In what she assumed to be the living room, photographs were arranged on a shelf. If she memorized them maybe she'd be able to recognize Bobo when he turned up. Not that it would help because he would know at once – unless he was high as a kite – that he'd never met her before. She examined the faces in their frames: the assorted groupings made it impossible for her to work out any identities, but everyone was joyful. Tempestuous was how Liddy had described Maresa Baldini, volatile; absolutely charming until you crossed her.

She was going to be found out. As soon as the others arrived Max would discover she'd lied to him. Well, not lied exactly, but there were truths and there were half-truths and there was falling face forward in the shit, which she had very nearly done. She took another two Peronis from the stock in the fridge and snapped off the tops. Keeping her breathing regular and even, a ploy she'd found useful in the moments before a performance, she returned outside. When he reached over for the bottle their fingers touched. She withdrew her hand quickly. 'I have to tell you something,' she said.

'Yeah?' He responded to her change of tone, looking quizzical.

'I don't actually know Bobo.'

'You don't? You mean one of the others invited you?' He stared at her. His eyes, which she had thought were brown, had flecks of bronze in them. He slapped away a fly that had landed on his torso. He might make out that he sat around in dim basements listening to indie rock and garage, but she could tell he worked out too: weight training and so on. She'd been forced to exercise so much in her childhood that she knew the signs.

'No one invited me.'

'No one?' He scratched his head as if taking some time to assimilate this fact. 'You're telling me you're a gatecrasher?'

'Yes, I suppose I am.'

'Fuck.'

'I'm really sorry. I should have explained earlier . . .'

'So why didn't you?'

'Well, you know what, I was tired and disorientated and when you woke me up . . . I couldn't think of anything more fabulous than a swim. But I know that was cheeky of me. Swimming first and confessing later, when you couldn't take it away from me. The swim, I mean.'

'Or the beers?'

She hadn't yet touched the bottle on the table. She pushed it away. A black beetle was crossing one of the flagstones, purposeful and unwavering.

Max whistled, a low single note, but he didn't comment. He was leaving her lots of rope with which to hang herself.

'I wanted to tell you earlier. Truly. But it was difficult when we got sidetracked and had so much to talk about . . . This isn't an easy thing I'm doing, coming clean, whatever, but I didn't want to con you any more. And I didn't –'

'– want to be shown up when Bobo and the rest of the gang arrived?'

'Well, I wouldn't have let that happen. I could have just walked out, left, thanked you for a free lunch and then you'd never have seen me again. But . . .' She paused. There were many things she could say to break the silence suspended between them – even more acute now the CD had ended and there was no driving guitar rhythm to bolster their connection – but she wasn't going to grovel. And she didn't care to dig her hole any deeper.

Max took a long swig of his drink and wiped his mouth with the back of his hand. 'So all that stuff about the music you're into was to string me along, get me on side?'

'No, no! I didn't lie about any of that. Come to think of it, I didn't lie about anything. You simply assumed I was one of Bobo's mates.'

'Why wouldn't I?'

'I know. I misled you. That's what I'm apologizing for and that's why I'm trying to square everything off now. Before I go.'

He rubbed his jaw again. 'You must have met him somewhere or how else would you know his name?'

'You called him Bobo,' said Allie. 'And someone told me this was the Baldini villa.'

'Someone?'

'While I was wandering about, lost.'

'What were you looking for?'

'It doesn't matter, it's not important.'

'Tell me.'

It annoyed her that he could steam ahead with his interrogation while she couldn't ask a single question, but then he was entitled to be idling on this sun-dappled terrace; she wasn't. Further half-truths came to her rescue. 'I was on a sort of recce. A friend's family used to have a place out here once and they'd been talking about how much it might have changed and whether they should have sold up. Lots of English people are buying villas abroad these days. It's like a new hobby. What happens is the budget airline companies stick a pin in the map of Europe and find some undeveloped runway where it's going to be really cheap to land. They start operating flights there and all the Brits take out mortgages and buy second homes because, you know, we're a nation of owner occupiers. Even I have my own house, as it happens.'

'Most of the foreigners who own property here are German, not British.'

'You sound very certain.'

He swatted away another fly. Until this point she'd assumed he was her age; now she realized he was older, more worldly-wise. 'Yeah, because I am. I've been coming here most of my life. The Germans are keen on spas and all that therapy and wellness stuff. I thought that's what you might have come for. Hydrotherapy.'

She liked to suppose that if a person hadn't said anything, if they hadn't averted their eyes or made any other reference, then they hadn't noticed. They always noticed. She might be draped in a towel now, but she'd been swimming lengths in the pool, parading around in her swimsuit: he'd have to be blind not to.

'I'm not one of those people who goes to Lourdes,' she said indignantly.

'Hydrotherapy is nothing to do with holy water! I'm not talking miracles.'

She clutched her arm behind her back. 'In fact, I manage damn well.'

'Well, obviously, if you really do play drums.'

'You don't believe me? You think all drummers are head bangers and I don't fit the bill?'

'Jeez! Let it go.' After an awkward pause in which they avoided looking at each other, he continued: 'So you're not here to take the waters? You want to buy some real estate?'

She'd been given another chance, she had to sound convincing. 'No, that's a pipe dream. I was just getting a feel for the place. I'd heard about Casa Colonnata and –'

'The development? I didn't think it was being promoted in the UK.'

'No . . . er, my friend mentioned it . . . Anyhow, there's no story to tell really. I got a bus, wandered about, thought I'd be able to get down to the beach –'

'It's a private beach club these days.'

'Oh right . . . Anyway, by then I'd been going round in circles and I was completely lost. So I sneaked in here for a peek at the pool, because it was so calm and I'd got myself into an awful dither. I didn't mean to fall asleep. What are the Italian laws on trespass? Do you shoot at first sight?'

She hoped he'd go easy on her. They'd hit it off so well at the start, like they'd known each other for ever.

Max was regarding her with great concentration. She felt as if he were seeing right through her. Abruptly he pushed back his chair and stood over her, his palms flat on the table, but she never found out what penalty he had in mind because a barrage of hooting bowled down the cinder drive and two cars, nose to tail, slalomed to a stop within inches of the veranda.

17

Allie didn't know what he told them. She couldn't understand any of the rapid Italian with which they greeted each other. They poured on to the terrace in such a torrent of suntanned limbs and colourful T-shirts and extravagant caresses, it felt like being mobbed in the mosh pit. In fact there were only six of them and Bobo – Bobby – she picked out at once. Chunky and solid as cedar wood, he had a green bandana tied around his temples, a manic glint in his eyes and an oddly high-pitched giggle. He walked with a confident swagger and an air that implied leadership: the rest of the party all deferred to him.

One after another they came up to shake her hand. '*Sono* Allegra – Allie,' she said six times over, to Bobby and Giulia and Sandro and Tommaso and Bianca and Laura. '*Piacere*,' they returned the greeting, kissing her on each cheek. Bobby said something provocative to Max, who responded, '*Vaffanculo*.'

Allie was tiptoeing on burning coals, over-sensitive to her situation. 'Don't let them tease you because of me. Really I should be leaving . . .'

He frowned. 'It's got nothing to do with you. He's having a go at me because of the car. When I picked it up from the rental place it was all they had left. Bobby's such an asshole. He's so into appearances, *quel cazzone!*' He slammed his fist into the crook of his elbow, directing the obscene gesture towards Bobby, who laughed. Allie had regarded Max as the all-round American, the sophisticated New York city dweller. Now, among his friends, he'd become seamlessly Italian. His intonation and speed of delivery matched theirs. His mannerisms – his hands rippling through his curls or describing shapes in the air, his toe tapping, his bursts of exclamation: *Figurati! Da morire!* – were in perfect harmony with the rest.

As she began to distinguish one from another, the impression of children let loose in a sweetshop diminished and the spectacle became a choreographed ballet. The young men helped themselves to soft drinks: cola or Orangina fizzing over ice cubes. They wandered around the pool, dipping a foot in the water, kicking a light spray at each other. One of them – Sandro? Tommaso? – found a shrunken rubber ball and batted it with dexterity from hand to hand and against the wall of the house. The young women went inside to claim their sleeping quarters and unpack. Their dance routine involved weaving adroitly between the men, the sun loungers and the various exits and entrances to the villa. If each had been attached to a skein of coloured silk, they would have created an intricate tapestry. They didn't keep still. They changed out of their clothes and into their bikinis. They fetched sun lotion and massaged it into each other's backs. They discarded the lotion and demanded more ice for their drinks. They took turns to question Bobby about their rooms, the beach or the locality. It was hard for Allie to be certain of the words, but the pointing, the shading of brows, and the body language were so expressive it was like being on the set of a silent movie.

The men decided to swim. Tommaso jumped in first, then Bobby, splashing like a noisy whale. And it was Bobby, the practical joker, who circled his hand around his girlfriend's (Giulia's?) ankle and pulled her in to join him. The pool, which had been such an oasis a few hours ago, fermented like a Jacuzzi. Max had gone to put on more music (White Stripes) and turn up the volume. Passing Allie, he muttered, 'Bobby's a banker, you know. Investors trust him with their savings.'

'And the others?'

'Giulia also. And Sandro. Bianca's a web designer, Tommaso's a pharmacist; not sure about the *fidanzata*.'

And where do you fit in? she could have said at this point. But before she had the chance, Bobby started hollering from the pool. In response Max snapped the waistband of his jeans against his torso. Bobby beckoned and unleashed a stream of adjectives which transported the girls into giggles. Max let his jeans fall; beneath them he was wearing swimming trunks. His calves tensed as he leapt, rather elegantly Allie thought, on to Bobby's head.

Both men vanished in an underwater tussle. Laura and Bianca, their bodies dry, their mascara intact, their lips, toes and fingernails still defined in glossy red, broke off their conversation for the space of a sentence and then smoothly rejoined it. The water whirled and boiled as if a geyser were about to erupt. Bobby thrust himself upwards, tore off his soaking bandana and called over to Allie. 'He says you are very good swimmer. Very speedy. You drive with your legs and the water makes no movement when you are in it.'

She shrugged as if this were unnecessary flattery and her style nothing special.

'Show us,' commanded Bobby.

Their faces were on her, eager for a display: these strangers whom she'd known scarcely an hour, whose house party she had gatecrashed. They had every right to expect her to sing for her supper. They weren't asking anything unreasonable; they were keen to admire. But she would have to explain why she swam the way she did, her one-armed crawl, and although she reckoned she was a good sport she wasn't an exhibitionist. 'No,' she said.

'*Dài!* We will move from your way.' He flung his arms wide. 'You have the *piscina* for yourself.'

She shook her head again. 'Sorry. Maybe later.'

Max hauled himself on to the side. He sat with his legs in the water, his chest gleaming as if it had been newly varnished. 'Why the heck not? You're good.'

She shouldn't have to justify herself. 'Because I'm not a performing monkey.'

His eyelashes were matted into wet clumps. He rubbed them with his fists, adding to his impression of disbelief when he challenged her. 'Not a performer?'

'No.'

How shameful would it be if they turned on her? If only her backpack were a little nearer she could grab it and run.

'Quit bullshitting,' Max said. 'If you play live music in front of an audience you're a performer. No argument.'

'Okay, but your mate wasn't asking me to smash a cymbal. He wanted to see me swim.'

Even Laura and Bianca had ceased chirruping, their attention caught by the crackle in the air and the stand-off they didn't comprehend. Everyone was looking at Allie. It was difficult to be dignified in a swimsuit. 'You're trying to turn me into a freak show,' she said.

Max scrambled at once to his feet. 'Hell no! You don't think I'd . . .' He tugged handfuls of his hair in exasperation.

Allie manoeuvred herself away from him and towards her bag. She pulled on her denim skirt and tussled with the zip. It was all so stupid. She would cheerfully have joined in swimming with the rest of them; it was the way she had been singled out that disturbed her.

The others were looking from her to Max as if they were watching a lovers' tiff, as if the signs to be read from the exchange were quite different from the actuality. But how would they know? How could these well-heeled fun-seekers imagine that she was a flagrant interloper who happened to get lucky with a guy who shared her interests? And why hadn't he told them he'd literally only known her for ten minutes? She concentrated on fastening the row of small buttons on her cotton top.

Giulia, tucked into a sarong, came over and touched her arm. '*Per favore, non piangere*,' she said.

Allie blinked. She hadn't intended to cry. She hadn't intended to blow herself out of the water like this. What a fucking eejit. 'I'm sorry,' she said. '*Che stupido*.'

'*Stupida*,' corrected Giulia. She offered one of her Marlboro Lights to Allie, who declined. Giulia lit up, took a deep drag and then held the cigarette at a distance so the smoke could trouble other eyes than her own. English came tumbling out as if she had cranked a wheel. 'To swim or not swim is not important. Massimo is good guy. Roberto also. They like fun, is all. You and Massimo are together long time, no?'

'No,' said Allie. 'Actually, we only just met . . .'

'You are not *fidanzata* from America?'

'No I'm not.'

'Ohhh . . .' Giulia considered and then came to a decision. 'Is not my problem,' she said. 'We are here to enjoy. Is enough.' She padded back towards the pool, trailing ash and the ends of her sarong. Her build, like Bobby's, was stocky, but her flesh was so tanned and supple she looked like golden syrup in motion. Quietly she passed this new information on to her friends.

The group had plans for the next day, Saturday, for taking the boat out on a fishing trip and bathing in the hot springs; a restaurant was booked for dinner and they were going on to a club. But this evening they were going nowhere, chilling. Bobby was organizing the cooking – not that there was much to cook. He whirled around the kitchen opening cupboard doors, invoking a person he called the sainted Rosaria, and criticising Max for being inefficient. Allie understood that he'd been supposed to obtain a decent range of foodstuffs, not just the beer, olives and panini he'd bought at lunchtime. In any case, more than half the panini had already gone, snatched and gnawed by guests passing through the kitchen – or used as ammunition in a mock fight between Bobby and Sandro; torn pellets of bread littered the terrace.

'I thought there was stuff in the freezer,' Max grumbled in English. 'They always have steaks or ribs or sardines or something.'

There followed a lengthy debate to determine whether they should eat out or stay in. Tommaso volunteered to drive to the nearest pizzeria to fetch takeaway pizzas and Bobby insisted on cooking his signature dish, so no one would go hungry in the meantime. This dish was spaghetti (of which there was no shortage) tossed with olio, aglio and peperoncino (of which there was no shortage either). Allie was accustomed to the powerful curries of the West Midlands, but Bobby's liberal use of flaming red chillies stripped all feeling from her lips and tongue. Giulia, wisely, refused the pasta. She lit another cigarette and insisted she was happy to wait for the pizza to arrive. After they had eaten, they danced. Bobby took charge of the music; it was in his nature to take charge of everything. His choice veered between classic Tamla Motown and emotional Italian ballads. Allie and Max sat out the ballads, mocking their host's questionable taste.

At midnight, there was talk of going down to the beach to swim in the sea, an activity for which the men were game, the girls less so. They complained the twisting path down the cliff would be dangerous, they might lose their footing in the dark or cut themselves on the rocks. The notion appealed to Allie – the inky, diamond-studded water – but after half an hour of argument, they were no closer to getting there. To settle the matter, Bobby declared, '*Che cazzo me ne frega!*' ripped off all his clothes and plunged completely naked into the pool. Giulia followed him, untying the ribbon of her halter-neck dress and letting it shimmy into a heap. Giggling, the two other couples undressed in the shadows and jumped.

Max and Allie were the only ones left standing, fully clothed, at the edge. It was at moments like these, she thought, watching a group of friends relaxing their inhibitions and having a grand time, that you remembered, yeah, that was me not so long ago. In the middle of things. Not a bloody wallflower.

They were calling for her and Max to join them. Well, why not? She wasn't going to repeat that earlier humiliating scene. The pool was too crowded for swimming anyhow: it was a porpoises' playground. She wasn't going to be stuffy about this. She imagined phoning Liddy and hearing her gasp of incredulity when she told her: 'That little boy you used to look after, the one called Bobo? Well, I spent last night skinny dipping with him and his friends.'

Last night . . . *Last night* . . . The lyrics hummed in her brain like an anthem, although the music had ceased a while ago. She tossed her clothes aside and plummeted into a forest of scything legs and ghostly white buttocks. She surfaced to cheering and Bobby flung a friendly wet arm around her neck.

Alone on the terrace, Max gathered up the glasses and empty plates, tipped the contents of ashtrays into the plant pots. '*Lasciali*,' commanded Bobby. '*Vieni con noi*.'

'*Dopo*,' he called back, continuing his operations with the same steady attention to detail as this morning, when she'd thought him a handyman topping up the water levels. His demeanour was that of an older brother, responsible for controlling his younger, hare-brained siblings (even if he had cocked up his shopping list). Then he went indoors for a long time and when he re-emerged the swimming had lost its charm and everyone had clambered out.

Allie was sheltering within her towel when Bobby came over to her. 'I think he was calling his girlfriend back home,' he said.

'Oh, right.'

'It doesn't bother you?'

'Bother me? Of course not.'

'It's best,' said Bobby, 'to be upfront, yes?'

'Yes. Absolutely.'

So they took her to be a temporary replacement – well, that was okay; not true, but okay. They also took it for granted she would share his sleeping quarters.

At one end of their room, facing the double bed, a small balcony jutted over a precipitous drop. Allie stood on it, inhaling the warm scent, the dreamlike quality of the night. 'You must think I'm dead cheeky, leeching on to you like this,' she said. 'I should have fucked off and found a hotel.'

'But you wanted to stay?'

'I was having a good time, yes.'

'Well then.'

'I could always go and crash on the sofa.'

'Bobby'd never let me live it down. Quit stalling.'

She leaned forward to fasten the shutters. She'd feel more comfortable undressing in the dark, even if he had already seen her strip naked.

'Don't,' he said.

'Why not?'

'You'll shut out the stars. You can never see them in a city, there's too much light pollution. It's another thing I like about coming back here.'

Either he had a romantic streak or he wanted her to think he did. She moved away from the balcony and pulled on the extra-large T-shirt she wore to sleep in, conscious that the words 'Too Hot to Handle' were branded in dashing colours across her bust.

'Come on, get in.' He'd already dived under the duvet. All she could see of him was his hair curling on the pillow, the prow of his nose and the angle of his collarbone. His hands, his ribcage, his slim hips, the jagged white scar she had noticed on his shin, were hidden. When she joined him he rested a hand on her cheek. '*Allora* Allegra,' he said.

'*Allora* Allegra, what?'

He moved his head forward as if to kiss her. She could smell the wine on his breath and taste it on her own: a dose of heavy red tannin mixed with garlic and chillies and the tart acidity of olives. She closed her eyes and felt his kisses grazing her cheek. She wriggled a little closer until her thigh was in contact with his. His left hand lifted her shirt and ran up her hips and over her waist until it settled and curved cup-like around her right breast. His mouth moved down and fixed on hers. His tongue foraged between her lips in much the same way as his knee pushed between her legs, encouraging them to part.

It was so easy, so pleasant, so downright enjoyable, the sensation of being aroused. Responsive. Desirable. And so hard to know what part was played by alcohol or inertia, or sheer desperation: the result of too many weeks – no, months – of celibacy. She extricated herself and pushed him away. 'What about your girlfriend?'

'What about her?'

'Is it serious? Did you agree it was okay to play around?'

He rolled on to his back, raising his arms behind his head. 'She's the other side of the ocean.'

'So?'

'So I don't know when I'm going to see her again.'

'Aren't you going back home?'

'Not for some time.'

'Oh.'

He turned his head to catch her eye. 'And she could have come out here but it didn't suit her, so you see, it's not me who's the deserter. We're in what you could call a state of hiatus.'

'Does she call it that too?'

'What's with the fifth degree?'

'I thought Americans took cheating on partners really seriously.'

'You keep forgetting, Allie, I'm Italian.' He laid a hand on her stomach, where there was all kinds of turbulent activity. 'If we didn't go around seducing women, we'd be letting the side down.'

'I didn't think you were such a walking cliché.' Perhaps that was going too far. Perhaps she should be grateful a man was taking an interest in her again. No: her confidence was not at such a low ebb she needed her ego stoking.

‘Point taken,’ said Max. ‘But you know, since we’ve ended up in bed together I was only doing what came naturally to me. For you, could be it’s different.’

‘I never do it on first meeting,’ said Allie.

‘What, never ever? Not even if you’ve been to the wildest party and thrown back, I don’t know, a quart of champagne, and met a guy who’s a total turn-on, whose path you might not cross again so it’s like a once-in-a-lifetime opportunity . . .’

‘No.’

‘What the hell, it’s only sex. No big deal.’

His hands roamed, his touch tantalized. But in the morning, when they woke with hangovers and dry mouths and matted hair, in sheets smelling of garlic, it might not seem so much passionate encounter as pitiful balls-up. A one-night stand that shouldn’t have happened.

‘It’s a good rule,’ she said, as much to herself as to Max. ‘Abstaining, I mean. This time yesterday I didn’t even know you existed.’

‘If that’s the way you want to play it . . .’ He climbed out of bed and she saw his erection slump. ‘I’m going to take a piss,’ he said. ‘And then we’re going to sleep, right, like babes in the wood?’

She drew the T-shirt over her hips and crossed her wrists and her legs. ‘Yes.’

‘But tomorrow’s another day and we’ll take it as it comes?’

‘Yes.’

18

Saturday. This will be a day to remember, Allie thought at the start of it, embracing the boat, the beach, the thermal springs and the chance to get to know Max better: discussing bands and books, exchanging confidences, spilling dreams and ambitions. And at the back of her mind lay the tentative thrill of spending another night with him; the possibility of saying yes. She didn't expect the happy equilibrium of the day to be disrupted so completely by a casual conversation with Bobby.

Sated with sunshine, fresh air and good food, they were sprawled around the restaurant table, waiting for the bill. Max had gone outside to take a phone call; Allie was pretending it wasn't important. Bobby leaned towards her, 'You are okay?'

'Yes, I'm good.'

'She should accustom herself to his absence I think.'

'Well, I suppose if it's just for the summer months . . .'

'No, no, for the year.'

'A year!' This was something she hadn't appreciated, but why should it make any difference? Her own ticket would soon expire.

'Yes, he will work in his father's practice.'

'Oh, I hadn't realized. Doing what?'

'He didn't tell you?'

'Well, you know, we covered a lot of things, but we didn't talk much about boring stuff like work. I mean, he mentioned labouring on construction sites but I thought those were holiday jobs.' She'd also suspected, with amusement, that he was trying to impress her with fake blue-collar credentials. 'He said he'd been a student for ever.'

'Yes, is true. But soon he will qualify.'

'As?'

'As architect. This is why he is coming to work with his father to, how do you say, widen the experience?'

'Right.'

The bill arrived on a saucer and was passed to Bobby. Allie rooted in her purse; she would not be beholden. She handed over a pile of euros.

'No, you are guest.'

'Everyone else is paying,' she said, looking around the table.

'Massimo wishes to pay for you, he has told me.'

'Well, I'd prefer to pay for myself.'

'Then have your fight with him.'

'No, Bobby, I'm having it with you.' She placed her notes squarely in front of him.

He raised his hands in a show of helplessness. 'So, you win. What can I do?' He took the money with a mock sigh and flicked his credit card on to the saucer. (Being Bobby, the flick was more of a spinning double somersault; he didn't do anything unobtrusively.)

'I thought Max's parents lived in New York,' said Allie.

'His mother yes, and his stepfather. My uncle has always lived in Rome.'

'You two are cousins!'

'Yes, you didn't know? That's why we often had holidays together. Fabrizio is my mother's brother. He used to own the villa close to ours and it was he who designed Casa Colonnata. There were some arguments about that in the family, as you may imagine, but at least the development is legal. Some builders are not so scrupulous.'

'You *are* joking?'

Bobby was probing the inside of his mouth with a toothpick. He set it down, puzzled. 'Why do you think this is joke?'

'Are you telling me Max's father is the architect who designed that whole new development?'

'*Sì*.'

'And his name is Fabrizio?'

'The practice, they use another name, but yes, he is Fabrizio Verducci.'

The group was rising from the table, ready for the next stage in their evening's entertainment. The table itself appeared to Allie in hyper-real detail: every wineglass, tumbler, bottle, napkin, knife, spoon, pepper pot, dispenser of oil or vinegar etched with fine distinction against the white linen cloth. Her shoulder bag was beside her chair but she couldn't trust herself to reach for it. She shivered.

'You have cold?' said Bobby. 'You spend too much time in water today, I think.'

She forced herself to stoop for her bag. 'I have to make a phone call.'

'You also?'

'Yes. I've just remembered. It's quite important. Quite urgent. I'll catch up with you later.'

'Is no problem. We can wait.'

'No, please don't. You showed me where you're going. I'll meet you there soon. I promise.'

She took out her phone and pretended to dally behind as they left the restaurant. At the last moment she dashed downstairs to the ladies' toilet and locked herself in a cubicle, where she forced her head between her knees and gulped stale air. But she couldn't confine herself there indefinitely and, below ground, there was no mobile signal. She had to speak to Liddy. For most of the day she'd been looking forward to making such a call, relating the effortless way she'd gained access to the Baldini household, comparing notes, analysing the differences between past and present. She'd been going to boast, she'd thought herself so clever – how wrong could a person be?

She splashed cold water on her face without looking in the mirror. As she picked her way between the tables of the trattoria she was convinced everyone was watching her. She imagined their heads swivelling and the word *incest* spurting through their grim lips. Guilt made you see things that weren't there – but she was *not* guilty. *Nothing* had happened. A waiter opened the door for her, bowing slightly from the waist as she left.

None of the others was in view, not even Max. They had taken her word and assumed she'd be following close behind. When they found out she wasn't, they might come searching for her. Needing time and distance she turned in the opposite direction and took a side street. Beneath a lamp illuminating an advert for Aperol – the Low-Alcohol Drink! – she scrolled through her address list. A thousand miles away Liddy's mobile warbled but wasn't answered. She could try her home number. She would not, dared not, contact her mother.

While she was considering the next move, her phone jumped excitedly in her hand: Liddy was ringing back. She pressed the answer button.

'Allie? Did you just try to call me?'

'Yes . . . I . . .'

'How are you? How's it going?'

'Well, I've made it to Ischia . . .'

'You have? Oh!' A short silence. 'It's spectacular, isn't it? Are you . . .?' Another pause, an edge of nervous caution when she spoke again. 'Did you, um, find the villas?'

'I've met Bobo,' said Allie.

'Oh my God! How extraordinary. I never thought . . . So the family still goes there after all these years? And did you meet Sara, his sister?'

'No. I think she's married. Lives in . . . actually I've forgotten where she lives; it's not what matters right now. Listen, I need to know, the other child, the little boy Mum looked after, the one who got kidnapped –'

'That was such a mystery,' said Liddy. 'And so absolutely horrendous at the time.'

Allie wanted to scream. There was only one piece of information that was relevant to her. 'What was his name?'

'Who? Mimmo?'

'Mimmo? You're sure?'

'Well, that's what everyone called him, but it was a child's nickname, like Bobo. He was Massimo really.'

'Massimo,' repeated Allie.

'Allie,' said Liddy. 'I can't hear you. Are you there?'

Distracted by her own powerful emotions, Allie was unaware of a shadow encroaching. She was standing in the circle of light with her new phone in her hand. The shoes of the youth closing in on her were rubber-soled and silent. In a second he had whipped away the phone to the sound of Liddy's plaintive: 'Allie, Allie? What's going on?' Then he grabbed the strap of her shoulder bag. *No!* she thought in fury, remembering Char. This would not happen to her. She refused to let go, yanking it back so fiercely she stumbled, twisting her ankle. A sharp pain shot up her left leg and she fell in the roadway, an easy target. The deserted street which had seemed a good idea five minutes ago had become a terrifying trap.

Perhaps Max and Bobby had noticed her absence, were even now turning back to look for her – but she couldn't afford to wait passively. Although one leg felt numb and useless she had plenty of strength in the other. She aimed a powerful kick at the figure lurching over her and connected with his groin. She hoped that if she was troublesome enough he'd give up and slope off. But after a yelp and a stagger he was back in the fray, raising his own foot as if to stamp her into the gutter. Allie, swinging her right arm forward to protect her face, made contact with a cold metal object. For a second she thought he'd dropped a knife and she could use it to defend herself. But the object had fallen from the bag she was still clutching and was round and stubby: Meg's whistle. She blew it at such an ear-splitting pitch that he wobbled on his single leg and had to lower his toe to recover his balance. Allie used this reprieve to roll on to her front but she didn't stop blowing.

There was a pounding in her ears, the vibration of oncoming footsteps. Then a touch on her shoulder, the crackle of a walkie-talkie. Rescue came too late for her phone or to catch her assailant, but she'd saved her battered bag with wallet and passport intact. She sat up by degrees. Her back was bruised, her elbow and knee skinned, and God only knew what she'd done to her ankle.

The response to her whistle had come not from Max and Bobby but from men in uniform, *carabinieri*. One had a bald head that gleamed like an acorn in the lamplight. The other was younger, hollow-cheeked, his jaw in constant motion as he chewed successive pieces of Nicorette gum. Neither spoke much English, but the older one managed to explain she would need to complete a *denuncia*. She tried to object, to insist it wasn't necessary, she had no charges to press (she'd had a bellyful of bureaucracy in Nice), but the younger one took the whistle off her and rolled it between his palms. He held it under the light and showed her the words *Comune di Firenze* stamped on the barrel. She understood him to be telling her this was state property, it belonged to some civic official in Florence.

Allie marvelled. It wasn't only Liddy Rawlings who could trip her up at such a distance, but complacent, self-righteous Meg too.

'I don't know where it came from. Someone gave it to me,' she said, fixing her shoes and wincing. She couldn't straighten her back or put weight on her left foot.

The older *carabiniere* settled her into their patrol car, tutting at the state of her clothes streaked with dirt and the blood dripping from her knee. At the police station she was allowed to wash the grit from her injuries and then taken, hobbling, to complete the forms describing the theft.

'*Indirizzo?*' said the officer at the computer screen, his fingers suspended over the keyboard. 'Address in Ischia?'

'I don't have one,' said Allie.

He said it again, patiently. 'Where do you stay?'

'I only just arrived. I need to find a hotel.'

The men looked at each other. There were five of them surrounding her now, all on her case. Ischia wasn't like Nice, a city that heaved with foolish tourists and sly pickpockets: it was old-fashioned and overlooked, always playing second fiddle to Capri, its more glamorous neighbour. Nevertheless, it suffered the same problems as the rest of the continent: poverty, unemployment, bored teenagers, drugs. Her assailant was a drug addict, they decided, probably come over from Naples to prey on the tourists. Truth to tell, she was lucky to be alive. Unmolested. They did their best to clean up the streets, make arrests. *Droghe!* Where would it all end?

Allie was wary of giving them too much information. She'd already been found in possession of a stolen whistle and although this had become a joke and the cause of much banter, Helena's experience hung over her like a warning.

'You are just now arrived? You come for day trip? You have address in Naples, *forse*?'

'I – I don't remember it. Anyway, I checked out.'

She couldn't let them put her on the ferry, even if it sailed this late, which she doubted. She needed her stuff. She'd have to collect it tomorrow from the Baldini villa, but she couldn't spend another night there. Nor could she seek Bobby out at the club: in such a state she wouldn't get through the door. If she had been thinking clearly, she might have realized they'd be worried about her. Max might even (too late) be scouring the streets. But she was thinking only of how easily she could fade away. Let them write her off as an erratic visitor. Bobby and his friends didn't *know* her; they had no loyalty to her. They'd been very kind. They'd probably be very kind to a lost puppy. She'd been attacked on the street and robbed of her mobile. It could have been a lot worse. She had cash and cards. She could book a room and review her options in the morning.

'I don't suppose the tourist office is open?' she said.

They laughed. 'At this hour!'

'It's like I've been trying to tell you. I need to find somewhere to stay.'

The tall, gaunt officer replaced an old piece of gum with a fresh one; his jaw rotated as he perused her. Allie read the message in his eyes and the expressions of the rest: no one was likely to want to take her in her present state, and with no luggage.

The men conferred, massaging their chins and tugging their earlobes. She could see the butt of a gun carelessly displayed in a holster. Then the one with the burnished acorn skull, whose English was the most adept, said, 'We have a colleague who runs with his wife an *agriturismo*. Is possible they have a room.'

'Hey, that would be fantastic. *Favoloso! Grazie mille.*'

People like to help, Allie had learned, and it was a truth she found useful. It was surprising how far gratitude could carry you if you played it right: just don't let anyone know how desperate you really are. She caught some of the words the officer used during his call. She heard his apologies for the late hour, for the disturbance; she heard herself being described as a *signorina con un piccolo problema*. Then she saw him smile and exchange a couple of insults before he replaced the receiver. '*Tutto a posto.*' He beamed, latching his fingers together.

Probably, she thought as she was ushered with some delicacy back into the patrol car, they were relieved to finish their form and get her signature. Plus it had been a diversion for them on an uneventful shift. Whereas her own evening had been more like an out-of-body experience, her mind in flight from information it couldn't accept. The girl whose hands had clawed suddenly at Bobby's sleeve and cried, 'You're joking!' seemed very distant from the girl lying in the gutter, emptying her lungs and kicking a man in the balls.

'*Agriturismi* can be hard to find,' said her driver, his headlights sweeping the dark tarmac. 'But our colleague's is one we know well.'

In the back seat Allie was picturing another, future scene. She could see herself in conversation with her mother, saying, 'You know, the police were really good to me on Ischia when I got mugged. They even went out of their way to find me a place to stay.' And Helena rising from her chair, shaking her head in disbelief, replying: 'Only you, Allegra, could sleep with your half-brother and get yourself robbed and still be grateful for small mercies. How do you do it, darling?'

Allie groaned inwardly. For the moment though, some small comforts awaited. They were approaching the long, low silhouette of a farmhouse and converted outbuildings. Cypresses lined the drive, the aroma of pine resin was soothing in the warm night. A golden glow seeped around the edges of the shutters and through the welcoming open door.

The driver got out, cupped his hands around his mouth. 'Ciao, Enzo! Cristina! *Siamo arrivati.*'

A woman stood in the porch and waved a greeting. A middle-aged man – the first thing Allie noticed about him was his furry black moustache – came out to carry her non-existent suitcase.

'*Senza bagagli,*' said the *carabiniere* with an expressive shrug.

Something to steady the nerves, thought Allie, that's what I really need. A calming smoke or a couple of Valium. Failing that, if they ask, I'll say, *Oh please, a bath would be absolute bliss.*

PART FOUR

FATTORIA LA CASTAGNA

19

Helena opened the door of her daughter's house to a man in police uniform. She was wearing spiky earrings, a green low-necked top and cream wide-leg trousers. He was wearing an old-fashioned helmet strapped beneath his chin and a reproving frown.

'You bastard!' she said.

The man clumped over the threshold in his heavy black shoes. He picked her up in his arms and staggered a little. 'Don't struggle or I'll drop you. Hold on.' He nudged the sitting-room door open with his foot. 'I'm not going to be able to manage the stairs, but this will be better anyway. Now, shhh. Don't say a word.'

He laid her out on the beaten-up old couch and closed the curtains. The room had a bleak, impermanent feel as if it were between lets – no pictures gave life to the walls, no personal possessions animated the alcove shelving – but the sun dipping through the red chenille gave it a rosy glow like a bordello.

'I had a problem with the music,' he said, crossing to the CD player. 'I couldn't decide what would suit you best. In the end . . .' – he took a disc from his pocket and slotted it into the machine – '. . . I decided to go for the obvious.'

The first bars of 'Every Breath You Take' murmured in the corner of the room, strengthening as he increased the volume.

'I was never a Sting fan,' said Helena.

'Be quiet! You mustn't interrupt or you'll spoil the act.'

She propped herself against the under-stuffed cushions and turned her head towards him. First he shuffled out of his shoes. Then he took off the plastic helmet and spun it on his finger. With a pious show of reverence he rested it at a jaunty angle on the mantel clock. To the lyrics of the first verse he began to unbutton his tunic. He kept his movements steady, unhurried, in time with the beat. His mouth didn't quiver, his eyes were impassive. He shrugged the tunic suggestively from his shoulders and whirled it around his torso before tossing it to the ground. By degrees he loosened his tie, pulling the longer end through the knot in a teasing motion. Starting at the collar he undid the buttons on his shirt, pausing as each one slipped its moorings and displayed another couple of inches of bare flesh. He unfastened his cuffs, let the shirt slither down his back and repeated the cape-whirling. As the melody eddied around him, he released the buckle on his belt.

Helena was choking on suppressed laughter. 'The song will be finished before you are.'

He ignored her, tugged the belt from his trouser loops and slowly drew down the zip of his fly. The final chorus hissed its warning into the room. He eased the trousers over his hips and let them fall.

'At this point,' he said. 'They'd all be purple with giggles and my dick would be shrivelled like a peanut shell so naturally I'd keep my underpants on. However, madam, for you alone, I'll make an exception.' He discarded the striped boxer shorts, knelt beside the sofa and kissed her.

She ran her hand down the sturdy plane of his back. His flesh felt firm but tender, like fillet steak, and the scent of him was strong and salty like anchovies. 'I can't believe you really did this,' she said.

'What?' said Simon. 'Just now. Or before?'

'Either. Both.'

'Needs must. When I was a poor student it was a way of making easy money. If you could put up with the hen humour.'

'Evidently you could.'

'It got to me in the end, though. I never imagined I'd be able to fit into the costume. It was a bit tight around the waist but, hey, not bad after sixteen years, wouldn't you say?'

'Not bad at all.'

As he tried to clamber on top of her the springs creaked and the cushions slithered sideways. The music was still playing but they no longer heard it. Helena held his face between her hands. 'This isn't going to work,' she said. 'It's too uncomfortable and neither of us is a teenager any more.'

'Then take me upstairs, girl.' He gave a parody growl. 'Dammit, just take me. Anyway, anywhere you want me.'

'Give me a minute,' said Helena, as they both got unsteadily to their feet. She moved the standard lamp into the bay and parted the red curtains a few inches so it could be seen. Then she replaced its shade with the imitation policeman's helmet. 'Honestly, Simon, you make me feel as if I'm playing a part in a P. G. Wodehouse novel.'

He feigned dismay. 'Sure you don't mean D. H. Lawrence?'

He ran ahead of her up the stairs, naked and exuberant. Helena followed him into her old bedroom – the bedroom where she'd lost her virginity so many years before to the seventeen-year-old schoolboy who'd been brave enough to scale the trellis to her balcony and claim it. Like Romeo and Juliet, he'd said, being romantically inclined. Helena recalled only a sense of bitter disillusion. In the decades since, she had made love in this room on two occasions. Both last week. Both with Simon. In the pub, after their meeting in Lee's, he had talked her into a date. After their banquet in Chinatown he'd got into her cab (although he only lived up the hill) and insisted on accompanying her home.

She hadn't intended to stay so long in Allie's house, but when a couple of new commissions were offered along with studio space, she'd collected some more belongings and made the temporary move. It was definitely temporary: her clothes were hanging from the picture rail, heaped on to surfaces, tumbled in two suitcases. And she missed the things she'd left behind in Oxford in oversight: her favourite panama, her clock radio, decent bath towels, nail scissors. But at least now she had the car with her and was able to take more rubbish to the tip, things that would have no meaning for Allie. In the loft she'd found bundles of rotted tablecloths, for instance, old school books and an Olivetti typewriter in a dusty case. She and Liddy had once written savage sketches mocking their teachers on the typewriter – or rather, Helena had written the savage bits; Liddy had moderated the language and corrected the spelling with Tippex.

'There's no point,' she'd said to Simon as he helped her pile the rubbish into her boot, 'in hanging on to the past.'

'That's why you fascinate me, Helena Ashbourne. For a conservator, you're a mass of contradictions.'

'Work's different. It's the challenge of fitting pieces together, finding the key. The objects themselves just prove how ephemeral we all are. It isn't about sentiment.'

'You're recreating what's dead and buried.'

'But from a stranger's past. Not mine. That's what they say about shrinks, isn't it, they treat everybody's hang-ups but their own?'

'Hang-ups?' he'd said. 'Like what?'

'Uniforms,' she'd said instantly.

'School uniforms?'

'All sorts. Nurses, traffic wardens, policemen, squaddies . . .'

'I'm sure a shrink would have something to say about that.'

'I'm sure you're right.'

He had manoeuvred her to the bed in the centre of the room and was lifting her top over her head. Through the gauzy green fabric she could see the blunt shape of his features, but not his expression. 'It's caught in my earring,' she said, raising her hands to disentangle herself. He left the task to her and concentrating on freeing her breasts from her bra, his tongue lapping at a nipple. As she finally stripped off her top he gravitated to her lower half. He tipped her on to the bed, sliding off her trousers and briefs with one easy movement, massaging her insteps with his thumbs and stretching her legs into a V shape, tucking them under his armpits.

'I've been thinking about this all day,' he said.

She raised her hips and locked her legs behind his back, bringing him closer. 'You were supposed to ring me, to tell me what time you were coming.'

'I wanted to give you a treat, to turn you on.'

He must know he'd succeeded. She toyed with the shaft of his penis, letting it buck and butt against her palm, and then guided it in the right direction, savouring the sensation of it pulsing inside her. It wasn't what she'd expected when she'd come back to Liverpool: to take up so quickly with a man who was not only younger, but – allegedly – unattached. She'd been fourteen years with Ian and although their parting was amicable she was in no rush for more. But Simon had the advantage of novelty and he brought her that essential ingredient in any romantic diversion: fun.

Afterwards, when he lay with his head against her heartbeat, she said, 'You're good at that.'

'What?' he murmured. 'Fornication?'

'Surprises.'

'Hey, did you really like it? The whole striptease thing? Naff as *The Full Monty*? I did wonder whether it might be going too far, but when I found the outfit I couldn't resist.'

'I'm amazed you kept it.'

'Not on purpose. It was in a box, under a heap of books I didn't know whether I might need again.'

'I suppose you found it amusing: criminologist dressing up as police constable. How did the hens react?'

'With staggering predictability.' He moved his hand over her abdomen and let it rest between her legs. 'With one exception. Poor girl thought I was going to arrest her. Burst into tears and was inconsolable. I went through the whole stripping lark to show her I wasn't for real but she sobbed throughout.'

Helena felt her stomach contract. 'Does anyone ever dredge it up? Your murky fanny-baiting past?'

'I'll admit it's undignified,' he said. 'But no one actually cares. They just think you're a bit of a lad. I know it's different for women. You ever been a lap dancer?'

'Too old.'

'Bollocks.' He pulled her into his arms. 'So you didn't find it too crass, the whole routine?'

'I loved the routine,' said Helena. 'In fact, I enjoyed it so much I'd like you to do it again – and piss into the helmet for good measure.'

'*What* into the helmet?'

'Urinate. It's plastic, isn't it?'

'Right,' he said. 'I will if you will.'

She sat up. 'I need a drink first.' She surveyed the welter of crumpled sheets and discarded clothes, as if a handy bottle of wine might be bobbing amid the debris.

Simon stroked the curve of her cheek. 'I've a confession to make.'

'What?'

'I know we were thinking of going out for a meal but, idiot that I am, I have no other clothes with me. Driving round to you was okay, but I cannot saunter the streets of Waterloo in cheap fancy dress. It will ruin my image.'

'Oh.'

'Haven't you got something that might fit me?'

'Certainly not!'

'It wasn't an insult. You have terrifically long legs.'

'I wasn't insulted.' She bit her lip. 'But I had a bad experience once, ages ago, with a boyfriend who borrowed my clothes. It wasn't an identity crisis I could handle at the time.' She could see his hair tumbled around the puffed sleeves of a cotton blouse. 'Don't ask,' she said. 'You don't want to know.'

He swung his feet to the floor. 'Then I guess I'll have to wear a towel as a loincloth. With your permission?'

She nodded. 'Anyway, there's no need to go out. I have booze downstairs and maybe some eggs or something, as long as you're not very hungry.'

With brimming wineglasses, they swayed around the kitchen, obstructing each other's efforts to make toast and scramble eggs. The rest of The Police's greatest hits serenaded them down the hallway. Helena had borrowed Allie's new dressing gown and her breast kept poking past its lapel. Simon's towel kept loosening itself from his hips. He was kissing the back of her neck when the bread caught fire and the telephone rang.

'Don't answer it,' he said.

She was busy flapping away the smoke with a dishcloth. He probed the interior of the toaster with two forks.

'Don't electrocute yourself.'

He laid down the forks and some black pieces of charcoal. 'Salvage complete. Dare we try again? Or is it knackered, d'you think?'

'I hope not. It's brand new.' The ringing stopped. 'I can't imagine who it would have been,' she said. 'Hardly anyone uses the landline.'

Half an hour and half a bottle later they were back in the bedroom with a tray containing two plates of scrambled egg and a bowl of bananas sliced into yoghurt, for which Simon had all kinds of ideas. When they had cleared their plates and emptied the bottle, Helena disrobed and disposed herself once more on the bed. Spread-eagled, she permitted him to decorate her with the banana slices and a creamy trail of natural yoghurt. When the phone rang for the second time she was in no position to respond; she could not have moved if she'd wanted to, tormented by a thousand licks. The CD had long since ended; in the distance was the faint grumble of a train; in contrast, the ringing was loud and persistent. She looked down at the top of Simon's head where the crown was thinning – and she welcomed his dedication. A great wave of released tension washed over her, a pleasant surfeit of repeating ripples. By the time they ceased so had the telephone.

'I have to bath now,' she said. 'Or I'll ferment.'

He followed her down the landing. 'I'll join you.'

'I'm not sure there's room for two. It's a poky little tub.'

'There's always room for two. There's also the matter of our business with the helmet. Shall I fetch it?'

'No, leave it!' she ordered, as the water trickled, then spurted from the taps and gathered force. 'I was only joking.'

'Helena, you disappoint me.'

'Your trouble,' she said, testing the temperature, 'is you spend too much time clowning around with your students. I'm way past all that now.'

He let her get into the bath first, then sloshed in behind her. 'I'm not interested in callow students,' he said. 'I've always preferred older women.'

'It's five years, Simon! I'm not your granny.'

He laughed and picked up the cake of soap. His hands skimmed over her skin, tiny translucent bubbles formed and exploded. She squirmed in an effort to avoid his tickling.

'Keep still now. Raise your leg.'

He was soaping the back of her calf when the ringing started again. She cocked her head to listen. 'I don't believe it! What's up with that goddam phone?'

'Someone must be very eager to get hold of you.'

'But there's nobody . . . Oh my God! Perhaps it's Allie. Perhaps something's happened.' She leapt up and nearly lost her balance. Water splashed over the sides and on to the cork tiles.

'Whoa there,' he said, steadying her. 'Wouldn't she be more likely to ring your mobile?'

'I don't know. I'll have to check.' She wrapped herself in Allie's robe again and went downstairs to dial call-back, but the number was withheld. In her bedroom, after taking some time to unearth her mobile, she scrolled through recent calls and texts: none new, none from Allie.

Simon joined her. 'It's obviously a wrong number.'

'I suppose so, but if it happens again you mustn't stop me answering it.' She felt agitated for no clear reason. She crossed to the window and peered out. 'Switch off the light. I think someone's outside.'

'What?' But he obeyed and came to stand beside her. Among the overgrown shrubs in the front garden there was distinct and sometimes violent movement. 'It's only a dog,' he said.

'Are you sure?'

'Quite sure. A person would be twice the height.'

'Not if they were crawling through undergrowth.'

'Look, you can see its tail.'

The dog bounded to the gate, then turned and headed back towards the house. They lost sight of it as it entered the open porch but they could hear claws skittering at the door.

'Bloody hell!' exclaimed Helena.

'Do you want me to chase it off?'

'No, I will.' She pushed her feet into an old pair of espadrilles. 'And I shall enjoy it.'

Liddy's first thought, when she saw the shape of the helmet in Helena's window, was that the police were already there. She was impressed by the speed at which news travelled, until she realized she was looking not at the body of a person but at some kind of pole with one of Helena's more eccentric hats on top. As she opened the car door she was knocked sideways by Rolo's sprint for freedom. She hadn't intended to bring him with her, but Rolo had a way of circumventing other people's plans. She'd thought he might try and vault the railings into the formal gardens or bound over to the grassy foreshore, sniffing out chip papers. She'd forgotten his attachment to Allie or his likely recognition of her house.

The evening sky wore a faint hue, a silky lilac she associated with summer. Street lamps cast a butterscotch glow. Rolo wriggled through the partly open gate and started ferreting about in the bushes. Liddy had been relieved in a way when the phone rang into a void. She didn't relish explaining why Allie had gone to Ischia and whether she might have met with an accident there. She had written a brief note outlining the situation and driven over to drop it off, duty discharged. What Helena chose to do next was her own affair.

She assumed Helena was out and the police helmet a bizarre decoy. Then her eye travelled up to the bedroom she'd known so well in her teenage years and she saw the faint light abruptly extinguished. Keeping close to the warm protective bulk of her car, she hissed: 'Come here Rolo! Here boy. Now!' He barked joyfully from the porch. With his lead in one hand and a slim ivory envelope in the other, she entered the front garden. In one quick manoeuvre she could post her note, clip on the lead and tear him away. A minute was all she needed.

She had only taken a couple of steps along the path when the door opened. An exposed bulb swung in the hallway illuminating the tall female figure in her rich aubergine gown. For a split second she thought Allie had miraculously flown home. Then the figure spoke: 'Beat it!' she shouted. 'What the fuck d'you think you're doing, you fucking tramp?'

She's been drinking, thought Liddy, as Helena flapped her hands and tried to chase Rolo away. He thought this a marvellous game and ran rings around her. She lunged a couple of times for his collar and failed. Liddy bent forward and succeeded. 'He didn't mean any harm,' she said. 'He's playful, that's all.'

Helena bunched her gaping lapels together in her fist. Her face was damp and wild and there was no colour in it. The garden with its phlox and its peeling silver birch, the parked cars, the street itself – all were monochrome. 'Liddy? Is it you?'

'Yes.' That gesture of Helena's: tilting her head to one side, sweeping her hair around the back of her neck so her ear was exposed, was so immediately familiar it was like hurtling back in time.

'Is that your dog?'

'Yes.'

'What the hell does he think he's doing?'

'I think he might be looking for Allie.'

'Oh.' Helena gazed down at her feet in the middle of what had once been a flower bed and moved gingerly on to the path. Her canvas espadrilles were rimmed with moisture from the dank weeds. 'I'm not dressed for this,' she muttered, heading back to the porch.

'Helena?'

'What?'

'I need to speak to you.'

Helena folded her arms. Lack of make-up gave her face an aura of youth and uncertainty. 'This isn't really a good time. It's quite late and . . .'

'I'm sorry about Rolo,' said Liddy. 'I'm sorry he disturbed you. He wasn't meant to come but he sneaked into the car before I could stop him. We're not out walking the block for a last pee before bed. I've been trying to ring you.'

'Oh . . .' Her eyes cleared, danced a little. 'It was you.'

'It's quite urgent or I wouldn't have bothered you.'

'Urgent?'

'It's about Allie.'

She caught it at once, the snap in Helena's features, the sudden tension in her stance, as if she were shielding herself behind toughened glass. This is what it's like if you have a child, thought Liddy. Love on another plane.

'Has something happened to her?'

'I don't know.'

'You must know something or you wouldn't be here.' She'd retreated to the threshold. Liddy hesitated, Rolo's lead wrapped around her hand like a bandage. 'Oh for God's sake,' said Helena. 'Come in.'

So after more than twenty years they were face to face again: Liddy and the person whose life she messed up. They were standing, inches apart, at the table where they'd cribbed each other's homework and customized their clothes on Mrs Ashbourne's sewing machine, where they'd shared their hopes and fantasies and listed the qualities of the men they were looking for. And Helena didn't seem any different: still fiery, still unpredictable, still beautiful in an untamed way.

A smell of burning permeated the kitchen. A pan was plunged into soapy water in the sink. Flaccid banana peel lay on the counter top, along with a salt and pepper mill, a Worcester sauce bottle, a butter knife freckled with toast crumbs, a corkscrew. Liddy was convinced she could hear movement elsewhere in the house, the pad of bare feet, heavy male breathing. She was nonplussed when a police officer entered the room.

'Everything okay?' he said to Helena.

Liddy's mind lost its focus. Could Allie's faraway dilemma possibly have been conveyed by satellite to the local nick?

'Simon, this is Liddy,' said Helena. 'We used to know each other.'

It was an accurate statement, but carried a sting in the tail: the unspoken message that nothing would change, affection would not be resumed.

'Is it your dog then?' said Simon.

'He hasn't done any damage,' she said defensively and wondered why he laughed.

'Shut up!' said Helena in a tone both ferocious and tender, so that Liddy understood at once they were lovers. She found this surprising from the woman who had such a distrust of authority, but he didn't look like a typical member of the force: there was something slapdash and random about his attire.

'So tell me, what's up with Allie?'

'I'm not really sure. She rang me and then we were cut off.'

'It's not exactly normal,' mused Helena, 'to go rushing round to someone's house in the middle of the night just because you lost telephone contact.'

'It was the *way* it happened. We were speaking and I heard her mumble something but when I asked her to repeat it because the line was poor, there were various background noises and then silence.'

'What does that mean? Various background noises? Music? Traffic? A Tannoy? Was she in a restaurant, or a taxi? Waiting at the station?'

'I don't know where. But she sounded upset and I thought I heard a scuffle and then a scream. I tried ringing back right away, but her phone was off. I'm here, Helena, because I'm afraid she might be in danger.'

There was the soft plop of a cork being pulled. A bottle appeared on the table along with three glasses. The man called Simon drew out a chair for Helena and guided her into it. He passed her a glass of Merlot and filled two others.

'I'm driving,' said Liddy, nervous that she'd already exceeded the limit at home. She wouldn't have taken the car in the first place, she'd assured herself, if she hadn't been so concerned. 'And I didn't think you were supposed to drink on duty.'

'Touché.' He nodded. 'Too right. But I'm not on duty.'

'You heard Allie scream?' said Helena.

'Well, I'm not absolutely certain . . . it was more of a cry of alarm. It was hard to work out what was going on.'

'How well do you know my daughter?'

'Well, I . . . didn't she tell you? We met, um, some weeks ago and until she went away she walked Rolo for me. Every day. I think, you know, she liked the routine of it, in between all the other things she was trying to set up. He became very fond of her, got wildly excited when he saw her. I'm afraid that's why he was rampaging around your garden.'

'That doesn't explain to me,' said Helena, 'why she would ring you up from wherever she and her friends are now.'

'Italy. She's in Italy. Apparently the other girls went east but she stayed on.'

Helena was frowning, twirling the stem of her wineglass. 'Why then?'

'Why did she ring me?'

'Jesus, Liddy, why do you need to have everything spelt out for you, etched in four-foot-high letters?' The flash of anger was almost welcome; at least she was no longer being treated with the cold formality of a stranger. 'What's so special about your relationship with Allie that she feels such an overwhelming need to touch base?'

'She's on Ischia.'

'She's *where*?'

Simon showed surprise at the shock in her voice. He doesn't know about any of this, thought Liddy. But then, who does? Not even Allie. Since meeting the girl she'd spent hours agonizing over her right to tell, and Allie's right to know, the truth. Helena pretending none of it had happened was neither healthy nor honest.

'She didn't know anything,' she said. 'You'd never told her.'

'I just didn't go into detail,' Helena said with mute rage.

'I mean, I don't blame you for wanting to put it behind you.'

'Just as I don't blame you for setting the charabanc in motion?'

Simon's chair squeaked as he scraped it away from the table. 'I get the impression three's a crowd here,' he said. 'I can call a cab and pick up my car in the morning.'

'No,' said Helena, not moving her eyes from Liddy's face. 'We're used to threesomes.'

Liddy knew she was blushing, that every reminder of Jake – even one so tangential – could colour her responses.

'Anyway, we're off the point,' Helena continued. 'What's Allie doing on Ischia and why did she ring you?'

'She met Bobo Baldini.'

'She what? Jesus, Mary and Joseph! Bobo was a little terror,' she said to Simon, who'd come to stand beside her with his hand on her shoulder, his polyester policeman's jacket hanging open. 'I can't imagine him as an adult.'

It was a question Liddy often asked herself. At what point did you achieve adulthood? Was it passing your driving test or starting your first job? Buying a property or taking charge of a hefty budget? Being the boss of two, four, or twenty people? She'd always supposed that it happened when you became a parent, that until you'd produced another generation you were in essence still juvenile. Which was patently ridiculous – you only had to look at half the feckless youth of the neighbourhood. You only had to look at Helena, for Christ's sake, who, while her daughter was in danger, was shagging some weird bloke in fancy dress.

'Bobo,' she repeated, 'and Mimmo too.'

Helena had been resting her chin on her hands; they collapsed to the table top as her elbows gave way. The Merlot gave a giddy jump in its glass. Rolo whined in the porch. She half turned so she was looking up into Simon's face, speaking with care as if she were assessing the weight of each word. 'Many years ago, Liddy and I were nannies to two little boys. My daughter appears to have met them by coincidence. Incredible, wouldn't you say?'

'He doesn't call himself Mimmo any more,' said Liddy. 'That's what she was ringing to ask me. I explained that his real name was Massimo, but we didn't get any further because of . . . whatever happened next.'

'Is this what we have to deal with?' asked Simon. 'What happened next? Do you know how to get in touch with anybody out there?'

'We could try the Baldinis' number,' said Liddy. 'The villa would have a landline. But at this stage I thought it best if Helena was the one to investigate. I didn't think it was my place . . .'

'So it's not your place to do anything now you've thrown the poor girl to the wolves, but it was when you thought you could mess with her head?' Helena rubbed her eyes and pinched the bridge of her nose as if she were trying to wake from a bad dream. 'And how do you know the Baldinis still own their villa? She could have met Mimmo and Bobo in a club or something. It wouldn't be any more outlandish than what you've told me so far.'

'Because I . . . um . . . gave her the address.'

'What on earth did you do that for?'

'Well, I didn't think they'd actually *be* there. But Allie was interested and, after all, everyone has a right to know their origins.'

'Ischia was a blip,' said Helena, 'in Allegra's origins.'

'But Fabrizio –'

'*What* exactly have you told her about Fabrizio?'

'Well . . . hardly anything,' said Liddy in desperation.

'You know what I think? It's *your* road trip you've sent my daughter on. Not hers. Not mine. What are you looking for, Liddy? A chance to turn back the clock?'

'This is not about me,' Liddy insisted. Her hand rose to her collar to check her top button. At least she was fully clothed, contained. She didn't have bits of her escaping all over the place like Helena. 'Please can't we be civilized and sensible about this? I came because Allie seemed distressed about Mimmo. I was worried when I couldn't get back in contact with her and I thought you should know.'

'I'm a thousand miles away. What the hell can I do?' After a moment's thought, she said, 'Simon can you fetch my phone from upstairs? I could try Jess or Nita.'

'Won't they be a thousand miles away, too?'

'I don't believe this. Allie always travels in a gang. I can't imagine why she didn't stay with them.'

'Maybe they fell out?' Helena gave him a sharp look. He went on, 'She'll get in touch again, won't she? From a call-box or something. And if she doesn't . . . well . . . would you consider flying over there?'

'I couldn't possibly do that,' Helena said. 'I don't fly.'

Liddy remembered Allie had told her something of the sort. Simon looked puzzled: there was plainly a lot about Helena he didn't know. Liddy said, 'Look, if there's anything I can do. I mean, I can't just drop everything, but we're in down time at the moment, so with a bit of notice I'd be happy to –'

'Happy to what? Ride a white horse to her rescue? You're acting like you think she's been kidnapped.'

Liddy was surprised she could spit the word out so easily. 'No, of course not . . .'

'She can look after herself. That's the one thing I made sure of, right from the beginning. I may have been a crap parent, but I was the only parent and she needed to learn independence. She overcame a whole load of hurdles and I'm proud of her for it, but I wasn't standing by to wipe her nose every five minutes.'

'Didn't Fabrizio . . . ?'

'What?'

'Help you out at all?'

Helena's expressive mouth stretched into a sneer. 'He helped me out of jail. He wasn't so keen on the hospital visits, he's a bit squeamish.' She placed her hand over Simon's, which had tightened on her shoulder. 'My friend here is a criminologist. Now that he knows my dark secret, I daresay he can come up with a theory to account for such deviant behaviour.'

How the hell am I supposed to know where it's safe to tread? wondered Liddy. 'Honestly,' she said to Simon, 'she's exaggerating. Nothing deviant at all. It was more a question of being in the wrong place at the wrong time.' When Helena didn't elaborate she ploughed on: 'Why didn't you write to me? You never answered any of my letters. I hadn't a clue what was going on or what happened after Naples. I didn't know about Allie or anything. Was it all hushed up? Maybe it was my fault for not trying harder to find out, but I was scared of . . . I don't know, making things worse? Scared and ashamed. I said I was sorry at the time, didn't I, and I'll say it again. I'm sorry for all that you went through and I'm sorry you wouldn't let me share any of it. It must have been really tough.' There, she hadn't lost her nerve, she'd done it: a full and frank apology.

'I won't pretend,' said Helena. 'That it wasn't incredibly stressful. The birth, Allie's injury. Everything.' She sighed. 'And then trying to settle in England again and earn a living, that whole working mother conundrum. You must know how it is.'

'No,' said Liddy, pushing aside her untouched wineglass. 'Actually I don't. I . . . I haven't got any children.'

The central lamp hung low from the ceiling and cast a cone of light over the table. Simon moved away from its beam and said, 'Coffee or cocoa?'

Helena and Liddy's eyes met. For a second they were fifteen again, squealing 'cocoa' in unison. Then they fell silent and shifted in their seats. He blundered around, opening cupboard doors, humming under his breath. Eventually he found a canister of drinking chocolate.

Who would have imagined a couple of heaped spoonfuls of brown dust could have this effect? The hot liquid felt sludgy against Liddy's teeth and tasted excessively sweet, but there was comfort in it too. She risked a smile. 'Allie is lovely. You must be very proud of her.'

'Thanks. Yes, I am.'

Liddy swallowed. 'When I mentioned the Baldinis' landline . . . I mean, I already checked the number with international directory enquiries. It's only the prefix that's changed.' She rescued the envelope she'd stuffed into her pocket – she hadn't liked to take off her coat without an invitation – and passed it to Helena. 'It might set your mind at rest if you could get hold of her.'

Helena accepted the envelope, rose and left the room without speaking. Simon tapped his fingers ruminatively against his chin.

Liddy sipped her cocoa. 'Have you known her long?' she asked, to break the awkward silence.

'Well, now . . .' He let out a breath. 'Long enough to find her intriguing, shall we say. An impression you've certainly reinforced.'

'I'm so sorry I interrupted your evening. Only it's difficult to know what to do for the best when things happen at a distance and you've no ability to control them. Your imagination goes into overdrive, doesn't it, picturing –'

Simon's eyes travelled over her shoulder and she turned to see Helena in the doorway, twisting the cord of Allie's dressing gown. 'Picturing what exactly?'

Liddy marvelled that she used to regard her as a Boudicca-type, charging about, trampling over people – whereas, in fact, beneath that challenging exterior, she was as vulnerable as anybody else. 'I don't know. I mean, I hadn't really . . . Weren't you able to get through?'

'No,' said Helena. 'There doesn't seem to be anyone in. Any idea where we go from here?'

20

For the first time since leaving home, Allie woke alone. For once she wasn't in a railway carriage or a backpackers' dormitory; she was in a room with white-washed walls and terracotta tiles, floating amid clouds of feather pillows and quilt. Wrought-iron curlicues, like music notation, flourished at either end of the high double bedstead. Swathes of white muslin were suspended above her from a coronet, like a bridal veil or an unusually decorative mosquito net. Morning light was poking through the shutters, picking out the bright, jewelled colours of the rug and the cushions on the ottoman. The tranquillity of her surroundings was unbroken by any mechanical noise; there was only the whirr of doves' wings and the soft throaty clucks of chickens.

She'd been worried when she'd first hobbled into the spacious reception hall of Fattoria La Castagna that she wouldn't be able to afford the rates. It was transparently the type of place where attention to detail and comfort were not skimped. After the warmth of their initial greeting, the owners, Enzo and Cristina, regarded her curiously as if they ran a refined and superior cattery and a mangy three-legged dog had turned up expecting a kennel. When she'd held out her passport Enzo hesitated before accepting and opening it. He then studied the pages for some time – so long, in fact, that she began to wonder if it had been defaced or tampered with.

'Allegra Ash-a-bourne,' he said in a heavy accent. She nodded. 'You are born in Roma?'

'Yes, but I'm a British citizen.'

'In nineteen hundred and eighty?'

She nodded again. Husband and wife exchanged glances. Cristina's small features nestled in the shiny dough of her face. She pursed her lips and muttered what sounded like '*Impossibile* . . .' Afterwards, Allie guessed they were debating which room to put her in, but at the time she feared they would refuse to take her. Her police escort had already left and she didn't know where else she could go. Then Enzo picked up a pen and recorded her details with painstaking precision and Cristina beckoned her up the stairs.

'Oh, it's lovely!' Allie had exclaimed when shown her magnificent bed and gleaming bathroom. 'But I don't know if it's too expensive for me. If you have another room that's smaller and cheaper?'

'We have not so many beds here,' said Cristina. 'This is not hotel. This is *un agriturismo*. Is different concept.'

At that point Allie's ankle gave way and she crashed on to a rustic elm chair. Cristina went in search of painkillers and there was no more discussion of cost.

With the help of the painkillers she'd slept remarkably well, despite her throbbing ankle, but when she threw off the sheets in the morning she saw it had swollen and turned blue. So here she found herself: unable to walk properly, trapped in a place well over her budget, with no spare clothes and no phone, on the run from Max who – actually, she didn't know for sure who he was . . . But she wouldn't be disheartened. You couldn't be for long in a spot as perfect as this. With her weight on her right foot she shuffled across the tiles and opened the shutters on to a canopy of fresh green vine leaves and the dark, enticing aroma of coffee.

The dining room was converted from a former barn and had a high, arched ceiling and glass double doors opening on to a terrace studded with lemon trees in pots. An immense refectory table ran down the centre. At one end sat a frail elderly couple; two families, one German, one Italian, occupied the middle section. They all looked around as Allie entered and, apart from one of the children, looked discreetly away again. She was aware that she didn't fit in: wrong nationality, wrong generation, unaccompanied, grimy (the dirt from the roadway embedded in her skirt and top had resisted superficial soaping). She sat at what she judged to be a civilized distance and smiled at the staring child, who was reprimanded by his father. A boy of about sixteen, the owners' son she presumed, brought her a cappuccino. A basket of fruit and a basket of pastries were pushed in her direction. The other breakfasts were all further advanced; one by one the guests crumpled napkins on to their plates and pushed aside glasses smeared with the residue of freshly squeezed oranges. Allie accepted the offer of a second coffee and waited for everyone else to leave. She didn't want to be watched limping out of the room.

She didn't expect, once she'd negotiated the corridor and reached the lobby of the farmhouse, to be tripped up by her own backpack. It was sloping against a carved oak chest and one of the straps flopped on the floor, as hazardous as any banana skin. Sprawling beside it, she recognized the dark stain at the bottom where her shampoo bottle had leaked, the frayed drawstring and scratched buckles. For a piece of luggage that had never left the continent of Europe it looked distinctly well-travelled.

The entrance hall was deserted, but through the open doorway she spotted the rear-end of a much-mocked Fiat Punto receding from sight. She couldn't chase after it; she'd never catch up. She felt a faint thud of disappointment that the person who'd delivered her possessions hadn't stayed to hear her thanks. Wincing, she gripped the chest for support, pulled herself upright and contemplated the difficulty of hoisting the bag to her room.

A shadow blocked the passage of the sun. Max was striding over the threshold in cut-off Levis and a black T-shirt, jingling his car keys. He looked exactly the same as he had done twenty-four hours ago. But then he *was* the same. It wasn't Max who had changed, but Allie's perception of him.

'I had to park out back,' he said. 'Can't upset the chicks.'

She cleared her throat with a self-conscious cough. 'Thanks for bringing my things over . . . How did you know where I was?'

'Well . . .' He slipped the keys into his pocket and leaned against the newel post at the foot of the staircase. A long woven runner, in vivid blues and greens, separated them like a swiftly flowing stream. 'How about we start with you? And what happened?'

'He – he came out of nowhere.'

'Who?'

'The guy who mugged me.'

'Yeah, they said you'd been attacked, but I don't get it. One minute you were with us, the next –' He snapped his fingers. 'Pouf! Vanished.'

'I don't know myself. I expect I fell behind because I was talking. You know how it is when you're on the phone. You hang back. I never saw him coming.'

'You didn't even call out.'

'Yes, I did. And I blew my whistle.'

'Your *whistle*?'

'You can't have heard it or you'd have come. I got the police instead and they were ages questioning me and then they brought me here.'

'Okay, so here's the part I don't follow. When they'd finished with you, why didn't you come on back to the villa?'

What was one more lie on top of all the rest? 'I didn't think you'd be there yet. I didn't think I'd be able to get indoors and I was so tired. I just wanted to sleep.' She paused, adding with emphasis, 'On my own. And that's what's been good here. It's so peaceful.' He was shaking his head so she raised her sprained foot. 'It's a bummer not being able to get in touch with anyone because I've lost all my contact numbers, but this is the thing that's bugging me right now.'

Max crossed the strip of aquamarine carpet and peered down at her ankle. 'You should get that fixed up,' he said. 'Have you asked Cristina for a bandage?'

He spoke the name with a casual intimacy that surprised her. 'Do you know her?'

'Her aunt Rosaria used to work for us when we came for vacation and she helped out from time to time.' He glanced around the hallway. 'I remember their wedding party here a couple of years before we left for the States. Enzo and Cristina had been courting for ages.'

'Oh, right. Well, no, I haven't asked for anything apart from pain-killers. I think they only took me in as a favour. I was going to check out this morning.'

'And head where?'

'Once I get back to Naples I can go anyplace I like. The railway network's my oyster.' She thrust forward her chin to accentuate her bullishness. 'I can rest up in train carriages for a whole week if I want to.'

He rolled his eyes. 'So you were planning to run out on us?'

'Of course not! I'd have to collect my stuff, wouldn't I? I'm really grateful to you for bringing it over.' She hoped she didn't sound insincere. 'I don't suppose you could carry it upstairs for me as well? Only I'd feel like a hundred per cent better if I could brush my teeth and change my clothes.'

'Sure.' He shouldered it in a light, supple gesture and followed her halting progress up to her room. He poked fun at the bed and enmeshed himself like a ghost in the muslin drapery. Allie locked herself in the bathroom. Sitting on the bidet she scrubbed her armpits and her teeth. She tugged on her crinkle-effect, no-need-to-iron sundress and tied back her hair. When she emerged Max had taken off his sandals and was lying in the middle of the bed, his curls a dark contrast to the frothy pillows. She sat on the ottoman.

'Here we go,' he said. 'I'm waiting for chapter two.'

'There's nothing to say really.' She picked at a loose thread on her dress. 'I didn't tell the police I'd been staying up at the villa because it wasn't any of their business. There was no point in dragging you and Bobby into this. I mean, you'd already been so good to me. Plus I needed . . . I needed some space.'

'Right . . .' said Max, clasping his hands behind his neck, drawing up one knee so that she was looking directly at the scar on his shin. Her brother's scar. Her *brother*: that was so weird. She'd grown up in shared houses, with a rota of lodgers and a tide of children ebbing and flowing, and as the only girl in the band she was used to fraternizing with men, but the idea of a constant presence, a sibling who shared your DNA – that was something else. Yesterday she'd been overwhelmed because obviously she shouldn't be fancying him, but now that initial reaction had passed. She was entering a new phase.

'So,' he continued. 'You figure that because a person's only spent, what, a couple of days with you, sharing your pool and your music and your drink and your dinner they owe you nothing. Not a cent?'

'I paid for the meal in the trattoria,' insisted Allie. 'Bobby tried to stop me but I made him take the money.'

'I'm not talking about the cash. I meant an explanation. I'm trying to say you don't just crash into some guy's life and then vanish like you're an alien from outer space. We were concerned, Allegra. Have you got that?'

'Gosh!' The vigour of his speech startled her. 'You were really worried about me? What did you do?'

'Do?' He looked sheepish. Allie's fantasy of a search party rampaging the streets by torchlight with vigilante coshes evaporated. 'We called the cops this morning.'

'Why?'

'Why? Because you hadn't come back. Because we hadn't heard from you. So, okay, maybe you're the type of girl who gets a better offer in between a restaurant and a club, but how would I know that? And because Bobby took a call from England.'

'Who was it?' asked Allie, though she knew it had to be Liddy. It couldn't possibly be anyone else.

'Whoever you were calling last night, I guess, whoever knew where you were staying. Anyhow, she raised the alarm so we contacted the cops. Soon as we said we wanted to report a missing Brit they told us you were here.'

A frisson of horror trickled along Allie's spine. 'You were going to report me missing? Oh, that's heavy. You thought I'd been snatched or murdered or something?'

'It happens,' said Max in a non-committal tone. 'It happened to me as a matter of fact.'

'What?' Her heart thumped against her ribs. Was she now going to hear the whole story? 'What do you mean?'

'When I was around three, here on vacation, I went missing, believed abducted.'

'No! Really?'

'In the seventies it wasn't so unusual. This country had a whole spate of kidnappings. Sometimes for money, sometimes for ideology. *Gli anni di piombo*. Did you ever hear of the Lead Years? It was a terrible period. There was a weak centre-right leadership and left-wing terrorist cells operating everywhere. The Getty kid was the most famous ransom bid. Bandits cut off his ear. Aldo Moro was the most atrocious political one – the Red Brigades assassinated him. And the islands made impenetrable hideouts, Sardinia and Sicily especially.'

'But why you? Was your dad really loaded?'

'Getty-style? No way.'

'Then why?'

He hopped off the bed and came over to her. He propped his arm against the window frame and rested his forehead on it, looking out. The sun had moved around the corner of the farmhouse but Allie could feel its benevolent warmth on her neck. The German family piled into their car in the courtyard and drove away through the cypresses. A bird of prey with a vast wingspan was poised in the sky as if it had been painted: a menacing blot on a bright blue canvas. Eagles nested on the craggy limestone peaks, she'd read. She imagined bandits hustling their blindfolded victims into the cold dark caves below.

'There she is!' he exclaimed, distracted by the sight of Cristina carrying a basket of eggs. He called out to her in Italian. She raised her head and nodded. 'I've asked her to bring you a crepe bandage,' he said. 'It should ease the discomfort. I'm surprised she hasn't offered you a poultice or whatever. These country types, you know, they have remedies for any condition you can name and quite a few you can't.'

'I don't think she likes me very much.'

'Why d'you say that?'

'Oh, you know. Like I'm not her class of guest. She did look at me a bit like I was something the cat brought in.'

'You're reading her wrong,' said Max with conviction. 'Okay, she's done well for herself, but that doesn't make her a snob . . . Still, I could be biased.' Leaning against the wall, his knees slightly bent, he tapped out a rhythm with both hands. Allie thought again how it might be to play together – it was what so many siblings did, fitting into a common groove, automatically in tune. After a few moments he said, 'She was the one who found me.'

'The one who found you what?'

'When I was a kid. My little adventure I was telling you about.'

She tried to remember if Liddy had mentioned the name Cristina, if this information would add another crucial part to the jigsaw. 'Have I got this right? Do you mean . . .?' Before she could say anything further, there came a knock at the door and Cristina entered. Although she was dumpy, she moved with such fleet-footed grace she could give the impression of being in two places at once. Within seconds she was cushioning Max's face between her palms and kissing him on both cheeks. She rattled through a succession of questions while he tried to keep up with the answers. 'She's asking about my mother,' he told Allie. 'And how everyone's been coping in the city since 9/11. *Senti,* Tina, we should speak English for your guest.'

'I have not seen this boy,' she explained with a dramatic heave of her tightly-packed bosom, a gold crucifix twinkling above its cleft, 'for five years, no, longer. And he is not a boy, not like my son. Massimo is a man.'

'I've been a grown man for close on a decade. Now did you check out your medicine cabinet?'

'I have here.' She pointed at the metal container she'd set down on a small table and sprang open the locks.

'Come on, Allie,' said Max. 'Let's see this ankle.'

She crossed her leg and held it stiffly forward, flinching as Cristina prodded the bruised soft tissue. 'This is painful, yes?'

'Yes.'

'You want to see doctor?'

'No. I'm sure it will be fine if I rest it. It's very kind of you to do this.'

'Ouf, for Massimo I run around like hen. Even when he is very small.'

'Yes, he was telling me about how you rescued him.'

'He has so many *incidenti* that boy. You remember, Mimmo, when you broke your arm and were so cross not to swim?'

'That was after we moved to the States. I'd been looking forward to coming for the summer – I missed this place so much – and on my second day I ballsed it up.'

Accident prone, thought Allie. Just like me. 'I meant before that,' she said to Cristina. 'The time he was kidnapped.'

Cristina was concentrating on tightening her bandage around heel and instep. Allie hoped she wasn't going to cut off her blood supply.

'Ah,' said Max. 'But here's the thing: I wasn't kidnapped.'

'You weren't? But you said –'

'No I didn't. They thought I'd been abducted but it was a false alarm.'

Cristina sat back on her haunches and decided her packaging could be improved. She unwound the length of crepe and started again. Looking down, Allie could see that her bushy hair was unevenly streaked with henna, but everything else about her was trim. And efficient. Yet rewrapping the ankle seemed to be giving her great difficulty.

'I don't understand,' said Allie. 'How long were you missing for?'

'About two days I think.'

'Not so long,' said Cristina.

'Long enough for parents to worry themselves crazy, I guess. Though to be frank, it's all a blur. I did this the same summer, falling from some rocks.' He bent to touch the narrow white scar. 'I've got a faint memory of being stitched up, otherwise it's as blank as the business of getting lost . . . well, apart from the candy.'

'Candy?' She pictured a stranger enticing him with a paper bag of jelly babies.

'We'd been having this treasure hunt on the beach, it was a fun thing for kids. And when we'd stuffed ourselves sick we had a game of hide-and-seek. That's when I went missing.'

Cristina reached for a large safety pin, clicking her tongue as though she were dealing with a troublesome hen.

Trying to make it sound like a throwaway remark, she said to Max, 'So, what, did you spend the night camping under a gooseberry bush?'

He grimaced. 'I was aiming to be really cunning – you know how smug kids get sometimes, thinking they've been really clever: ha ha, you won't find me now? I scrambled up to the top of the cliff, which was exactly what we'd been forbidden to do, by the way, and then, it seems, I climbed into the trunk of a car.'

'But isn't that how they operate?' said Allie. 'Bundling their victims into car boots?'

'Heck, I recognized the car! It belonged to Cristina's father. He used to drop Rosaria off in it all the time. I was a bit *pazzo* but I wasn't stupid. My problem was that I fell asleep and they drove off and no one knew I was there. *Vero*, Tina?'

'*Sì, è vero*,' she agreed.

'What happened when you woke up? Didn't you yell for help?'

'I guess I did but nobody heard me.'

'And they didn't open the car boot for two whole days?' The point of the pin jabbed into Allie's flesh and she yelped. Cristina apologized and tried again to dig through the layers of crepe.

'I was lucky there, if you can call it that. The catch was faulty – which was how I'd crept in in the first place. Only by the time I managed to get out it was dark and I was so disorientated I got myself lost all over again in the woods.'

'You must have been terrified!'

'I don't know. I don't remember.'

'What, none of it? I'd've thought an experience like that would be indelible.'

'Or I blanked it out.'

'Poor Mimmo,' said Cristina. 'When I find him, I want to make him well to return him to his mama, but he cannot speak and this is big problem.' Finally she pinned the bandage successfully.

'Now you walk,' she said.

Allie rose gingerly and took a step. She'd have to wear trainers, but the pain was bearable. 'Thank you, that's much better. Couldn't he tell you anything at all?'

'Not one word. We make him clean and warm. We feed him minestrone, sing songs. *Niente*.'

'Trauma allegedly,' said Max. 'It took me days to get my speech back.'

'But were you okay physically? You weren't suffering from exposure or –' she glanced down at her foot '– a sprain or some other injury?'

'Just a few cuts and bruises. It seems I took care of myself pretty well. The crisis was more of a psychological one.'

'Did it really screw you up? Did you have to see a shrink?'

He laughed. 'This was Italy, not the States. People believed in old-fashioned cures. Rosaria offered up a million prayers. My mother kept putting me to bed, so at least she'd know where I was.'

'And it worked? You must have had nightmares?'

'Well, yes. I didn't come through unscathed. For years I had to sleep with the light on.' He spoke casually, but Allie's mind flew back to the night they had spent together and his desire to see the stars, which she'd taken as a seduction ploy. Perhaps, instead, it was the vulnerability of a little boy, resurfacing. She longed to probe deeper, but it was like inching along a narrow precipice. She had to pretend she was only half-interested – even though there was something about the whole story that didn't ring quite true. The nub of it eluded her. She chewed at her thumbnail and then said, 'But hang on, if it was your own doing, getting yourself lost and carted off, why was there a ransom note?'

'Did I say that?'

'Yes, I'm sure you did.'

Cristina's face was sphinx-like. She appeared to be having trouble with her skirt, which had twisted on her hips when she'd knelt to attend to Allie. She fidgeted and wriggled until the zip was settled neatly centre-back. She flicked invisible specks of cotton wool from the fabric and replaced scissors and dressing in their compartments in the first aid box.

'Right, yeah, there *was* a note that put the wind up everyone. But it turned out to be a hoax. No doubt they figured Fabrizio was good for a few bucks so they'd try it on. People do some sick things sometimes.'

'*Scusi signorina*,' said Cristina. 'You will inform us before midday if you wish to stay another night?'

Allie had the impression she was anxious to get away. Already one hand was poised on the doorknob: she probably had a million other errands to run, she was entitled to resent being sidetracked by nursing duties. Although Cristina tried to be scrupulous about treating her visitors as house guests, Allie felt once again that she didn't fit the mould.

After she'd gone, Max said, 'Afraid I can't offer you a bed at the villa, because we're all going back to the mainland tonight. Working tomorrow morning.' He faked a sigh. 'But you don't want to sleep with me anyhow.'

'It's not that . . .'

'No, it's against your principles to encourage a guy to cheat. Fair enough. I shall respect them.'

Allie said ruefully, 'I hoped we could be friends.'

'Given our countries of residence, do you think that's practical?'

'Whereas if we fuck it makes all the difference?'

'It gives you a connection. And a pleasant memory.'

'Don't we already have a connection?'

She'd been limping from one side of the room to another to gauge how far she might be able to walk. As she finished speaking, she stumbled. He reached out to stop her falling and she grasped both his hands to steady herself. An idea came to her. 'Sing with me,' she said.

'Sin with you? Now you're talking.'

'No. Stop taking the piss.' But she didn't withdraw from his touch: holding hands was innocent, childlike. 'I'd like to see if we can harmonize together.'

'Like how exactly?'

He had a way of narrowing his eyes to convey scepticism, but in Allie's view it gave him the look of a thwarted goblin and she wouldn't let it deter her. She plunged in. 'Okay, so we've no instruments and I'm not going to choose a specific song. It's more of a warm-up exercise. It's very effective when you're in a group, getting everyone into the right frame of mind so you're on the same wavelength and in the same mood. Last summer holidays I ran these percussion workshops for kids and I always used to start this way.'

'Sounds kind of new age to me.'

'No excuses,' she insisted. 'Don't pretend you're an inhibited Englishman when we both know you're not. Just try it.'

Singing in harmony could be as intimate and as revealing as touch. Would he be uncomfortable exposing his vocal chords or would he follow her lead? She began to vibrate her tongue against the roof of her mouth and the notes emerged in a clear and swelling stream. She held his gaze and after a moment he unlocked his throat, at first a beat behind, but then catching up in a low and tender counterpoint. We can do it, she applauded, drawing him on, leading him through a vortex of sound so that the music they were making filled not only her ears and her brain but the whole room: springing from the canopied bed to the beamed ceiling, reverberating around the walls, flowing like honey through the open window. Nothing else could compete until Max broke the spell by laughing.

'Wow,' said Allie. 'That was good. You see, it works as long as you absolutely forget everything and follow the tune. Connection? Check. Pleasant memory? Check. We can do it! I suppose you think I'm crazy but I just had to . . . had to try it with you.' Max's expression, the slight upward curve of his lips, was enigmatic. 'Plus,' she added when he didn't say anything, 'it helps me forget the mess I'm in. Shit, I haven't even got a phone any more.'

He dug into his pocket. 'You can borrow my cell if there's someone you need to call.'

'Oh, Liddy!' she said, remembering. 'Did anyone ring her back after the police told you where I was?'

'Bobby was supposed to,' said Max, 'after I left with your stuff, but Giulia was giving him grief over something so I don't know.' He'd been turning the phone over in his palm, rubbing its surface as if a genie might appear. He held it out to her. 'Do you want to try?'

'Thanks.' She could only remember the home number, but she'd probably be in on a Sunday morning. She pictured the calm, spacious house, the background ticking of the clocks, Liddy with the Sunday newspaper on her lap and Rolo thrashing his tail at her feet. She imagined those perfect oval fingernails twirling a pencil like a baton over the crossword puzzle; the husband she'd never met would be reading the sports pages or brewing more coffee. Allie felt a sudden urgent nostalgia for a landscape she knew; no matter that the weather would be dismal and the sky grey. She pushed buttons and waited. 'Liddy? Hi, it's me.'

'Allie! Oh thank heavens.' The line was surprisingly clear, not a crackle of interference. 'I've been so worried about you. What happened? Are you all right?'

'My phone was snatched while I was talking to you, that's all.'

'All? *All*?' A high pitch of disbelief.

'Honestly, if I'd been at home I wouldn't have bothered reporting it. I wouldn't have reported it here either but the police got to me first and made me spend hours filling in their forms. I think they didn't have anything else to do. Anyway, I expect Bobby explained all that when you rang him.'

'I didn't speak to Bobo.'

'You didn't?'

'No, it was your mother . . .'

'Mum!' This was unexpected. 'But she doesn't know where I am.'

'Yes she does. I . . . I went over to the house because I thought you were in trouble. Luckily she was in and I was able to tell her –'

'What, exactly?' Allie was annoyed. What rights did Liddy think she had? 'You've no business interfering. It's got nothing to do with you.'

'I don't think that's quite the case, actually. I felt responsible.'

'Why? Because I wouldn't have made it over here without your input?'

'Something like that, I suppose.'

'I'm old enough to look after myself, you know! I've been around a bit. I've handled worse situations than bloody phone muggers.'

'Yes, but Allie, I didn't see that I had a choice. She's your next of kin. If something dreadful had happened to you . . .'

'Well, it *didn't*. I was perfectly okay and Mum should have heard about what's been going on from *me*, not you.'

'Then you ought to ring her,' said Liddy firmly. 'Let her know you're safe. Where are you anyhow?'

Max was leaning out of the window as though the activities of the front courtyard were of absorbing interest, as though – the angle of his back was informing her – he was doing his very best to be discreet, to avoid listening. Allie suppressed her anger. 'As it happens, the police found me somewhere to stay, Fattoria La Castagna, up in the hills. And by quite a coincidence . . .' She paused.

'What?'

'Well, you know how I met this . . . guy whose American name is Max but in Italian it's Massimo? It turns out he knows the woman who runs the place. She's called Cristina and her aunt used to work for his family.'

'Cristina?' repeated Liddy. 'Rosaria's niece?'

'That's right.' She tried to sound nonchalant. 'He's known her for ages. Ever since he was a little boy and she discovered him when he went missing.'

'Good Lord, you're actually staying with Cristina! Surely I told you about her, producing Mimmo like a jack-in-the-box? She wasn't very keen on us. Helena was rather rude to her – she was probably glad to see her get into trouble.'

Allie glanced towards Max's back view and under cover of a sudden squawking of hens from the courtyard she said quickly, 'You didn't tell me he hid in her car.'

'He hid in her car? I didn't know that!' Liddy became distinctly animated. 'I didn't even know she could drive. But if she'd been on the beach too, why didn't she come forward when they asked for witnesses? And why didn't she bring him back right away?'

'Afraid I can't really . . .'

'Is Mimmo with you at the moment?'

'Yes. He's lent me his phone.'

'Oh I see. It was outrageous really, the way Cristina got all the glory and Helena was made a scapegoat. This is a gift, Allie, it's been handed to you on a plate. You have to follow it through.'

'How on earth can I do that?'

'Ask some questions? Scout around?' She gave a small sigh of disappointment. 'No, you're right. What's the chance of finding anything out after so long? One per cent? Two if you're lucky. Forget it. The most important thing now is to ring your mother, let her know you're safe.'

'I will, I promise, right away.'

She'd make it quick, casual, non-committal (Hi, Mum, I'm fine, no worries); Helena wasn't the only person who could keep secrets. But then she'd take a punt on that two per cent: she'd find her hosts and tell them she was staying another night.

21

After Max left, Allie found herself engaged in a bizarre battle with Cristina. In the afternoon, while she was reading on the terrace, the rest of her clothes went missing. She tracked down Enrico, the son, who suggested his mother might have taken them to wash. 'That's very kind of her,' said Allie, who didn't care to be held to ransom for some faded denim and a selection of cotton tops from H&M. 'But I didn't ask her to. I wouldn't want her to go to the trouble.' He assured her it was no trouble at all, but he was hazy about when the laundry would be completed and she was left with the disquieting notion that her wardrobe would either vanish mysteriously or turn up as motley rags.

That evening, dinner was served to the guests at the long refectory table where they had breakfasted. The occasion was sociable and over the antipasti – platters of salami and ham, roasted peppers and pickled artichokes – everyone joined in with halting but friendly conversation. When Cristina served the pasta, Allie noticed she'd been apportioned twice as much as the rest of the company. 'She needs to build her strength,' Cristina explained, to general agreement.

Allie resolved that she would not be intimidated. She floundered through the coils of *fettucine della casa* while the stout German couple sitting nearby grunted encouragingly at her laden fork. But when Cristina dished out the main course, and a rocky mountain of potatoes and bales of *involtini* swamped her plate, she tried to object. 'Honestly, that's more than enough.'

'You are hungry,' insisted her hostess. 'I do not wish you to return to England and say we are not generous here with our portions, *non é vero*?' The others nodded in approval, declaring how refreshing it was to see a young woman with a good appetite. There were too many girls these days whose limbs were like sticks, who lived on air and leaves. Cristina's capacious hips swayed as if in assent and she added a haystack of green beans. Allie reckoned she was being tested, or bullied, or both, but she would hold her own: she would polish her plate to an empty shine. As a result she spent the second night in her bridal bed suffering acute indigestion.

In the morning she was sluggish, in no rush to get up; she'd no desire for breakfast and only yesterday's clothes to wear. She waited in her room until the hum of activity subsided: the clatter of crockery, the squabbles of children, the exodus of cars. When all was quiet she would start her voyage of exploration – even though her mission was hazy, her evidence negligible, and she didn't know what she was looking for. Was she expecting to find a whole heap of ransom notes hidden somewhere? A cache of bones from another kidnap that had gone wrong? A signed confession sealed and buried in an old tobacco tin? But Liddy's reaction had alerted her: something was not quite right. Cristina had driven Mimmo away from the beach, allegedly by accident, and taken two days to return him. No one else had questioned the time lapse once the boy had re-emerged; Helena was the only person directly affected.

Allie began by undertaking a circuit of the farmhouse. She shuffled across terrace and courtyard, peeping over walls and behind potted plants. She learned nothing. She could see Enzo's back and shoulders at the computer in the private office. Even if he left his post she could hardly sneak in and rummage through papers. She headed for the outbuildings, a complex of barns used for storage and as a garage. This was quite possibly where Cristina would have parked when she'd come back from the beach. Surveying the barn's position on the estate, Allie did not believe a child could have remained trapped in a boot without someone hearing his cries.

The barn doors were open, beckoning her inside; as she entered she heard a rustle and felt a stab of panic. Stop it, she told herself, there's no reason to get spooked. When her eyes grew accustomed to the gloom she saw the rustling came from a chicken nesting in the corner. A range of old-fashioned farming implements, oiled and sharpened, were suspended from a row of hooks. On the one hand, these indicated the loving attention to detail that characterized Enzo and Cristina's hospitality; on the other, they were strangely menacing: what might they be used for? She was reaching to touch the shining blade of a long-handled scythe when a shot rang out. At the edge of her vision a heap of hessian unfurled into a human shape. Allie screamed. '*Che sta facendo qui*?' Enrico seemed as startled as she was.

She crossed her arms over her thumping chest in relief. 'I'm sorry, I don't . . .'

'I ask what you do here.'

'Oh . . . nothing.' She indicated her bandage. 'I can't go very far till this gets better. There aren't any buses and I can't afford a taxi to take me anywhere, so I guess I'm stuck really, just wandering about. That noise gave me a fright.'

'Ah – *la macchina*.' He laid a hand on its high wheel arch and she could see now that it was a quad bike. 'There was problem,' he said proudly, 'but I have fixed it.'

'You must be a good mechanic.' Flatter him, she thought, win his confidence.

'*Ottimo*,' he agreed, leaping into the driving seat. He pumped the accelerator until the tools shook on the walls and the hen flapped outside to safety. Over this noise he yelled at Allie. 'You want to ride?'

'Oh yes please.' He let the roar diminish as she clambered beside him. 'Where will we go? I'd love to see the whole estate. Is that possible?'

'You want I will be your guide?'

He didn't give her time to answer but careered through the doorway into the blinding sunlight and bowled down the broad track that bisected the vineyard. A fine chalky powder sprang up in their wake. The trunks of the stubby vines were gnarled and weathered but the leaves were a soft fresh green and the grapes were embryonic, bunched in hard, tight clusters. Wild fennel flourished between the rows and, as Enrico sped past, traces of aniseed pursued them.

'First we see the pigs,' he bellowed. 'We keep far from house for the smell.'

He slowed to a halt by their pen and described how in the autumn they'd be fattened with chestnuts from the family's woodland, how the nuts gave the meat a sweet, mellow flavour and buttery texture. '*Dopo*,' he said with his eyes sparkling. '*Il coltello*.' He drew his hand in a slicing gesture across his throat. 'The salami you have for breakfast, the pancetta in the pasta – this comes from last year's pigs.'

'Who kills them?'

His voice was tinged with regret. 'The butcher from the village. Before he died, was always my grandfather. He have the farm for many years. Even when the harvest is bad, when the animals sick, when there is no money, he will not give up. He was hard man, very strong.'

'Can we go into the woods?'

'*Certo*.' He stamped on the accelerator, rising to a standing position as if he were navigating a motor launch, spinning the wheel through his hands as the vehicle lurched up a twisting gradient. He swerved past an outcrop of rock, screeched through two more switchback bends and stopped within inches of a five-barred gate, where he cut the engine and leapt from the driver's seat. He wiped his palm on his trousers and held it out to help her descend. 'In the wood we must walk,' he said. 'I am sorry.'

But Allie wasn't thinking about her limp. 'Tell me more about your grandfather. He was very strong, you said.'

'He frighten everybody,' said Enrico simply. He picked up a fallen stick and snapped it across his knee. 'He can break a chair like this if he is angry.'

'Did he often get angry?'

'*Boh!*' The boy was puzzled. 'Why do you want to know?'

'Because things have changed so much,' said Allie. 'You've given me this picture of someone who's very determined. I was wondering how he felt about the farm being turned into an *agri*-whatever, when he'd struggled to keep it going for so long.'

'It is after Nonno die we open. Tourists make good money for us.'

He unhooked the gate and led her through it. Dead leaves and the husks of last year's chestnut crop crackled underfoot; the shade was deep and cool. 'Oh this is marvellous,' she said, drinking in the sweetness of sap and nectar.

'In autumn,' he said, 'we are very busy here, to harvest the *castagne* and the *funghi*. When I was little I used to come with Nonno and he show me the *funghi* that are safe to eat. I learn well and I never make mistake.'

The lad was a curious combination, Allie thought, of naïvety and bravado. Impatient to demonstrate that he had adult interests, adult skills, yet still impressionable. He treated her as if she were part honoured guest, part clueless visitor and part potential girlfriend. It was tough being a teenager; she wouldn't want to be back there herself – in that soup of confusion, yearning for independence but needing protection. Cristina must have been caught up in it too – taking her father's car to the beach as an act of defiance but not looking ahead to the consequences. She doubted the old man had been the hero Enrico depicted; wasn't it possible he was more of a tyrant? Terrorizing his family by battering the furniture? Maybe that wasn't all he battered.

'He must have taught you a lot of things. Was he very strict? I mean, like a disciplinarian?'

'I don't understand.'

'If you got something wrong, did he hit you?'

'No.' The boy shook his head. 'This is the job of father, not grandfather.'

'Oh . . . right.'

'Come now. I have something I think you will like to see. Your foot is not problem for walking?'

'I'll be okay if you don't go too fast.'

He kept forgetting, charging on ahead through the trees and having to hang back to wait for her. Although they hadn't covered much ground, they were soon immersed in the velvety chamber of the forest; the distant trails down the mountainside, the gate and the quad bike were out of sight. There were no clearly trodden paths, but twining lengths of honeysuckle and arched whips of brambles stretched like tripwires. Allie started to recall childhood fairy tales. This was a place in which you could easily become lost; if Enrico decided to abandon her she'd never find her way out.

Along the route she thought he had taken she could see only piercing shafts of sunlight, discrete as spots on a stage set. 'Enrico!' she called. 'Where are you?' She half expected him to emerge from behind a tree with hairy legs and horns poking through his scalp, transformed into a satyr. 'I can't keep up.'

His words floated some fifty yards ahead. 'We are nearly arrived.'

Arrived where? Then for a few moments she thought she must be hallucinating because she could see it ahead in a clearing: a gingerbread house.

'Is cool, no?' said Enrico.

Her eyes adjusted themselves, quelling the antics of her brain. Where she had seen gingerbread there was mud and thatch, rotten wood instead of slabs of chocolate, fungus instead of marshmallow; she was looking at a tumbledown goatherd's hut. He led her inside. The floor was beaten earth and smelled of mould, not sugar and spice. A bench ran along one wall with a shelf above it. In the corner lay a heap of ash and charcoal.

'Does anyone ever use this?' she asked.

'Many years ago when we have *cinghiali* in the woods and goats on the mountain. And sometimes I come with Nonno for *la caccia*.' He cocked his hand into a pistol and picked off imaginary vermin.

'What did you shoot?'

'Small animals. I do not know name.'

'Squirrels? Weasels? Rabbits?'

'Also birds.' He mimed impaling a creature on a spit and poked the ashes with his toe. 'We roast in flames. Delicious.'

Boy's Own stuff, thought Allie. Charging about with ammunition, killing things. The type of activity you could do nowadays on a games console without leaving your warm sitting room, without getting dirt or blood on your hands. Nature's small and vulnerable creatures might enjoy a longer life.

'So nobody comes here any more?'

'Nobody know this place. And I have not enough time. *Peccato*.' He broke off a piece of door frame, which crumbled in his fingers like cake. 'But I have idea. First we have to build swimming pool, I know this is important. Is priority. But for next project I want that we restore this house for barbecue and picnic, even for *la caccia*. You think is good idea?'

What Allie was actually thinking was that if you were frightened of getting into trouble for something you shouldn't have done, and you wanted to hide someone for a day or two, a hut like this (in better condition naturally) would be as good a place as any. Especially if that person was so traumatized they'd lost their speech. And who, in any case, would expect a three-year-old to have a sense of time or location?

Enrico repeated his question.

'Oh yes,' said Allie. 'Excellent. A brainwave.'

'You will tell my father?'

'What?'

'Is good idea for development. Swimming in summer. Hunting in winter. No?'

'Yes, absolutely. I'll tell him with pleasure.'

As it happened, Enzo was waiting as the quad bike rattled into the courtyard. He looked disconcerted to see the two of them together. He barked at Enrico, who answered in sulky monosyllables. To Allie, he said, 'You have telephone message. If you will come to office, please.'

'A message?'

She followed Enzo through the entrance lobby and into his private cubicle. She didn't recognize the number he handed her, written on a post-it note in looping cursive, but she saw it lacked an international prefix. A delicious light flutter inside her drove away the nagging remnants of her indigestion. Max. It couldn't be anyone else. This was what happened when you felt a strong kinship with another person: you did not lose touch. Your brother did not want to let you go.

'Is it okay to ring him back?'

Enzo pushed a pile of folders to one side and indicated both the phone and a swivel chair for her to sit on. Created from the cubby-hole beneath the stairs, the room was too small for two people. A fan spun in a corner; it moved the air but didn't replenish it. If only he would leave, if only she could think of some errand to distract him. She didn't want him listening to her conversation. He settled himself again at his computer screen. She punched in the number.

'*Pronto*.'

Allie put on an accent to make her English harder for Enzo to follow. She broadened her vowels and swallowed her consonants. 'Max? Hi.

I'm returning your call like you said, only I'm ringing from the office so I can't take too long.'

'Who is this?'

'It's me, Allie.'

'Must be a bad line. How's the injury?'

'Bit better, thanks.'

'Did you get around much?'

'Enrico gave me a ride on his bike, showed me the pigs. And the woods and stuff.' She was watching the dome of Enzo's bowed head, but it didn't jerk forward in alarm or display any other emotion. 'I have a theory, Max.'

He was in the street. She could hear the hooting of stalled traffic, the wheezing doors of a bus, the cry of a child. She imagined a place crammed with noise and people and urgency – the very opposite of this isolated retreat – and wished she could be there.

'I didn't catch that, what kind of a theory?'

'Later. Tell me why you're calling first.'

'To check you're okay I guess and to say that when you leave, if you're passing through Roma . . .' There came the rattle of a metal canister across cobbles, a medley of hooting, then the heavy clunk of a latch and a moment's silence before his footsteps echoed on a marble staircase.

'Rome? Is that where you are now?'

'Yeah, I'm working here, remember? Anyhow, like I said, if you're passing we could get together, grab dinner or a drink someplace . . .'

'And talk?'

'Well, sure we can talk. What is this? You don't trust me not to jump you?'

'It's not that. Max, I really want to see you. There's so much –' No, this was going too far. This could make her sound flaky or plain unhinged. She discarded her failing, indeterminate northern accent and said with careful formality, 'I could come tomorrow if it suits you.'

'Great. If you have time to call before you catch the train I'll try to make the station. Otherwise let me know when you get in and I'll figure out a place to meet. Have you been here before?'

'Actually I was born in Rome.'

'No kidding?'

'No kidding.'

'So was I!' She imagined him balancing against the banister on the way up to the office as other people passed by, shaking his head. 'You never said before.'

'I suppose it didn't come up.'

Enzo shifted in his seat, clicked several times on his computer mouse.

'I have to go,' said Allie. 'I'm using the office phone here. I'll ring you again tomorrow when I'm on my way.'

'You won't get cold feet or chicken out like last time?'

'No, I promise.'

'It's a date?'

'It's a date,' she agreed, replacing the receiver in its cradle. She scooted backwards on her chair and thumped into Enzo's. 'I expect you've understood,' she said, 'that I'm travelling on to Rome tomorrow. Is it all right if I stay one more night?'

'We shall be most happy,' he said, although his eyes continued to look mournful, 'to accommodate you. What hour do you wish to leave? I can order a taxi.'

'Well, after breakfast, I should think.'

'Ah, breakfast. Today you do not eat.'

'I . . . I couldn't.' She pressed her right hand to her abdomen. 'I was so full after yesterday's dinner. In England, you know, we have pasta *or* we have meat and two veg. We don't have one after the other. Both together. I'm not used to it.'

'We want you to have good experience,' said Enzo. 'This is important to us.'

She wasn't clear where the emphasis of his words lay. Was it you or good? Important or us? 'I think your wife,' she began. And then stopped. What on earth could she say? And what would Enzo understand anyway? What could he possibly know of events that had happened probably way before he'd even met Cristina, let alone married her? 'I'm afraid she thinks I'm a nuisance,' she finished lamely.

'*Assolutamente no!*'

'Oh . . . right . . . Well, I meant, you know, having to find me painkillers and bandages. And now she's taken all my stuff to wash and I'm not even sure I can pay for it.'

'There will be no charge.'

'Look here, I don't want special treatment. I mean –'

Enzo chewed his pen. She glimpsed for the first time the depression of a dimple at the side of his mouth. Damp patches of sweat discoloured the cloth of his shirt. 'We know who you are,' he said.

Allie blinked. 'Excuse me?'

'You look much like your mother.'

'*You* knew my mother?'

'A little,' he conceded. '*Comunque*, the circumstances were . . . complicated.' What on earth was he trying to say? 'Ash-a-bourne,' he continued. 'I have good memory for names and faces, is all. Is useful in my work.'

'Your wife knew her too, didn't she?'

'*È vero*. In a manner of speaking she has brought us together. And for this we are grateful.'

Allie didn't know what to make of this. Was he referring to the search for Max? She took a gamble. 'Your son's also been very kind, showing me around. I loved the little goatherd's hut, but it's very remote isn't it? Gosh, if you had an ankle like mine, you could be stuck there for days and no one would find you.'

She was intrigued to see his colour deepen. 'I do not know this hut.'

'You don't? But Enrico said – '

Shuffling the files on his desk, he corrected himself. 'Please excuse my English. I mean that I *did* not know this hut.'

She frowned and started to speak but he cut her off. He tapped some figures into a pocket calculator. 'While you are in our home we wish for you to have first-class treatment. I will adjust your bill so the stay is not expensive for you. We can give special offer at this moment: three nights for price of two. Is good, yes?'

'Oh . . .' She was startled. 'Very good. Thank you.'

'*Prego*.' He turned his back, dismissing her.

She went upstairs to her room. It had been cleaned and tidied in her absence. At the head of the bed, the pillows were crisp and puffed as meringues. And at the foot, the stained and crumpled clothes she'd hauled around Europe for the past two weeks were folded into sweet-smelling piles.

22

The view from the cathedral tower was renowned for its scope: the sweep of the Welsh hills across the wide grey channel of the Mersey, the clash of spiky Victorian gothic and florid neo-classicism, the narrow red-brick terraces like lengths of taut rope – and lately an outcrop of ambitious new monuments with steel frames and mirrored glass, a gaggle of cranes dangling crows' nests and wrecking balls. Just as a city's grandeur is best appreciated from a height, mused Helena, the past is better understood from a distance.

She was gazing at the great sandstone bulwark of the cathedral through the window of Simon's top-floor flat in Gambier Terrace. 'I hadn't imagined you in a place like this,' she'd said on her first visit. 'I thought you'd be in one of the swanky modern apartments they're building, all spotlights and chrome.'

'Ah, but I took this on before those developments got off the ground and I'm too lazy to move. Besides, I'm walking distance from work.'

Helena raised the sash, inhaling estuary sludge, a whiff of salt and the tired flowers of unpruned privet.

Simon was packing. He was moving between rooms, taking down books from his bookshelf, assembling razor, adaptor, phone charger, assessing clothes for cleanliness and soliciting her opinion. 'I suppose I'll have to take some ties.' He draped half a dozen over his arm. 'Which do you think?'

She'd been trying to peer into the nooks of the sunken graveyard, but from this height and with the shrubs in full leaf only shadows could be seen. In contrast, the dancing tails of woven silk were astonishingly vivid. 'I'm not sure that I have an opinion on ties.'

'Helena without an opinion? I don't think so.'

She perched on the sill. 'Well, no one's going to accuse you of understatement, are they? But, since you're going to America, I guess that's fine. You should flaunt yourself.' She swooped on one that had a jagged design like forked lightning and knotted it around his head. 'Now you look like a schoolboy playing Cowboys and Indians!'

He trapped her hand between his. 'I'd have more fun if you'd come with me.'

'Fun? On a conference about effective deterrents within the penal system? Are you sure that's allowed?'

'You could stand in as exhibit A.'

Helena turned her back on him, and gazed with increased concentration at the cathedral. Simon wrenched off his headgear and threw it on to the sofa. He stood behind her, rested his hand with caution on her hip. 'I didn't mean to offend you.'

'It's okay, I'm not offended.'

'It was a really tactless thing to say. What happened to you should never have happened.'

'That's beside the point.'

'Actually,' he said, 'I've got a confession to make.' With gentle pressure he swivelled her to face him again. 'I have a guilty past myself.'

She stared at him blankly. 'You?' Then she roared with laughter. 'I knew it! You know, the first thing I thought, when you accosted me in Lee's, was that you must be a pickpocket.'

'Fucking hell. Why?'

'Because of the creepy way you pretended I'd dropped something and then commandeered my suitcase.'

'Creepy?' He looked hurt. 'I was being a good citizen.'

'So what were your youthful misdemeanours then? Cheating in exams? Dope-peddling? Joyriding? All of the above?'

'Yeah.' He nodded. 'Pretty much. But mainly I was shoplifter supreme. Woolies, HMV, WHSmith, you name it. Independents are easier than high-street chains because they can't afford sophisticated security, but even as an angry adolescent you can feel a bit shit about taking advantage of a small business.'

'What about the joyriding?'

'Oh, we only nicked rich men's cars. No cachet in a Ford takeaway.'

'And you never got caught?'

'Nope.'

'Christ,' said Helena. 'Doesn't look like the wages of sin worked out quite fair, does it?'

'We shouldn't have got away with it. Had some hairy moments. But young boys can leap over walls and outrun most adults so we were lucky, basically. And then when I'd grown out of the whole phase, it got me thinking I suppose, got me into what I do today.'

'Being careless. That was my mistake.'

'We stole,' said Simon, 'for the thrill of it. The buzz. The loot was a by-product really. But you, you like to go head-to-head, don't you?'

'I don't like being told what to do if that's what you mean.'

'I think it's more a deliberate distaste for authority that motivates you.'

'Fuck off, Simon. Stop treating me like an object lesson for a seminar.'

'Yes, but seriously, back then, if you'd –'

'If I'd what?' There are so many ifs in a lifetime; she happened to have a concentrated bunch that summer. She ticked them off. 'If I'd never fallen for Fabrizio? If I hadn't left my passport with Liddy? If I'd watched where Mimmo went to hide? If I'd smoked all Jake's dope and not left a few crumbs for a rainy day? If I hadn't aggravated Enzo?'

Simon's chin jerked up. 'Enzo? Who's he?'

'Just a *carabiniere* who liked to cut a dash rescuing damsels in distress. He wanted a date and I was a bit of a cow. He probably couldn't believe his luck when he got me in handcuffs. Look, can we forget it, please? I am not your piece of research. I am totally unsuitable.'

'Totally,' he agreed, slotting his fingers beneath the waistband of her trousers. 'Great piece of arse though.'

'Fuck off,' she said again. 'And finish your packing.'

'I'll be as quick as I can,' he promised, pausing only to change the CD on the system. R.E.M.'s 'Losing My Religion' quavered into the room. Helena sank into a leather armchair, which sighed beneath her weight. She kicked off her sandals and settled her feet on to a leather footstool. To her left were the windows overlooking Hope Street. Around the other three walls, hung at carefully measured intervals, were reproductions of Hogarth's *The Rake's Progress*. Simon told her he'd been collecting them for years, hunting down bargains in back-street print shops.

You could spend hours observing the details of the depravity Hogarth portrayed, examining each rung of the descent into destitution in an age of rough and random justice. She chewed at her bottom lip reflectively. You didn't have to accept a downward spiral. You could dig yourself out of a hole if you put your mind to it. She'd proved that, hadn't she? It was why, despite the ordeal she'd been through, she'd stayed on in Italy after her release.

She didn't intend to be seen as a victim – so there was no point running home to the pitying whispers of local gossip, accompanied by Allie the albatross. It was different in Rome. She wasn't mixing with the Catholic bourgeoisie; she was on the expatriate fringe. Her flatmates – Chilean Milagra, Syrian Samira, Australian Greg, Irish Kevin, and the host of *stranieri* who passed through the squat, metal-clad entrance to their shared apartment – were happy to take a turn with the baby. Communal living, they all agreed, was good for young children. Their attitude meant that she hardly noticed when Fabrizio's visits became less frequent; she didn't need him in her life. She hadn't forgiven him for his reaction to Allegra.

'Why is her arm twisted like that?' he'd said.

'Because her shoulder caught on my pelvis and they didn't do a Caesarean in time.' (You realize you could have sued the hospital? people told her afterwards, but Helena felt she'd had quite enough of the Italian legal system.) 'They said the nerves aren't damaged beyond repair. If she exercises, she can build up her strength and do everything other people do and more.'

'She looks . . .'

'What?'

'Ouf . . . I don't know. Like a bird of some kind?'

She had the barrel ribs, the scrawny limbs, the large, wobbling head of any other newborn on the ward. 'You're making her sound like an alien! Your precious Mimmo must have looked like this too.' In truth, Mimmo was the albatross, the unspoken weight that had scuppered what was not, as it turned out, a satisfactory love affair.

Fabrizio did try to take a scientific approach to Allie's treatment, to see it as a counterbalance of stresses and load-bearing joints, but a baby was not a building with clean harmonious lines, to be taken apart and put together again, reinforced with steel ties and concrete. Progress was slow and frequently disheartening. Soon after Allie's second birthday Helena gave up on him. She moved to Wales at the invitation of a woman ceramicist she'd met, who'd bought a sprawling farmhouse and was establishing a studio complex. This rural idyll of potters' wheels, creative partnerships and country-reared children didn't last either.

Simon stood in the doorway. 'All done.' He crossed the room, knelt beside the footstool and began to fondle her bare foot. 'I wish you'd reconsider,' he said.

'Reconsider what?'

'Coming along.' When she groaned, he continued, 'I have the hotel room booked already, you know that. You've admitted you've got no urgent commitments. You could spare a few days. I know you're a carpe diem sort of girl.' He stroked her sole. 'I will lay the sights of Chicago at your feet.'

'There's the problem of the flight.'

'Yes, I've thought of that, but I reckon you could get one on standby quite cheaply. Give it a whirl – you've nothing to lose.'

'It's not the money, Simon, you idiot.'

'Then what? Oh, bollocks . . .' One hand cupped her heel; the other, running up the back of her leg, tightened around her calf. 'Explain something to me,' he said. 'You told me you have a kiln in the shed at the bottom of your garden. You work in highly dangerous conditions in a tinder box that could go up any minute. Why the hell doesn't *that* freak you out?'

'The conditions are only dangerous if you're stupid,' she said, 'which I'm not. But anyway, it isn't the small enclosed space that's the problem, it's the *moving* small enclosed space.'

'A car?'

'A car's different,' she snapped. 'You can see out, get fresh air if you need it.'

'It *is* the result of being locked up, then?'

'Actually, the worst bit was when they took me across to the mainland.' She could speak about it now in a detached way, as if it had happened to somebody else – even though she was still handicapped by the effects. 'It was a horrid day, overcast and windy. I was in a hold in the boat, below the water level, and the sea was quite choppy. I was dreadfully sick, I mean really disgusting – it went everywhere – but I'd no other clothes to change into. When we disembarked they shoved me into the back of a van. I didn't even know where they were taking me. We were rattling around all these hairpin bends and the stench of vomit was unbelievable. I thought I was going to suffocate.'

'How long were you in there?'

'An hour or two, I suppose. The journey seemed to go on for ages, there were traffic jams and all kinds of hold-ups. It was bad enough at the time, but I didn't find out how bad until later . . .'

Simon sat on the arm of her chair and took her hand. 'How much later?'

'Oh, months afterwards, when I was back in Rome. I was visiting a friend who lived in a modern tower block on the outskirts – the sort they threw up for people who couldn't afford anything better. I had Allie with me. She was four weeks old, strapped in a sling. I wasn't going to traipse up eight flights – anyway, I wasn't aware at that point I had a problem, so I got in the lift and pressed the button.'

'Surely you'd used a lift since the arrest?'

'I suppose I must have done. But this one had an odd smell – maybe there was a ventilation problem – and it felt to me like it was tilting. Then the metal walls started to move inwards, crumpling the way polythene does when you vacuum-pack something. That was what was happening to Allie and me: all the air was being sucked from around us. First I couldn't breathe and then I blacked out. Apparently we went on up, collapsed together in a heap, until we were rescued by some guy on the top storey. An angel stepping off his cloud and into the lift.' Afterwards, she couldn't get it out of her mind that she might have killed her baby, literally crushed her to death because of the way she'd fallen. The damaged baby she hadn't wanted in the first place? That was her turning point.

'And you've never tried since?'

'To take a lift? Yes, I've tried. But I hyperventilate as soon as the doors start to close so I avoid them. It's called risk assessment. Anyway, stairs are good for you.'

'*I* could be good for you,' said Simon with conviction. 'I shall make it my mission.'

'What?'

'To get you on a plane.'

'Why?'

'So that you can go places! You're not the only person to have been afflicted: there are ways and means.'

'You think I don't know that?'

'What about tranquillizers?'

'Useless.'

'Cognitive behaviour therapy?'

'That didn't work either.'

'Not at all?'

'I wasn't the right subject. Whatever.'

'You will find,' he said, tracing the lines on her palm, 'that I don't give up so easily.'

'Well, it's nice that you're so keen to help me,' said Helena, pushing him away. 'But don't let's rush things.'

'Who's rushing?' Then he tapped his watch and said with a grin, 'Only I was hoping we could manage a quick fuck before the taxi comes. Something for me to remember you by.'

Later, lying on his bed – catching from a different window the gleam of slate rooftops and a fanciful display of chimney pots – she watched him strut around the room, getting dressed again. She liked his unabashed nakedness, the slick way he zipped up his chinos, slotted his arms into his shirt. There was, in all his movements, the easy confidence of a man not much troubled. Researching the darkest recesses of deviant minds, the depressing triviality of the petty criminal, the wearisome predictability of the repeat offender, might not have given him a rosy notion of human behaviour, but it hadn't dragged him down. Cocky bastard probably thought he had it all under control. She'd observed this with academics: lecturing, posturing, confabulating, they soon considered themselves minor deities.

She stretched her legs and arched her spine. Her clothes were pooled yards away. He came to sit beside her, tweaked a nipple. 'I'm going to miss you.'

'I know what conferences are like. You won't be deprived. You'll be bed-hopping for four days.'

'I wouldn't if you were with me.'

'Why do we keep going round in circles?'

'You can do it, Helena. You have to find the will.'

'It's the end of the world as we know it,' she sang in imitation of Michael Stipe. 'Change the record, Simon.'

'You don't realize how much you're restricting yourself.'

'Why, because there are now all these ridiculously cheap flights to godforsaken places I don't want to visit anyhow?'

'The United States?'

'I've managed so far. No one invited me to an unmissable international conference until today.'

'Suppose your precious one-and-only daughter decided to live there?'

'Why would she do that?'

'Because she met someone? Or to follow her musical ambitions?'

Helena sat up and began to pull on her underwear, rejecting his teasing attempts to help her.

'Well? You'd never see her, would you?'

'I don't believe in crossing bridges until you get to them.' She finished fastening her trousers and reached for her bra.

'Or oceans, it appears.'

At this, at what she interpreted as his snide manner, she stuffed the bra into her pocket and yanked her top over her head, ignoring the fact that it was the wrong way around. Was he deaf? Had he not paid attention to anything she'd told him? Storming into the sitting room, she seized sandals and bag, sniping at him over her shoulder. 'I shall get a fucking boat. In spite of what happened in the bay of Naples I'm okay on deck. I *like* the water.'

'Hey!' he protested, in pursuit. 'I'm not trying to pick a fight.'

'Well, don't let me stop you.'

'Helena, I've got to leave in ten minutes. The taxi's on its way. Please let's not quarrel . . . I could get blown up mid-Atlantic.'

She snorted. 'That's planes for you.'

He wrapped his arms around her. 'Will you wait for me?'

'I might have gone home to Oxford by the time you get back.'

'I'll have to come and find you then, won't I? Any last wishes? Final demands?'

He was holding her in his bear hug. She was trying to break free. Hogarth's Rake was declining into pox and penury. The cathedral tower was filling the window. 'Bring me a hat,' she said. 'Not a baseball cap. A Stetson. Haven't got one of those. But now I have to go. Have a good trip.' She kissed him lightly on the lips and sprinted down the stairs to avoid a protracted goodbye.

Gambier Terrace had a private forecourt, separated from the road by tall iron railings. A taxi was turning in through the gates as she left the house. Moments later Simon appeared at the doorway and slung his case and laptop into the boot of the cab. She gave him a final wave, then went to her own car, parked around the corner, and found a ticket on the windscreen. Five minutes, five bloody minutes over. Annoyed, she ripped it up, switched on the ignition and accelerated into the mercifully empty street. No doubt Simon and his colleagues would have a theory about her subversive inclinations, point out it was useless to argue over a pathetic parking ticket. Maybe when she'd calmed down she'd Sellotape the scraps back together – or maybe she wouldn't.

As she neared her front door, she could hear the phone ringing. Her first thought was that it was Liddy again. She didn't hurry to answer, taking her time with the key, wondering why she was feeling so uncomfortable until she realized she wasn't properly dressed. In the hallway she stripped off her backwards top, restored her bra, selected a fresh T-shirt from the pile of laundry at the foot of the stairs, and only then picked up the handset.

'Is this the right number for Allie Ashbourne?' asked an unfamiliar male voice.

'Er . . . yes.'

'Man, that's a relief. Is she there? Only her friend Jess told us she'd heard nothing either and we've been, like, worried that she had problems of some kind.'

'Problems?'

'She doesn't answer her phone.'

'Oh . . . that's because it was stolen. She rang me from the place she's staying. She's fine. Though I think she might come home a bit earlier than planned so you could try calling again next week if you want to see her.'

'We're not in England,' said the voice. 'But we wanted to check she hadn't gone missing.'

'Missing?' It was impressive the way Allie managed to cause such concern.

'She seemed a bit strange, though we didn't know what was normal so we didn't want to, like, force the issue. We thought, well, she's just looking to chill, but then she was talking about going after her dad and when she didn't return our calls, it put the wind up us a bit. Thinking, you know, she could be vulnerable on her own out here.'

'Her dad?' said Helena.

'Are you her mother?'

'I think you should tell me who the hell you are first.'

The young man sounded aggrieved. 'I'm Dom. Me and Meg, she's my partner, we –'

'Well, Dom, what exactly has given you the idea that Allie is looking for her father?'

'Only that she *said* so, that she was quite worked up about it. And we weren't sure she was going about it the right way. I mean, a mate of ours who was adopted, he had counselling and everything and even then –'

Helena didn't want to hear any more. 'I'll tell her you called,' she said, hanging up.

Less than two miles away, in the heart of Crosby village, Liddy entered the delicatessen in search of goat's cheese and truffle oil. She found flyaway Felicity turning from the counter with a small package of shortbread. 'Mother insists,' she said. 'It's her favourite and frankly I'll do anything to keep the peace. Not cheap, though.'

Liddy didn't like to ask for truffle oil in front of Fliss. She'd wonder why on earth one might need it and balk at the price. 'She's keeping well?'

'Well enough. And how are you? Is the back better?'

'The back pain was a red herring,' said Liddy. 'It's basically more of the same, if you know what I mean . . . Actually, they're taking me into the Women's next month.'

'For an op?'

How she hated that word, the inconsequential sound of it, like 'hop' or 'pop'. 'I'm afraid so. For another shot at decluttering my womb.' It was not something she cared to discuss in a public place.

A young couple came into the shop. Liddy and Felicity moved to make way for them. The man had his arm around his girlfriend's waist; the bulge of her pregnancy strained against her cotton top. She twirled her hoop earring and giggled. 'You got anything minty?' she said. 'I'm totally obsessed with peppermint creams right now. Kendal mint cake, that sort of stuff.' Her tongue flickered forth like a cat's, a silver stud bobbed at the centre of its tip.

'I haven't seen you since the last book group,' said Felicity. 'Did you make any progress?'

'Progress?' The prospect of going into hospital certainly focused the mind: it had sent her into overdrive. 'Well . . . since you ask. Yes, I did fire off a few emails and I've just managed to set up a meeting.'

Felicity was perplexed. 'I meant with the book. Whether you'd finished it yet.'

'*Under the Volcano*? Oh . . .'

'Why, what did you think I was asking about?'

A dainty box of chocolate peppermint creams was being tied with a yellow ribbon. The girl was seeking advice on the different kinds of mint tea. 'I get such terrible heartburn, y'know. Food repeating on me and everything.'

Liddy decided she would get the goat's cheese somewhere else. And a different flavoured oil: hazelnut or walnut.

'Of course!' exclaimed Felicity with a sibilant whistle on the *s*. 'I remember now. You've unearthed the old boyfriend?'

The young man stared at them over his partner's head as she dipped her nose into the different leaf teas.

‘I managed to make contact with an intermediary, that’s all,’ said Liddy, trying to downplay any significance. ‘We’ll take it from there.’

‘You’re not actually going to meet him, are you? Wouldn’t that be dangerous, open a whole box of tricks?’

‘It won’t be a problem,’ said Liddy, ‘because he’s the other side of the world. In Australia. This, um, colleague is based in the London office and I’ve got to go there anyway to give a presentation, so I’m taking advantage of a spare couple of hours. I’m the type of person who likes to dot i’s and cross t’s. I know some people call it anal, but I can’t bear unfinished business.’

PART FIVE

ROME

CHAPTER 23

As Allie crossed the glittering marble concourse, a raft of destinations rotated on the departure board: Trieste, Salzburg, Vienna, Prague. These cities she might have visited were now erased from her itinerary. They conjured all kinds of exotic images but they would remain dots on a map. Her journey was taking her elsewhere. She scoured the crowd for Max, who had arranged to meet her. She expected to identify his loping gait, but in fact he was standing still and she was jolted by her failure to recognize him. In a dark suit, with the shirt collar white against his brown neck, his hair slicked behind his ears, eyes masked by sunglasses, he was no longer a hippyish New Yorker but a suave Roman businessman. She had to look him twice up and down.

'Hey, what happened to you?'

He whipped off the glasses. 'What do you mean?'

'I guess you're not on holiday any more,' she said sadly.

'Oh, this?' He swung his jacket from his shoulders and looped it over his forefinger. 'I had a site visit with some clients. But I got off early and came here instead of the office. I hope you appreciate that.' He picked up her luggage and began to steer her towards the taxi rank.

Less than a week ago, she was following this very route with Dom and Meg. She half expected to catch sight of them, their shoulders bowed beneath the weight of edifying reading matter in their backpacks. She regretted she'd lost possession of Meg's whistle – a useful talisman – but the police had confiscated it.

Max ushered her into the back seat of a black and green cab and issued instructions to the driver. 'I'm taking you for *gelato*,' he said, climbing in beside her.

'Oh, why?'

'You didn't want to go sightseeing? You already know the city.'

This wasn't quite true, but she let it pass. Her walking was still slow and painful and she'd no desire to join the troops of tourists. The crush in Piazza di Spagna last week had resembled the aftermath of a football match or a stadium rock concert. Meg, whose Ph.D. was something to do with the crisis of individual identity in western capitalist society, had had much to say on the subject of crowd generation.

'It's too early for dinner,' Max continued. 'And some people might say it's too early to start drinking. So I'm offering you a classic Italian pastime to fit the bill. Where are you staying?'

The taxi driver clamped his hand to his horn as he negotiated a route through a clogged junction. Allie fidgeted. 'The hostel we were in before was gross. I hoped you could recommend somewhere.'

'For how long?'

'I'm not sure. A couple of days? I want to find out where my friends are and whether it's worth meeting up. Mum was going to email their numbers, so I'll need an internet café.' She spotted one through the cab window but already they were past it, leaping across a set of traffic lights.

'You can use the internet in the apartment if you want.' Then he nudged her arm so she would turn and look at him. 'And I was only teasing about the hotel. You're welcome to stay.'

'Is that a good idea?'

'I don't know. Why not?'

'Are you sure you have room?'

'Jeez, yes. My father isn't even there at the moment.'

'Your father?'

'I haven't lived with him since I was a kid, apart from vacations. This time around it could be a while longer if we can stand each other's company.' Catching the expression on her face, he added, 'Don't worry. Like I said, he's out of town. His current girlfriend's based in Perugia.'

This was difficult territory, and fraught with anticipation. Allie felt as if she'd boarded a rollercoaster. 'Right, well, I really appreciate the offer. Thanks.'

He inclined his head. 'You're welcome.'

With a melodramatic swoop, the taxi lurched into the path of a tram, careered across a bridge spanning the sluggish waters of the Tiber and finally stopped outside a small bar. A brown awning shaded a handful of cane tables and chairs, set out on the pavement. 'This is it,' said Max. 'One of the best *gelaterie* in the city. And the apartment's only a couple of blocks away so we can walk from here if you're up to it. Hop out.'

'You know what I really like about Rome,' Allie said, appraising the graffiti on the wall opposite, the crumbling stucco, the badly parked *motorini*, the build-up of litter. 'It's scruffy as hell and it just doesn't care.'

Max stared for a moment and then burst out laughing. 'It's that European sense of superiority,' he said. 'Or a lack of ready cash. The Vatican's the only place around here with any money.' He rested an arm across her shoulders and propelled her into the bar. Below a long glass counter were dozens of ice creams in a myriad flavours, few of which she could understand. 'Most people,' he said, 'take hours to make a decision with a selection like this.'

'Not you?'

'Not me.'

'Fine,' said Allie, accepting the challenge. 'Do I get any help with the translation?'

She picked ginger, pineapple and apricot and took pleasure in the subtle combination of their colours in her paper carton. Max went for strong contrast: bitter chocolate and an intense purple bilberry.

'Well now,' he said. 'There's food for interpretation.'

'I chose flavours I hadn't tried before,' said Allie. 'That's all. What about you?'

'Oh, these are my favourites. You see, I know what I like.'

They went to sit at one of the cane tables. Max loosened his tie and undid his top button. Along the pavement a pair of youths dribbled an empty Coke can back and forth. An agitated woman teetered past with a small dog tucked under her arm and a phone to her ear. A group of girls in tight jeans and bright tops, shaking clusters of bracelets down their wrists, entered the *gelateria*. They bunched around the display, giggling and squealing, changing their minds every ten seconds.

Allie plunged her plastic spatula into the frozen creamy pineapple. 'Are you ready to listen to my theory now?'

'What theory?'

'The one I couldn't tell you on the phone because Enzo was there. About getting to the bottom of your disappearance? And Cristina's part in it.'

'I don't get why you're obsessed with something that happened so long ago.'

She sampled the ginger and coughed as the spice caught the back of her throat. 'I'm not obsessed.'

'That's how it seems to me. Like you've got a grudge against Cristina when all she's done is take care of you. I don't see that it's any of your business anyhow.'

'Will you take those sunglasses off?' Allie said.

'Do they bother you?'

'I like to see a person's eyes when I'm talking to them. Especially . . .'

'Especially?'

She had to come clean. She couldn't procrastinate any longer. 'There's stuff about me, Max, that you don't know. I mean, that I haven't told you, that I should have told you.'

He laid the dark glasses on the table top and his frown deepened. 'I thought there was something. The way you turned up at Bobby's was altogether too neat.'

Her heart was hammering. This wasn't going to be easy. She savoured a spoonful of apricot and was immediately reminded of the flushed, golden fruit overhanging the pathway in Casa Colonnata. 'You might expect it to be tricky to trace people or their addresses. But it's surprising what you can manage if you put your mind to it . . .'

He waited.

'So . . .' The apricot was her favourite flavour, definitely, but its iciness numbed her tongue, made her teeth tingle. 'I admit that guff I gave you, about a friend looking for a villa to buy, was a cover story. In fact, I was on a quest. A pilgrimage, if you like.'

'A *what*?'

'Not in the religious sense,' she said quickly. 'And I wasn't trying to con you or anything. But the fact is, I already knew about the time you went missing and I was trying to discover –'

The laden spatula was halfway to his mouth. 'How did you know? Who told you? And why would you care?' A cross between a laugh and a splutter. 'Fuck, you're not a private dick, are you?'

'No, no, not at all. I never lied about what I do. I *am* a musician. Haven't I proved that?'

'With a quaint little sing-song?'

This was not going quite the way she'd hoped. 'If you think –'

'Hell, I don't know what to think.'

'Then listen to me! I came over to Ischia because I wanted to find out what had happened to my mother.'

He seemed to be scowling as he scraped at the bottom of his tub and pushed it aside on the table. But when he raised his face she saw his expression was one of bewilderment.

'Your mother? I don't get it. She's around, isn't she? You called her. You're going to pick up her email . . . Look, d'you fancy a beer? I could sure do with one.'

'I'd rather have a cup of tea.'

'A cup of tea,' he mimicked. 'How very British.'

'She was your nanny,' Allie said.

'Who was?'

'My mother.'

'Let me get this right. *Your* mother used to take care of *me*? She was my babysitter?'

'That's what I said, yes.'

He tapped a cigarette from his packet of Marlboro. She was reminded of Sam dribbling tobacco strands into his roll-ups, his nails kept long to pluck guitar strings, the pads of his fingers stained yellow with nicotine: a scene from another life. Max's lighter flame flared. 'I had a whole bunch of babysitters,' he said. 'None of them lasted very long. To tell the truth, my mother's a bit of a pain in the ass.'

Allie nodded swift agreement. 'Yeah. Mine can be too. Her name's Helena Ashbourne.'

'Helena? No . . . I don't think . . .'

'Everyone says we look alike.'

'Really? I must have been too young to appreciate her.'

'You *were* very young,' said Allie. 'You were three. That's what I've been trying to tell you. She was the person responsible when you went missing during that game of hide-and-seek.'

He regarded her with a detachment she found unnerving. 'You've known this all along and yet you haven't said anything till now?'

'First off,' she said, 'when we met I'd no idea you were Mimmo. How was I supposed to know the boy I'd heard about had gone to live on another continent and Americanized his name?'

'You let me think . . .'

'That I was up for it? A loose floozie.'

'A what?'

'Someone who'd shag you to win a bed for the night. And I suppose you're still thinking the same thing?'

'Cool it,' he said. 'I'm going to get those drinks.' He strode to the entrance of the bar, drawing heavily on his cigarette. Then he dived inside and was gone for so long Allie wondered if he'd found a back exit and deserted her. She'd intended to build up to her revelation more slowly. She'd spent three hours on the train imagining this conversation, predicting his likely reactions, composing her phrases so they sounded as neutral as possible. At the time she'd thought that, as long as he didn't attempt to kiss her, she'd be all right, she'd muddle through. He had such a lovely mouth. She could picture it blowing gently into a harmonica, the tautening of his lips on an intake of breath.

'They're coming,' he said, returning to a different chair, directly facing her. 'You'll have your tea.'

A few yards away an old man waved his walking stick in greeting to another; a scooter zigzagged between them. The girls were finally trickling out of the bar and down the street, scooping dollops of coffee, pistachio, lemon, kiwi and *crema* on to their hot, greedy tongues.

A waiter brought out a tray containing a tall glass of lemon tea and a bottle of Nastro Azzurro. His long white apron brushed the leather of his shoes. He reminded Allie of Enrico: not yet grown to his full height despite the shadow on his upper lip.

'Right,' said Max, bending forward, elbows on the table. 'So what I want to know is why you've been stringing me along here. You turn up at the villa, all smiles and eyelashes. You get us on side without a hint of what you already know. Why so devious?'

'I didn't mean to be devious. I was nervous. And confused.'

'I still don't get it. You said you were looking for information. But it was me who was the lost babe in the wood, right? The kid who couldn't speak for a week. And if I could get over something like that I sure as hell can't see why anybody else has to drag it all up again.'

She fixed her gaze on the beer frothing gently down the side of his bottle. 'Maybe you didn't know this – but my mother ended up in prison because of what you did.'

'Because of what *I* did?'

'Yes, basically. Hiding in that car boot.'

'Goddamit! What are you looking for, Allie? Revenge?'

'Don't be so sodding ridiculous!'

'Quit yelling, will you?'

'I'm not yelling.'

'Sister, you *are*.'

This brought her up short. It was a figure of speech, she knew, delivered in this instance with a biting sarcasm. Her hand tensed around her glass of tea. She didn't notice the heat of it, the steam rising, but she saw that his eyes were striped with amber, like a tiger.

'Brother,' she said with equal sarcasm, 'I wasn't out to get anybody. I didn't intend to gatecrash your house party, I just sort of trapped myself there, but actually you were the one who came after me.'

'Like I had a choice!'

'Will you listen to me, please?' He looked sulky and flapped his hands as if in defeat. Allie would not be deflected. 'I didn't really expect to learn anything from my trip to Ischia, but I was amazingly lucky. Being able to stay with you and then Cristina. And when Enrico took me for a ride around the farm everything fell into place. I was able to work it out.'

His toe tapped a rhythm on the pavement. 'Work what out?'

'What happened to you, of course.' She paused but when no encouragement came, she rushed on. 'I think Cristina took her father's car down to the beach that day without permission. I bet she didn't get many afternoons off.'

'That's true, I guess. They were different times.'

'And everything might have been okay, if you hadn't found your hiding-place.'

'What's this? Pass-the-blame game again?'

'I'm not saying it's your fault. Mum should have gone to look for you sooner. She always leaves everything to the last minute. Anyway, the official story – am I right? – is that you finally manage to escape from the car boot because it has a faulty catch. But that's just bollocks, isn't it?'

Now he pushed his beer aside and folded his arms, giving her his full attention. 'Is it?'

'You know what? I think that eventually Cristina hears you screaming, but you've been trapped for so long you're a gibbering wreck. She's scared to return you because of the state you're in and because her father will find out she took the car. Wasn't he a bit of a bastard, a control freak?'

'Yeah,' Max acknowledged. 'He was a bully. Even Rosaria was frightened of his temper.'

Triumphant, Allie steamed on. 'So she decides to hide you somewhere until she can calm you down and get you acting normally again.'

'Hide me? Where?'

'There's a hut in the woods. Enrico took me to see it. It's falling down now, but it could have been a nice little Wendy house for you.'

'And how long did I spend in this cute little Wendy house?'

'A day and a half, I reckon.'

'And she doesn't stop to think about a family going off their heads with worry?'

'No, because she panics. She's only a teenager, Max. She has a tyrannical father and she's stepped way out of line. Perhaps she's even got a grudge against your pain-in-the-ass mother? Maybe she had a row with her. Or mine for that matter. The point is, she knows you're safe, as will everyone else soon enough. I've been running all kinds of possibilities through my head, but this is the one that makes the most sense to me. Can't you remember anything?'

'Like what?'

'Well, it would be like camping out, wouldn't it? She'd have to smuggle you food and stuff. Some kids would find that exciting. Unless, of course, she kept you sedated. Did you see her first aid box? I bet she has chloroform in there.'

'Whoa, Allie, you're going way off-beam.'

Reluctantly she reined herself in. 'Sorry. But there must have been some kind of plan hatched. Else why did everyone think you'd been abducted?'

'Because of the ransom note, you mean?'

'Yes.'

'But it was a hoax.'

'How can you be sure?'

'Because they got a confession.'

'Really?'

'It was just a sick stunt. One of the original suspects actually, some guy caught for stealing motorbikes. It took a while, but they got it out of him eventually.'

'That sounds dodgy. Could he have known Cristina? Or where you were hiding?'

'Jesus, Allie, I wasn't even four and you expect me to have the memory of an elephant! But it takes a while to live down an adventure like that. People point at you in the street and you just wish to hell it would go away. So, in answer to your question: no, I don't believe they had any connection.'

'But when the note turned up it was quite specific, wasn't it? About what you were wearing and stuff?'

'Half the *paese* had been out looking for me. It wasn't a secret.'

'I still think . . .'

'What, that Cristina wrote it? No way!'

'Okay, *she* didn't.' She stirred the long-handled spoon in her tea, creating a spinning whirlpool. 'But how about this? She wouldn't have gone to the beach by herself, would she? She'd have gone with a friend or a boyfriend – maybe he was the one who drove the car.

Now suppose he was greedy or just plain skint. If he was dirt poor or had debts to pay off, he might think the money was worth the risk. He could have written the note without even telling her until afterwards. Which may also be the reason Cristina took you back when she did: she was scared of getting into even deeper trouble. She must have realized you'd tell them about hiding in the car at some point and she'd have to face her father. But think how much worse it would be if she was found guilty of – what d'you call it – extortion? Instead of which, she was treated as a bit of a heroine, wasn't she? Did she get a reward?'

His expression was quizzical. 'I think my mother took her to buy a dress. And they gave some cash to the local church. They were always giving cash to the church, to save themselves the trouble of turning up to Mass.'

'It's amazing she got away with it. You've seen the barn where they keep the cars, it's right near the house. If you'd sprung the lock of the boot from the inside, why on earth would you run off into the woods instead of knocking at the farm? Even for a three-year-old, even if it was pitch-black and you were being chased by a wild boar, that would be crazy. I wonder why no one thought of it.'

'They were probably too busy celebrating the happy outcome. There were some horrific crimes back then and kidnapping was a real threat. Or maybe somebody *did* suss Cristina, but didn't see any reason to take it further.'

Allie recalled Enzo, the ex-policeman with his upright bearing and treacly eyes. What was it he had said yesterday? *In a manner of speaking she has brought us together. And for this we are grateful.* But then he'd clammed up. 'When you brought my stuff to the *agriturismo*, you talked about Enzo and Cristina's wedding party. You said they'd been courting for ages.'

'Well, that's not uncommon here. She was very young when they met.'

'Through finding you?'

'Yeah, they used to joke about it. Called me Cupid. Well, Enzo did. I don't know if Cristina thought he was a bit old for her at first.'

'Was he a catch, d'you think?'

He mulled this over. 'I guess. I mean, he had a steady job with a good pension and the family approved. Poor Rosaria was always held up as a bit of a warning.'

'What was wrong with Rosaria?'

'Oh, she married the wrong guy. He died without leaving her a cent, which was how come she worked for us.' His eyes brightened. 'She was a fantastic cook.'

'So Enzo's welcome, but the boyfriend before him could have been a bit of a chancer?'

'If he existed in the first place.'

'Oh come on! There had to be somebody else involved. She couldn't have managed everything by herself. Have you any idea what might have happened to him?'

'Well, most young men, if they're from the lower classes and can't afford to buy themselves out of it, get hauled off for military service. Maybe he left Ischia and never came back.'

'Do you think he was even questioned? They never arrested anybody, did they?'

'They rounded up a bunch of suspects initially, but the case would have collapsed once I started talking and they learned the whole thing was an accident. They couldn't charge anyone.'

'Except my mother –'

'Who was jailed for something she didn't do?'

'Um, no, not exactly.'

She toyed with the string of her tea bag; he stroked the neck of the beer bottle with his thumb. The sun moved behind the awning and cast them into shade; a couple of streets away car horns blared.

After a while, Max said, 'If I'd been missing for any longer, it would have been a different story. My mother and aunt can create the biggest drama you've ever seen, but on that occasion the only evidence the police had was a cack-handed note –'

'So they pick some random guy to do a deal? He confesses, they close the file and the enquiry just fizzles out?'

She wondered if she was pushing things too far, but finally he was looking at her with a kind of respect. 'Wow, Allie. You don't give up, do you? You're a ferret, like my aunt.'

'I'm not a ferret.'

'Maresa, she gets an idea in her head, she doesn't let it go.' Then he said: 'But even if you are right about there being some kind of cover-up – and I'm not trying to make excuses for anybody – the problem is, it happened so long ago I don't see how you can get any closer than this.'

Allie prodded the slice of lemon at the bottom of her glass. It might be an unproven theory but she was pleased with it. She felt a quiet sense of satisfaction. And they'd come through the experience, after all: Max, Helena, herself (though this was not, she reflected, the moment to mention her mother's pregnancy). If an act cannot be undone you have to move on.

He rocked back in his chair. 'Shoot! And there was I thinking we'd have dinner and take in a movie.'

'Sorry.' She smiled. 'If I got a bit carried away. But we can still have a meal, can't we? You're not mad at me?'

'Well, I think you're nuts, but where's the harm in a bit of unpredictability?' At the precise moment he finished speaking something shot from the sky and landed on his shoulder like a squirt of *stracciatella* ice cream. He leapt to his feet and the beer bottle rolled to the ground where it smashed. 'What the fuck!'

'Bird lime,' said Allie, suppressing a giggle. 'Is it a terrible omen?'

'It's a goddam nuisance,' he said, sitting down again and pulling a raft of paper napkins from the dispenser.

'Here, I'll do it.' She stood over him, dabbing at the stain. She could feel the ripple of pectoral muscle beneath her touch, inhale the muskiness of his skin. Part of her would have liked the hand hanging over the arm of his chair to tickle the inside of her leg. Instead she reached to clasp it, interlacing her fingers with his. 'Still friends?' she said.

He returned the squeeze. 'Sure.'

24

They'd had a good night (Allie had been careful not to drink too much; there were no awkward lunges when Max showed her gallantly to her bedroom door), but it took her a long time to get to sleep. Band practices had often lasted through the small hours and she'd grown used to collapsing at dawn and being stirred into wakefulness by the chatter of children trotting home from school. She'd never found mornings easy. She surfaced to the sound of conversation – which confused her until she realized Max must have switched on the television. A large plasma screen occupied a corner of the open-plan living area. She hadn't yet come across an Italian TV programme where the participants spoke at less than excitable full volume. She'd have to get up; she couldn't loll around in bed until he banged on her door to inform her he was going to work. She pulled on her jeans and hobbled barefoot into the living room.

The television was silent, although a radio murmured on a shelf. Max was standing at the counter in his shirtsleeves tossing back a cup of espresso. The long windows, which gave on to the balcony and an interior courtyard, stood open. The air was fragrant with coffee and freshly watered vegetation, not yet contaminated by the fumes of petrol or decaying garbage. Max put down his cup. 'Good morning,' he said with exaggerated politeness.

She disguised a yawn. 'Hi.'

'Sleep well?'

'Yeah, great thanks. You're looking perky.' She tried to massage the creases from her face. 'Not groggy like me. I should try a bit harder.'

'No rush. Take your time. I thought we could meet for lunch if –'

He broke off and she sensed a movement on the balcony, followed by an eruption of Italian.

'*Aspetta un attimo*,' Max called back.

Allie's feet felt unaccountably cold, rooted to their square of Carrara marble.

A man strode through the sliding doors with a faint air of exasperation. Like Max he was lanky and loose-limbed. His grey hair was cut as sharply as his trousers, black-framed glasses rested on a prominent nose. He peered over the top of them at Allie.

'Oh,' said Max, 'this is my dad, Fabrizio. He wasn't supposed to be back for a couple of days but, whaddya know, he sneaked in last night while we were out.' His manner was flippant but there was circumspection in it too, as if he needed to be wary in his father's presence.

'*Piacere*,' said Fabrizio, inclining his head.

'And this is Allie,' continued Max as she accepted the hand extended to her. 'She's from England.'

'Allie?' said Fabrizio. He'd let her hand fall and was staring at her left arm. Most people didn't stare, some didn't even notice. Curious children might probe and question why the one didn't quite match the other and she was always upfront with them. The brutal honesty of children was preferable to the cautious oversensitivity of adults. At this moment, however, she would have welcomed a bit of sensitivity. She felt as exposed as she'd done at the Baldinis' swimming pool. Her arm had frozen by her side as if it were paralysed; she couldn't move it if she wanted to.

'Allegra,' Max was saying. 'We met just recently and I suggested she stopover while she was passing through town. Turns out she was born here.'

'*Veramente?*'

'*Veramente*.'

She didn't follow the rest of the exchange, which had resumed in Italian. She was awaiting a response from Max. *Oh my God!* or *You've got to be kidding!* When neither came she guessed that his father was berating him for picking up strange girls and letting them stay over. As if she couldn't be trusted not to walk out with a four-foot plasma screen under her good arm. But she must have got that wrong too because, although Max's response had been deferential, they were soon joking and synchronizing watches.

'I have to run,' Max told her. 'My dad will fix you a coffee or show you how to use the machine or whatever. Call me later. You've got the card I gave you yesterday?'

She nodded, unable to speak; afraid her voice would float away from her, as high and false as if she'd swallowed a dose of helium.

'Okay, cool.' He gave her shoulder a brotherly pat on his way to the door, too busy slotting his laptop into his briefcase and checking for phone messages to puzzle at her rigid stance.

She was alone with Fabrizio Verducci. A man, that's all he was. A middle-aged man with piercing eyes and an assertive manner. As Max's father he held a degree of interest; as her own, he amounted to nothing. It wasn't as if a father figure had been absent from her life: Ian had played a significant part in her upbringing. She wasn't deprived. She had come to see how much she might appreciate a brother, to recognize the shiver of excitement whenever she thought of Max, but this man – well, he shouldn't even have been here. It was unlucky timing for both of them.

Fabrizio moved towards the sink. 'Sit down,' he said in English. 'I will make the coffee. The machine can be temperamental and I have one hour.'

An hour, she thought, balancing on the edge of a chair so stylized it resembled a one-legged flamingo. The furniture had an insistent quality, demanding admiration for its clean-cut masculinity, for its classy components of leather, smoked glass and brushed steel. There was an expensive array of audiovisual equipment along one wall and a stack of architecture magazines on a low table. The only touch of colour in the room, the only concession to nature, was a dish of vibrant lemons and limes.

Fabrizio increased the volume on the radio and waited for the steam to build up pressure, to force the coffee drip by drip into the cup below. Then he pushed it across the counter to her. She could have done with something to eat, but this wasn't an apartment where cooking took place. The cupboards were unlikely to contain cornflakes and, anyway, there wasn't any milk. She stirred in two spoonfuls of sugar.

'You have known my son for long time?'

'Well, no, not really.' His expression was expectant, so she added, 'A week.'

His eyebrows flew up. 'Quick work!'

'It was . . . I don't know . . . the way everything happened – very quickly. We have . . . I think we have a lot in common.'

Fabrizio was silent. He was examining her closely, as if registering each eyelash, each freckle, the angle of her bones beneath her skin; as if making sure there could be no doubt. As if he hadn't known, from the first moment of their encounter, who she was.

'How is your mother?' he asked at last.

Right, thought Allie with a measure of gratitude. No more beating about the bush, thank goodness. 'She's fine, thank you.' She hesitated. 'Actually, she doesn't know I'm here.' He was inspecting the back of his hands, hands that must have held her as a baby; he wore no rings. 'It was just that Max invited me, like he said, when we met on Ischia.'

'You have been in Ischia?'

'I don't believe I need anyone's permission to go anywhere.'

'This is true.'

Did she imagine a softening of the lines that ran between his nose and mouth? Maybe he liked the idea of a grown-up daughter. He had several years on her mother and it was the sort of thing men of his age could get sentimental about.

'I admit I realized there was a possibility, once I'd met him, that I might meet you too. But I only got into Rome yesterday and I don't feel I've completely woken up this morning. It's all a bit sudden, a bit overwhelming . . .'

'For me also.'

She wasn't going to apologize. 'Obviously my head is . . . is full of questions . . .'

'Elena had difficult times,' he said. 'I have tried to help her.'

Not tried hard enough, Allie would have said – if she hadn't known too well the steel of Helena's resistance. As a reaction, Allie had gone through life allowing people to think they were being useful. She'd noted the flush of pleasure that often results from a minor good turn.

'I suppose things were different in those days,' she mused, as if a lack of tolerance at the time – for illegitimacy, for disability – could excuse his behaviour. 'Is that why you used to be a communist?'

This startled him. '*Comunista?* Certainly not.' He rolled his eyes in an expression of contempt. 'Political extremism is the curse of our country.'

'Oh . . . right.' This confirmed what she'd already suspected, from Liddy's information, that her mother had been trying to throw her off the scent. Holiday villas, nannies and ransom demands don't figure in the lives of the penniless. She couldn't help wondering what it might have been like to have grown up with some of that affluence. Helena claimed she'd left Rome because it was preferable to be a single parent in England, but why hadn't she forced him to support her? Perhaps he'd done something unspeakable. After all, Max's mother had left him too. Might he be a violent man?

'I don't know where she got that from. Actually, she told me practically nothing about you. Not even your name.'

'You have done some detective work, if you have found my son.'

'Don't say anything to him,' she pleaded. 'I've been trying to tell him, but I haven't quite worked myself up to it yet. I'll do it at lunch. But if you're worried it puts you in a bad light . . .'

Fabrizio's laugh vibrated through his body. 'He knows my weakness.'

'Weakness?'

'Women . . .'

This made her angry – as if being a philanderer was something to be proud of. 'I wasn't talking about sex! I'm talking about dumping a girl and leaving her alone to get on with it.'

'What do you mean, Allegra?'

He was leaning on the counter and steepling his fingers as if in prayer. His glasses had slipped further down his nose. She sat erect; she would not be daunted. 'I mean bringing up a baby on her own!' Her eyes smarted and she blinked. 'You have to believe me when I say I don't want to get all emotional about this. I never really expected to meet you, not face to face. Max said you were in Perugia and I wasn't intending to hang around until you came back or anything. But now that it's happened – you can hardly blame me for wanting some answers.'

'We are talking of blame?'

'Well, yes. Like I said, I haven't been told much, but the little bit I do know . . .' What did she have to go on? Lies from Helena, guesses from Liddy. 'Let's just say you don't come out of it very well.'

'I have done what I could,' he said. 'Your mother's mistake was very expensive for me.'

'Mistake? You mean me?'

'Also she did not take good care of Massimo.'

'Is that why you let them arrest her? Because you were angry with her? You couldn't possibly have believed she had anything to do with his abduction! And once he was found, if you'd acted faster . . . I mean, why didn't you rush over and get her released? Make them investigate properly what happened?'

'My position was compromised,' he said. 'It was not so easy.'

'Last weekend,' said Allie. 'I stayed in an *agriturismo* run by a woman called Cristina. Max told me she was the one who drove him away from the beach. She was as much at fault as Mum, so why didn't *she* get into trouble?'

'Cristina?' He paused. 'Ah yes, Cristina. At that time she was a girl young in years, but not so much in other ways. She knew things she should not have known. She knew how to make problems and there was my wife to consider. Gabriella was greatly upset. In a small community one must think of the family's reputation and the business of the drugs was unfortunate. Elena made it hard for me to help her. But in the end I paid for her freedom. I paid for the hospital. I paid for her rent. Is this not generous?'

She gave him a probing look but he didn't flinch. Did he really not feel any remorse? 'It wasn't enough though, was it?'

Someone called out from a neighbouring balcony; staccato heels clicked across the courtyard; the radio burbled. I'm in this high-gloss apartment, thought Allie in wonderment, bawling out a stranger. Though at one time he must have known her quite well. She might have clutched at his finger or the flap of his tie. He might have stroked her dimpled knee, or the curve of her downy head. As far as she could tell, he wasn't cowed by her accusation. 'You knew how tricky things were. Because that was how you recognized me, wasn't it? From my arm?'

He stalked outside and back in again; his movements were restless like Max's, but his shoulders were more stooped. If she were being clinical about it, she would say he was a man past his prime.

'Not only your arm,' he said, 'your name. Your' – he described some indefinable shape in the air – 'comportment.'

'Didn't you ever think that one day this might happen? You'd open the door or pick up the phone and there I'd be, confronting you? Isn't it the sort of thing men who abandon their children worry about?'

'I abandoned no one,' he said.

'Well, that's a matter of interpretation. I know it was Mum who ran off and shut you out of her life or whatever, but she must have had a reason. And chances were I'd find you eventually, so this isn't exactly a surprise, is it?'

'What do you want, Allegra?'

'I don't *want* anything. I already told you, my coming here, meeting you, it wasn't *planned*.'

'You must think I am very stupid.' His face darkened. 'But I have to tell you, the wealth of the family was Gabriella's, not mine. And we divorced many years ago. An architect cannot succeed unless he is also good at business. So, I have some success, but I am not a rich man.'

'Money?' said Allie in incredulity. 'Why would I want your money? I have an inheritance. I have my own house.'

'Well . . .' Was he relieved? 'That is good.'

'But, since you're asking, what I *do* want, what I *would* like to know is what you did to drive her away, what happened between you?'

'A relationship is a private thing. If Elena has not already told you, it is not my place.'

'I suppose it was because you were already married. I suppose she gave up waiting for you.'

'She was free to do as she pleased.'

'And you didn't try to stop her leaving? You didn't care.'

'I loved your mother, truly.' He repeated: 'But it was not my place.'

'Why not?'

He approached and took hold of her left hand. He uncurled her fingers and studied her palm as if he might read something there. She resisted the impulse to pull away.

'Because, my dear,' he said calmly. 'You are not my daughter.'

25

Liddy disposed of the paraphernalia in the bin. She'd already held the indicator up to the light and examined it from all angles to make sure there was no mistake. Then she washed her hands several times. She brushed her hair, wondering whether she could detect an extra bounce. She ran a fruit-flavoured lipgloss over her mouth and decided her lips looked fuller, redder. She pressed the electronic button that operated the toilet door and almost expected it to crank open on to trumpets and bunting, a flock of dancers, trapeze artists and circus acts. Instead the Cheshire countryside rolled past. She pressed another flashing button and settled back into her seat.

Half of the carriage was declaring: 'I'm on the train.' The other half was trying to block them out: a low level buzz, insistent and monotonous as bees preparing to swarm, filtered from their ear-pieces. Liddy had switched off her phone. She needed to focus, to analyse exactly what she was doing here, in forward-facing seat 32A en route to Euston. Her presentation had been cancelled at the last minute, but she was the only person who knew this. Michael was expecting her to spend the day in London; so were her colleagues. She would have to pretend she hadn't received the cancellation email, that it was still hurtling around the ether. She'd earn sympathy – 'Oh you poor thing, all that way for nothing' – and would accept it graciously. The fact was she'd already bought her ticket and arranged the *other* meeting before she'd set out this morning.

She'd arrived early at Lime Street Station and hadn't been the least bit tempted by giant muffins or a cardboard cup full of sugary froth. Instead, she was drawn to Boots. For the past week, she'd been extraordinarily patient; she had developed the art of not-hoping to an advanced level. But she hadn't been able to contain herself any longer: curiosity overcame her and she bought the pregnancy testing kit that she'd just taken into the train loo. And (she was trying *not* to get over-excited about this) it had come up with a blue line. A blue line. Could this finally be the beginning? Could you have a final beginning? Well, why not? They'd have to cancel the myomectomy operation and that alone was a relief. The young man opposite, whose earphones were sending out thumping bass rhythms like coded messages, turned to stare at her and she wondered if she'd spoken aloud.

This was not where she wanted to be, trapped in a train when she could be outside turning cartwheels. But she'd have to go through with it now: the *other* meeting. How was she going to justify it? Because it was technically work-related? Because, as she'd claimed to Felicity, she couldn't brook unfinished business? Because, when you've been waiting over twenty years for a contact you don't turn it down when it comes? (Even though, strictly speaking, she'd initiated it.) Anyway, she wasn't going to see Jake himself. She was going to meet his business partner, the one who'd recently opened up the London office. She'd kept the correspondence brief, signing herself Helen Rawlings. The name would mean nothing to Jake, who was probably still in Australia where the production company had begun. And, if at some point, she put work his way and they got to talk on the phone he might be amused to find out who Helen Rawlings actually was. She'd done well for herself and this would be proof that she bore no grudges for the way he'd treated her, for not loving her enough. If she were about to enter a new phase of her life, she wanted to tie up loose ends, leave all the messy complicated stuff behind.

'Any drinks or snacks?' The trolley attendant was hovering over her with a hot water jug. The trolley itself crackled with packages in Cellophane and foil, as bright and garish as Christmas decorations. Liddy ordered a green tea and took a banana from her briefcase (she had brought sheaves of work with her to collate and annotate, which she might address on the way home if it suited her mood, but not now, not in this state of suspended animation). Eating healthily was important, everybody knew that. Michael, her loyal beloved Michael, had murmured something about dinner being bland but she hadn't explained. When it was his turn to cook, when he conjured a red-hot curry, she might have to say something, but it was too early yet. She shouldn't be tempting fate.

The train arrived on time at Euston. She dawdled along the platform and across the noisy concourse to avoid being too early – and because her legs were curiously reluctant. The address she'd been given was on the border of Islington and Hackney, an odd location for a film production company – she'd have expected a more central office. She had a suspicion (confirmed when the taxi dropped her off) that the business was operating out of someone's front room. The terraced street was at various stages of gentrification. Fresh paint, gleaming brass and potted shrubs predominated, but there were pockets of resistance too: corroded gutters, cracked doorsteps, peeling woodwork. The house she faced had vertical blinds drawn across the front window. Liddy gave a tentative ring on the doorbell. She wasn't encouraged when the gaunt man who responded seemed surprised to see her.

'I have an appointment,' she said. 'To discuss training material? I'm Helen Rawlings.'

He clapped his hand to his high forehead in a theatrical gesture. He was more faded-looking than she'd expected of an Australian. 'Oh, sure, come in. We're still getting settled, as you can see.'

She followed him into a room which was a shambles of boxed equipment. 'This is only a temporary office,' he said, leafing through a desk diary. 'Until we've sorted out the lease downtown. I know I have your name here somewhere, but my PA's on leave this week and I'm *so* falling behind.' He gave an unexpected smile, which illuminated his face and caused Liddy to think twice about turning around and walking out and chiding herself for her misplaced curiosity. She would stay and see it through. 'I hope you haven't had far to come.'

'Oh no,' she lied.

'What can I do for you?'

'That's what I'm here to find out. First, though, you *are* the person I've been corresponding with? Grant Fielding?'

'That's me.' He was very thin, she couldn't help noticing. Like a pipe-cleaner. He wrapped his pipe-cleaner arms around some box files and shifted them so she could sit down. She supposed that he, too, had been an actor. He had an ethereal, androgynous quality; his accent was indeterminate, unplaceable. 'Can I get you something to drink, Helen?'

'Tea please, no milk.'

'Kettle's next door. I'll only be a jiffy.'

A photograph frame lay face down on the desk and when he left the room she turned it over. Two men, windblown, their arms flung casually around each other's shoulders were grinning at the camera. The exposure was grainy; the light so bright it bleached the detail from their faces, left their complexions unmarked by age or worry. One of the men was Grant Fielding; the other, scarcely different from the way he'd looked all those years ago, was Jake. Until this point, she'd had no certainty. All her evidence was circumstantial. She wouldn't have been surprised if her search had yielded no results. Now that her hunch was proved correct, she was torn between elation, excitement and the anxiety that perhaps, after all, sleeping dogs should not be provoked. She heard the clatter of a teaspoon falling and a mumbled curse. The phone rang three times and was diverted to an automated message. She replaced the photo upside down.

One of Liddy's private tests for a well-run office related to the quality of the china. Chipped and mismatched mugs were as much an indicator of sloppiness as scuffed shoes. The test wasn't foolproof – people who were more than competent at a trivial level could be incapable of focus and efficiency on a larger scale – but it was useful to file away in the process of information gathering. When Grant handed her an elegant white cup and saucer, he rose in her estimation, even though the tea itself was far too strong.

He sat at the other side of the desk and toyed with a pen. She tried to look relaxed. 'So, you're expanding your operation into the UK sector. Have I got that right?'

'That's the aim,' he said. 'Though if we do well enough in London we may close down the Sydney branch. For various reasons we'd like to focus our resources here. I think we have a lot to offer.'

'You realize you'll be up against extensive competition?'

'Have you seen our work?'

'I came across it by chance,' she said. 'But I was impressed. I'd like to see more.'

He pushed a DVD across the desk towards her. 'Be my guest.'

She picked it up and glanced at the cover. Unable to identify the face she sought among the medley of images she tucked it into her briefcase. 'Why don't you show me an excerpt while I'm here? Talk me through it.'

'The new premises will have a screening room,' he said. 'I would set up a temporary one out back but it's chock-full of clobber right now. Next week, when Mandy's here . . .'

Liddy prickled with annoyance at the spectacle of yet another man unable to function without his sidekick. She waited in silence while he booted up his laptop and fed in a disc. It was possible that within minutes she would see Jake on screen, performing some absurd role-play, pretending to be a useless middle-manager. He'd never made extravagant claims for his talent – he admitted he'd been on the bottom rung at Cinecitta – but surely this cannot have been the career he had in mind? Surely he had more ambition?

'Excuse me,' she said, as the title music started up. 'I need my glasses.' Fumbling for them gave her an excuse to look away from the screen. She should not have put herself in this position, flushing with shame on Jake's behalf. It was a fantasy scenario that had misfired and she needed to extricate herself swiftly and politely. She heard the beginning of a voiceover and was relieved not to recognize it. For the next nine minutes she sat twisting her wedding ring as Grant pressed pause and play and talked about camera angles, and split-screen techniques, the importance of snappy script editing and taking a holistic approach. There was no sign of Jake.

'Thank you,' she said, though she'd barely noted the content. 'That's given me enough to be going on with. Your production values are very high.'

'Absolutely essential,' Grant said. 'We don't cut corners. We hire the best actors and I think we have an inventive take on direction. I can guarantee that viewers will not be bored. Did you read our testimonials?'

'Doesn't this make you expensive, though? Don't you find your competitors undercut your fees?'

Grant sighed. 'Don't *you* find, Helen, that in life you get exactly what you pay for?'

'Let me make my position clear,' she said. 'I wouldn't be hiring you directly, but if I thought it appropriate I could recommend you to my clients. I really need to be sure that you can deliver what you're offering and it seems to me you're not quite up to speed here.' She indicated the boxes and the stacks of files.

'All under control within a couple of weeks,' he promised. 'As soon as Mandy's back from leave I'm signing the lease on the office space.'

Liddy couldn't help being distracted by his mannerisms, by their odd similarity to Jake's: tossing his fringe and letting his eyes rest upon hers with intense sincerity. Grant was like an etiolated version of the man she'd known – as if an impression of the original Jake had been taken and rolled out to near transparency: a faint, cloned shadow.

'A couple of weeks?' she repeated. 'And what's happening at the Australian end?'

'We'll keep that ticking over for the time being.'

'We? Who are your other business partners?'

'We have backers in Sydney who've invested in us. Sleeping partners. And then . . .' With one hand Grant pinched the bridge of his nose. The other was piercing a piece of paper with a pen. Liddy waited, horrified. 'Sorry,' he said. 'You hit a raw nerve. It's the reason I'm sitting here right now, actually. Back in the old country.'

'You're English?'

'Yeah. My partner was English, too. Jamie and I set up the business when we grew tired of being a couple of beach bums. We took it a helluva long way.' As if realizing this was not a topic to be expected at a business meeting, he added, 'Sorry for going off target, Helen. This is not what you came to hear.' The pen had stopped piercing. His grip around it was so tight his knuckles blanched.

'Jamie?' said Liddy. '*Was* English? What happened?' She couldn't help her eyes straying to the back of the photograph frame. Grant lifted and regarded it before showing it to her. She knew what he was going to say before the words came; she knew with complete conviction that the worst thing she could possibly imagine had already taken place.

'There was an accident.'

'What sort of accident?'

'Not while we were filming, you understand. We have very high health and safety standards. He wasn't on location. It was a personal trip. Kayaking. Not long after this picture was taken.' He paused. 'Jamie got into difficulties and we couldn't rescue him in time.'

'He drowned?' If Liddy shut her eyes she could see them all in the boat: herself, Helena and Jake, Mimmo, Bobo and Sara. She could feel the water rocking beneath her, glittering and treacherous. They'd laughed at her for being scared, but she'd been proved right. Small boats were dangerous things.

Grant bowed his head. 'Two and a half years ago.'

She'd wanted to draw a line but she hadn't expected it to be this final. During the past few months, since meeting Allie, memories of Jake had surfaced and tugged at her. She could see him spinning turntables, lighting a cigarette, lying on the tumbled bed in one of his black moods. Sometimes she could hear his persuasive charm; feel the deft play of his clever fingers. For so long she'd looked out for him, wondering whether she might see his face on a screen or his name in the credits, or read an interview in a magazine. That wouldn't happen now. Jake wasn't part of anyone's life. He'd been dead for over two years.

'That's terrible,' she said, because all useful words had forsaken her.

'It was tough,' Grant said. 'We put so much energy into setting up the business and he was an ace director. Losing your other half is kind of difficult to overcome. But hey, I'm conquering new territory here, that's what it's all about. Come back home and make a new start . . .' He crumpled his ravaged paper into a ball and hurled it at the waste-paper bin. 'Strewth – how d'you get this stuff out of me? I didn't mean to be, like, so unprofessional.'

'It's how I get the full picture,' said Liddy. 'Listening to people.' And ferreting about in their accounts and their filing systems and their desk drawers; forever breaching the defensive barriers they put up when they suspected someone was coming to spy on them. Sometimes she hated what she did.

'Well, I've already said too much. I swear to you we're a going concern. New projects lined up and a handful in the final stages in the editing suite. You've caught me at a moment of hiatus. The new website goes live next week, but meantime let me find some copies of our brochure for you. They should be in the back office.' He shambled out again.

Liddy was sifting his words, examining them as if they were three-dimensional objects, as if from a different facet she might get a different analysis. Had she heard correctly? 'My partner . . . a couple of beach bums . . . losing your other half.' She'd classified Jake as one of those intriguing itinerants who can't bring themselves to settle down, but clearly he and Grant had been long-term lovers. It irked her that he'd chosen a stringy pipe-cleaner over soft, curvaceous womanhood – but it was nothing compared to the tragedy of his early death. Poor Jake. For all that he'd appeared to promise, what had he left behind? A handful of workplace DVDs, soon to be superseded. No glory.

This was too much to take in. When Grant returned with a fraction more colour in his cheeks and a pile of A4 folders, her stance was still rigid, frozen.

'I have to apologize,' he said, 'that you found me in such disarray. To be frank, I wouldn't have made the appointment if I'd remembered Mandy was going to be off. We could have sorted all this on the phone.'

He was right. She'd been foolish. She forced herself to speak. 'I like to make a point of meeting new contacts face to face. I hope you don't think I've taken advantage of your . . . um . . . circumstances. I'd be happy to reconvene when you're more organized.' This wasn't true. She had no intention of keeping any association. Future emails would be deleted, unanswered.

'And I hope, Helen, that you'll think our work speaks for itself. I can assure you I haven't let standards fall. That DVD I've given you is a new one. Jamie wasn't the only talented director in our stable.'

'It's so sad when talent is cut short. And it's my turn to apologize' – she had to say this, however difficult it was – 'if I probed too far into your personal life. I didn't mean to. It's just . . .'

'Are you okay, Helen?'

She seemed to be glued to her seat. She rested her hand on her abdomen as the nausea rose in her throat. 'Yes, I'll be fine. It will pass in a moment. To tell you the truth, I've always been afraid of water myself.'

'Oh, but Jamie didn't have much fear. And if he did, he'd face it head on. Exorcize his demons, as it were.'

Liddy swallowed. 'Did he have many? Demons, I mean.' They both wanted to talk about him, that much was obvious: she and Grant Fielding and heaven knows how many other lovers. Grant smiled again, the smile that transformed his face from nondescript to handsome. It contained within it an echo, a fragment of Jake. 'Hundreds,' he said.

Shaking his hand on departure, noting its dry warmth, she marvelled at the power of touch, its ability to awaken other fleeting memories. She had to get back home, to something that resembled reality. She didn't know which direction to take for the Tube and she couldn't see a taxi. Perhaps she should ring for one. As soon as she switched on her phone, several text messages rumbled into her inbox. There was also a voicemail, surprisingly agitated, from Allie.

26

Helena had fired up the kiln she kept in her garden studio and was waiting for it to reach the required temperature. Summer was tipping into August. There was a languorous feel to the hawthorn hedge and the high grass was rampant with clover. The apples were reddening and starting to drop. She'd come home determined to harness a spurt of creative energy, to produce a ceramic collection that was shockingly gaudy – in complete contrast to her meticulous restoration projects. She thought she would welcome an uninterrupted period of concentration, but already she longed for distraction. She was finding Bryony Cottage, a square, detached twenties house with quirky Arts and Crafts touches, a little too quiet. It was different in term-time, when charming overseas lodgers turned her kitchen into an international canteen (she'd never relished the nuclear family unit, not even during those relatively stable years with Ian) and promised reciprocal hospitality should she find herself in Tokyo or Tangiers or Buenos Aires – which was most unlikely to happen.

She wondered whether it was too early to ring Simon in Chicago. The plenary sessions wouldn't have started. He might be eating breakfast. Pancakes and maple syrup? Soufflé omelette with bacon rashers so crisp they crumbled on impact? He might not be alone. He might have picked up another delegate. You couldn't rely on them to be frigid blue-stockings, particularly not in criminology. She imagined a Californian with long, red fingernails and platinum hair. Or a Brazilian sitting astride his lap with her toffee-coloured legs outstretched. Her pace quickened as she crossed the lawn and re-entered the house. She picked up the handset, sat at the foot of the stairs and dialled the number of his hotel. At the reception desk they tried but failed to put her through to his room. His mobile didn't appear to be functioning.

Really, this was stupid. What was she going to say to him anyway? I didn't expect to miss you? She was chiding herself for her impatience when the phone rang in her hand before she'd had a chance to replace it on its rest.

'Faultless timing!' she exclaimed. 'How *do* you manage it?'

'Mum?' said Allie. 'How did you know it was me?'

'Telepathy,' said Helena without missing a beat. 'I've been waiting to hear from you.'

'You have?'

'You upset quite an apple cart.'

'That's not fair.'

'Well, I suppose Liddy had a hand in it too, but you should have told me what you were up to. I shouldn't have had to call Bobo bloody Baldini to find out where you were. Plus, the other day when I was at your place, this bloke, this complete no-mark, comes on the line and starts interrogating me . . .'

'Who?'

'I don't know. I can't remember his name! As if it's any of his business. And God knows –'

'I don't believe this,' said Allie. 'Are you *angry* with me?'

Helena flexed her shoulder blades, straightened her spine; she was no longer bored. 'Of course I'm angry – with the pair of you for cooking up this expedition behind my back. This is only the second time you've contacted me since it all blew up.'

'I emailed. Didn't you get my email?'

'I don't think so, but I've been in the studio. Which account did you send it to?'

'Here's the thing,' said Allie, and it was at this point that Helena detected a flatness, a dull monotone that was quite uncharacteristic and which could not be explained by the physical distance between them. 'I'm phoning you now because there's stuff I need to know. Like why did you lie to me?'

'Lie about what?'

'The guy . . . The man who . . . my father.'

The day was muggy. Thunder flies drifted in a black cloud in the open doorway. Helena said, 'I cannot possibly have this conversation with you on the telephone.'

'Well, we've never managed to have it any other way. I thought it might be easier if you didn't actually have to look me in the eye.'

'Allie, what's got into you?'

'*I just want to know.*'

Helena was taken aback by the hostility she could hear in Allie's voice. She took the phone into the sitting room and launched herself on to the sofa, scattering cushions. 'We've managed pretty well up to now, you and I. You need to think carefully about what you're asking.'

'I *have* thought. I've been super-sensitive. I've never pushed this before. But, the fact is, I have a *right*.'

'If you yell at me, Allie, I'll cut you off. I've already told you this isn't the subject for a phone call.'

'Why? You're at home, aren't you? It's not like you're walking down the street with everyone listening in.'

There were no background noises at Allie's end either. 'Where are you?'

'I'm in an apartment in a district of Rome called Prati. It belongs to someone you used to know. Fabrizio Verducci.'

She should have guessed this would happen: she had instilled in Allie the value of perseverance. She punched one of the cushions but it gave her no satisfaction. 'What on earth are you doing there?'

'I was invited by his son.'

'Mimmo?'

'Max. I already told you about him.'

'You only said he was lending you his mobile. And I couldn't get back in touch with you afterwards.' She could sense an incipient headache. She held the handset a little further from her ear. 'So you've actually met Fabrizio, have you?'

'Yes.'

'How is he, the bastard?'

'I think he's probably still a bastard,' said Allie.

'I used to be fatally attracted to the type,' Helena said. 'You should know I was only trying to protect you.'

'Actually, he's agreed to take a DNA test.'

'Really? They weren't easy to come by in those days.'

'What I don't understand,' Allie said, 'is why you gave me all that bollocks about the romantic, feckless, left-wing musician. Where did he come from?'

Helena stood up and stared at her reflection in the mirrored overmantel: the lines that bracketed the upward tilt of her mouth and crimped the corners of her eyes. It was not a miserable face, nor a defeated one. If your will was strong enough you could deal with all kinds of flak and come through cheerful.

'Mum, are you there?'

'It was a solution of sorts,' said Helena. 'When you're stuck between the devil and the deep blue sea. Creative licence.'

'What does that mean?'

'You weren't going to meet him, after all. A charming, talented wastrel seemed to fit the bill and isn't far off the mark anyway.'

'You made him up? You *invented* him! Why?'

'Why do you think?'

'Why *would* somebody lie about a person's father?' Silence stifled the line. At length Allie said in bewilderment, 'Unless he was a murderer or a rapist or something. Oh shit . . .'

'You see!' exclaimed Helena. 'That's exactly why we need to talk this over in person. You're making things worse than they need be and whatever I say now you won't believe. You'll think I'm fobbing you off.'

'Try me.'

The thermometer on the kiln would be rising steadily, building heat. The blast when she opened the door would be awesome. She should be getting back to the studio. 'You have to remember that my dates were confused because of the pill. The simple fact is that I didn't know who got me pregnant.'

An astounded pause. 'You didn't know!'

'I don't believe I ever sprouted wings,' said Helena.

'No but . . .'

'It didn't seem so outrageous at the time. I'd met Fabrizio soon after I arrived in Rome – the practice was sponsoring an exhibition we had to visit – and I daresay I got involved with him too quickly. There was a period when I tried to break it off – because he was married for goodness' sake – and I had a short-lived fling with someone else . . . When you were born and Fabrizio refused to acknowledge you I thought it was because of the palsy. You can't believe how angry I was.'

'Someone else?' demanded Allie. 'Who?'

'An English actor called Jake Knight.'

'So I'm not half-Italian?'

Many of Allie's friends had such a rich cultural heritage they were like one-man multinationals. She was bound to be disappointed. 'Possibly not.'

'An actor?'

'You won't have heard of him. He slipped under the radar years ago.'

'Did he ever see me?'

'No. He left Italy before you were born. Got some bit part in a film on location in Spain. We didn't keep in touch.'

'But you could track him down now, if the DNA . . . I mean . . . ?'

'Well, that would be your prerogative, though I'm not sure it would be a good idea. Look, Allie, I've had some crap boyfriends, but actually you were lucky with Ian. He was a much better dad than either of your supposed biological fathers would have been.' Fourteen years of compromise was how she saw it now.

'You know he left us because he wanted his own kids. And that was your fault.'

At times like this, Helena regretted she no longer had a twenty-a-day habit. The buzz of nicotine (or something stronger) to kindle her brain, the primitive comfort of her mouth sucking the filter. 'Yep, that's me, responsible for all the shit in the world. Shoot me, why don't you? Or you could just come home . . . Darling? Please.'

'I have to go,' said Allie abruptly. 'I'm running late.'

In fact she was early. She'd thought about not turning up at all, but she didn't want to earn an undeserved reputation for bottling stuff. She wasn't a bottler; she faced things head on. She scanned the tables set out in front of the restaurant, all occupied by strangers. She'd expected Max to arrive before her, but he wasn't in the smoky interior either. She accepted the waiter's invitation to dine in the back courtyard and was placed at a table that rocked on the uneven paving and was a little too close to the drains. She spent ten minutes trying to translate the menu, wondering how long she should give him and whether he'd be able to find her.

'Jeez, I'm sorry. Have you been waiting for ever?'

She looked up. She wished he'd ruffle his hair a bit, like when she'd first met him. When it was sleek and slicked back, the echo of his father was too strong, unnerving.

'Is this the best table they could offer you?'

She indicated the rest of the courtyard. 'They're quite busy.'

'I should have booked ahead.' He slid into the seat opposite. 'Hey, but it's a privilege these days, don't you think?'

'What is?'

'All this: the leisurely lunch. Back home everyone's walking around with take-out coffee in one hand and a hot dog in the other. Or maybe, if you're the Wall Street end of the city, a tuna wrap. What would you go for, Allie, tuna or lox?'

'What's lox?'

He laughed in apparent delight. 'Smoked salmon. You've never been to the States, right?'

'We had plans,' she said. 'Me and the others, but –'

'You'd love New York. Everybody does. It's so full-on, charged with excitement. Nowhere compares really . . .'

'I grew up on *Friends*,' said Allie. 'I've spent hours in Central Perk.'

He grinned and raised his arm to hail a waiter. 'Have you chosen yet?'

'I don't know.' She wasn't even sure she was hungry. 'I'll probably just have a salad.'

'Lox or tuna?' he joked. He was keyed-up; animated. He'd had a good morning, solved some difficulty with a staircase return in a renovation project that had been bugging him, which was why he was late and he was sorry, but it had been worth it, to fix the problem. His explanation sounded too mathematical for Allie to trouble with.

She couldn't keep all his figures in her head as he talked and moved the cutlery into different positions on the tablecloth. A knife fell to the ground and when he bent to retrieve it, he spotted her backpack. She'd tried to push it under her chair, but the end stuck out.

'Hey, you're not *leaving*, are you?'

'I think I should.'

'Why? Is something the matter?'

'I don't think I should stay in your flat while your father's there.'

'Why not? He won't care.'

'Well, then, I probably shouldn't stay in it anyway.'

'What's making you so squeamish all of a sudden?'

'It's, like, your family home,' said Allie. 'And I'm an interloper.'

Max lifted an eyebrow. He pulled over the waiter to take their order. Allie chose a salad niçoise because she knew what it was. Max ordered pasta with pancetta and *funghi*. They both agreed to drink mineral water.

'So are you going to tell me what's really bothering you or do I have to play twenty questions?' He snapped a breadstick in half and held a piece out to her.

The sunny courtyard was a warm, intimate space. The light tinkle of glass and china, the muted throb of conversation floated gently to the blue canopy of sky. This was what Italy was good at: creating seductive tableaux that made you think you could stay for ever. A family had reached dessert stage; an older child was spooning ice cream into a toddler's mouth. A group of office workers was teasing a colleague who kept taking calls on his mobile. Three Scandinavian girls flirted with a man alone with his newspaper. A middle-aged couple, tourists with peeling complexions, held hands across the bread basket. What would an observer think of us, Allie wondered. Friends? Partners? Lovers? Ships passing? Siblings? No, probably not.

Max crunched the end of the breadstick. 'Well?'

'It's to do with my mother,' she said. 'I spoke to her just before I came here. It was a kind of heavy conversation.'

She'd intended to follow Fabrizio out of the apartment. He had explained to her, with irreproachable courtesy, that he had an appointment; he was sorry their encounter was so short. He also made it clear he didn't want to see her again until the DNA results had been analysed and the nature of their relation established. He had no doubt he would be proved correct. This was the deal they had struck, but she couldn't find the words to tell Max. It had taken all morning to mull over their meeting and square up to ringing Helena.

'Your mother? Is she ill or something?'

'No, no. Don't you remember? She used to look after you. I mean, she was your family's employee. It makes things embarrassing.'

'Why? I'm an employee, come to that.' He stopped and narrowed his gaze. 'Oh, wait a minute. She lived with us the summer I got lost, right? And –'

Allie interrupted, still bitter towards Helena. '– Yes. She was no good at her job, was she? A complete liability, in fact. It wouldn't be surprising if there were hard feelings. Not that she admitted any of this to me. I learned it from a friend of hers, Liddy, the one who gave me the idea of coming out here.'

He brushed Liddy aside. 'But that's not all you're saying, is it? She wasn't just my babysitter. She was having an affair with my dad, wasn't she?'

'Well . . .'

'It's okay; she wouldn't have been the first. Or the last . . .' He put his fingertips to his temples and squeezed as if trying to contain the realization: 'That summer I was what, three? Nearly four? And you, how old are you now?'

'I'm twenty-three.'

The arithmetic was simple, wasn't it? You didn't need a degree in mathematics or architecture to work it out. 'Fuck,' said Max.

The waiter set down the salad and the bowl of pasta. He unscrewed the bottle of mineral water and poured it into their glasses where the bubbles hissed and exploded. He wished them *buon appetito*.

Allie said, 'You've got it wrong.'

'What have I got wrong?'

'Well, I'm guessing that you're jumping to conclusions.'

'Adding two and two and making four? That kind of thing? Like suddenly discovering you're my –'

'Five,' she said. 'You're making five.'

There was a pause, an interval readily filled by the babble of other diners. The middle-aged couple called for their bill. Max's cell phone beeped and he switched it off. 'What's going on here? What is it you *want*, Allie?'

Fabrizio had asked the same question.

'Why do I have to *want* anything? Why can't I have a natural curiosity? Or be on a voyage of self-discovery like most other people my age? All those backpackers.'

'But why are you being so evasive? You've already talked me through everything else that happened that summer, so talk me through this. In 1979 you were what, in utero? Only luckily for all concerned you had X-ray vision?'

'That's unfair! This hasn't been any easier for me than for you. My mother never told me the truth until today.'

'Jesus Christ!' His glass halted halfway to his mouth. The expression in his eyes was appalled.

Allie felt immediately defensive. Helena had, in a misguided way, been trying to shield her. 'I told you we had a heavy conversation. You want me to go over it with you?'

'I think maybe we should get some things straight, yeah.'

She tried to keep the story simple, despite the loose ends yet to be woven and knotted. Max occasionally interrupted with questions or snorted in disbelief. He didn't touch his food; the cream of his sauce congealed. 'You're saying my dad had a problem with your arm?'

She rested the offending arm on the tablecloth, curling her bitten fingernails from his view. 'People want perfect babies, don't they? What's the Italian – *bella figura*?'

'*La bella figura* doesn't mean beautiful figure, you know. It's more, like, a concept: how you present yourself. A certain style.' When he shook his head she supposed this was a style she lacked; she was too scruffy. But he said, 'I can't believe my dad would be so crass.'

'Well, that was how my mum chose to interpret it.'

'From what you've told me he supported her, didn't he? Supported both of you. It wasn't like he dumped her in the shit. If he really thought you were someone else's kid, you could say that was honourable.'

'I got the impression he wasn't around much, the whole situation made him uncomfortable.' She imagined furtive visits, the curiosity of Helena's flatmates, Fabrizio's reluctance to linger. 'Even so, he could hardly have kept it a secret. *Your* mother must have known about us. Is it common in Italy for men to have two families?'

'Not common exactly, though back when my parents first married you couldn't even get divorced.'

'Do you think she gave him an ultimatum?'

'Like what?'

'Like threatening to take you away if he didn't stop seeing my mother? Fabrizio wouldn't want to lose you, would he? For a baby who might not be his.'

'Also ironic since in the end we left anyway.' His lips stretched into a grin. 'Do you suppose we ever met, you and I, in an earlier life? You in your stroller in the Giardini Borghese, me riding alongside on my bicycle?'

The notion was appealing. Was that why she'd felt she'd known him for ever? 'That would have been something! Do you remember it?'

'Riding my bike, yeah. Baby sister, not so sure.'

'Don't! He was absolutely adamant this morning that I wasn't his daughter. Those were his words. In English. No mistake.'

'And you believed him?'

'He was very convincing. About the likely dates and so on. There was a short period, you see, when he and Mum split up.' His certainty had been impressive. 'I didn't know whether to be relieved or disappointed.'

'About what?'

'About us. The possibility we're related.' She reviewed the unlikely image of an older brother playing with her in the park. 'Up to that point, I'd sort of hoped we might be.'

His eyebrows lifted. 'You did?'

'God, I've said the wrong thing, haven't I?'

'There isn't a right or a wrong here. There's just stuff that needs figuring out.' Belatedly he spooned a snowfall of parmesan over his pasta and sampled his first mouthful. 'You wonder how some guys' parents can make such an unholy mess of things . . .'

The tourist couple paid their bill and left the restaurant, still holding hands. Allie wistfully watched them go. Max rapped on the table top to recapture her attention. 'So then . . . you and I . . . where do we go from here?'

'We just have to carry on, don't we? Till we get the DNA results. Stick to the original plan.' Now it was all in the open she could relax a little. She picked up her fork and turned over a lettuce leaf. You could spend as long as you liked toying with salad and it wouldn't spoil.

'Which is?'

'Well, to start with I was going to book into a hostel, check out a few places I've been wanting to see, and then . . .'

'Check out where, what places?'

'Well, there's Keats' grave in the Protestant Cemetery and the church, San Pietro . . .'

'You've never been to San Pietro!'

'Not *that* Saint Peter's.'

'*In Vincoli?* Michelangelo's *Moses*?'

'No! The one on the Gianicolo, I've forgotten the name –'

His face cleared. 'Ah, San Pietro in Montorio. And Bramante's Tempietto. That is the most stunningly perfect building. It may be small but the proportions are exquisite. Really you should see it with someone who knows the score, who can tell you –'

'Like an architect, you mean?'

'Yes. Exactly.'

'Thanks. I might take you up on that.'

When he had finished chewing, he said. 'Afraid I'm busy the next couple of days, but if you can find out what time it closes . . .'

'I'll probably go there tomorrow after I've picked up some more emails. And leave in the evening. I can get the train and be in Paris for breakfast.'

He shovelled some more rigatoni from plate to mouth. 'Making a quick escape?'

'My ticket's running out so I'd have to leave soon anyway.' She speared a morsel of tuna and a shred of cucumber. 'But you could come to England whenever, now that you're staying here. It's only a couple of hours by plane.'

'I was going to spend vacations back in the States.'

'Just for a weekend?' She tried to sound casual. 'It's easy these days. We could go to a gig, check out some upcoming bands.'

'Are you inviting me?'

'If I did, would you accept?' She salvaged an olive pit before she choked on it and laid it at the side of her plate. 'You could email me. Or call. I'll send you my number when I get a new one.'

'You think we should keep in touch?' He paused. 'Whatever happens?'

'Why not?'

'And how long would we keep this up?'

'You mean, after we've found out for certain who I am?' This was ludicrous. She knew perfectly well who she was: Allie Ashbourne, percussionist. 'How am I supposed to answer that?' Since he was waiting, she offered: 'Till Christmas? Till we're bored? Or maybe we'll get the bug and carry on for five years. You'll be fielding major commissions and I'll be thumping away on backing tracks – if I'm lucky.'

'Five years!' He wiped a piece of bread around his plate.

Allie couldn't imagine that far ahead either. She couldn't even imagine boarding the train or entering Bryony Cottage and confronting her mother. This was now. A shutter in her head clicked on the composition of the courtyard, the angle of the light on Max's cheekbones, his fingers twirling the stem of his glass, the sardonic curve to his lips, as if he were merely humouring her. 'We could give it a go,' she said.

27

The man Helena was following seemed at home in the hospital corridor, his manner proprietorial. As he paused every now and again to greet a member of staff she wondered if he were a consultant en route to his clinic. He was a large man, substantial in his suit and brogues, and yet he had an air of disarray: a trailing shoelace, untamed hair, a patch of grease on his worsted elbow. He jingled the coins in his pocket and veered suddenly into the shop, into a crush of pastel rabbits, teddies in bow ties and silver helium balloons. Not a doctor after all then; a visitor. She was amused to see him collide with a stand of cards to welcome Your New Baby. The stand tottered and the cards floated to the ground like leaves. No one else paid any attention, but Helena joined him in his attempt to collect and replace them in their racks.

'Size thirteen feet,' he said. 'Unlucky for some.'

He was putting most of the cards back upside down so that babies fell out of their prams and storks perched beneath chimney pots. She didn't alter them.

'Thanks.' He towered his bulk upwards again. 'All I'm after is a copy of *Elle Decoration*.' She laughed outright at this and the man said quickly, 'For my wife, of course.'

'Of course.'

'These magazines come with so much baggage, don't you find? All that extra bumph.'

They both stood gazing at their Cellophaned ranks.

'It's how they con us into paying more,' said Helena. 'Worthless freebies that go straight into the bin. Candyfloss. Popcorn. Spinning out the molecules. That's marketing for you. Hot air.'

'Is that your speciality? Marketing?'

'No, just a hobby horse.' She inclined her head and had to adjust her cloche hat.

'You could grow plants in that,' he said, running his hand through his own unruly hair, increasing its resemblance to thatch.

'I suppose you think you're the first person to make that crack?'

'Well, I warned you. Size thirteen feet.'

He had a manner that put you so much at ease you felt as if you'd known him for ever. He was nearly fifty she guessed – the lines around his eyes, the grey hair at his temples gave him away – though there was a boyishness about him. If you had strongly developed maternal instincts (which Helena didn't), you might be tempted to take him in hand, knot his shoelace securely so he didn't blunder into things, point him in the right direction. His smile was lopsided like the way he walked, with his weight falling on his left foot. He lolloped away from her towards the magazines and brought a spark to the face of the girl at the till as he counted out his change. She watched him wander off, checking his Blackberry, tangling with a buggy pushed by a bald-pated father.

In her bag Helena carried a punnet of nectarines. She hadn't wanted to visit Liddy empty-handed, but now she wondered if her choice of nectarines was less a peace offering than a dig, whether she should play safe and buy some chocolates. The selection on offer was depressingly predictable. After contemplating the boxes of Cadbury's Black Magic and Terry's All Gold and the queue building up at the till, she decided chocolates were such a cliché she'd stick to the fruit. Back in the corridor, she headed to the reception desk for directions.

There was no sense of urgency in the Women's Hospital. Any evidence of operating-theatre drama was well hidden. She recognized the smells, though. They tried to disguise them with freshly brewed coffee, bunches of lilies, newsprint, but she could pick them out like a draught of cold air under a door. She couldn't help her guts knotting as she recalled the frenzied panic of Allie's delivery, the uproar among the nurses who made no attempt to lower their voices. She couldn't understand what they were saying because her mind couldn't access the language, couldn't make sense of anything except the conviction that something was wrong: giving birth should not be *this* difficult. Why wasn't the baby slithering out with a satisfying squelch? Why was everyone screaming at each other?

There had been no cause for concern: she was young and healthy, her pregnancy for the most part untroubled. They knew the baby was large for its dates (whatever they were), but Helena was tall. Nobody had been concerned about the width of her pelvis until it was too late, until the baby had beaten against the bone for several hours, until its head had ripped through her vagina into the world and its body had jammed. This was the point at which she ceased to be a person and became a piece of meat to be hacked at and manipulated. And nothing could dull the intensity of the pain. The birth took place overnight, the lights in the labour ward so dazzling she was convinced she was in a torture chamber. She rarely spoke of it, but it was not an experience she would ever forget.

At reception they looked up Liddy's details. Apparently she had her own room. Many patients were allotted private rooms, but Helena suspected Liddy would have insisted on privacy in any event. She progressed along the broad, bland corridor and up a staircase. She marvelled at the security, at the number of intercoms and the necessity for identifying oneself. She was not expected and she had no idea how she would be received. She was making this visit on Allie's instructions. She knocked, a decisive rap, at the door. It was opened by a man she knew at once.

'You must think I'm stalking you,' she said.

'You're a friend of Liddy's!' he exclaimed in delight, pumping her hand. 'Mike Rawlings. I'm sorry, but I don't think we've met. That is . . . apart from . . .' He grinned at her like a conspirator. 'Come in.'

Liddy was sitting up in bed in an ivory silk nightdress with *Elle Decoration* on her lap. Her face was pale and drawn. When she saw Helena she blinked rapidly as if in disbelief. 'Good Lord,' she said. 'How did you . . .?'

'Allie told me.'

'Oh, are you staying with her? Only I thought –'

'No. I'm at a friend's in town. Simon. You, um, met him that time you called round.'

'The policeman?'

'He's not really a policeman.'

'Yes, I know. I didn't mean . . .'

'The old house is full of plumbers. But Allie isn't there anyway. She's back in Birmingham helping to run some epic gig. I guess you know that since you've been advising her.'

'PR and marketing?' said Mike Rawlings jovially.

'Music promotion.'

Liddy turned to her husband, wincing as if the movement were painful. 'Darling, you know Allie – she's been so good with Rolo. Helena's her mother. We were at school together, but we lost touch until . . . recently.'

'You're her *mother*?'

'Yes. I started young.'

He looked as if he were trying to recollect what he'd heard about her, but gave up, shaking his shaggy head. 'Right then,' he said. 'If you two are catching up, I'll be off.'

'You don't have to go on my account,' said Helena.

'No worries, I'll be back this evening. And I was leaving anyway – hence the mag.' He bent over Liddy in her high bed and laid his palm against her cheek. The stiff set of her jaw relaxed at his touch and the action was so gentle, so tender, the expression in his eyes so full of emotion that Helena had to look away. She sauntered over to the window as if to stress she'd no wish to interrupt their leave-taking. She looked out on to a parade of evergreen shrubs, strung with bright autumnal berries, glinting with scraps of tinfoil and trapped bottle-tops. The sun was already low in the sky. She heard the scrape of the bed as Mike rose; turning, she caught the warm intensity of his smile. Lucky Lid, she thought.

'It was good of you to come,' said Liddy, when the door had closed on his heels.

'Simon's place is only down the road. A stone's throw. So how are you?'

Liddy grimaced. 'Who'd be a woman?' Her complexion was translucent, like water overlaid with a film of chalk dust, her eyes bitter and cloudy. 'What did Allie tell you?'

Helena pulled off her hat and pulled up a chair beside the bed. 'To stop fucking about and come and see you.'

'Oh, right. Well, you just made it. They're sending me home tomorrow. Did she also tell you . . .' Her fingers plucked at the sheet. 'They'd had to delay the operation because I thought I might be pregnant?'

Helena nodded. Allie had been eloquent on the subject of Liddy's disappointment.

'I shouldn't have got my hopes up. My womb was so cluttered with those damn fibroids there was probably no space for a baby anyway. Really it's stupid how much emotional energy one wastes thinking, maybe this time . . .' Liddy's fingers stilled; the copy of *Elle* slid gracefully to the floor. 'I know I have to grow up and get over it, but it's so hard . . . I don't think anyone can understand quite *how* painful – unless they've been in this situation.' She muttered so quietly that Helena could hardly hear her: 'I can't help thinking how things might have been different.'

'But that's the way stuff happens, isn't it? Totally random. Like my getting pregnant on the pill.' Helena spread her arms in a gesture that encompassed the entire gynaecology ward. 'No way could I ever go through something like that again. I got my tubes tied after Allie was born. Once was enough for me.'

'Was it really so awful?'

'Let's say I don't have any regrets about the decision.'

Liddy poured a glass of water from the jug on her bedside cabinet and held it to her mouth. She seemed to have difficulty swallowing. Helena opened her bag and took out the nectarines. 'I bought these for you,' she said. 'It's marvellous what you can get out of season nowadays, isn't it? And they felt as if they should be ripe. Hope you enjoy them.' She placed the punnet next to the water jug.

'Thanks.' Liddy put down her glass. With an effort she said, 'I'm sorry I encouraged Allie to go off to Ischia like that. I know I shouldn't have interfered, only when I met her it felt like I was being given the chance to put things right, make amends . . . I wouldn't be punished any more.'

'*What?*'

'Well, I know it sounds a bit Old Testament, but –'

'You're a rational educated person, for heaven's sake!'

'Yes, I know . . .' Liddy looked so frail and vulnerable that Helena bit back the further cutting remarks that tempted her. 'It's just, you see, when you want something really badly and this need grows out of all proportion and there simply isn't any logical reason for failure, then your brain loses its logical function too. You start to make stupid bargains with fate. You start to dredge up all your misdemeanours. You assume it's your fault, so you feel guilty.'

'*I* don't,' said Helena. 'And I think you'll find men don't either. It's a female handicap and I'd banish it if I were you.'

'So you've forgiven me?'

'For my jail sentence?'

'You didn't actually get sentenced, did you? I thought you were let off.'

'Let off, let out, whatever. I should bloody well hope I've moved on by now.'

Liddy had gone back to pinching folds in her coverlet and smoothing them flat again. 'After everything, it came as quite a shock when I heard the DNA results for Allie and Fabrizio . . .' She faltered. 'It had honestly never occurred to me, but surely you must have . . .'

'What?'

She hadn't thought it possible for Liddy's face to blanch further. 'Surely you must have wondered if Jake might be her father.'

How many times had she pored over the calendar for summer 1979, calculating the chances? She sighed. 'I couldn't be certain, though. And frankly, I couldn't bear the thought of her being rejected a second time. That might sound paranoid, but imagine how awful it would have been! At least Fabrizio was prepared to offer us support and a bit of stability.'

'Is that why you let Jake go?'

'God, Liddy, you knew what he was like. He didn't welcome encumbrances. He always travelled light, remember?'

'I tried to keep in touch with him. He didn't have an address so I'd write poste restante. I got a couple of breezy postcards, but he never replied to an actual letter.'

'He wasn't very reliable. Lots of charm, totally self-centred.'

'You always acted like there was an unmentionable secret between you.'

'Did I?'

The room was overheated. Helena slung her jacket over the back of the chair. On a high shelf a blank television screen was angled at the bed. An extravagant autumnal bouquet wilted on the trolley beneath it. From Mike, she presumed. The walls were buttermilk, the curtains and upholstery a soothing sage, the washbasin spotless. It was still a hospital room, though; an artificial capsule from which time was absent.

'There was something, wasn't there?' said Liddy. 'Something you were keeping from me – but I never understood why.'

'Basically because you wouldn't have believed me. You'd have thought I was being vindictive. You were so besotted you wouldn't listen to any warnings. You didn't want to hear a word against him.'

Liddy gave her a stricken look, as if she were deliberately trying to withhold information. 'Then try me now.'

'Well, it was trivial really. He always said I overreacted and he may have been right. It was the end of May, just before the course finished. I came home one afternoon after lectures, thinking the place was empty.' If she shut her eyes she could see the images unspooling: her girlish self meandering down the narrow street, spared from the sun's strength by the height of the apartment buildings, trotting up the staircase, poking the oversized key in the lock, entering the dim shuttered space. 'In fact, someone must have let Jake in. My room had a huge antiquated wardrobe which took up the whole of one wall. He was standing in front of it.'

Liddy had been leaning forward to listen; she flopped against her pillows and waved her hand dismissively.

Helena said, 'I suppose you thought I'd found him in my bed rogering some bit of fluff he'd picked up? He'd a reputation for screwing anything that wasn't nailed down.'

'He was faithful to me,' said Liddy.

Helena let the comment pass. 'Anyway, he wasn't that predictable. He was admiring himself in the mirror.' Beyond the double glazing there was the wail of an ambulance siren, the squeal of a brake; in the corridor the clip of footsteps. She broke off until they had passed the door. 'And he was wearing my clothes.'

'He was an actor. Actors dress up.'

'The thing was, he looked quite like me. Similar height, similar complexion. Long hair. Not like a drag queen or a tranny. He looked like a woman. I flipped, ended it there and then. I wanted a proper *man*, Liddy. Not the competition. Not someone who kept switching sides. He tried to excuse himself, laugh it off, but sometimes there's stuff you just don't want to hear.' It had unnerved her: the sight of Jake filling her clothes with such style and swagger; she didn't enjoy being outshone. 'So I stormed off and called Fabrizio. We got back together and I had the brainwave of getting him to employ us in Ischia . . . It was meant to be a treat, to seal our reconciliation.' She gave a rueful smile. 'I hardly expected Jake to end up there too, but I reckon we acted pretty civilized in the circumstances. We managed to stay friends, didn't we?'

After a moment's silence, Liddy rallied. 'However Jake behaved, it didn't alter the way I felt. I couldn't forget him . . . and I'd always half expected his name to show up somewhere . . . That was why I tried to find him through the internet.'

Helena was glad she could feel calm, composed. 'Yes, Allie said.'

'Even though he'd gone back to using the name James, it was horribly easy. It wouldn't have been ten years ago, but with Google . . . Anyway, I discovered he'd been living in Sydney for ages, making educational-type films. And that he'd drowned in an accident.' Tears brimmed on her lower lashes.

It was ironic, Helena thought, that Liddy had cared so much more for Jake than she did, was so moved by her memories that she could weep for him. 'Of course it's tragic when someone dies young, but Allie never even knew him – she can't mourn a stranger. And she has an extremely good relationship with the man who actually brought her up.'

'Yes, but –' Liddy closed her lips on a little blurt of pain.

'It seems to me,' said Helena, 'in the two minutes I saw him, that you have a fine husband yourself.'

'I know. I only wish –'

'So don't cry over Jake.'

'There's more,' insisted Liddy. 'Something else I found out.'

'Nothing I learned about Jake would surprise me –'

'He'd been living for years with a male partner. Happily, it seemed.'

'– except that he settled down at all. Though that's good, I suppose.'

'I haven't told Allie. I thought I should leave it to you. I see quite a lot of him in her, actually. His good qualities. Don't you think?'

Liddy's arm flailed in her direction and Helena moved to catch hold of it. In the process of connecting they knocked the punnet of fruit from the cabinet; the nectarines spun and rolled like giant marbles. Helena stooped to collect them up, reminded of Mike Rawlings and the card rack. Was this her fault, the effect she had on people?

'Oh dear,' said Liddy. 'They'll be bruised now.'

'Not if we eat them right away. Come on.' She rinsed two nectarines under the tap and handed one over. They took simultaneous bites. The flesh was dry and woolly. Helena was tempted to lob hers into the bin. 'Shit, I'm sorry. What a letdown. That's the trouble when stuff's forced and not allowed to ripen naturally. What you really want is to pick a fresh, juicy fruit straight off the tree.'

'Like we did in Italy,' said Liddy in a plaintive whisper and then, because she was clearly not at her most sanguine, Helena tossed away her nectarine and settled on the bed. She took Liddy in her arms and let her rest her head against her collarbone. Her hair was newly washed and carried the fragrance of aloe vera; a trickle of tears soaked through Helena's shirt. They stayed in this position, in fragile harmony, until a cleaner clattered in to empty the rubbish.

A light wind was blowing as Helena left the hospital, and she tugged her hat closer around her ears. It was a short walk downhill to Simon's flat. In the distance, silvery patches of river nudged the clouds. A phalanx of new buildings was unrolling along the dockside but from this vantage point all she could see were the cranes dominating the skyline. She turned into Faulkner Square. The street was tranquil, deserted. The trees were changing colour, shedding flakes of copper and gold. In her youth, Faulkner Square had been a crumbling eyesore, its gracious terraces partitioned into squalid bedsits, kerb crawlers almost as numerous as the rats that ran in the back alleys. Now the area's restoration programme was complete. The Georgian Quarter would never recover its past magnificence: the once-grand mansions were unlikely to revert to single dwellings, but their stucco had been repaired, their façades repainted, their interiors refitted; their weathered beauty was still imposing.

The walk was less than ten minutes, not long enough to dwell on her reunion with Liddy, if that's what she was to call it. Perhaps next time we meet we'll both be fully clothed, she thought in a moment of levity and buzzed Simon's doorbell.

He was waiting for her on the top flight. She'd hardly gathered her breath before he'd ushered her into his kitchen. There was a mug in the sink, a used tea bag, but the counter tops were scoured. She knew he was tidier than she was.

'Fancy a drink?'

'It's a bit early.'

'How did it go?'

'Okay I think.'

'The rift is healed? The hatchet buried?'

'Don't mock. We've made contact, all right? That's what she wanted. I didn't, to be frank, feel I needed her friendship, but there *is* something comforting about the company of someone you grew up with.'

'Whereas you and I, we have no history?'

'I'm not making comparisons, Simon. What are you getting at?'

'You might want a drink anyhow.'

'Why, have *you* got some awful confession to make?'

'I'm afraid so.'

She couldn't interpret his expression – a hybrid of penitence and defiance – his mouth wry and his eyes serious. It put her on edge. She liked to think she could be one move ahead; she liked to be the first to dump. 'Don't spare my feelings,' she said. 'I can handle bad news. I've had plenty of practice. And if you want to call it a day –'

He seized her arm below the elbow and covered her mouth with his other hand. 'Don't say anything you might regret. Let me finish.'

She pulled herself free and sat on one of his leather-topped bar stools. She crossed her legs and waited.

'I applied for a new job,' he said.

The relief was like the tickle of soap bubbles bursting in a warm bath. 'Oh? You didn't tell me.'

'I wasn't sure I'd get it, but I did. I start in January.'

'Well done. Onward and upward?'

'Yes . . . but here's the thing. It's at Queen's.'

'Queen's College, Oxford?' So close to home. 'Wow, that's terrific.'

He shook his head.

'Cambridge?'

'No.' It occurred to her that she'd rarely seen him flustered. 'Queen's University, Belfast.'

'Oh . . . right.'

He moved towards his fridge, which was twice as large as any of the other appliances in the kitchen. 'Beer? Wine? Vodka?'

'Vodka. Thanks.'

He topped it up with ice and tonic.

'Well,' said Helena. 'I guess we'd better call it quits.'

'Is that what you want?'

'No, but then I'm not pissing off anywhere. I've been in the same house for seven years now, which is a record for me. And I'll probably stay there, thanks very much. I don't imagine you were inviting me to share your pad in Northern Ireland, but even if you were, the answer's no. Coming back here is different, obviously, because of Allie. Though she may sell up after she's finished renovations, the way house prices are going.'

'Lots of people have long-distance relationships,' said Simon. 'We could visit weekends. And there are holidays. It's not impossible. Heathrow's not so far from where you live. The journey needn't be any longer for us than it is at the moment.'

Helena hoped he wouldn't touch her. She couldn't be certain how she'd react. She thought of Liddy and Mike with a flicker of envy.

Simon left the room and returned a couple of minutes later with a sheet of paper. 'Don't shout at me,' he said.

She was nursing her drink in her lap. Her palms were cold and slippery and the ice was melting. She took a long draught of the vodka and felt the alcohol churn in her empty stomach. She put down the glass and accepted the paper print-out. It was an email confirmation of two return flights from Liverpool to Belfast. 'What's this?'

'It's the first step,' said Simon. 'You can do it.'

'What makes you so sure?'

'It's the shortest possible flight. You're practically no time in the air. A hop and a skip across the Irish Sea and you've arrived. I shall be with you. I shall hold your hand all the way.'

'Don't you think anyone else has tried this?'

'With you? No. You're too stubborn.'

'As it happens . . .' She rested her cheek against the windowpane. Four storeys below a cat was leaping across the dustbins. '. . . It hasn't been a problem for me up to now. If you live in the south and want to go to Europe, it's just as easy to take the Channel ferry. Or Eurostar.'

'It's also because no one ever stands up to you, Helena. Listen, this is the deal. You give it a whirl. You let me take you on board – I've got sedation if you need it – and I won't get embarrassed, even if you try to scream the plane out of the sky. And if it doesn't work, if you really truly turn into a gibbering wreck, then we'll come back by boat, I promise.'

'Simon, don't you realize this could be *damaging*? Haven't you done any fucking psychology?'

'A Master's actually.'

'Then you're a bully.'

'No more than you.' He came up to her stool, parted her thighs and stood between them; his face poised a few inches from hers.

'When?'

'You didn't read the reservation properly. Tomorrow morning.'

'It's not going to work.'

'We have all night to prepare,' he said.

EPILOGUE

2008 ANOTHER PLACE

Black was not Liddy's colour. Her palette was tawny: russet, olive, chestnut, with accents of white or cream that freshened up anybody's look. Black drained her. However, there were times when it was expected. She squeezed into a shift dress she'd had for some years and felt the seams stretch. She added high heels and a short rope of faux pearls. She'd taken the afternoon off work even though she had a million things to do (including preparing to go away). She was only attending the funeral out of a sense of obligation – and because she'd ended up organizing most of it anyway.

Rolo had been responsible for finding Daphne. He had bounded unbidden on to her veranda and Liddy had awaited the booming reprimand. When none came, she'd followed the dog around the corner of the house and through a side door. The flat was no less cluttered, the air heavy with essence of alcohol and anchovy paste. Daphne was slumped in her well-padded chair, her chin folded on to her chest. Rolo was licking her palm. Liddy crossed the room, avoiding the trailing lamp flex and the footstool on castors. She noticed something white and crumpled had fallen to the ground and thought perhaps it was an important message or letter – but it was only a handkerchief. Gingerly she dabbed at Daphne's brow and felt a faint pulse. While she was phoning for an ambulance, Daphne stirred a little and uttered something unintelligible. A chemical equation might have been appropriate, Liddy thought afterwards, a sophisticated expression of 'ashes to ashes'. But too much emphasis was placed on last words. She probably just said, Help me.

The paramedics diagnosed a stroke. It was hard to know how long ago it had happened, or how severe its effects would be. They suggested Liddy should collect together some of the patient's personal requirements, lock up her flat and follow on to the hospital. They praised her observant dog, her good neighbourliness, and her prompt actions: she may have saved Miss Myers' life. As it turned out, she didn't. Another seizure saw Daphne expire in her emergency bed before there was time to rally distant relatives or even local acquaintances.

Managing a temporary crisis was one thing, and Liddy knew she had a knack for it, but she hadn't expected to have to follow it through. In tandem with a second cousin who'd inherited the furniture, she'd met with the vicar and helped make the necessary funeral arrangements. They'd chosen a couple of hymns, a reading from the Psalms and one from Saint Paul's Epistles to the Corinthians. She'd also ordered and paid for flowers because no one else seemed willing to do so.

Liddy sat on her own in a row towards the front of the crematorium. She didn't like to turn her head, but she sensed there were not many mourners. She felt uncomfortable, not just because of her tight dress, but because it was so long since she'd been to any kind of religious service. The readings were bland and impersonal; she didn't know the tunes to the hymns and the singers warbling behind her sounded querulous. It was a relief when the coffin rolled through the curtains.

The vicar had arranged for tea and refreshments back at the church hall, but she didn't plan to stay long. She couldn't wait to change into a pair of walking shoes and tramp through the dunes with Rolo.

'Liddy Rawlings?' said a woman at her elbow. She'd been eating egg and cress sandwiches and strands of cress lodged at the corner of her lips. 'Is it you?'

Liddy peered. 'Oh, my goodness. Janet!'

'It must be years. How are you?'

'Fine, thanks.'

'You abandoned us,' said Janet.

'Well, not exactly. But I was out of action for a while and it can be difficult sometimes to pick up where you left off.' She'd thought of going back to the book group but, while deliberating, had been invited to join another. This was a mixed group, younger, more irreverent, less intimidating. 'I'm sure you've managed without me.'

'You were always an asset,' insisted Janet, though Liddy wondered how she could say this since she never gave much shrift to other people's opinions. 'I didn't realize you knew Daphne.'

'She taught me. Years ago, of course. What about you?'

'We were colleagues for a while. Must have been after your time. Lord, she was dominant in the staff room.'

'I can believe it. She terrified us girls.'

'We often awarded her the wooden spoon, you know,' Janet said with a confidential chuckle. 'She so liked to stir up trouble.' She launched into a fund of anecdotes, none of which showed Daphne in a particularly good light, tempting Liddy to feel sorry for her – for the person who could only win attention by courting unpopularity. She wasn't sure she wanted to hear any more. 'So sorry, Janet, but I really ought to be leaving. I'm in the middle of packing to go away.'

'Anywhere nice?'

'America.'

'Holiday or business?'

'Bit of both. My husband's identified an opening he thinks will be good for his company.'

'Ah yes, I remember those magnificent clocks.'

'They're real works of art, aren't they? And in America they don't have many fine clocks on public buildings like we do in Europe. I think there's scope for something a bit retro . . .'

'Time,' said Janet, tapping her wrist, 'marches on for all of us. Did you know Daphne was over eighty?'

Liddy clucked her tongue against her teeth. She backed herself by degrees along the trestle table until the exit was only a yard behind her. She said, 'It's been lovely to see you again,' and assured Janet that she would try to keep in touch. Then she flitted through the door with a nod and a wave. She drove home rapidly to change and collect Rolo. She threw on her mac, picked up his lead and set off for the beach. The packing wasn't finished, it was true, but before she went back to it she needed to clear her head. She always walked briskly these days.

She no longer had any fear of being felled by a sudden savage attack of cramp or the embarrassment of shedding blood. She was fit and well and pain-free and she was never going to end up like Daphne Myers. That prospect in itself was cheering.

Along Crosby beach a hundred naked iron men now stood and stared out to sea. Some had sunk to their knees as if a giant finger had pushed them down into shifting pockets of sand, but most waited for the waves to swallow them, lapping by degrees at their ankles, their thighs, their shoulders, and sweeping over their heads. The iron men were as impervious to the tide as they were to the prodding of children's hands or the snuffling of dogs' noses. They allowed themselves to be draped with football scarves and Halloween masks, garnished with buckets and spades and wreaths of seaweed, photographed at the centre of family groups. Liddy and Rolo threaded a route between them; he scampered towards the water, she stopped and gazed across the Irish Sea.

She wondered if, on the other side, Helena was visiting her policeman. Liddy tried very hard to think of Simon as a serious academic or sociologist or whatever he was, but she could never quite banish her image of the man in his hired navy uniform. She wasn't sure how often Helena went over to see him, but sometimes she'd come back via Liverpool and spend the night. Michael liked Helena and that pleased Liddy, stopped her fretting about whether their friendship had been worth reviving. On a previous visit, two months ago – 'Capital of Culture, my giddy aunt!' – Helena had decked one of the iron men in a straw bonnet. She'd tied the wide ribbons tightly under his chin and planted a nosegay of wild mallow in the brim. It had lasted all of three days. Either the wind or a mischievous youth had loosened the ties and the hat was long gone. Liddy couldn't be sure which figure (although they were all numbered) had worn it.

Three thousand miles away, on the other side of the Atlantic, was Allie. Allie bounced back and forth over the ocean like a yoyo. Promoting gigs mostly. She'd inherited Jake's talent for making people like her; she was good in the room. Her schedule included other countries, other concert halls, other festivals, but it was to the States that she was drawn most often. Whenever Liddy had asked, 'And Max, are you still seeing him?' Allie would reply, 'Of *course* I see him. We're good friends, mates.' But now that Liddy was actually coming over and they were meeting up in Manhattan, Allie had admitted, 'Actually there's been a new development.'

'Really?'

'I haven't told Mum, at least not yet. You're the first to know.'

'What?'

'Max has broken up with the *fidanzata*.' (She always called her the *fidanzata* even though she must have known her real name.)

'The girl he's been going out with all these years?'

'Not the first one. The second one. It was less than three years, as it happens. But she was clingy and neurotic and it was kind of hard to extricate himself.'

'And?'

'And what?'

'What about you? Have you managed to find yourself between boy-friends? In the right place at the right time?'

'We'll have to wait and see,' said Allie in a voice that was positively creamy.

'I suppose . . .' – Liddy hardly knew how to broach such a delicate subject – '. . . it might be awkward for you, meeting his mother. She is, um, around?'

'Gabi? Yes, she *loves* America. Max says she's the laziest person he knows. Most people here work really hard but she swans about from beauty salon to soirée . . . You should *see* her fingernails!'

'So you have met her? How did you get on?'

The cream frothed and gurgled. 'Great! Because I wasn't the mad *fidanzata*. If you like, I could fix for us to go out for a meal with her while you're over.'

'I'll think about it,' Liddy had said. 'I'll let you know.'

Rolo careered up to her and laid a bleached stick at her feet. As she bent to pick it up, his tongue lapped her cheek. Briefly she buried her face in his silky soft fur. Then she hurled the stick inland so they could head in the right direction. When her phone vibrated in her pocket she knew it would be Michael letting her know that he too was on his way home. She pulled it out to read and reply and, as she did so, a white handkerchief fell on to the sand. She couldn't think where it had come from, until she remembered she'd been wearing the mac the day Daphne had suffered her stroke. It was a clean, serviceable cotton handkerchief, the sort that was donated in presentation packs to school fairs and tombola tables. She knotted the four corners to create a dome shape and, before leaving the beach, she arranged it jauntily on the bald head of iron man number thirty-six.

Acknowledgements

I would like to thank Alan, Luke and Melissa for their enthusiasm, support and guidance in the shaping of this book.

About the Author

Photo: Stephanie de Leng

Penny Feeny has lived and worked in Cambridge, London and Rome. Since settling in Liverpool many years ago she has been an arts administrator, editor, radio presenter and advice worker. Her short fiction has been widely published and broadcast and won several awards. *That Summer in Ischia* is her first novel. She is married with two sons and three daughters.